THROUGH THE NIGHT

#7 THE WINDSOR SERIES

TAMSEN SCHULTZ

To everyone out there who struggles to balance it all, this one's for you

ACKNOWLEDGMENTS

I'd like to acknowledge fatigue, my constant companion during the journey that was this book. I'd also like to give special thanks to doubt, guilt, and neuroticism—self-publishing a book for the first time is not for the faint of heart.

Thankfully, I've also had people like Angeli Weller, Eileen Rendahl, Spring Warren, Lisa Nalbone, Catriona McPherson, and Kris Calvin to keep me motivated and focused. And laughing (mostly at myself, but sometimes just because we've had too much wine).

I'd also like to thank my new PA, Stephanie Thurwachter who has gracefully (and extremely competently) guided me through this journey—and by "guide," I mean tell me exactly what to do and when—seriously, do NOT underestimate the importance of having someone who will break everything down for you into digestible, and doable, pieces when it sometimes (most of the time) feels overwhelming.

And then of course, there are my editors...lots of learning going on with this book and JC Wing, Kay Springsteen, and Mitch Workman have been gracious about it all.

And last, my family. There have been a lot of changes in the past few years and I love you all for traveling this journey with me.

CHAPTER ONE

Naomi DeMarco stepped out of the elevator directly into the foyer of her Beacon Hill apartment. She set her computer bag down gently, then with a sigh, dropped her duffel onto the floor beside it. Rolling her shoulders back, she paused to feel the warmth of her home wrap itself around her. Slowly, the tension caused by more than just the strain of carrying her bags fell from her body.

Smiling to herself and happy to be back in Boston after ten hellish days in Washington, DC and Quantico, Virginia, Naomi slid out of her heels, flexed her toes, and made her way into the kitchen. Draping her cashmere wrap over the back of a chair, she flinched as a gust of wind hurled rain at her windows.

She cast a glance in their direction. The drops of water streaking down the pane caught the glow of the streetlamps and headlights five floors below, illuminating them into a miasma of yellow, red, and black. Her eyes tracked the falling streams as she debated whether to pour a glass of wine and curl up in her living room in front of the fire or stick with her original plan and make a good cup of tea before heading to bed. As the stress of the past few days continued to drain away, the thought of sipping her favorite Chianti and doing nothing more than watching the gas flames dance in her fireplace won out—truly, it hadn't been much of a debate.

Selecting a bottle from her wine rack, Naomi reached for the drawer that held the opener. A neatly stacked pile of mail sitting on her kitchen counter drew her gaze and she paused. The fact that Brian, her twin, must have been in her apartment before leaving for his own work trip didn't bother her—they'd been in and out of each other's space since the womb, not to mention they worked together and lived in the same building—but the card he'd placed on top caught her attention.

She reached for the smooth, pastel, yellow envelope then slid her finger under the flap and unsealed it. An illustration of a goofy bunny greeted her as she pulled it out, its paws imploringly clasped in front of it, big sad eyes looking out. The caption beneath the picture read, *"Some bunny misses you."*

Setting the card to the side, she turned her attention to the envelope and noted the postmark date—ten days ago, the day she'd left Boston for DC. A sense of urgency tightened her chest, and she dropped the envelope and opened the card.

"It's hard to believe it's been nine years since we met. October 14th is a day I will always remember. Wish we could catch up more often, but I know how life can sometimes get in the way—still, every now and then, I wish we could pop out to the Cygnet like we used to. Take care and hope to see you soon. XO Smitty."

Naomi glanced at the clock; eight forty-five. "Shit," she grumbled to herself, already moving toward the foyer, snagging her wrap as she passed. She hit the elevator call button as she shoved her feet back into her heels. The doors slid open just as she grabbed her keys.

The ride down to the ground level took approximately four years longer than it normally did, or at least that's how it felt as she noted each familiar bump, jostle, and creak along the way. Finally, the doors opened into the apartment she and Brian used to house their company's visiting consultants and advisors. It was empty now, and Naomi made her way quickly toward the back of the room. Passing through a secure door that led out onto a small enclosed porch, then through another door and onto a covered patio, she followed the pathway to the garage. Thankful it wasn't yet winter and she didn't have to contend with snow, she hit two buttons simultaneously on her key fob—the first started her car and the second opened the garage door. Less than five minutes later she was pulling onto Storrow Drive, her windshield wipers at their highest setting.

Glancing at the clock on her dash, she swore again. At least the major commute hours had passed. Even so, she was never going to make it to Salem in time—especially not with the notorious Boston traffic and especially not with the weather.

"Call Kate," Naomi said, bringing her Bluetooth to life as she merged onto Interstate 93 North. The spray from a passing truck pelted her window, drowning out the first ring. Keeping her attention on the surrounding cars, the phone continued to ring until finally, her cousin answered.

"I thought you were out of town," Kate said by way of greeting.

"I was. I just got back tonight. How'd you know?"

"Your folks were in two days ago on their way back from leaf peeping up in Maine," Kate answered.

It didn't surprise Naomi at all to learn that her parents had stopped by Kate's upscale-yet-homey pub, The Swan and Gander. Kate's mother and Naomi's father were brother and sister—two of seven siblings. Despite its size, though—there were almost too many cousins to count—the DeMarco family was tight.

Naomi's eyes darted to the clock again. "Is Smitty there?" she asked.

"Not anymore," Kate answered without hesitation.

That gave Naomi pause. Her clock had just turned to nine,

the time Smitty's note had cryptically indicated he'd wanted to meet her. Why had he left?

"But he was there earlier?" she asked.

"Yeah, around lunch time, came in for a couple of hours, had a meal, we chatted and caught up." Smitty was a business contact of Naomi and Brian's, but he'd been in and out of their lives for nearly a decade and had met most of her family members at one time or another.

"I don't like the sound of that," Kate said, bringing Naomi back from the questions that had come pouring into her mind after hearing her cousin's response.

"The sound of what?" she asked.

"That silence. Is there a problem?" Kate asked.

Yes, there was a problem, probably a big one. Now that she was a couple miles north of the Tobin Bridge on Highway 1, the traffic was starting to ease and despite the rain, Naomi picked up her speed.

"Is there anyone hanging out at the Swan you think looks, well," she paused, not quite sure how to phrase her next question.

"Yes," Kate said into the silence. "There are two. You're on your way, I assume?"

"I'm about twenty minutes away," Naomi confirmed.

"Good, it will be good to see you," her cousin continued, and Naomi gave Kate props for maintaining her cool. Both her tone and her manner remained unchanged despite the fact that not only had she instantly known that Naomi was inquiring about anyone who looked out of place but also that she'd also recognized two people in her pub who fit the unspoken description. It might seem a stretch to be concerned about two random people sitting at a pub, but the DeMarco clan had blue running through their veins. And though neither Naomi nor Kate were law enforcement themselves, that didn't mean they didn't know a thing or two about spotting questionable characters.

"I think I'll make a scene when I come in, do you mind?" Naomi asked.

Kate let out a soft laugh. "I can't wait. It's pretty quiet tonight, it will be good to have the company," she said before clicking off.

By the time Naomi had exited Highway 1 and turned into the downtown area of Salem, she had a plan in place. Passing shop after shop peddling to the tourists who visited the town hoping to have a brush with its dark past, she kept a cautious eye on all the Halloween revelers. Tarot readers, psychics, costume shops, and good old-fashioned tchotchke stores lined the street. More than once, Naomi had to slow to let a group of dressed up tourists, some more *celebratory* than others, cross in front of her.

Shaking her head and not suppressing a smile, she waited as three women dressed like the witches from *Hocus Pocus* passed in front of her. Once they were safely on the sidewalk, she maneuvered her car toward the end of the main drag and turned left toward her cousin's pub.

Located two blocks off Main Street, The Swan and Gander came into view. Lit with soft white lights that created pale shadows, it was evocative without being attention seeking.

Three blocks past the building, Naomi slowed her car, made a U-turn, and pulled into a spot along the curb in an area that marked the transition from commercial to residential. The few businesses located this far off Main Street occupied houses rather than mercantile buildings. To her right sat a cute little Tudor owned by a family therapist; across the street in a quintessential beach cottage, a sweet café that she knew—from more experience than she'd like to admit—baked the most amazing croissants.

A soft quiet filled the car when she turned the engine off. The lashing anger of the storm had passed and though the rain still fell, it was only a gentle patter now. Not ideal for what she had planned, but it would do.

Tossing her wrap in the back seat, Naomi then grabbed a leather jacket she'd left there days ago. Her gaze lingered on the beautiful leather as she pulled it on and zipped it. As part of her plan, it would be sacrificed tonight; it was a small sacrifice as far as sacrifices went, but still, she and this jacket had seen a lot together.

The wind gusted, sending water from a nearby tree cascading onto her car and drawing her attention away from the supple leather. Glancing up at the sky through the front window, Naomi took a deep breath and wished she could call her brother. She couldn't—Brian was on a business trip and was unreachable other than through channels of command she didn't want to invoke—but that didn't mean she didn't want to.

With another fortifying breath, she opened the door and slid from the seat of her SUV. Quickly closing the door behind her, she stood unprotected in the rain, letting the drops land on her hair and slide down her scalp. Ignoring the cold and the urge to shrug and hunch her shoulders against the wet, she closed her eyes and turned her face to the sky. Naomi knew exactly what the rain would do to the little make-up she wore—she only hoped she'd look more bedraggled than psychotic when she finally walked into The Swan.

When she felt the telltale damp on her shoulders that let her know her jacket had been soaked through, she started walking toward The Swan. A burned out light across the street and one block up flickered to life then died again. The street wasn't a busy one—not this time of night—and for the most part, it was more charming than anything else. But with the weather, the dark of the night, and the echoing sounds of inebriated ghost hunters and ghoul seekers filtering down toward her, the sudden hint of light from the street light as it buzzed and flickered made the darkness that followed carry with it an ominous feeling.

Turning her attention back to her own plan, Naomi scanned the area, looking for what she needed next. Spotting it at the next corner, she quickly made her way to the storm grate. Pausing at its edge, she slipped off her left shoe then squatted and jammed the heel into one of the squares of the metal grate. With a tug, she yanked back.

And nothing happened.

Groaning at the fact that she bought such high quality shoes, she gave up trying to keep her jeans clean and knelt on the sidewalk. Using the leverage her new position gave her, she jammed the shoe in farther into the grate and yanked again. This time it gave with a snap and she lurched back from the momentum, nearly tossing her prize in the process. When she found her balance again, she set her now defunct shoe down and wriggled the heel out of the grate. The sound of voices coming closer filtered toward her and she stood quickly, shoving the errant heel into her pocket. After brushing the bits of dirt and gravel from her jeans she wiggled her foot back into what was left of her shoe and turned to walk the last block to her cousin's.

Click, thump, click, thump. She sounded like a peg-legged pirate as she made her way down the street.

"Hey, you okay?" a guy dressed as a puritan called from across the street. The woman at his side wore a blood red, hooded cloak.

Naomi kept walking but she held up her heel. "Fine thanks, just a little malfunction," she called back. She shoved an estimated four hundred dollars' worth of her shoe back into her pocket and continued the last half block to The Swan.

Pausing just outside, she braced herself for the performance she had planned. It didn't take long to get into character and before she knew it, she was flinging the door open with more force than necessary. As she hoped, all eyes in the pub turned toward her. Two guys having a drink in a booth to her right quickly dismissed her, and a man at the bar took in her disheveled appearance and frowned—though to be fair, it looked more like a frown of concern rather than one of judgment. A group of four women sitting at a table to her left looked to be empathizing with her misfortune—as if they'd all been there at one time or another—and deep in the far left corner of the cozy room, another woman sat alone. The woman's eyes were on Naomi, but Naomi got the feeling she wasn't really looking.

"Well, well, well, look what the cat dragged in," Kate said, walking through the door that led from the kitchen to behind the bar.

Naomi flashed an annoyed grin. "I was having dinner with that blind date your mom set me up on. It didn't go well. I left before the second glass of wine was poured—well the second glass for me, it would have been his fourth."

She *click, thumped* her way farther into the pub and pulled out her heel again.

"And then your heel broke. I always tell you not to buy those cheap shoes," Kate added. Naomi fought back a laugh at that. Kate knew very well that Naomi didn't shop often but when she did "cheap" wasn't how she rolled.

"And got caught in the rain," she said. For emphasis, she shook her head as she spoke and water sprayed from the ends of her hair. She also took the opportunity to scan the room. The woman in the corner had gone back to her drink, and the two men in the booth seemed uninterested in the conversation happening in front of them. The man at the bar had his attention on the baseball game playing on the TV mounted on the wall at the other end from where he sat, but his eyes dropped down a time or two and bounced between her and Kate. The four women at the table had gone back to their conversation, but like the man at the bar, their eyes darted up every now and then.

"I have a bag of gym clothes in the back," Kate said with a jerk of her head toward the door marked "Employees Only."

"Gym clothes?" Naomi didn't have to try too hard to sound disappointed.

Kate rolled her eyes. "Do I *look* like I go to the gym?" she said gesturing to herself. Kate was bigger than Naomi, but Naomi had always envied her cousin's curves. Where Kate often got compared to the bombshells of the forties, Naomi was more often than not compared to a pixie.

"I might get the urge someday," Kate continued, shrugging off Naomi's raised eyebrow. "That's why I keep a bag of gym clothes here and pay forty-dollars a month to a fitness center I have yet to see the inside of. But as that hasn't happened yet, the clothes are clean." At that, Naomi did chuckle.

"Go on back, I'll bring you a hot toddy," Kate directed.

Naomi nodded her thanks then *clicked, thumped* her way across the room and through the "Employees Only" door. Once through, she toed off her shoes and walked barefoot the rest of the way to Kate's office. Stepping inside, she closed the door behind her and immediately stripped off her ruined leather jacket and hung it on a hook on the back of the door. A hot-pink duffel sat in the corner and Naomi moved toward it, hoping she'd find something to fit. Kneeling beside the bag, she dug out a towel, a T-shirt, a zip-up hoody, a pair of yoga pants, and ankle socks.

When she was down to her skivvies, she toweled her body off then wrapped the small terry cloth around her hair. She had one leg in the yoga pants when Kate knocked on the door and let herself in, a steaming hot toddy in hand.

"I know you didn't walk far, but you still must be cold," she said setting the mug down on her desk. "So, what gives?"

Naomi finished pulling the pants on and, while they were

9

probably Capri style on Kate, on her they fell to a weird length about two inches above her ankle bone. She would not be winning any style awards this evening.

Reaching for her drink before answering, Naomi inhaled the smell of lemon, cinnamon, and whiskey before taking a sip. The hot liquid trailed warmth down her throat.

"Mmm, you always did make the best hot toddies," she said, reaching for the T-shirt. "Smitty sent me a letter wanting to meet tonight at nine," she started to explain as she pulled the shirt over her head. "I've been away for ten days so didn't get the letter until I got home about an hour ago."

"Your production," Kate said with a gesture toward the pile of wet clothing on the floor, "leads me to believe you're more than just a little concerned about missing a meeting with a friend."

Naomi nodded and zipped up the sweatshirt. Dragging a chair over to the desk so she could sit near her drink as she put on the socks, she continued. "I was just in DC for ten days, in and out of the FBI office both there and in Quantico. The fact that he didn't try to contact me while I was in his neck of the woods raises a flag in my mind, not to mention that he coded the letter he sent."

"Coded? As in cryptography? Isn't he an accountant?"

Naomi nodded. "He's a forensic accountant, to be exact, and his letter wasn't coded cryptographically. It was just written in a way that only I would know the meaning. To anyone else, it would just sound like a sentimental letter to an old friend."

"And in it, he told you he wanted to meet you here, but you have no idea why?"

"I don't," she confirmed. "What time was he here, exactly?" Naomi asked as she opened a drawer she knew held Kate's hair supplies—with a mass of curly hair, Kate always had supplies on hand.

"He came in around one and was here for a little less than an hour and a half. Sat at the third bar stool from the left."

Naomi tugged her damp hair into a ponytail as she contemplated the information. The only reason she could come up with as to why Smitty would arrive hours before their scheduled meeting was if the situation—whatever it might be—had become more concerning than he'd originally anticipated when he'd sent the letter.

"Why the production?" Kate asked interrupting the path Naomi's mind had wandered down.

"I wanted to make enough of a scene that people's attention would be drawn to me—normal people's," she said.

"Ah, so you could see whose attention wasn't on you," Kate finished.

"Exactly." Naomi took another sip of her drink, appreciating the warmth now seeping into her body.

"Those two men in the booth who barely acknowledged your entrance were the ones I mentioned," Kate said.

Naomi met her cousin's eye. "Why did they catch your eye to begin with?"

"They've been here nearly two hours and are still nursing the one drink they ordered. If people aren't drinking when they come in here, they are usually at least eating or catching up with friends."

"And those two aren't?"

Kate shook her head. "They hardly speak to each other at all. And one of them is definitely carrying in a shoulder holster."

Naomi blinked at her cousin.

"The bulge," Kate said, gesturing to her side. "I noticed it when he went to the bathroom about an hour ago," she explained.

"Ah," Naomi said, trusting her cousin's judgment. "I agree," she continued. "They noticed me, but as soon as I mentioned your mom and the fake blind date, they dismissed me. All the other folks in the bar, with the exception of the woman in the corner who looks incredibly sad, noticed me. Even if their attention wasn't fixed on me, it flickered to me, which was just what I would have expected from normal folks out for a night."

"So, what now?"

Naomi leaned back in her chair and took another sip of her drink. If Smitty had been in earlier, maybe he'd left something for her, but that wasn't something she could check while the two men of questionable character were sitting in the pub.

"Were those two men here when Smitty was?" she asked.

Kate shook her head. "No, the first time I saw them was when they came in this evening."

"There's some good news," Naomi murmured over the rim of her mug as she cradled its warmth between her two hands. "Any chance you can get that guy at the end of the bar to move? I want to sit at that end so I can use the mirror over the TV at the other end to keep an eye on them. But I think it might seem weird to sit right next to him when there are so many other open bar stools."

Kate's lips quirked into a smile. "That guy?"

Naomi frowned. "Yeah, you know the one. Jeans, blue T-shirt, New England Rebels hat," she said.

Kate let out one of those half-laugh-half-huffs. "Yeah I know the one and no, I can't get him to move. Seriously, what do you think I'd say to him? 'Can you please move to make way for my cousin who doesn't want to sit too close to you because she thinks you'll think she's hitting on you?'" Kate rolled her eyes. "Besides, I think he's pretty into the game. It *is* the last game of the American League title. Whoever wins tonight plays the Rebs in the World Series," she added.

Naomi refrained from uttering a not very adult-like "whatever," and turned her mind toward how she could finagle a seat where she needed without appearing weird. Or like she was hitting on the guy.

Finally Kate sighed, then rose as she spoke. "Look, I know it's the best place for you to be. I'll see what I can do to get you set up there. But remember, I'm your favorite cousin."

"Actually, Vivi is my favorite cousin," Naomi shot back with a grin.

Kate's brows went up. "You still need shoes," she pointed out.

"But now you're my favorite cousin. Always have been."

Kate laughed. "That's better. Look in the cabinet there," she said motioning to a tall armoire that sat behind Naomi. "My shoes won't fit you but nearly every family member has come through here at some point, and it's like a graveyard of discarded and forgotten shoes in there. You'll probably find something closer to your size than my tens."

"You're the best," Naomi called as Kate exited the office.

"I know," Kate called back as she shut the door and returned to the front of the pub.

Naomi gave herself a minute to finish her drink and prepare for the rest of the evening. She didn't know what it would entail, and she didn't know what to think about Smitty's no-show, but the foremost thought in her mind was the fact that the last time Smitty had done something similar, she and Brian had been able to use the information he'd given them to thwart one of the biggest attempted cyber-attacks against the FBI in the agency's history. It had been a close call, even with the advantage Smitty's information had given them. Would this failed meeting mean that she might already be too late to fix whatever Smitty had wanted to bring to her attention?

Setting her mug down on the desk with a definitive *thunk*, Naomi rose from her seat and opened the armoire—whether she and Smitty would ever catch up tonight was anyone's guess, but sitting in the office alone certainly wasn't going to answer her questions.

CHAPTER TWO

THREE MINUTES LATER, Naomi pushed back through the door leading to the main room of the pub, wearing a pair of her cousin Kiera's black ballet flats. They were a half-size too big, but a way better option than the pair of her own knee-high, high-heeled boots she'd found in the armoire that she hadn't even realized weren't sitting in her own closet back in Boston.

"Here," Kate said, sliding a mug of what looked like tea onto the bar top. She'd set up a seat for Naomi right next to the opening used to move between behind the bar and the front of the pub. It was one seat away from the guy in the hat.

"Thanks," Naomi said taking a seat. The guy glanced her direction then turned his attention back to the game.

"Some of the ghost tours around town are ending in about twenty minutes, you can help me behind the bar if I need it," Kate added. Naomi nodded, knowing that while she would help her cousin if needed, Kate had likely come up with the idea as an excuse to keep her on that end of the bar.

"Tea?" Naomi asked, glancing at the liquid in front of her. "And my favorite, black mango if I smell correctly?" she said after taking a sniff of the steam.

"Yes, because I'm your favorite cousin. And I know you had a glass of wine with dinner and the hot toddy I made you, and I need you sober if you're going to help me," Kate responded, flashing Naomi a cheeky grin as she reached for a glass resting in the drying rack.

"I may be petite but I'm not *that* much of a lightweight," Naomi muttered as her cousin walked to the other end of the bar. The guy beside her glanced her way again; his eyes lingered, as if assessing the truth of her statement. She thought she might have seen a hint of a smile in his gaze when it met hers, but he causally slid his blue eyes away and focused on the game. In turn, Naomi switched her focus to the other side of the bar as well, only her attention didn't fall on the game but rather on the reflection of the two men seated in the booth behind her.

Ten minutes passed before one spoke to the other. Naomi couldn't hear the comment, but she could guess the topic when the other man glanced at his watch and replied. Now past ten, if they were waiting for Smitty—or whoever they thought might be meeting Smitty— they had to be wondering by now if the night was a bust.

"You like baseball?"

It took Naomi a moment to realize the guy beside her was talking to her. Her eyes flickered to the clock before turning toward her neighbor. She'd been watching the two men intently for about fifteen minutes. He must have thought, as she'd intended, that she'd been watching the game.

She shrugged. "It's okay," she answered, her eyes going back to the mirror.

"It's the great American pastime, how can you say it's just 'okay'?"

She heard it then, the hint of laughter she'd seen in his eyes earlier. She turned in her seat and picked up her now tepid tea, cringing as she took a sip. "I don't *dislike* it. It just doesn't seem like the game it used to be when I was a kid is all."

"At the risk of sounding too existential, everything changes," he countered.

Naomi smiled. "Is it even possible to be too existential? Doesn't that just make you, well, existential?"

The hint she'd seen and heard earlier finally made an appearance, and his eyes creased as he smiled. Taking in his tanned skin and ruggedly weathered face, Naomi recognized a man who spent a good deal of time outside and probably a fair bit of it laughing, too. Her own smile grew in response, she liked that his face seemed to reflect a life enjoyed.

"Fair enough," he replied. "But what makes it so different now from the game you knew?"

Naomi shrugged again. "I don't know really. There is just so much money involved now. I don't mean to get preachy, but it's hard to get excited about watching a bunch of guys who make millions of dollars hitting a ball with a stick when the average family, who *should* be the target audience, can't even afford to go to most games. I guess it just feels like we've lost a little bit of the soul of the game in the last several decades."

As she spoke, she turned her attention to the game for the first time. Her dad had taken her and her brother to games all the time as kids. She remembered her dad being able to spend a hundred dollars for the day and that covered three good seats, hot dogs, and drinks. The last time she'd gone to a game, it had been a birthday gift for the man she'd been seeing. Granted, she'd purchased good seats, but between the tickets, the parking, the food, and the drink, the day had cost close to a thousand dollars.

As she watched a batter for the West Division champion belt a ball out of the park, she realized her neighbor had been silent for an awkwardly long pause in their conversation. She turned her head to find him looking at her, maybe studying her.

"That's, well, that's just my opinion of course," she said, hoping she hadn't offended him. "Like I said, I don't have anything against the game, and I know players aren't just talented but work hard, too—no way could they be that good if they didn't—but, well, I just wish it were more about the game and less about the personalities and money." Naomi paused then laughed out loud. "I sound like a crotchety old man, don't I? Complaining about how much better the good old days were."

He smiled again and chuckled. "Maybe a little, but I don't disagree with you. Still love the game, mind you, but don't disagree with you. I'm Jay Evans," he said holding out his hand. More out of surprise than wariness, Naomi hesitated before reaching out. Warm, rough skin enveloped hers, and though his grip was gentle—firm but gentle—she felt a sudden awareness of her own petite size. Her fingers felt almost delicate in his, and *delicate* was not how she was used to feeling.

"Naomi DeMarco," she said, withdrawing her hand. "So, who do you want to win?" She nodded toward the game, which gave her a chance to check in on the two men in the booth, one of whom had just finished his beer. Her stomach revolted at the thought of what a two-hour old beer must taste like.

"You okay?" Jay asked.

"Um, yeah," she said, realizing her distaste must have shown on her face. "I just caught a glimpse in the mirror of one of the guys behind us finishing his drink. According to my cousin, he's been nursing that same drink since he came in about two hours ago."

Jay blanched at her observation and to his credit, he didn't turn around to look at the man but rather used the mirror, just as she had, to eye the offender.

"There ought to be a law against that," he said.

"If his taste buds and stomach don't object, clearly the laws of mere mortal men will have no impact."

Jay chuckled. "Fair point."

"So, who do you want to win? Clearly you're a fan," Naomi said, returning to the slightly more palatable topic of baseball.

"Who I want to win and who I think will win are two different things," he said, his attention going back to the game in progress. At the bottom of the seventh inning, it was tied three to three. "The West Division team has a lot of flash and some phenomenal talent, but they play more like individuals on the same field rather than a team."

"And the East Division team?"

"Good, strong players, no flash but a strong team effort—they'll win or lose as a team."

"So, you want the East Division to win but think the West will?" she asked.

"Actually," he said, another smile dancing on his lips. "I want the West to win. If they win, the Rebs will easily be able to take them in the World Series. It won't be an easy fight, but the Rebs have more experience, more grounding in the game as a team."

"But if the East wins it will be like two giants pushing against each other until one gives."

Jay nodded. "The two teams are evenly matched, although if you ask me to admit that to anyone else, I'll deny saying it," he said, flashing her a grin. "But the truth is, you put the East Division team and the Rebs together and the series is going to come down to pure luck and which team happens to wake up on the right side of the bed that week."

"You're a Rebs fan I take it?"

That grin again. "Who isn't? No one I know, that's for certain."

Naomi couldn't help the laugh that bubbled out, but then movement in the mirror caught her eye. Nearly two hours past the time Smitty was supposed to be meeting her, the two men looked to be calling it a night. One man threw a bill on the table and they both slid out of the booth without a word. The one wearing a dark blue windbreaker was definitely carrying on his left side, but Naomi suspected the other man also had a weapon, a small one, tucked against his right hip.

She watched them as they made their way out of the pub. For three seconds, she considered following them. But while she worked for the FBI on a regular basis, she wasn't an agent. And while learning how to handle a gun was a family rite of passage, her weapon of choice had a motherboard and a keyboard.

So, there was no reason why she should feel like she was letting Smitty down. Right?

"So, what brings you to Salem?" she asked Jay, abruptly cutting off her own thoughts.

"Just getting away for the night," he answered. At that odd reply, Naomi raised an eyebrow. Jay smiled. "I live south of Boston, but I'm working with my team in the city right now on a big negotiation. I needed to get away from it all for a little while, so I just took a drive and ended up here," he added.

It was on the tip of Naomi's tongue to ask what kind of deal he was negotiating, but since she generally disliked talking about her own work—the pieces of it that were declassified enough that she *could* talk about—she was disinclined to ask probing questions about other people's jobs. Besides, she'd learned over the years that who a person worked for or what they did for a living tended to say very little about the actual person.

"So, is this your first time to my cousin's pub?" Naomi asked, sliding from her seat and stepping behind the bar to make herself another cup of tea.

"Actually no. I found it last year when my mom was visiting. She decided she wanted to see the infamous Salem, Massachusetts so we drove up for a day. She'd read about this pub on some blog and we ended up here for dinner. I liked it, kind of out of the way but not too out of the way, if you know what I mean. After that, I came up here maybe once or twice a month with friends. But then my travel picked up and this is my first time back in a while."

The door jangled open and both Naomi and Jay looked over as a party of four walked in. Naomi shivered as a gust of chilly air swept through the room reminding her of her still-damp hair. On the other side of the bar, Jay grabbed a dark blue hoody that had been hanging from the back of his bar stool and slipped it on.

"Time for the post-tour revelers," Kate said coming back to their end of the bar carrying a tray of glasses. "Jess leads a tour, but she'll be in to take over the bar once she's done—shouldn't be more than twenty minutes," she said referring to one of the bartenders Naomi knew worked several nights a week for Kate. "I'll manage the front of the house and serving..." She paused as another group of three women walked in.

"Can you cover the bar until Jess gets here?" At Naomi's nod, Kate added, "There are more glasses under the counter, but start with these" She gestured to the tray she'd placed on the back bar.

"Can I make a quick trip to the bathroom before I start?" Naomi asked, only half teasing.

Kate rolled her eyes. "So long as you wash your hands."

Naomi made a face at her cousin then grinned at Jay as she stepped back from behind the bar. Crossing the pub to reach the restrooms, Naomi paused in front of the seat Smitty had taken during his lunchtime visit and leaned in. "Hey, Kate," she called as she slipped her hand under the lip of the bar, her body blocking anyone's view of her task.

"Yeah?"

Naomi's fingers slid along the underside of the bar until she felt something like gum. Fighting an instinctive urge to yank her hand back, she smiled. "Can you finish making me another cup of tea?" she asked as her fingers found their grip and pulled the tacky substance from where it had been stuck. Kate would no sooner allow gum to gather under her bar than she would allow colored Christmas lights in her windows—which was to

21

say never. Naomi tucked the small blob into her pocket as her cousin shook her head and muttered something uncharitable even as she reached for a mug.

"You're my favorite," Naomi called back as she continued on to the ladies' room, her hand wrapped around the substance in her pocket. She didn't know what she had, but she felt fairly certain she had something Smitty had left for her.

Stepping into a stall, Naomi closed the door behind her and pulled the item from her pocket. About three inches long and rectangular, it looked like a simple brick of blue tack. Turning it over, Naomi examined it further, finding nothing but the small seams where the tack had been joined together. Deciding to dive right in, she started to pluck some away. Within moments, she knew exactly what she had, what Smitty had wanted her to find. It took a few more swipes to clear all the tack away, but in the end, Naomi held in her hand a small, black thumb drive.

The triumph she felt at correctly guessing what Smitty had been doing in the pub earlier that day—leaving something for her—quickly quelled when she thought about why he must have felt the need to leave it rather than wait to meet her. Her stomach turned with anxiety; hopefully, he was just on the run and it wasn't anything worse than that.

Taking a few deep breaths, she exited the stall. After washing the tack off her fingers, she used one of the soft towels Kate stocked to dry her hands then rejoined her cousin behind the bar.

"You okay?" Jay asked as she familiarized herself with the taps in front of her. Kate kept a good rotation of local beers going and Naomi spotted three new ones that hadn't been available the last time she'd been in.

"Yeah, fine, thanks," Naomi forced a smile. "Can I get you another drink?" she asked, gesturing to his nearly empty glass.

He eyed her before shaking his head. "It's the bottom of the eighth, I have to drive home tonight. How about a glass of sparkling water instead?"

Naomi glanced at his tab on the bar computer. "It's on the house," she said sliding the water over to him. "You've only had two drinks since the game started—hmm, Ardbeg, good choice," she said, then grinned. "I'm a sucker for a responsible driver."

He took the glass and raised it to her. "That's not something I hear very often."

"Yes, well, I'm also a sucker for puppies, hikes on a crisp fall day, cozy fires, a good night out on the town in my favorite little black dress that isn't black, and Giuseppe Zanotti shoes, I'm a complex woman." She poured and handed over a pint of a local stout for a woman waiting. The woman placed a ten on the counter and walked away.

"Layers, like an onion," Jay said.

Naomi made a face at him. "Word of advice, don't ever liken a woman to an onion. I like to think of myself more like a kaleidoscope—full of color and ever shifting, but the essential parts remain the same."

"Existential much?" he teased.

She laughed. "All part of my dubious charms."

She turned to help another customer, but hesitated when she thought she heard Jay mutter something like, "Nothing dubious about them." She glanced back, but his eyes were focused on the game.

She chanced a few surreptitious looks at him as she served a couple more people. His eyes were lined with dark lashes, making the light blue color stand out even more against his tan skin. From what she could tell, his build wasn't lean but not bulky either, he appeared fit and solid. And strong. She'd noticed the muscles in his arms flexing under his T-shirt before he'd pulled on his sweatshirt. Perfectly proportioned cheek bones, full lips, and just a little bit of a beard all contributed to an appealing package. But that's all it was, Naomi knew—a package. She didn't underestimate the importance of physical attraction, but she'd always had an unreasonable need to actually *like* the men she chose to spend her time with.

Turning her attention to a couple waiting to place their order, she looked up as Jess came through the door, still dressed in the period costume she wore while giving her tour.

"Naomi!" Jess exclaimed, placing a kiss on Naomi's cheek as she scooted behind the bar and reached for an apron. "I didn't know you were coming tonight. I got this," she said, taking a glass from her mid-pour. "You go sit down." That was Jess, all take charge and a whirlwind of energy.

"Bad blind date tonight. Decided to stop in and drown my sorrows," Naomi responded, re-taking her seat near Jay.

"In tea," he interjected, pointing to her mug.

"I have to drive tonight, too," she said.

He grinned. "It's a good thing I'm a sucker for a responsible driver, then."

Jess's eyes bounced between them as she filled the pint then handed the drink to the customer. Stepping closer to Naomi, she reached for the mug and wrapped her hands around it.

"It's gone cold," she said with a frown. "I'll make you another one." Before Naomi could respond, Jess whisked the drink away.

"Are you flirting with me?" Naomi asked once Jess was out of earshot.

One side of his mouth lifted. "Yes. Is that a problem?"

Naomi drummed her fingers on the bar top. "That depends. What else are you a sucker for?"

He smiled then answered without hesitation. "Thunderstorms on a hot summer night, a woman's smile when it's just for me, the way my mom always acts surprised when I meet her at the airport with flowers, and a good clean curve ball."

Naomi laughed. "One of those things is not like the other."

"I'm a complex man." He shrugged and smiled.

"And puppies? How do you feel about them?"

In response to her question, he pulled out his phone, unlocked it, hit a few icons, and handed it to her. A gorgeous golden retriever looked back at her, a goofy grin on its face.

"That's Goo," he said. "I rescued her when she was six weeks old. She's seven now."

"She's adorable. You said you travel though, what do you do with her when you're away?"

"I take her with me when I can. The company owns a plane and she's allowed on it. When I can't take her or it doesn't make sense, my sister comes and stays at my place. Goo likes people, I wouldn't want to kennel her," he said. Naomi handed him his phone back and he glanced at the picture and smiled to himself before shutting down it down and sliding it back into his pocket. A little bit of her heart thumped at the adoration she saw on his face for his dog.

Yes, it was quite all right if he flirted with her.

But his wasn't the only device that captured her attention. Naomi reached down and fingered the thumb drive in her pocket; she'd be out the door already if she hadn't promised Kate she'd help. Kate would understand if she hightailed it home, but even so, a promise to family wasn't something Naomi wanted to go back on.

"Why 'Goo'?" she asked. More people filed in and Naomi slipped back behind the bar to help. Jess had all the drinks covered, but Naomi could help prep the cocktail accoutrements.

"Depends on who you ask, me or my sister."

Naomi began to peel a lemon rind into strips. "What would you say?"

"That the puppy melted into a puddle of Goo the first time I picked her up," he answered.

Naomi had no issue picturing an adorable little puppy, maybe a scared one, melting in has arms, probably feeling safe for the first time. "And if I ask your sister?"

He rubbed a hand over the back of his neck and ducked his

head before meeting her gaze with a self-deprecating smile. "She'd tell you I was the one who melted into a puddle of Goo the first time I picked my puppy up."

Naomi laughed. "I think I might like your sister."

"Probably, Allie is hard not to like."

Another point in his favor—based on the way he spoke about both his mom and his sister, he had women in his life he liked and seemed to respect. And they were family too, family was everything to Naomi. She understood that "family" didn't always mean family by blood, but over the years she'd noticed that those she kept close to herself, those she'd drawn into her inner circle, all had strong family—and family-like—bonds with people.

"Tell me about her," Naomi said as she topped off his sparkling water.

He shot her a look that let her know she might regret asking, but for the next hour or so, they chatted about Goo, which led into stories about siblings and family. They also watched the end of the game, a game—and series—won by the East Division, much to Jay's dismay.

Closing time came faster than she'd anticipated, and a few minutes after the last patron left, Kate shooed them out the door. Standing on the darkened street beside Jay, a borrowed coat from Kate wrapped around her, Naomi realized that while she wanted to be home exploring the thumb drive Smitty had left her, she wasn't quite ready to say goodbye to Jay. She lingered outside the Swan, contemplating this dichotomy and fully aware that the longer she stood there, the more awkward the end of the evening became.

A couple of young men whooped and hollered as they turned the corner and began walking toward the now closed pub. Making a decision for them both, Jay grabbed her hand and tugged her across the street and down the block. Not surprisingly, the burned out streetlight hadn't been repaired yet.

But what had earlier seemed an ominous yawning darkness now provided an opportune place to say a proper goodnight to a man she was most definitely attracted to.

Apparently, Jay had the same idea. After leading them deep into the shadow cast by a row of hedges, he stopped then turned and slipped a hand to the back of her neck. She tilted her head up and met his gaze as he pulled her gently toward him. She could see him asking permission with his eyes and as her consent, she slid a hand up his chest until her palm curled around his neck, her thumb grazing his jaw line. Going up on her toes, she pulled him down until his lips settled on hers.

She felt his hand tighten against the nape of her neck as he brushed his lips across hers; his other hand finding its way to her waist. She dropped her own hands to the hem of his sweatshirt then underneath the soft material to feel the heat of his skin against her fingertips. As she slid her hand across his lower back, the gentle goodnight-kiss turned into a heated dance.

Slowly, after who knew how many minutes, Jay ended the kiss and drew away a few inches. Their breaths mingled in the night, and they eyed each other for the space of a heartbeat. And then their lips met again.

Although he made no move to do anything beyond the kiss, his arm tightened around her. Wanting more of him, an undeniable urge to run her hand up his back, to feel the flex and pull of his muscle, gripped her.

Just as she started to follow through on that urge, the squealing tires of a car taking a corner too fast startled them apart. They were nowhere near the street, but Jay shifted a hand to rest on her hip, as if he wanted to be ready to push her behind him if needed.

They both watched as an old hotrod careened down the street, its headlights bouncing like two spotlights. It sped past them, illuminating the cars parked along the road. Naomi followed its progress with disinterest but when the lights fell, ever so briefly, on a dark colored sedan, a shard of panic lanced through her.

She jerked in shock and in response felt Jay's hand tighten on her hip.

"What's wrong?" he asked. His voice fell softly in the sudden quiet of the night, the hotrod having turned a corner and disappeared.

Still in shock, not believing she'd seen what she'd thought she'd seen, but knowing that she had, she stuttered.

"I…I." She paused, took a deep breath, and dug out her phone with her free hand. "I thought I saw something," she said, moving out of the shadows and onto the sidewalk. Jay followed but reached for her hand, keeping her anchored by his side.

She led him onto the street and walked alongside a sporty little convertible until she reached the back of the sedan that had been illuminated for mere milliseconds. She leaned down to get a better look through the window and her heart skipped several beats. She didn't need her flashlight to see what she knew she'd see, but she brought it to life anyway, shining its beacon toward the ground.

"Stay here," she said, withdrawing her hand from Jay's.

"I don't think so," he said, taking a step closer. She didn't want him involved in what she knew would follow, but she also recognized the undeterred tone of his voice.

She moved toward the front of the car as she stepped farther onto the street. When she came perpendicular to the door, she let her flashlight illuminate the street between her and her final destination. After sweeping it back and forth along the ground, she brought it to a rest on a small spot just below the door. A few bits of glass glistened in the light. The beam from her phone hovered there, and she felt Jay move to stand behind her, the heat from his body radiating against her back.

Slowly she moved the light up, then up some more to the window. Smack dab in the middle, a hole glared back at her.

The tempered glass had done its job and not shattered, but cobwebs and cracks emanated from the small, deadly gap.

Taking a step forward, Jay right behind her, she finally let her light fall on the interior of the car.

Even knowing what she'd find didn't save her from the shock that rocked through her. Her hand started to shake and tears, ones of anger and denial, sprang into her eyes. Suddenly, she was spun around and pressed against Jay's chest, tucked away from the horror before her.

Tucked away from the sight of Smitty's body slumped over the console and the single bullet hole through his head.

CHAPTER THREE

WITHIN THIRTY SECONDS, Naomi had pulled her shit together and stepped out of Jay's embrace. Not that it hadn't been welcome, but this was one of those moments she needed to put her own emotion aside and deal with the situation. She pocketed her phone, plunging them back into darkness.

Jay's hand lingered on her shoulder and he ducked his head to look her in the eyes.

"You know him, don't you?"

She nodded even as she glanced over her shoulder.

"We need to call the police."

Yes, they did. But still, her hand came out to stop his as he reached for his phone. "Let me," she said.

He paused. "Why?"

She let out a deep breath. The night had chilled enough to turn her exhale into a puff of fog. "It's complicated."

"Wrong answer." His response came swiftly. Under other circumstances, she might admire his fortitude, but now... well, hell, she kind of admired it now even though it was a pain in the ass.

She took one more deep breath and exhaled as she straightened and met his gaze. "I don't mean to sound dramatic, but what I'm about to tell you isn't general knowledge. It isn't classified, but it's not widely known, either. Do you understand?"

He hesitated then nodded.

"I told you I work in the tech industry and I do, but it's not quite as simple as that. I consult with a number of government agencies, including the FBI—we have for a number of years. Both my brother and I," she clarified. "The projects we work on are, well..." It was her turn to hesitate. She didn't ever like to talk about the classified nature of her work, but she couldn't figure out how to get around it.

"Are the kind of projects people are better off not knowing about," he offered.

She closed her eyes then nodded. "Exactly."

"And him?"

She took a deep breath. "His name is Smitty," she said. "He wanted to meet with me tonight, but I just got back into town from a business trip and didn't see his message until about fifteen minutes before the time he'd suggested meeting. I live in Boston and well, I knew I'd never make it in time, but I needed to come anyway."

"And?" he prompted.

"When I got on the road, I called my cousin to see if he was already at the pub. She told me he wasn't but that he'd been there earlier. I didn't like the sound of that," she said, then paused. "There are certain things about Smitty that, well, that make him more valuable than the average agent," she continued. "And then when my cousin mentioned the two men in the pub—"

"The two men in the booth behind us?"

"Yes," Naomi confirmed. "Kate didn't like the look of them."

"I didn't either. They weren't there for a night out, and at least one of them was carrying."

"They both were," Naomi responded, not allowing herself to

wonder how he'd recognized that. "I figured they were either there waiting for Smitty or waiting to see if they could identify whoever it was he was supposed to be meeting."

"Which is why you played up the family connection—"

"And generally made a spectacle of myself," she said. "There was no way they'd see me in the state I was in and think I was the FBI contact Smitty knew."

"And it's why you took a seat so close to me, so you could watch them in that mirror?"

"I did try to get my cousin to get you to move because I thought it would be weird to grab a seat right next to you when the rest of the bar was empty," Naomi admitted.

"I'm glad she didn't," he said. "But why shouldn't we call the police?"

"That's not what I said. We will call the police. But I want to call my dad." She raised a hand, cutting off the objection she saw rising in his eyes. "My dad is a retired cop, and I have a good dozen cousins on forces all over the area. My dad will know who to contact so that this," she waved over her shoulder, "is efficiently and quietly handed over to the FBI. I want to keep both our names out of it, and he'll know the best way to do that."

He eyed her dubiously, then finally nodded. She let out a breath she hadn't realized she'd been holding and pulled out her phone. Her instinct told her to turn away while she talked, but she forced herself to stay rooted to her spot, holding Jay's gaze the entire conversation. For reasons she didn't have the luxury of exploring at the moment, she wanted him to know she had no intention of hiding anything from him.

She ended the call and gestured him back to the sidewalk. They'd only bring attention to themselves standing in the road.

"Why do you want to keep our names out of it?" he asked when they'd stepped back into the shadows.

"Not to sound like a coward but it's safer that way. I may be wrong, but I'm going to assume those two guys in the pub are the ones who did that to Smitty," she said, gesturing toward the sedan. "And I think they were at the pub looking for whoever he was meeting. I don't know who they are, not yet anyway, but if they have access to police and FBI reports, I don't want our names connected to Smitty's. At least not yet."

"Why does that sound reasonable but wrong?" he asked.

"Because sometimes that's how life is," Naomi said. Jay didn't respond and the silence stretched between, turning the moment into an awkward one.

"You can go now if you want," Naomi said. "I wouldn't blame you if you don't want to get mixed up with this. With me."

In response, he took her hand and pulled her close. Wrapping an arm around her shoulder, he dropped a kiss on the top of her head. "I knew you were smart when I first started talking to you, don't be dumb now."

She couldn't stop the laughter that burst from her—quietly, of course, but still unexpected.

"So, if you and Smitty never actually met, and he didn't have a chance to tell you whatever it was he was planning on telling you, so long as your name stays unconnected, you're safe, right?" he asked.

She meant to state an emphatic yes, but she hesitated. She heard him sigh.

"He did manage to tell you something, didn't he?" he asked.

"Yes, but I don't know what. Not yet, anyway," she answered.

"Can you tell me what that means?"

She hesitated. He didn't press, making it clear with his silence that it was her decision. He wasn't all wrong about being concerned with her safety. If something were to happen to her, it might be a good idea for someone else to know about the device.

Taking a breath, she took a chance and told him. "He left me a thumb drive."

He blinked. "How could you have possibly found that?"

She told him about finding the blue tack and embedded drive under the bar. He took in her recitation—seemed to be taking in the entire series of events—with an almost unnerving calm.

"I'm not going to ask you if you have any idea what's on it, but should I also assume that I shouldn't mention it to the police?"

She cleared her throat. She hadn't yet asked him to actually break the law, but avoiding mention of the thumb drive, the information on which may have very well kicked off the events of the evening, definitely straddled that line.

"I won't mention it if you make me one promise," he said.

She drew her head back to look at him. "What's that?"

"I don't want you to be the only one who knows whatever it is that guy was killed for so when you start looking into it, promise me you'll bring in someone else you trust. I'd say your brother, but I know he's traveling right now, so someone, anyone, you can trust."

She stared at him for a long moment. "That sounds reasonable, almost too reasonable. Why are you so calm about this?" she asked, trying to pull away from him. She didn't suspect him of having any part in what had happened to Smitty, but his response was a little unusual.

He tightened his arm around her shoulder and reached for her hand, preventing her from drawing away. With her hand in his, he placed her palm over his heart. Through his shirt and sweatshirt, she felt a strong beat racing under her touch. "I work in a business where it's essential to remain calm and focused even when you don't feel like it," he said. "Believe me, I am *not* calm about this."

The rapid beat of his heart attested to the truth of that statement.

"But I'm working my ass off right now to keep a clear head

because in my line of work, that's the only way to succeed," he continued. "I've also found that pretending to be in control is a pretty good fallback approach when I don't know what the hell else to do."

She let her hand mold to his chest as she absorbed the feel of his heartbeat under her palm. "Are you going to be okay?" she asked.

"I'll be fine." His response was a bit stiff and she tried to pull back again, but he pulled her against him. "I'll be fine," he repeated, this time more convincingly. "We'll get through tonight and then after that, well, I told you that my team is negotiating a big deal. Prep will start tomorrow, and my job always helps me put things in perspective. It also gives me a healthy way to cope with the shit that life sometimes deals. And I think we can both agree that this is some weird shit we've encountered tonight," he finished.

Naomi wasn't so sure about the strength of his reasoning, but he'd trusted her enough in the last thirty minutes that the least she could do was return the favor.

"Wait," she said, as she heard a car turning onto the road. "That sounds like we won't be seeing each other during the negotiations?" He opened his mouth, but she cut him off with an uncomfortable laugh. "That sounded way needier than I meant it," she said.

"Believe me, I get that work sometimes demands one hundred percent of your attention," she said. "I travel enough and go off the grid enough to understand that, and I expect the people in my life to accept that, too. I guess I've just never met anyone else with the same need and it caught me off guard," she clarified.

He chuckled at her words as a car approached. She poked her head out and saw a nondescript police vehicle approaching. "They're here," she said.

"To be clear," he said, pulling her back when she made to

move toward the street. "I have every intention of seeing you again, but while I won't be totally off the grid, I won't be available in person for a few weeks."

She searched his eyes, looking for any hint that he was holding something back, but his steady gaze met hers. "So, no face-to-face meetings for a few weeks?" she asked.

He nodded.

She inclined her head in acceptance. "But after?"

His hands slid up and cupped her face, "Like I said, I have every intention of seeing where this goes."

She smiled. "Fair enough, if this goes anywhere, I'm sure I'll be asking the same of you at some point. If you can live with that, so can I."

He gave a curt nod and let her step away toward the street. But before she could fully move out of the shadows and into view of the woman emerging from the car that had pulled to a stop at the curb, he yanked her back.

"I may not be able to see you, but that doesn't mean we can't talk," he clarified.

She felt her smile grow. "Here," she said pulling her phone out of her pocket, unlocking as she handed it to him. "Add your number to my contacts. I'll get it back from you as soon as I talk to this detective."

The look of shock on his face when she entrusted him with access to the tiny device that contained so much of what she held dear was one she knew she'd remember.

* * *

*J*ay watched Naomi walk away, her borrowed clothing looking odd, almost childlike on her—the pants a little too short, the sweatshirt a little too big, and every now and then her feet would slip out of the flats she wore. He smiled as she shook hands with the detective and began talking, gesturing toward the car with a quiet efficiency—nothing so superficial as clothing was going to impact her confidence.

He entered his name and number into her contacts then hit the call button, bringing her number on his phone. After saving it on his device, he locked both and headed toward the back of Smitty's car where Naomi and the detective now stood.

"No, we didn't touch anything," Naomi said as he approached.

"We didn't get closer than three feet from the car at any time," Jay added, coming to a stop at Naomi's side.

"Detective Patel, this is Jay Evans," Naomi said, not offering any more commentary on who he might be. But then again, what would she say? *"This is Jay Evans, the man I was making out with in the hedges?"*

"Detective Patel made the unusual leap from the FBI back into local law enforcement, but she worked with my cousin on a few federal cases before coming here to Salem," Naomi added.

"Detective Patel." Jay held his hand out.

A beat passed before she took it. "Mr. Evans."

"Did you hear anything or see anyone else when you approached the car?" the detective asked as she dropped his hand and moved toward the front window.

"No," Naomi and Jay answered. "Other than the hotrod," Jay added. Judging by the look of disinterest in Detective Patel's face, he figured Naomi had already mentioned the car.

With her hands in the pockets of her leather jacket, a jacket not dissimilar to the one Naomi had been wearing earlier that night, the woman took the last few steps and stopped before the shattered window. Both Jay and Naomi stayed silent as she gazed inside the vehicle.

"And your cousin said he left her pub around 2:30 in the afternoon."

Naomi nodded. Then, with the detective's back still to them, she added, "Yes."

"And you have no idea why he wanted to meet you? He didn't sound worried or anxious?" Now she turned her eyes back to the two of them.

Naomi shook her head. "I told you, all I received from him was the letter. I can't comment on his state of mind as we hadn't spoken recently. Although the fact that he didn't reach out to me when I was in DC, well, my guess is he *was* anxious about something but whatever it was, he wanted to keep it quiet."

Surprising him, she slipped her hand into his and squeezed. She might be worried he'd let slip about the thumb drive, but he had no intention of saying anything. He would, of course, make sure she kept her promise to him. The thought of her being the only possessor of information someone might have killed for did not do good things to his stomach and reflexively, his hand tightened on hers.

Detective Patel turned to look at the man in the car one more time, her long, sleek ponytail swinging as she moved. She held her stance, just gazing at Smitty, then raised a hand in their direction.

"You can both go now. I know how to reach you if I need to."

"Thank you, Detective," Naomi said at the same time as he said, "But how are you going to explain this?"

The detective flashed a smile at Naomi who, in turn, wrapped her arm around his and started nudging him away from the car. "The less we know the better. Detective Patel can manage it from here."

He let Naomi lead him away but realized, as they crossed the street and headed away from the pub, that he'd reached his limit on all the unknowns he'd been confronted with that night. Naomi couldn't tell him exactly what she did for a living. He didn't know who Smitty was other than that he was someone Naomi had been supposed to meet. He didn't—and wouldn't—

know what was on the thumb drive. And now it appeared he'd know nothing of the investigation into the shooting itself, other than what he might glean from the news. If the news even reported it.

They stopped in front of a cream-colored hybrid Lexus SUV, and just as he opened his mouth to voice his unease, Naomi slipped her hands to cup his face and pulled him into a kiss. Well, there was one thing he *did* know—he knew he liked kissing Naomi. He knew he'd like doing a whole lot more with her, too, when the time was right.

"You did that to distract me," he said when they drew apart.

Naomi smiled and brushed a finger over his lips. "Maybe a little bit, there's been a lot for you to take in tonight. But I also did it because I wanted that to be how I remember this night ending."

And with those few little words, he decided he *really* didn't want the night to end.

But he knew it had to; she had things she needed to sort out and he had, well, he had work to focus on for a few weeks before he'd really be able to give her the attention she deserved. He dropped another kiss on her lips then forced himself to step away.

"You'll keep your promise?" he asked.

Her hand slipped inside the pocket of her sweatshirt where she must have been keeping the drive as she nodded. "There are a couple of folks I can reach out to once I have an idea of what it is."

"Text me when you get home?"

She nodded, her eyes dropped to his lips. He shoved his hands in his pockets and took another step back. A smile flitted across her face.

"Good luck with your deal," she said, pulling her keys out of her pocket and unlocking her door—the *beep, beep*—echoing in the still of the night.

"Thank you. It's going to be a tough negotiation, but in the end, I think we'll walk away with what we want."

She looked about to say something then seemed to change her mind and simply said, "I hope so," as she slid behind the driver's seat. He shut the door and stepped away as the car came to life. Then, with a little wave, Naomi DeMarco disappeared from his life.

But only for the next few weeks if he had anything to say about it.

* * *

*N*aomi blamed the shoes and not her own exhaustion as she stumbled out of her garage and made her way back to her apartment. Stepping into the elevator, she listened to the muted sounds it made as she rode it up to her apartment. Years ago, when she and Brian had first started their business, they'd purchased the six-story historic residence that fronted on the edge of the Public Garden and had views of the Charles River from the back. It was one of just a handful of properties that had views of both iconic sites and now, the former single-family residence included a mix of work and residential space. They'd created a ground floor apartment for consultants to use when in town and had transformed the first floor into a common work area. The second and third floors were Brian's private residence and the fourth and fifth were hers. Each of the two-level residences had a staircase within it, but an elevator—and a service staircase—also connected all six floors. Although, without the right biometric indicators, or an invitation, none of it was accessible.

The doors slid open on the fourth floor and she stepped out, kicking off the too-big shoes and not caring where they landed. Her feet sank into the thick carpet and, as the doors closed behind her, she took a deep breath and let the comfort of her space sink in.

Pushing aside her fatigue, she walked into her bedroom at the back of the building. The city lights reflecting off the Charles River—visible through the floor-to-ceiling windows—created enough ambient light for her to move around the familiar space in the muted darkness. Setting the thumb drive on the bedside table, she paused and eyed the small device. What secrets did it hold that were worth killing Smitty for?

At the thought of her friend, tears started to gather and she pressed her palms to her eyes to stop them. There would be a time for grief, but now was not it. Now was the time to focus on finding what Smitty had wanted her to know, and there was only one way to do that.

Quickly, Naomi stripped out of her borrowed clothes and slipped into her favorite flannel pajamas. Retrieving the thumb drive and her phone, she headed upstairs, texting Jay on her way. His reply came quickly, and though the thought of him did give her a little bit of the warm fuzzies, knowing that she might be carrying the cause of Smitty's death in her hand dampened her smile.

After setting the teakettle on the stove, Naomi pulled an old laptop out of a hutch in the dining room. Not connected in any way to any of the secure systems she and Brian had set up in their building—not even the internet—the device was the safest way to see just what Smitty had left her.

She watched the computer go through its booting sequence as she made her tea, well aware that her attempts to be "cozy" were just her way of throwing up a shield against whatever she might find. When her drink was suitably creamy and sweet, she carried the tea and the laptop into the living room, flicking the gas fireplace on as she passed. Sinking into an upholstered chair, she set the two items down on a side table then reached for a throw blanket and tucked it around her legs. When she was feeling settled, she picked up the computer again and propped it on her lap. As it came fully to life, she removed the last of the blue tack from the thumb drive, took a deep breath, and inserted it into the USB port.

Two files popped up in the file reader—one dated just over two weeks ago, and one dated the day before he'd sent his letter requesting to meet her. The first date was one she was familiar with; there had been a glitch, a ripple, in the IT system used by the FBI financial analysis team, the team Smitty had belonged to.

The disruption hadn't been a full hack, but Naomi and Brian had been called in to investigate. Their initial examination hadn't uncovered any evidence of an actual data breach, and so rather than pay them to conduct a full investigation, the FBI had asked that they just bolster security. Neither she nor Brian had loved that idea, but they'd done what they could within the FBI's restrictions.

Naomi quickly scanned the file, which consisted of the logs from Smitty's computer. Not the most technical of people, Naomi was impressed with the information Smitty had been able to pull together, although the actual content came as no surprise given what she already knew about what had happened.

Opening the second file, she found logs similar to those in the first file, but this time it also included the results of a security scan performed by the FBI's internal security team.

This gave Naomi pause.

Smitty's computer, and certain systems he had access to, had a few extra security bells and whistles—including a few new ones she'd added after the disruption event. All of those additional security systems were set up to alert Brian and her in the event of any unusual activity. But she'd not received any alerts from Smitty's computer or the network on which it sat. So why had he called internal IT in to run a scan?

She skimmed through the log lines looking for anything obviously off. She hadn't really expected to find anything with such a cursory look—after all, hackers were notoriously subtle. But even so, she still felt a shard of disappointment lance through her when nothing jumped out as being out of place.

With a yawn, she glanced at the clock in the corner. At nearly two in the morning, she'd been up for twenty-one hours. Her eyes dropped back to the log files in front of her. She needed to do a deep dive, but she needed sleep to do that. Making a quick decision, she copied all the files from the USB onto the laptop then encrypted them before removing the USB device and shutting the computer down.

She stared at the fire contemplating her next move. Jay hadn't been wrong in that she needed to make sure someone other than she had the information Smitty had given her even if she didn't yet know what the information meant. Normally, she'd team up with Brian, but since his current assignment was scheduled to run for six weeks, she needed to figure out who her second go-to would be.

Sipping the last of her tea and watching the flames dance in the hearth, it didn't take long to land on a name—Damian Rodriguez. Damian was an agent she both knew and trusted. He also happened to be visiting her cousin Vivi and Vivi's husband Ian. And while Vivi would have been a good candidate to bring in as well, she was still on leave after the birth of her and Ian's second child.

Naomi smiled, thinking of Vivi and Ian's children. Technically, Jeffery and Anna were her cousins, but since Vivi was like a sister to her, Naomi tended to think of them as her niece and nephew. She missed them—it had been three weeks since she'd been to Windsor.

She looked at her clock again even though not five minutes had passed since she'd last checked. Doing some quick calculations, she figured that between tying up some loose ends in

Boston and avoiding the morning traffic, she could be in Windsor by noon tomorrow and could kill two birds with one stone, or maybe even three. She could bring Damian up to speed, spend some time spoiling her niece and nephew, and, if she could finagle it, maybe even tap into Vivi's enormous intellect a bit.

Not one to linger in regrets, Naomi smiled. She had hoped to spend some time at home after having been away for nearly two weeks. But she had a new plan and now couldn't wait to get back to Windsor.

CHAPTER FOUR

"Naomi, it's good to see you," Damian said, opening the door for her as she crossed Ian and Vivi's back patio.

"You too, Damian," she responded, kissing him on the cheek as she passed by carrying her computer bag, a bouquet of calla lilies, two bottles of wine, and a box of pastries from Vivi's favorite bakery.

"Need a hand with those?" he offered, closing the door.

"No, I got it. Just a few more steps anyway," she said, passing through the mudroom area and into the kitchen where she set everything on the counter. "Besides, I have this for you." She dug into her pocket and handed him a USB, a copy of the one Smitty had left her.

Damian held it up between his fingers. "Do I want to know? And by the way, Vivi just went to drop the kids with Ian's parents for a few hours. She'll be right back."

"Perfect," Naomi said, pulling the pastries out of the box and placing them on a platter. "I'm sure she's been up since the crack of dawn. I know she'll appreciate the sugar when she gets back. And as to your first question, probably not."

"But you're going to tell me?"

She finished setting out the goodies and made her way to the family room, flopping herself down into a comfortable chair and curling her legs underneath her. "I am. I'm trying to decide whether to wait for Vivi to get here or to just tell you and then pretend that the only reason I'm here is to see her and the kids. And Ian, of course."

"May as well wait. She'll know you're keeping something from her anyway. For someone who can't lie her way out of a paper bag, she's remarkably adept and seeing it in others."

"All her training at your esteemed FBI," Naomi responded with a grin.

"I hate to tell you this, but your cousin was recruited into the FBI *because* of her unnatural abilities. I suspect their training had little to do with it."

"Actually, it was a little of both," Vivi said, making both Damian and Naomi jump at her sudden appearance.

"Jeez, you scared the crap out of me, how'd you get here," Naomi said, standing up to give her cousin a hug.

"I walked. I needed the exercise and maybe some quiet time in the woods, too. Coffee? Tea? I see you brought some of my favorites," she said, inhaling the scent of the pastries.

"You sit," Naomi said. "I'll make coffee and we can have it with the pastries."

"That assumes I'm sharing," Vivi said, picking the plate up and sitting down with it in the family room.

"You both sit," Damian said. "I'll make the coffee."

"Yes, sit, Naomi, and you can tell me why you're here," Vivi added, taking a bite out of a cinnamon sugar crescent. "Oh my god, these are good. Sometimes I desperately miss living in Boston."

"Well, it's a good thing you have me, then; you know I love playing delivery girl," she said, curling back up into her seat.

Naomi remained silent, allowing her cousin to enjoy the treat and listening to Damian making the coffee in the kitchen.

A few minutes later, he returned, carrying three cups of black coffee.

"Did you remember this is how we like our coffee or are you just too lazy to offer cream and sugar?" Naomi asked taking her mug from him with a grin.

Damian rolled her eyes. "Ma'am, a Ranger may be many things, but lazy ain't one of 'em," he said, referring to his days as an Army Ranger, where he'd met Ian.

Vivi laughed as she set her coffee down. "Why don't you tell me why you're here? Other than to visit me and my adorable, but exhausting, offspring," she said, picking up another pastry and tearing it in half.

At the reminder of Smitty, Naomi looked down at the dark liquid in her mug. Both Damian and Vivi gave her the space she needed to gather her thoughts before speaking.

"Do you know Michael Smith? In the financial analysis group? The forensic accountant?" she asked.

Vivi nodded. "Smitty, right? You introduced me to him several years ago when I was working that kidnap and extortion case."

Naomi nodded then turned to Damian who shook his head. "I don't know him, the anti-terrorism team works with the finance guys more than my team does."

Naomi cleared her throat and took a deep breath. "I've known him for years and, well, we were supposed to meet last night in Salem only someone killed him before we had the chance."

Neither Damian, a current agent, nor Vivi, a woman who'd been consulting on and off with the FBI for over fifteen years, reacted. Their utter control over their emotions and reflexes always took Naomi a moment to adjust to—and the more interested they were, the more controlled they became. Right now, both were watching her closely, and she was fairly certain that the only thing moving in the room was her own gaze as it bounced between the two.

"I assume *this* has something to do with it?" Damian finally spoke, raising the thumb drive for Vivi to see. Her cousin glanced at the small device then back to her.

"What can you tell us?" Vivi asked gently. Naomi let out a deep breath and for the next few minutes told them everything that had happened from the moment she'd received the letter to when she'd left for Windsor that morning.

When she'd finished, Vivi was frowning in thought, her eyes turned toward the windows at the front of the house that framed a view of the small valley. Damian was gently jiggling the USB between his thumb and forefinger.

"And you have no idea what this Smitty was trying to tell you?" he finally said.

Naomi shook her head. "Not yet. I haven't started my deep dive into the data in the second file, though, so I may have a better idea after that."

"Want me to look into it?" he offered.

Naomi began to shake her head but Vivi cut her off. "Yes, but not in the same way Naomi is," she said.

Damian's eyebrow went up in question.

"It's weird that there was a scan when neither Naomi nor Brian received any security alerts," she said. "I'd be curious if Smitty requested the scan or if it was performed at someone else's prompting," Vivi said.

Naomi frowned, "I hadn't thought about that," she said. "I went straight to the 'why' there was a scan, from a security perspective, rather than to the 'how' it might have come about."

"Or what it would mean if Smitty didn't request it," Damian added.

"You mean that it would imply someone in the FBI may have been involved in Smitty's death?" Naomi clarified.

Damian nodded. "Or if not his death, the circumstances surrounding it."

"Actually, I did assume someone from the Bureau was involved," Naomi said. "All his cloak and dagger didn't make sense unless Smitty was really concerned about someone in the Bureau finding out. What I didn't consider was that it might be someone connected to the IT department."

Damian chuckled. "We all have our blind spots."

"Is there anything else we can do? Do you need Damian to take a look at that?" Vivi asked with a nod toward the device he still held between his fingers.

"No, he doesn't need to," Naomi interjected. "You can, of course, but it's just a lot of technical logs and code. I wanted you to have a copy because a friend suggested that if Smitty's death was connected to what was in the files he left for me, then it might be a good idea if I wasn't the only one who had the information."

"A good idea. And who is this friend?" Vivi asked, trying to sound not curious at all as she took a sip of her coffee.

"Just someone I met last night at Kate's. He happened to be with me when I found Smitty."

"Interesting you didn't mention that part before," Damian said.

"Does his name happen to be Jay Evans?" Vivi asked. Naomi stared at her. "Kate texted last night," her cousin added, not bothering to hide her amusement at all now.

"It's official, Kiera is now my favorite cousin," Naomi said.

Vivi laughed. "She's not really a cousin at all, you know."

"Close enough and you know it," Naomi shot back. Kiera's father had been a cop with both Naomi and Vivi's dads—the three men had been as close as brothers.

"So, you met this guy last night?" Damian asked. At first, Naomi thought she heard suspicion in his voice, but then she saw the glint of humor in his eyes. "Just how much meeting did you do?"

Naomi tossed a pillow at him—they didn't call them "throw pillows" for nothing. "None of your damn business you perv."

A laugh rumbled from Damian's chest. "You have had quite a dry spell, haven't you?"

Naomi opened her mouth to snap back but Vivi cut her off. "I assume you're staying here tonight?" she asked.

"No," Naomi answered. "I knew Damian was here, so I called Rob and booked a room at The Tavern."

"You didn't have to do that, we have the room now," Vivi said. When Vivi and Ian had first met, Ian had lived alone in the home they now called theirs. With two bedrooms and two bathrooms, it had been perfect for two people. When Jeffery had come along it had been doable, but a squeeze, and then when Vivi had gotten pregnant with Anna, they'd decided they needed more space. Thanks to Ian's connections in the community, in the span of about four months, they'd been able to design and build an entire second floor that added three bedrooms, two more baths, and great room over the new, connected garage— and all while maintaining the charming, Greek revival style of the original home.

"I know," Naomi said. "But you don't really need another guest. In fact, why don't you go nap and I'll clean up around here a bit then go pick something up for dinner. Maybe Damian can take Rooster for a walk or something. Where is Rooster?" Naomi asked suddenly, scanning the area for the big gray fluff ball of a dog.

"He's not here," Vivi answered. "He needed his annual shots so Ian dropped him off at Dash's," she said, referring to a friend and local vet. "He'll pick him up on his way home. He was also planning on putting some steaks on the grill tonight. I think he wants one last hurrah with the grill before winter sets in. And did you just drop a hint that my house is a mess?"

"Ha," Damian barked out, making Naomi laugh. Ian had left a good many things behind when he'd left the Army after an IED had nearly blown him up, but his propensity toward tidiness wasn't one of them. In fact, despite having two kids, Vivi's place looked only *slightly* more lived in than her own.

"No, and you know it. But with kids, there is always laundry to do, dishes to put away and that kind of thing. Just go lie down, I'll take care of all that, and maybe Damian can pick Rooster up and take him for a walk."

Vivi looked hesitant then finally, she nodded "That would be amazing. Anna is teething already and isn't sleeping very well."

Damian stood and began collecting their mugs. "I'll just copy the data from the drive onto my computer before I go get the beast. You know, so your *friend* can be assured you're not an isolated target." He flashed Naomi a cheeky grin.

"Hey, when you go for a walk, I hear the path around Diller's Pond is nice. It goes by the back side of Dash and Matty's property. I bet Charlotte will be out in the garden," she shot back. Damian and Charlotte Lareaux had dated for nearly a year. Their break-up hadn't been Damian's idea.

"Bite me," he responded as he moved toward the kitchen.

"Such a sweet talker. No wonder Charlotte is with Matty and you're staying here." Despite his back being toward her and his hands full of dishes, he managed to give her the finger as he walked toward the kitchen. Naomi grinned at Vivi who just rolled her eyes.

When Damian disappeared into the kitchen, Vivi turned to her. "How are you?" she asked, somehow managing to be both the trained psychologist she was and Naomi's best friend.

Naomi lifted a shoulder and looked out the windows. "You know how I am. I'm not in denial, I know what happened, and I know whatever I discover probably isn't going to be good. But I also don't want to linger on the specifics, I don't want to think about Smitty truly being gone or what he might have been feeling in those last few seconds. I don't want to think about all the what-ifs—what if there was something wrong with the security layer I put on his computer and I missed something, what if I'd run into him when I was down in DC." She paused and let out a deep breath.

"All those thoughts are big thoughts with big emotions, and I just need to let them trickle into my life rather than flood it," she said. "And so, in the meantime, I'm going to focus on one step at a time."

"And the first step is figuring out what those files mean," Vivi finished, and Naomi nodded.

"Why don't you spend some time doing that? I can clean up around here and you're right, it's the laundry. There is an endless stream of laundry in this house," Vivi said with a smile.

Naomi waved her suggestion off. "Not a chance. Whatever dishes Damian doesn't do will take me ten minutes, I'll throw a load of laundry in, fold what's in the dryer, and then spend some time looking things over. Once the laundry is done, I'll pop out for a little shopping and drop my stuff at The Tavern. I may fit in another hour or so in my room before coming back."

Vivi looked to be about to object, but Naomi rose from her seat and started shooing her cousin toward the stairs—in an odd way, Naomi felt she needed the comfort of simple tasks to help her focus, to help her manage.

Vivi's lips pursed, but she stood then started toward the stairs, pausing to give Naomi a hug. Of all the things that had happened in the last eighteen hours, it nearly brought Naomi to tears.

Vivi pulled away. "Don't do too much cleaning. Ian will be distraught if he comes home and finds there's nothing for him to do," she added with a smile.

"Your husband is weird, you know that?"

Vivi laughed. "He feels guilty going off to work every day and leaving me to manage the rest. It makes him feel useful."

"Because being the sheriff isn't useful?"

Vivi lifted a shoulder but Naomi didn't miss the special smile Vivi reserved for her husband—she might think her husband was a little over the top too, but she still adored him.

"Go get some rest and let me get to my chores. I'm going to have this house sparkling by the time he gets home just because it's fun to see him flustered."

"You're terrible," Vivi said through a laugh as she turned back toward the stairs. "At least leave him a dish to do or something."

Naomi watched her cousin leave then Damian popped in to let her know he was off to get Rooster. She remained standing, alone and quiet in the house, just listening to the muted sounds of Vivi getting ready for her nap. When the sounds from upstairs ceased, Naomi glanced around, assessing what to tackle first. The house really was mostly clean; a few toys lay scattered in a corner, a couple of Anna's blankets and a sweater were draped over a chair, and unless Damian had done them, the lunch dishes sat in the sink.

After tidying the kitchen, Naomi settled in the living room with a load of laundry. Picking up an impossibly small pair of leggings, Naomi began folding. As she made her way through the clothing, her computer, still tucked away in its bag and sitting in a chair across from her, seemed to taunt her. She couldn't help but feel anxious about diving into the files Smitty had left her. Based on Vivi's suggestion, she also wanted to look into the IT department and maybe even Smitty's phone log.

She paused, a small sweater dangling from her fingers, and eyed her bag. She had a longstanding security clearance that allowed her to go into the systems and retrieve information like Smitty's phone logs, but Jay had been right to force her to think about her own safety.

She folded the sweater and placed it on a pile of Anna's clothes as she considered her next step. Digging into Smitty's records wouldn't be the first time she'd courted danger, or even faced it, but it would be the first time she'd done so when the danger felt more real, more personal—seeing Smitty's body had removed any distance she might have been able to keep under other circumstances. Even so, the anger and the sorrow she felt about his death outweighed her own reticence.

Reaching for a pair of Jeffery's jeans and wishing Brian were around to bounce ideas off of, she startled when her phone vibrated on the table. Moving aside some piles of clothes to find the device, she hit the answer button.

"Hello," she said.

"Hi, it's Jay," came the warm voice through the line.

She smiled to herself. "Hi," she said again. "How are you?"

"Good, just did some prep work with my team. I'm taking a break so I thought I'd call and see how *you* are doing. I don't know if Smitty was a real friend or just a work colleague, but still, he was someone you knew."

Naomi set the folded jeans down in the pile and leaned back against the soft cushions of the couch.

"He was more than a work colleague, but not quite a friend," she said. "We didn't hang out on weekends or anything, but we worked a few cases together over the years and spent a fair bit of time together. I always liked working with him, he was smart, kind, and one hundred percent committed to his job." She paused, thinking about the man she'd known. She dabbed the corner of her eye with a finger then answered Jay's first question. "I'm sad, of course. Horrified at what happened, but I'm also angry and wanting to do my part to figure out why what happened to him happened," she finished.

"Yeah, I'd probably be feeling the same thing. I won't ask what was on the USB, but I assume you're looking at it and I assume it's something that might help you?"

Naomi let out a little laugh. "Actually, I'm folding baby clothes right now."

A long pause followed her announcement. "Baby clothes?"

"Yes, since you like baseball so much, I figure we should have at least enough kids to field a team and, in that case, I should start collecting clothes now."

"Do they make little catchers' masks, too? And mini mitts? Because that would be damn cute," he said without hesitation.

Naomi laughed. "I'm at my cousin's house in Windsor, New York. I drove over this morning because I wanted to see her. It's a small town on the western side of the Berkshires, just over the Massachusetts border."

"And she has kids, I take it."

"Two. Jeffery, my godson, is three and Anna is nearly eight months."

"You just got home. I thought you were looking forward to being back in Boston?"

She shrugged even though he couldn't see her. "I made you a promise, and even without the promise, it was a good idea. I told both Vivi and Damian about last night and even gave Damian a copy of the data on the USB."

"You trust this guy?"

"I do and I'm not the only one. He saved Ian's life back when they were both in the army, and aside from being a close friend of the family, he's also helped Vivi out a few times over the years when she needed someone on the inside."

Jay paused then seemed to accept her answer and changed the subject. "When do you think you'll head home?" Jay asked.

"Maybe tomorrow night. I haven't decided yet. When do your negotiations start?" she asked, changing the subject.

"We've all relocated to a central hotel, but everything starts the day after tomorrow."

"And are you ready?"

He paused before answering but she didn't hear any hesitation when he spoke, but rather something more like pride. "Yes, we're ready, we're all ready."

They chatted for a few more minutes then ended the call, agreeing to touch base again the next day. Naomi was smiling as she loaded the folded laundry back in the basket and Vivi came down.

"I know you like to clean but folding laundry did *not* put that smile on your face," her cousin said.

"It didn't, but I don't want to talk about that right now," Naomi responded.

Vivi arched a brow but didn't pry any further. "Ian invited Dash and Matty and the twins over for dinner tonight, I need to run into town and pick up some more food for the grill," she said.

Naomi handed her the basket. "Why don't you just go put those away, and I'll run into town to pick up a few things. I need to stop by and see Drew, anyway," she said, mentioning a mutual friend who happened to be a former CIA operative. After retiring earlier in the year, he'd set up a mini-training facility on the several-hundred-acre farm he and his wife, Carly, ran.

"Drew?"

Naomi nodded and started gathering her things, tucking her computer bag under her arm. "I was going to stay at The Tavern, but after spending some time thinking about it, I'd feel more comfortable if I were at The Grange," she said referring to the highly secure facility Drew had built for his program.

Vivi studied her then nodded. "Probably a good idea. I know Carly is home this afternoon because she offered to have Jeffery out to ride Pony, the little, well..." Vivi paused and laughed. "The little pony she bought a few months ago in Ireland for all the kids to ride. I'm sure Drew is there, too. Why don't you invite them to dinner? May as well make an evening of it. Come to think of it, if you go to Kirby's to get the meat, you'll be close to Kit and Garret's place, pop by and invite them, too. Kit's editing her next book and could use an excuse to shower."

"Since you seem set on getting the gang all together, what

about Jesse and David and Cate and Caleb?" Naomi asked, picking up her keys.

"I'll call them both and text you if they can come so you can be sure to get enough food."

Naomi agreed with the plan. Then, after forcing a promise from Vivi not to touch the clothes in the dryer, she headed out to track down Drew.

He turned out to be an easy person to find. When she pulled up to the Carmichaels' horse farm, she could see Drew standing in a field, his back against a fence, a heel hitched up on the lower rail. Wearing jeans, a sweater, and work boots, he didn't look like the same man she'd met just over two years ago—back then she was fairly sure he wouldn't have been caught dead in jeans.

He glanced over his shoulder as she approached and smiled, his blond hair falling over his forehead as a breeze blew up from the field. "Naomi, I didn't know you were in town."

"Just arrived a few hours ago. Are you out here contemplating life, the universe, and everything," she said with a nod toward the empty field he'd been watching.

"No, just my wife," he said turning back to the field as Naomi came to stand beside him. Five seconds passed, and then Naomi saw what Drew had been waiting for. Carly, riding hell bent for leather on a gray horse that looked to be eating up the ground with his enormous strides, came tearing out of the woods across the way and flying up the far side of the pasture.

"Holy shit," Naomi said, her heart rate kicking up despite the fact she was doing nothing more than watching the pair.

"Yeah, not my favorite thing to watch. But at least now she tells me when she's going so I can keep an eye out for them. I can see them for most of the run, but there's about a five-minute stretch when they go into the woods. She's an amazing rider and I don't doubt her ability, but those five minutes on that beast have given me more gray hairs than I care to admit."

Naomi watched as Carly, now at the far end of the field, began to turn back toward them. "She do this every day?"

"Every time she rides him, which is about three to four days a week," he said. "I think she's planning on taking him to his first show in a few weeks."

"Three weeks, to be exact," Carly said, bringing the horse to a trot as she circled around them. Dropping the reins, the horse lowered his head and stretched his back even as he continued to move. Naomi didn't know much about horses, but the animal looked relaxed and happy. Eventually Carly brought him to a walk, and though she kept him moving as he cooled down, she turned her attention to the pair.

"I saw Ian this morning in town. He mentioned you were coming for a visit," Carly said.

"I am, for a day or two. I've been sent to ask you both if you'd like to join us for dinner. Vivi is inviting the gang over," Naomi said.

Carly looked to Drew who shrugged, leaving it to her. "I'll bring some dessert, then. What time?" she asked.

Naomi named a time much earlier than she typically ate, but with the gaggle of kids attending, all ranging in age from Anna at eight months to Emma and Elise, both kindergarteners, such was life—then again, starting the evening early meant ending it early, which would give her more time to look into the lead she wanted to explore.

"I was also hoping you might have some room at The Grange?" she asked Drew. His pale blue eyes studied her.

"Anything I can help with?" he asked.

"I'll leave you two to it," Carly interjected before Naomi answered, no doubt knowing that whatever might be discussed would be way above Carly's own clearance level. In silence, Naomi and Drew watched as she walked away, occasionally reaching down to pat the stallion on his neck.

"It's a long story," Naomi said when Carly was out of earshot.

"It usually is."

Drew's security clearance was almost as high as hers so telling him wouldn't be an issue, but she also knew that he'd just retired, and he'd retired for a reason—the world of deceit and betrayal wasn't one he had wanted to inhabit any longer. That was also why he now focused on training newer agents, agents he could help prepare for their missions but also for the toll the job could take on a person.

"I just need some extra computing power and a bit more security than The Tavern offers, do you have room?"

Drew wagged his head. "I do, and of course you are welcome to it on one condition."

"What's that?"

"Carly wouldn't like it if anything happened to you so if you *are* in danger, you'll let me know?" he asked as he stepped through the fence.

"Damian is working with me," she responded.

"Good enough, then." Drew knew Damian from when the agent had helped Carly track down and capture the men responsible for killing her mother. He also probably knew that if Naomi did get into trouble, Damian would tell Ian, who would tell Vivi, who would tell Carly, and it would get back to him. Because that was how things worked in their circle of friends here in Windsor.

"I have one agent staying at The Grange right now," he said as they made their way toward her car. "I'll let her know you'll be by later tonight."

Naomi nodded her thanks then paused by her car as Carly came out of the barn. Drew held out his hand and she came toward them, slipping hers into his and leaning into his side. They chatted for a few minutes more then said their goodbyes. Ten minutes later, she was on her way to Kit and Garret's then on to Kirby Farm to pick up some extra steaks. Once she was loaded up, she swung by the grocery store before finally pulling back into Vivi and Ian's drive two hours after she'd left.

A whirlwind of activity followed her arrival and before Naomi realized it, the house was overflowing with all her favorite Windsor residents. Ian grilled the steaks to perfection, because that was what Ian did, and salads and sides were laid out alongside loaves of fresh bread, wine, and some local beer. People spilled out onto the back patio, and Damian built a fire in the fire pit, giving some warmth to the cool evening for those who'd opted to eat outside.

By the time everything had wrapped up, with the leftovers put away and the dishes done, the kids—all six of them—looked ready to crash. Naomi, Vivi, Ian, and Damian saw all the guests off before turning their own attention to Anna and Jeffery.

Forty-five minutes later, Damian and Naomi stood in the clean kitchen, the house quiet in the unique kind of stillness that falls once children have gone to sleep. "Do you think if I ever have kids, I'll fall asleep by nine every night, too?" Damian pondered, folding a tea towel and hanging it on the oven handle.

"God I hope so," Naomi said, searching for her jacket on the hooks in the mudroom. "I'm such a night owl but I get to sleep in. I know how early Vivi and Ian get up now. If I end up not being able to get to sleep early *and* I have to wake up early, well, let's just say it doesn't bear thinking about."

Damian chuckled and followed her out the door. "You okay to drive?" he asked as she pulled her keys out.

"Two glasses of wine all night, that's my limit," she said sliding behind the wheel. He opened his mouth to no doubt remind her of the few times she might have exceeded that limit —by just a little bit—in his presence. "When I'm driving," she added, cutting him off.

"Right, well drive safe, and I assume you'll need me to don my FBI persona tomorrow?"

"Yes, please. I have a couple of things I'm going to look into tonight, and hopefully by tomorrow I'll have some leads."

"You know I took a week's vacation to come up here, right?"

"Vacations bore you and you know it. If Charlotte weren't here, too, you would have gone back to DC two days ago."

He rolled his eyes and shut her door but not before she heard him mutter something that sounded like, "brat."

She shot him a cheeky grin in return then wagged her fingers at him and drove off into the night.

CHAPTER FIVE

"His name is Corbin Beekman," Naomi said, handing Damian a file. He looked aggrieved but he took it nonetheless. Glancing at his sweaty shirt, muddy shoes, and basketball shorts, she could kind of see why—she'd barely let him in the door before thrusting the file at him. But he'd been out on a walk with Rooster when she'd first arrived at Ian and Vivi's that morning and then, when she'd returned after taking the kids to the park for a few hours, he'd been out on a run.

And truly, there was only so much patience a woman could demonstrate.

"Talk to me," he said, tossing the file down on the counter and reaching for a glass in the cupboard. With Vivi and the kids upstairs getting ready for naptime, they both spoke in hushed tones.

"Based on Vivi's suggestion, I ran a scan last night of Smitty's cell and desk phones," she said.

"His desk phone at the Bureau?" Damian's hand paused halfway to raising a glass of water to his lips.

"Yes, and while I do have the clearance to do that, I'd rather not have anyone else find out if you don't mind."

Damian regarded her. "You are far scarier than you appear, woman."

She smiled. "I think that's part of the reason all the alphabet agencies like me."

He inclined his head then took a long drink of water before speaking again. "So, what did Corbin do?" he asked, leaning against the counter.

"Corbin works in the IT department that manages the computers for Smitty's division. There were no indications that Smitty placed a call to IT, but Corbin *did* call Smitty and then showed up and ran the scan included on the drive Smitty gave me," she said. "And now that I know Smitty didn't request the scan, I want to know if Corbin ran it on his own or if someone told him to run it, and if so, who and why?"

"Why don't you just ask him?"

"Because first of all, that would be weird to have someone he doesn't know call and ask what he was doing in the financial analysis department, and second of all, he hasn't been back to work since the day he ran the scan on Smitty's computer."

Damian let his head fall back and rest against the cabinet. For a brief moment, his eyes closed, and Naomi felt a twinge of sympathy. She didn't know what they would find next but, like Damian, she knew it wouldn't be good.

"Can I go shower and change?" he asked, not moving his head or opening his eyes. "I feel like I'm going to need to be more prepared for whatever we're going to talk about next."

Naomi nodded then added "Yes," when she realized he still had his eyes shut.

"My vacation is over, isn't it?" He didn't sound particularly surprised or even all that put out, but she did hear a hint of resignation she wished she hadn't.

"I can ask someone else for help," she offered, though they both knew she didn't want to and he wouldn't let her.

"Give me fifteen minutes," he said, pushing off the counter and heading to the guest room.

Naomi was just placing Damian's glass into the dishwasher when Vivi walked in. "Did you finally get a chance to talk to him?" she asked.

Naomi moved toward the cabinet that held the canister of ground coffee. "Coffee?" she asked.

Vivi nodded.

"I started," Naomi continued, "but then he asked to take a shower before I finished. I feel kind of bad about ruining his vacation, but since I think he's really only up here because Charlotte is, I'm trying not to feel too bad."

"Actually," Vivi said, taking the coffee pot and filling it with water as Naomi measured out the grounds. "He's here because it's the anniversary of the IED that nearly killed Ian five years ago. He came up to make sure Ian was okay."

Naomi's hands dropped, landing on the counter with a heavy thud. "Okay, now I feel like a shit."

Vivi let out a soft laugh. "Don't. Ian appreciated the gesture and likes having Damian visit, but he's been managing his PTSD really well over the last few years."

"Therapy, an amazing wife, and two great kids might be helping a bit," Naomi said, turning around and resting her back-side against the counter as the coffee pot began to gurgle.

"Therapy and time, probably more than anything. And his own will. But I'll take some credit if you're offering," Vivi said.

"As far as I'm concerned, Ian would be a shell of a man without you," Naomi answered dutifully, making Vivi laugh.

"I might argue the same could be said for me without him, but enough of all this. Are you going to head home tonight? I assume you won't be able to pursue the lead you're about to tell Damian about sitting around Windsor."

"We won't be sitting around Windsor, will we?" Damian said

as he entered the kitchen wearing clean jeans and a T-shirt, his hair still damp.

"No," Naomi said, shaking her head. "But we'll need to discuss the best place for us to go. Here," she said handing him a cup of coffee. "Let's go sit down." She poured a cup for Vivi then one for herself, and all three took their steaming drinks to the family room. Naomi and Damian sat on opposite ends of the couch while Vivi took a seat in an upholstered chair, tucking one leg underneath her.

"So, Corbin Beekman," Damian prompted.

At Vivi's questioning look, Naomi filled her in on the little bit of information she'd already shared with Damian.

"So how did you settle on him?" Damian asked.

"I know the date and time the security scan was run, so I searched the two hours prior to that. Not surprising, there isn't a lot of activity coming and going from that floor, especially at four in the afternoon. There were only four people who entered the area that aren't on the team and Corbin was one of them. I then ran a phone search and found a call logged from Corbin's phone to Smitty's earlier that day."

"And he hasn't reported for work since when?" Damian asked.

"Since the day before Smitty sent me the letter, twelve days ago," Naomi answered.

"Maybe he's on vacation?" Damian suggested.

"None of his credit cards have been used," Naomi responded.

"But no one has filed a missing person's report, have they?" Vivi asked.

Naomi shook her head. "He's an only child and his parents, who had him late in life, live in Florida. I don't know if there is any love lost there, but I checked Corbin's personal phone records, too, and it looks like he only calls them about once a month or so. And the last time he visited them was three and a half years ago."

"So even if they haven't heard from him, they are unlikely to be worried," Vivi surmised.

"Friends?" Damian asked.

"Mostly online friends. He does a lot of gaming, although he hasn't been participating in that either since that day. Most of his credit card charges look to be for take-away food—not from the kind of places you'd meet friends and have a meal together. Unless he pays cash, which judging by his banking activity is unlikely, I don't think he goes out much."

Damian stared at her for several seconds then shook his head, presumably at her information dump. "So, I take it we're going to DC?" he said.

Naomi grinned. "I was hoping you'd say that. Drew has a private plane flying down tomorrow. He said we could hitch a ride."

"Your clothes?" Vivi asked, ever practical.

Naomi lifted a shoulder. "I'll take Jeffery into town when he wakes up and buy a few things. Other than that, I have a couple pair of jeans and I always travel with at least a week's worth of underthings."

Her phone vibrated, cutting the rest of the conversation off. Naomi glanced at the number, and though she didn't recognize it, she did recognize the area code.

"Detective Patel," she explained to Vivi and Damian as she rose from her seat. She headed for the front porch to take the call, feeling the need to be alone when she heard whatever the detective had to say.

"Hello, this is Naomi," she answered.

"Ms. DeMarco, this is Detective Patel," the voice said, confirming Naomi's assumption.

"Please call me Naomi," she said.

"I hope you don't mind, but your dad gave me your number. I thought you'd want to hear the results of the autopsy of your friend. Well, as much as anyone would want to hear those details, anyway," she said.

The detective was right; Naomi wasn't keen to hear the details but knew she needed to. Fifteen minutes later, with some questions answered and new ones raised, the two women hung up. Rather than return to the living room right away, Naomi took a minute to gather herself, using nature as her anchor.

The autumn pageantry that usually filled the month of October in this part of the Northeast had been cut short this year due to the unusually cold temperatures and a few short, but powerful, rainstorms. Even so, a field of green grass dipped away from the porch and the edges of the property were lined with trees, some of which still clung to a few colorful leaves here and there. Despite the sparseness of the landscape, her eyes drank in the landscape and its gentleness soothed her.

Feeling more grounded, Naomi stepped back toward the door but paused when her phone rang again. Glancing at the number, a subtle anticipation lanced through her.

"Jay," she answered.

"What's wrong?" he asked immediately.

Caught off guard that he'd read her state of mind in just one word, she stumbled to answer. "It's nothing, well, not nothing. Actually, it's pretty awful. I just got off the phone with Detective Patel. She called to walk me through the autopsy results."

She heard Jay suck in a breath. "Anything you can talk about?" His voice was gentle and she heard two questions in one —the first about whether the security clearance would allow her to tell him anything and the other about whether she could emotionally talk about it or not.

She exhaled and wandered back to the front of the porch. "Cause of death was as we thought, a single gunshot wound to the head," she started. "No DNA on the outside of the car, but they're still running everything they found inside. It's unlikely the killer sat in the car, so testing the interior of the car itself

isn't likely to yield anything, but they are checking that too."
She paused and let her eyes drift over the bright fall colors.

"They're also running the bullet through the system to see if
they can match it to any others used before. Other than that,
there were a few more specific things that point to what he did
the day he died, but I won't go into those." A hawk took flight
from a tree to her left, startling a rabbit in the field below.

"And how are you?" he asked again, just as he had the night
before.

Naomi took her time in answering, wanting both to be
honest with herself and Jay. The first wasn't a surprise, she tried
to be honest with herself as much as possible. The second, well,
she wasn't one who shared her emotions easily and that she
found herself wanting to with Jay was a new experience. What
was an even newer experience—perhaps even a unique one—
was the feeling that talking with him wasn't just something she
wanted to do, but something that would be *good for her* to do.

"The information didn't come as a shock, not really," she
started. "It's just that sitting out here in Windsor and doing my
computer searches and talking with my family and Damian
about next steps—about the *future*—it just felt a little like
reality slapped me in the face." She paused and Jay remained
silent, letting her find her words. "I *know* everything I'm doing
now is to help find whoever killed Smitty and why," she said.
"But it's easier to focus on what needs to be done next rather
than..."

"Rather than what brought you to this point?" he finished.

She let out another deep breath. "Exactly. I know that
doesn't sound too healthy, like I'm in denial or something—"

"You're not in denial. If you were in denial, you wouldn't be
doing any of this. I've never lost a friend or colleague the way
you did, but I do know a little something about compartmental-
izing, and sometimes it's what we need to do to survive. So long
as it doesn't turn into denial, so long as when you feel you can,

you go back and let yourself mourn what happened, it isn't necessarily a bad thing, Naomi."

Naomi let those words sink in. She wasn't the kind of person to wail and lament over a tragedy—when Vivi's parents and brother had died in the same day, in two separate incidents, it had taken her three weeks to shed a tear. Once she'd started, she hadn't been able to stop for nearly a week. But until then, she'd been focused on being with Vivi, on organizing first her aunt and uncle's funeral and then the return of her cousin's body from overseas where he'd been stationed, and then finally, his memorial. It had truly been the worst three weeks of her life, and she'd been like an automaton, answering calls, making calls, filling in forms, driving Vivi wherever she needed to be. Yet she hadn't cried once during those days, and she'd always wondered if maybe there was just a little something missing about her that she hadn't.

Maybe she was justifying her own lack of empathy, but maybe there was something to what Jay had said.

"How are you?" she asked, clearing her throat from a sudden thickness that had formed in the last minute. Maybe Jay was right, but now was not the time to analyze it and no, the irony of that train of thought was not lost on her.

"Good, we had some good prep sessions this morning," he said, rolling with the change of subject. "We have one more team meeting this afternoon and then we'll go our separate ways until we start tomorrow."

"You nervous?" she asked.

He paused before answering, "Not so much nervous, but I do feel anticipation. I'm looking forward to this. It's been a long time coming. But while it's exciting, I also don't want to get distracted by that feeling."

"A little compartmentalization?"

He chuckled. "Maybe a little, though on a different scale than yours at the moment."

"Not everything is relative, sometimes it just is or isn't," she said. "So, will it be fun?"

"Fun?"

"Yeah, you said you're ready, you said it's been a long time coming, and you sound like you're looking forward to it. Will it be fun, too?"

"I haven't really thought of it as fun," he responded slowly.

"Will anyone die if it doesn't go your way?" she asked.

"No…" He drew the answer out.

"Will anyone lose their house or livelihood?"

"No," he repeated.

"Then maybe you can have some fun, too?"

He paused then answered. "I…" He hesitated again then continued. "Maybe I can."

Naomi laughed at his tone—part tentative but part recognizing the possibility. "Well, I hope you do. Work—life—isn't always fun, and sometimes it deals us some real shit storms, but if you don't really have anything to lose, I mean nothing so serious as life or livelihood, it seems like maybe we should try to have some fun where we can."

"I think that's probably something you do well," he pointed out, and she heard the smile in his voice.

"I have a loud, crazy, boisterous family, and we're very rarely, if ever, allowed to forget what is truly important. The rest is just stuff to be enjoyed or dealt with, depending on the situation."

"Do you think we should invite Oprah onto our next call?" he said with a chuckle, making her laugh too.

"Go, go do your deal, kick some ass and have some fun," she said, still smiling. "I'm headed to DC tomorrow to follow up on a few leads. I'll probably be traveling while you're in meetings but call me if you have the chance—and no, I don't expect it to be tomorrow and won't be upset if you're focused on doing what you need to, just call whenever you can," she said.

"Deal," he said. "And be careful," he added.

"Will do," she agreed. "I'm making Damian come with me, too. I know I'm pretty tough but still, it's always nice to have an ex-special forces FBI agent around when you need one."

Naomi had expected a witty quip to follow but when silence fell, she paused and realized how that might have sounded. She cleared her throat again. "Just to be clear, there is nothing going on between Damian and me. There has never and will never be anything. Ian, my cousin-in-law is like a brother to me, and Damian is like a brother to him, so in more ways than one, we're more like family than anything else."

"You don't have to—"

"Yes, I do," she cut him off. It had been months since she'd met anyone who even remotely interested her, and she wasn't about to allow any miscommunications to get in the way of what might be happening between her and Jay—a man who more than interested her.

"I do need to say what I said because it's important to me that you hear it. I can't tell you how to feel about it or whether or not to believe me, but I can tell you the truth." She'd told him a lot of truths during this call—some related to the case that she felt he had a right to know, some about herself that took a much bigger leap of faith on her part. Both of which she knew, in her heart, were important for her to share with him. She didn't know why it felt so important, but she knew that she wanted a solid foundation with him for whatever the future might bring and the only way to ensure that was to be open and honest.

A beat passed. "Fair enough," he said.

She wished he'd say more, she wished he'd reassure her that he trusted her, but she also knew she had no right to expect that after just a few days. Not in the way she wanted, emotionally. All she could do was speak her truth.

"Now, as I said, go kick some ass tomorrow, and we'll talk whenever you can catch a break."

"Sounds good and, again, be careful. I have no intention of letting the other night be our first and only date."

She liked the sound of that. "It wasn't really a date, you know."

"Whatever, Miss Smartass. I kissed you goodnight, and I have no intention of letting that be our last kiss. If it's a real date you want, give me ten days, at the most, and I'll be happy to oblige."

"I don't really need a real date, but a night out that doesn't require calling in a homicide detective would work for me."

"It's a deal," he said again. She smiled, they said their final goodbyes and hung up. She took one last look at the peaceful valley then turned and headed back inside.

* * *

Jay hung up the phone and set it on the table in front of him. Naomi's words, "have fun," echoing in his head. How long had it been since someone had told him to have fun? He thought about it, he really did, then realized the last time someone had said those words he'd probably been about twelve. Well, if he was honest with himself, his mom used to say it to him all through high school until that night he and a couple of teammates toilet-papered the rival high school's coach's house. She'd stopped after that and started admonishing him to be good instead.

He smiled at the memory then glanced at his phone. With a little jolt of surprise, he discovered that he wished he had a picture of Naomi—wished he'd taken one before they'd parted ways. His empty hotel room echoed as he laughed at himself. If he had a picture, would he stare at it moodily? Longingly?

The more he thought about it, the more he knew it would just make him smile. A picture of her wearing an oversized sweatshirt, her hair that seemed to be a mix of brown, red, and blond pulled into a ponytail. And her laughing green eyes. It had been her eyes that had caught his attention that night; Naomi DeMarco had marched into the pub, wet, bedraggled, and limping along. And yet there'd been a confidence in her eyes that had caught his notice. She was a beautiful woman and she wasn't one to pretend otherwise, but in her eyes, he had seen her own knowledge of what made her unique, what made her who she was, what made her someone to value—and it wasn't her appearance. No, her looks were a part of who she was, but not a big part and definitely not the most interesting part.

And then when she'd taken the seat beside him, he'd decided to strike up a conversation just to see if what he'd glimpsed in her was anywhere near the truth. He had to admit to feeling a little cocky about just how well he'd pegged her. There was *much* more to Naomi DeMarco than what she'd presented. And most of it was reflected in her eyes.

He stood and stretched his back, raising his arms overhead and leaning from side to side. Not bothering to look out the window to the view that sprawled before him, he instead glanced at the clock. He had a meeting with his team in twenty minutes. In the meantime, he was going to think about having a little fun.

CHAPTER SIX

"MAYBE I SHOULD GO to work for Drew," Damian said, stretching out on the leather sofa twenty-eight thousand feet above somewhere in New York.

Naomi heard the comment, but remained focused on her laptop. Kate had finally sent her the file of the closed-circuit camera feed of the two men in the pub that night. The picture was a bit fuzzy, but nothing Naomi couldn't work with.

"Whatcha doing?" Damian drawled.

Naomi glanced at him then returned her attention to the frame on her screen. Hitting a few buttons, she sent it to Damian. His phone beeped a few seconds later and he pulled the device out.

"These are the two men you think killed Smitty?" he said, the mock antagonism gone from his voice.

Naomi nodded. "I'm cleaning up the image and then I'm going to run it through facial recognition."

"Have you sent it to the detective on the case yet?" He frowned as he used his fingers to enlarge the image on the screen.

She shook her head. "She has the footage from Kate, but I

need to figure out a good story as to why I think these two men, men who by all accounts just happened to be doing nothing other than sitting in a pub having a drink, should be suspects in Smitty's murder. I doubt Detective Patel will fall for the 'I've spent my life around some of the best law enforcement officers and agents in the United States, so I know how to recognize bad actors' spiel." After a beat she added, "Well, Detective Patel might believe me, but that doesn't mean her police chief will give her the resources to pursue it. I'd rather figure out who they are first and then hand her the info."

Damian seemed to mull this over for a bit, then nodded and slipped his phone back into his pocket. "You have another computer for me? I left mine at home."

Naomi looked up and frowned at him.

"What?" he demanded. "I figured as long as I'm just sitting here, I can help. Surely there are local traffic cams I can tap into around the pub? Maybe I can help figure out where the two men came from, their car, or even get evidence they were in the area at the time Smitty was killed."

Naomi blinked at the onslaught of options. "That would be great, thank you," Naomi replied feeling sluggish. She'd been so hell-bent on getting lost in her own searches that she'd overlooked the fact that Damian was more than just a good body to have around.

"I think Drew keeps one in there," she said, nodding toward a closed door that she knew led to an office. "The login credentials are taped to the cover, then you should be able to use your own credentials to get into whatever system you need."

Damian stood, saluted, and headed into the office. Naomi turned her attention back to her computer and the image of the two men. Then, as it often did when she was in front of a computer, time seemed to fly, and the next thing she knew, they were wheels down in DC.

After dropping their bags at Damian's Georgetown apartment, then grabbing a quick lunch at a diner around the corner, the two parted ways. Naomi returned to Damian's to continue looking for information on Corbin Beekman while Damian opted to take his own laptop to Beekman's IT department and feign an issue that required their assistance.

To help his story, Naomi had coded in a little glitch that would time bomb out of his system five minutes after he logged on. It would leave no trace or damage, but the blue screen it would produce would give the IT person something to investigate while Damian used that time to ask around about Beekman.

Apparently, it gave him *a lot* of time, and it was after six when he finally returned, storming back into his apartment with a string of muttered curse words shooting from his lips. Unceremoniously, he dumped his computer bag on the floor and glared at her.

Sitting crossed legged on his couch, her own computer in her lap, she blinked up at him. "Problem?"

"Three hours," he said, throwing himself into the chair across from her. "I got there, made up some song and dance. By the way, it's easy to lure an IT person into looking at a computer. Too easy. They were all over it once I insinuated that if they didn't have the time, I'd figure it out on my own." He rolled his eyes as if he'd never had an attack of The Pride.

"My computer did that thing you said it would when I logged on," he continued, "And then they refused to let it go for *three hours* after everything returned to normal. They practically took it apart piece by piece." He closed his eyes and let his head fall back against the chair. "And then there was a problem on the metro, and I ended up walking from Foggy Bottom," he grumbled.

"Awww, does the FBI agent need a drink?"

His head snapped up, and he glared at her again. Then his expression slowly changed to a smile. "Actually yes, I do. Let's go," he said, standing and gesturing for her to wrap up her work. She looked down at her screen—she had enough information for now, she could finish after dinner. After hitting print and sending the document to Damian's wireless printer, she powered down her device.

"I'll just go change. Can you grab those papers I printed?" she asked as she moved past Damian. She didn't bother to wait for an answer as she shut the door behind her.

Thirty minutes later, she and Damian were standing at the entrance of a Thai restaurant that looked more like an English pub than almost any other pub—including those in England—she'd seen. Rather than contemplate the anomaly, Naomi's attention caught on a framed article about Bletchley Park, and she was halfway down the first column when a voice startled her from behind.

"Damian!"

Naomi spun to see a man approaching. Damian wore a welcoming smile and her heart rate, which had kicked up in surprise, slowed.

"Jack," Damian said, reaching for the man's hand. "It's good to see you." The handshake quickly turned into a bro-hug. When he stepped back, he introduced her. "This is Naomi DeMarco, Ian's wife's cousin," Damian said. "Naomi, this is Jack. He served with Ian and me."

Naomi smiled and shook his hand.

"Keeping it in the family, then," Jack commented with a teasing grin, his eyes going between the two.

Damian rolled his eyes. "I love her like a sister, and I'd rather have the plague than have it any other way."

Jack's eyes widened then darted to her warily. Naomi shrugged. "It's not worth getting worked up over his insult when I feel the same way."

Jack regarded them, then a smile split his face. "Okay then, let me get you seated. And judging by your hair, Rodriguez, I'm guessing you need a drink too?" He turned and led them toward a table in the back.

"What about my hair? You didn't tell me anything about my hair," Damian said to her as they wound their way back.

"It's sticking up in front. Straight up, right about here." Naomi answered pointing to a spot above her own right eye. He'd run his hands through it in frustration more than once during the recitation of his encounter with the IT department.

"And you couldn't have told me?" he muttered as they reached their table, him patting his hair down.

"Of course I could have. I just didn't feel like it," she said, making Jack laugh as he pulled out a chair for her. She smiled at him and sank down into the seat. "Thank you, Jack."

Jack smiled back, all handsome charm.

"Do not get that speculative look in your eye, Jack Zhang. Trust me on this one," Damian warned his friend as he took his own seat.

Jack raised an eyebrow at Damian then turned his attention back to her.

"I hate to say it, Jack," she said, "because, like most of Ian's army buddies, you're very good looking, but he's probably right."

"That's a shame. Perhaps I can change your mind over the course of dinner," he replied good-naturedly.

"You can try, and I'm not above flirting a bit if it will lead to a good meal, but don't get your hopes up it will mean any more than that," she said with a smile.

Jack laughed. "Fair enough. I'll bring you both a drink and get you started on dinner," he said, then turned and walked away.

He'd not provided them with menus nor asked what they wanted. Naomi considered asking Damian what to expect, but just then he pulled out the papers she'd asked him to grab for her and handed them over. More serious topics took over after that.

"Corbin Beekman was scheduled to take several days off but was expected back today," he started. "He didn't show. No one seemed worried about him and everyone seemed sure he must have just called HR to let them know he wouldn't be in."

"In other words, nothing going on to ring any warning bells," she said, unfolding the papers Damian had handed over.

Damian inclined his head. "They did say his vacation was sort of sudden, but he claimed to have won the trip and so again, no one seemed to think much of it."

"Did they say where he was going?"

"A beach somewhere was all I could get." He shrugged and quirked one eyebrow.

Jack brought two drinks, and Naomi and Damian both leaned back a bit as he set them on the table. Jack paused, his eyes going between the two. "I've seen that look before, Rodriguez. You'll let me know if you need anything?"

Damian gave a half nod, half head bob. "I think we're covered, but thank you."

"If you change your mind, or circumstances change it for you, you know where I am."

"I do, and that means a lot. Now go away so I don't get any sappier."

Jack shook his head but turned and left them alone again.

"He seems nice," Naomi said, lifting the drink he'd given her and smelling it. It had a whiskey base and an orange peel, but other than that, she couldn't place any other scents.

"He is. He's great. Opened this restaurant with his dad when he got out. His mother is English, his dad Thai, hence the some-what odd blend of cuisine and décor."

She took a sip of her drink to find it surprisingly more herbal than she'd anticipated. Letting out a satisfied moan, she took another sip then set it down. "So, did you get any insight into Beekman's character?"

"A bit," Damian said setting his own drink down. "They seemed to know more *about* him rather than know *him*, if you know what I mean." Naomi nodded and Damian continued. "He's diligent, quiet, doesn't socialize with the team much. But he's made no secret of the fact that he wants to eventually become an agent in the cyber security division. And because of that, he's always taking on extra work."

"He's pushing the age limit a bit isn't he? He's thirty-five. If he wants to be an agent, he only has a few more years left to try," Naomi commented, rubbing her fingers along her glass and collecting the condensation.

"It could be motive for him to do something rash," Damian suggested.

Naomi took another sip of her drink, mulling over Damian's comment. Desperation was always a motive to do something rash, but was Corbin really desperate, and was what he did—running a security scan on Smitty's computer—rash? She didn't know enough about him or how much he truly wanted to be an agent to answer the first question. As to the second, a simple security scan didn't appear rash at all. Then again, Smitty was dead, and it was possible Beekman was now missing, so maybe it was rash. She just had to figure out how.

Two dishes filled with food slid onto the table under her nose, and two empty plates landed in front of her and Damian. She looked at the food, inhaled deeply, then glanced at Jack. "Blistered beans," he said pointing to one dish, "and papaya salad." He left without another word, and she and Damian started digging into the appetizers.

"That's all I have on Beekman," Damian said, placing a healthy helping of the salad on his plate. "What did you find?"

She nodded to the papers sitting beside her as she popped a

forkful of beans into her mouth. He picked the sheaves up and scanned the contents. "This looks like a career plan for a criminal. Starting out with petty theft and working his way up," he said.

Naomi nodded. "Kevin Farlow. He's one of the guys from Kate's place," she said. "The larger of the two," she added.

"You managed to identify one of them?"

"Just one though, and it's killing me that I can't find the other," she said, stabbing at the papaya as if her failure was its fault.

"Talk to me about him."

Naomi set her fork down and picked up her drink, though she didn't take a sip. "He's from the British Virgin Islands. He spent most of his youth in and among all those islands in the Caribbean, and he started to be picked up for all those petty crimes at age fourteen," she said with a nod toward the papers Damian still held.

"How'd you find him?" he asked.

"Interpol, actually. He popped up in enough police files in different countries that he has his own file. The interesting thing, though, is that none of his crimes have occurred on the US mainland. He does have an assault charge in Saint Croix, but he doesn't appear to have ever worked on the mainland. And, if one were to examine Homeland Security immigration records —which might have happened today—he's not even in the United States."

Damian made an "mmm" sound as he perused the list of crimes Farlow had been implicated in. As he did, a young man came to clear the appetizer plates, and Jack dropped more food on the table. He pointed to one dish, telling Naomi it was a style of chicken curry, then to the other, saying it was a pork and noodle dish, then he left them again.

"He's never been implicated in anything like what happened to Smitty," Damian said, his attention still on the papers while hers had drifted to the food. "His crimes aren't that violent, but—"

"But there's a pattern of escalation, and there's always a first time for everything," she finished as she dished some of the pork and noodles onto her plate. The aroma of the garlic, onions, chili, and basil was so intoxicating that she contemplated stealing the entire dish for herself.

"Don't even think about it," Damian interrupted her thoughts. She gave him a wide-eyed look of innocence. He reached across the table and extracted the noodle dish from her hand.

"So those are his crimes, what about him?" Damian asked, dishing some of the entrees onto his own plate.

She considered how to respond as she savored a bite then, after taking a sip of her drink, she answered. In chronological order, she told him what she'd learned about Kevin Farlow and his life. Starting with his father—a businessman who'd been convicted of embezzling investor funds when Farlow had been twelve—and ending with his most recent stint as a "bodyguard" to a man who'd raised millions of dollars for a hotel investment in the Caribbean and then simply disappeared with the money six months ago.

"It's interesting that most of his life and his crimes have centered around money and the financial industry," Damian said once she'd finished. Empty plates cluttered the table before them, but their drinks had been refreshed. This time hers was something warm and not quite sweet but not sour either, and she held the glass between her hands as she considered Damian's observation. With the exception of a few things here and there, Damian was right—Kevin Farlow tended to work for, with, or around people who possessed, invested, or managed money.

"I didn't find any link between him and Smitty so I don't think Smitty was investigating anything Farlow might be involved in, but it does give us some reason as to why he might have been interested in Smitty in the first place. We may not *know* the reason, but it's not a stretch to see Farlow targeting someone who worked in the financial analysis division of the FBI."

They continued to mull over the implications of Kevin Farlow's involvement—tossing ideas back and forth as they finished their drinks and desserts and, after Jack refused to let them pay, they started their walk back to Damian's apartment. They'd barely gone a block when Damian suggested the possibility of dropping by and visiting Beekman. She didn't love the idea but reluctantly agreed it might be the best next step.

But that was about the only thing they agreed on—Damian wanted to go that night, under the cover of darkness, she wanted to go in the morning, in the light of day when it wouldn't appear as if they were skulking around.

They debated the pros and cons of each option the rest of the way back to the apartment. When they still hadn't come to a consensus, Damian decided to give her some peace and head to the gym down the street for a few hours. As soon as the door closed behind him, Naomi curled up on the couch with her computer.

Damian's comment about Farlow's sphere of conduct made her wonder if maybe the second man from Kate's—a man she had yet to identify—might also be in that sphere. His picture hadn't shown up anywhere, and she hadn't yet been able to get a bead on him, but going with the assumption that maybe Farlow and the other man had worked together at some point before, she began revisiting each of Farlow's crimes and activities.

Starting from the most recent, she worked her way back. She'd just found a promising lead—a man who had ties to a rather sketchy investor who lived the life of Riley in the Caymans—when her phone rang, startling her. Glancing at the clock, she realized nearly two hours had passed since Damian had left. She gave a fleeting thought as to whether she should be worried about him, but when she picked up her phone, the thought fled and she smiled.

"Hey," she said to Jay.

"Hey yourself. Staying safe?"

"I am, thank you. And you? You kicking ass and taking names?"

He laughed. "Why yes, it was a good day today."

"And are you having fun?" She settled back against the cushions and set her computer to sleep.

"Surprisingly, I am. Anything new today you can tell me?"

She had just started telling him about their few leads—not mentioning any names—when Damian came strolling back into his apartment. She raised a hand in greeting then returned to her call, telling Jay about the debate she and Damian were currently having about when to drop by and visit the absent IT guy.

"You're staying with Damian?" Jay asked. It took Naomi a few seconds to switch tracks from the missing Beekman to the question Jay had asked. Part of her winced, knowing she probably wouldn't be happy if the tables were turned and Jay was staying with another—single—woman, but another part of her knew she had nothing to hide and so nothing to defend.

"Yes, he has a huge three-bedroom apartment in Georgetown that really should raise questions as to how he affords it on a government salary," she said as Damian strolled back into the living room after having disappeared into the kitchen. He carried a glass of water in one hand and flipped her off with the other.

"His grandmother left it to him. She lived here sixty years, raised Damian's dad here, then left it to Damian when she passed away six years ago. It's a great place—a little dated, but in an excellent location, and kind of retro now, too." She flashed a grin at Damian who stared flatly back. He'd never told her any of that. Every now and then it was good to remind people just what information she could find on them.

"Is that Jay you're talking to?" Damian asked as he leaned against the wall and eyed her. "The guy you met the other night but didn't meet as thoroughly as you wanted to?"

"The place may be great, but the company sucks," Naomi said to Jay as she glared at Damian. Damian gave her a toothy smile.

"I overheard you tell Vivi you've had a ten-month dry spell, maybe he'll be the one to end it?" Damian said then raised his glass in a mock salute.

"I swear to god, Damian, I can make your pension disappear," she shot back.

"I swear to god, Naomi, I'm a former Ranger, I can think of a dozen ways to make *you* disappear without anyone knowing any better." He rolled his eyes at her, clearly unimpressed by her go-to threat.

Her eyes narrowed into slits. Then, opting to acknowledge that retreat was sometimes the better part of valor, she rose from the couch, juggling her computer in one hand and her phone in the other, and managed to make it to her room. That she happened to stomp the entire way, and that maybe she managed to shut her door a little harder than necessary, didn't mean he'd won this round.

When she finally settled on her bed, she let out a long breath. "Sorry about that. He annoys me."

"You did start it," Jay pointed out.

"Aren't you supposed to sympathize with me?"

"You two sound like me and my sister but the meanest thing I've ever threatened was to put Rogaine in her body wash," Jay said.

"Eww," Naomi responded, crinkling her nose at the image his comment conjured.

"So, uh..." Jay cleared his throat. "Was Damian telling the

truth? About when we met, that you, well, that had I asked you we could have, well, spent more time together?"

Naomi knew the answer before he'd even finished asking the question, but voicing it seemed to require her to find her inner goddess—the goddess who didn't mind taking chances with her heart, knowing that even if it broke, she'd be a better person for it.

She cleared her throat and dove in. "Yes, you kissed me, and I turned into a great big hussy, and I mean that in the best possible way. If you'd kissed me again, we might not have made it farther than the back seat of my car." She wanted to sound flip, she wanted to *be* flip, but the truth was, she found herself anxiously waiting for his reaction to her admission.

He groaned. "Maybe I shouldn't have asked. I haven't been in the back of a car since I was a teenager, but it's probably going to be the only thing I think about all night now."

Slowly, Naomi smiled.

"So, does that mean he was right about the ten-month dry spell too?" Jay asked.

"I swear to god I'm going to erase at least one zero from his pension," Naomi muttered.

Jay laughed. "I ask, because I know I can't be the only one in the last ten months that's been interested, so why me?"

"Fishing for compliments?" she teased as she tucked the comforter over her legs.

"Maybe, I want an ego rush before another big day tomorrow."

Naomi let out a soft laugh because she knew he didn't need her to feed his ego—first of all, he didn't really have one. Well, everyone had one, but on the scale of egos, his was pretty humble. And second, she'd heard him talk about his team. she knew he had every faith in them and that they didn't need any help from her to do the job they had set out to do. But, all that aside, she could still have some fun.

"Because you're cute and wear a pair of jeans better than any man I've met. I've been surrounded by military and law enforcement my entire life, so I think I have a lot of data on which to base my judgment," she said, answering his question.

Jay let out a bark of laughter. "So, you want to break your dry spell because I have a nice ass?"

"It's a very nice ass," she emphasized. "But if you need a more real answer, I liked the way you talked about your mom and sister."

That seemed to give him pause. "You like the way I talk about my *mom*?"

"And sister," Naomi added.

Another silent beat. "Huh, I wasn't expecting that." Naomi smiled at the surprise she heard in his voice.

"You've heard enough about my family to know how important family is to me—whether it's family by blood or by choice. I like that you're close to your mom and sister, I like that you *like* them, that you seem to enjoy spending time with them, that you respect them. How you talk about them told me a lot about who you are. And so far, my first impression hasn't changed."

Silence fell and Naomi was pretty sure she'd either embarrassed him or given him something to think about.

"Well, on that note, with the introduction of my mom into the conversation I think it's pretty safe to say my former preoccupation with the back seat of your car has, well, taken a back seat."

Naomi laughed. "Yeah, well, back seats were fun when we were kids, but honestly, can you imagine trying that now?"

"Actually, yes. And again, on that note, I think I should go. I have another big day tomorrow and need to get some sleep. As much as the haunting idea of you and me together in a back seat will allow me to sleep."

"You going to kick ass tomorrow?" she asked.

"Yes, and you're going to stay safe?" he shot back.

"Yes. And you'll have some fun, too?"

She heard the smile in his voice. "Yes, I'm going to have fun. I'd kind of forgotten how much fun *fun* can be when it comes to work."

"I know, *fun work* sounds like an oxymoron but for the most part, I haven't found them to be mutually exclusive. Not always, anyway."

"Well, I'm not going to tell you to have fun. But be careful, and whatever you decide with Damian, whether to go out tonight or tomorrow, be safe."

Underneath his casual words, she heard his concern. Concern for her, she had no doubt; but she also sensed that what he felt was amplified by the fact that he knew very little about what she and Damian were doing—nor could he. And sometimes the unknown made things even scarier. She'd almost forgotten the toll that *not knowing* could take on a person.

"I will," she promised. "I'll let you know how things go. I know you'll be in meetings all day, but I'll shoot you off a quick text when we get back."

He let out a long exhale. "Thank you," he said. A few seconds later, they ended the call and Naomi set her phone down. Leaning back against the headboard, she contemplated Jay. Had the tables been turned and he was staying with a woman doing all sort of things he couldn't tell her, she didn't think she'd be taking it with nearly as much grace and good humor as he seemed to be taking it.

Mulling over this not very flattering assessment of herself, she started when Damian knocked on her door.

"Come in," she called.

He opened it and stood in the threshold wearing a pair of jeans and zip up sweatshirt, having obviously showered. "Let's go, Juliet."

"She dies at the end, Damian, not a good analogy. And I thought we were going to Beekman's tomorrow."

"Fair point on the Juliet reference, but *you* decided to go tomorrow. I'm going tonight. I know that neighborhood, it's primarily older folks. They'll be asleep or, even if they are awake, the darkness will obscure their vision. That won't be the case during the day."

Naomi eyed Damian. She didn't like the idea of skulking around at night, but she wasn't about to let him go by himself. He might be a former Ranger and trained FBI agent, but he was still her friend.

She sighed. "Give me ten minutes to change."

CHAPTER SEVEN

NAOMI SAT in the passenger seat as she and Damian cruised by Corbin Beekman's nineteen-sixties split level in a working-class neighborhood halfway between DC and Baltimore. Like Damian, Beekman had inherited his house, only his was left to him by his very much alive parents who had simply moved to Florida when Beekman's dad had retired four years earlier.

"Look, all the houses are dark, the street is dark, everyone is asleep," Damian pointed out, not a little smug.

"Until a dog barks and then all the nosey neighbors wake up," Naomi countered as Damian pulled around the block and stopped at a stop light. Beekman's house backed onto a green space, but on the other side of the green space was a shopping center. They planned to park in the big lot then pretend to be a couple out on a late night—possibly inebriated—walk. They'd then *accidentally* stumble across the field and, lo and behold, find themselves in Beekman's yard. Well, not exactly in his yard, he did have a fence. But it was a chain link fence and easily managed.

Thankful for once for the cold weather, Naomi tucked her hair into a dark knit hat, tugging it down over her ears. When they pulled into a spot and parked, Damian donned his own cap and, reaching behind them, grabbed both their jackets.

"Ready?" he said, holding hers out.

"Ready," she answered, grabbing her jacket and opening the door. Tucking her arm in his, she let him lead the way across the parking lot. Crossing the street, they began walking in the direction of Beekman's home. She followed along as Damian ventured off the pavement and onto the grassy green space. The line of trees that separated the busy shopping area from the neighborhood beyond loomed in front of them. She stumbled as she stepped into a groundhog hole and Damian righted her, pulling her up against him. If anyone happened to be watching, they'd see what she and Damian had wanted them to see, a couple out for a walk late at night. It didn't hurt that they'd timed their adventure for about twenty minutes after the bars let out for the night.

A few minutes more into the woods, Beekman's fence came into view. The houses on either side were dark, as were all the houses they could see from where they'd come to a stop inside the tree line. In silent consensus, they stood and watched for several minutes. Their breaths came out in puffs of fog, but other than that, in the still of the night, nothing moved, not even the tree branches.

"Once we approach the house, the neighbors won't be able to see anything," Damian said. Naomi studied the layout, noting, without surprise, that he was right. The houses on either side of Beekman's were set a little closer to the street on the front side, which meant that the back of Beekman's home sat closer to the tree line than his neighbors, and once they were up on the back patio, they'd be out of sight of any neighborly prying eyes.

She glanced behind her. Unless someone was up to no good or confused as to their location, it wasn't likely they'd be surprised by a visitor stumbling through the woods. As much as it galled her to admit it—even if only to herself—it was possible Damian had been right about this visit.

"Well, there's no point in waiting any longer, shall we?" she asked, stepping forward.

Damian nodded and followed her to the property line. Interlocking his fingers together, he made a cradle and adjusted his height so Naomi could step into it. Setting her foot in the palms of his hands, he boosted her over the five foot fence. She landed softly on the other side and he vaulted over after her, making the fence look like no more of an obstacle than a child's toy. Grabbing her arm, he pulled her silently to the back porch.

She stood still and quiet as he withdrew a small lock pick from his pocket. Less than a minute later, they stood in the three season porch that led into Corbin Beekman's home.

"Are you sure he's not here?" Naomi asked in a hushed voice.

Damian shook his head and motioned for her to stay put. Fighting the impulse to tell him he could stick his order where the sun didn't shine, she pursed her lips and watched as he moved off into the house. Leaving her alone. And cold. On the sun porch that wasn't really a sun porch at two in the morning.

"I cleared the house," Damian said, speaking in normal tones as he strolled back onto the porch a thousand minutes later— okay maybe it was three, but whatever.

"At least we won't find a dead body," she snarked.

"Not here anyway, but the night is young," Damian said gesturing with his head for her to follow him. "How'd you know there wasn't a dead body somewhere in here?" he asked as he led her into the kitchen, which lay immediately off the sun porch. "I just said the house was clear, not that no one was here."

"No smell," she answered looking around. The kitchen looked mostly tidy; there were two dishes in the sink, but no food left out or pots on the stove. "Did you find a computer?" she asked.

Damian flipped on a small flashlight. "All the curtains I saw were closed. I don't want to turn on any lights, but we should be okay with our flashlights. And as to your question, I didn't look for one specifically as I was focused on discerning whether or not we were going to have to deal with an actual person."

"Underachiever," she muttered as she turned on her own flashlight and made her way deeper into the house. They spent the next twenty minutes combing through the split level, finding very little. Well, very little with one big exception she discovered.

Seven monitors, four hard drives, and two laptops occupied what, judging by the posters on the wall, must have been Beekman's childhood room.

"Nothing," Damian said jogging up the stairs from the lower level and joining her at the doorway to the room.

"Not quite," she said, swinging the door wide open. She knew Damian had been in the room earlier, but only to assess if Beekman had been present. He wouldn't have had time to truly take in what the room contained.

He came to a stop beside her, and after a moment, let out a long whistle. "This is a lot of hardware," he said.

Her eyes scanned the room again. "It is," she agreed. "But it could be anything from an elaborate gaming set-up to, well, something more nefarious."

"Is there any way you can tell from here?"

She smiled in the dark. "From here?" she repeated. "You mean from here in the doorway?"

"If you could not be a smartass while we're breaking and entering I'd appreciate it."

She winced. "Sorry. And to answer your question, no, I won't be able to tell what he does with this system until I get into it."

"And will you get into it?"

Her eyes tracked the cords crisscrossing across the floor; pinks, blues, and blacks creating a web of power. "I can, but I'm not entirely sure I can erase my access. I can try, but I can't guarantee it until I know just what he's got going on."

"Meaning if you access it and for some reason some time down the road someone else does—"

"Someone like your colleagues at the FBI when they investigate Beekman's murder," she interjected.

"We don't know he's dead." Damian said, his voice curt.

"I think we're pretty certain whether we want to admit it or not," Naomi countered.

"Always so chipper," he said under his breath.

"You know I'm right," she said.

"Just because I know doesn't mean I can't wish it were otherwise," he shot back.

"You are the most complex FBI agent I know."

"I'll take that as a compliment," he responded. She stood, waiting for him to make his decision. She could power up the devices and see just how good Beekman was and maybe leave a trace of her presence. Or they could leave it be.

"There might be another option," she said, as a blinking light caught her attention. It hadn't been blinking consistently, which was why she hadn't seen it before, but sure enough, it had blinked once. Which meant something was on, and if something was on, chances were it was connected to the internet somehow.

"Yeah? I'm open to ideas, no need to hold back."

She elbowed him. "I think the power is on. If it is, I should be able to hack in from my own computer, which will let me control access a bit better."

A beat passed in silence. "You didn't think of that before we illegally entered the house?"

"I don't know whether to be indignant at that challenge to my ability or complimented that you think so highly of me that this oversight is a surprise."

"Which will make you make a decision faster?"

"Indignation. Definitely. And to answer your question, no, I didn't really think of it before. I checked his work computer of course. And I tracked his movements and any other electronic footprints he might have left, but when I *did* check his home network, his electricity usage had dropped so significantly in the past ten days that I made the erroneous assumption he'd shut his house down completely. Thankfully I'm a quick learner, such an oversight won't happen again."

"Woohoo for the future, but what about now?"

She ignored his tone and again eyed the cords, only this time she stepped deep into the room. Reaching out for one and holding it gently between her fingers, she followed it until it ended at a router. She paused then did the same with another cord and then another. Finally, she straightened and met Damian's gaze.

"I'll go at it from my computer. It's an elaborate, but not complex system. At least based on the hardware."

Taking her assessment as the final word, he nodded and gestured her out of the room. Quietly, they made their way back to the kitchen where, by unspoken consent, they paused.

Naomi let her gaze travel around the room as she leaned against the counter. "So, no signs of foul play, no signs of struggle, nothing to indicate that Corbin Beekman did anything other than go on vacation," she said.

Leaning against the refrigerator on the other side of the room, Damian crossed his arms as his own gaze drifted. He looked as if he bought into that theory as much as she did. Still, she wouldn't have minded if he surprised her and said that maybe things weren't quite as sinister as they might appear. But then he suddenly frowned and leaned down a bit, his eyes locked somewhere below her knees.

"What?" she said, turning to see what he might be looking at.

He cocked his head then slowly crossed the room to her side and crouched down. She took a couple of steps away so she could see him. He was poking at something underneath the lip of the cabinets by the floor, but she couldn't see what.

"It's a bullet hole," he said.

Immediately, she dropped to his side. Sure enough, there was a hole approximately three quarters of an inch deep in the baseboard. Keeping her head down, she turned her attention to the linoleum floor and shined her light along the surface. Damian did the same.

"It's been mopped recently," she said.

Damian inhaled. "And likely with bleach. I didn't smell it before but this close to the floor there are hints of it."

Naomi's eyes scanned the area of the floor then returned to the baseboard. "Do you have a handkerchief or something?"

"Do I strike you as a guy who'd carry a handkerchief?"

"What was the thing about not being snarky when we're breaking and entering?"

"Sorry," he said surging to his feet again. "But will this do?" he said tearing a paper towel off a roll sitting on the counter.

"Yes, thank you." She took the paper, folded it then ran it under the lip of the cabinets by the baseboard. Glancing at it as she pulled it way, she then held it up for Damian to see. Brown, dried blood. Most likely, anyway. Whoever had cleaned up after themselves had forgotten to check behind the narrow strip of wood at the bottom of the cabinet that faced the baseboard rather than the kitchen.

"Shit," Damian said.

"Yeah, my thoughts exactly," she said, rising to her feet. Not only had Corbin Beekman likely met a bad end, but as they had no legal right to be in Beekman's house, they couldn't even report it—not without things getting complicated.

"We can't keep this to ourselves," Damian said.

Naomi drummed her fingers along the countertop, grateful for the thin gloves Damian had given her in the beginning of the evening. "I agree, but we need more evidence, more *legitimate* evidence, if we want people to take us seriously."

"No one doesn't take you seriously, Naomi. But I agree, we do need evidence that doesn't rest on information gained from our B&E."

They stood in the silence of the kitchen for a minute; she and Damian nothing but shadowed forms in the dark room.

"We need to find Beekman," she said.

Damian inclined his head. "What did you have in mind?"

"We need to find out when Beekman died. This neighborhood may be quaint but that," she said, pointing toward the greenspace and the road behind it, "is a busy road. A fairly big commuter route."

"And commuter routes have traffic cameras," he finished.

"You're catching on, Watson," Naomi said. She thought she saw him roll his eyes.

"And do you have an idea of how to figure out when he was killed? He hasn't been to work for nearly two weeks, that's a long timeframe to be looking at traffic cams."

"It is," she conceded as she began drumming her fingers again. "But I ran his credit card activity, and it hasn't been active since the day before Smitty sent me the letter. No unusual activity in any of his accounts since then either."

"Do you think it's possible Smitty might have witnessed Beekman's murder and that's what sent him running?" Damian posited.

Naomi's first thought was that there would have been no reason for Smitty to be at Beekman's house—he didn't live in the area, they weren't friends, and as far as Naomi could tell, Beekman had never worked on Smitty's computer before the scan he'd run—but something niggled in the back of her mind.

"I need to get to my computer," she said. Five minutes later they found themselves walking at a casual pace back across the field toward the car. When they were seated inside, she grabbed her laptop out of her bag and powered it up. They had no particular direction in mind, but Damian pulled out of the lot and began driving.

Quickly opening the files she'd stored about Smitty, she began to scan documents. Ten minutes later, she found what she wanted. "Here," she said, rotating the screen toward Damian while they were stopped at a red light.

"I have about ten seconds before that light turns green and there looks to be about forty lines of credit card charges. I'm going to need a little help on this," he said.

She brought the screen back to face her with a dramatic sigh. "The day before Smitty sent me the letter—the day of the scan—he charged six dollars and thirty-two cents at a gas station less than a half mile from Beekman's place at eight fifteen in the evening."

Damian made a left turn into the parking lot of a twenty-four-hour diner. When he pulled to a stop, he killed the engine and turned to face her. "What kind of car did Smitty drive?"

"A 2002 Jeep Cherokee."

"And he bought gas? Not coffee or a soda?"

"Gas," Naomi confirmed.

"That's not a lot of gas for a Jeep. Do you think he was leaving you a trail?" he asked.

She pursed her lips. "I think he was. Smitty was nothing if not a cautious man. I think he might have gone to talk to Beekman about why he'd run the extra security scan, and I think he left a trail just in case. If he had his chat and nothing happened then he would have just bought gas he'd eventually need anyway. But if not..." she let her voice trail off.

"But if something happened to him, he knew you'd dig in and find that charge an anomaly I take it?" Damian finished.

She nodded. "If he'd been that concerned, I wish he would have just reached out to me," Naomi said, suddenly fatigued with sadness. If he had, maybe he'd still be alive.

"Don't," Damian said. "What ifs can destroy you. I think the more important question is, did Smitty leave the gas station and then witness Beekman's death? And if so, what did he do with himself between the time he witnessed Beekman's death and the day he went to meet you?"

Naomi took a deep breath and let it out. "You're right about the what ifs, even if it's easier said than done. And as to what he might have done in that time, I think that's a question for tomorrow, or later today as the case may be. Right now, I think we need to focus on finding Beekman. It's going to be a long night, Rodriguez, let's go get some coffee. And maybe some pancakes," she said with a nod toward the diner.

"You practically just ate Jack out of house and home tonight and you're hungry again?" he grumbled even as he exited his car. "Is it going to be safe to do whatever is you need to do on that computer here?" he asked gesturing toward the restaurant.

Naomi scoffed. "I have certain ways to make sure that no matter where I am, I can maintain at least a minimum level of security."

"And by minimum, you mean the equivalent of what's in place to protect Fort Knox," he held the door to the diner open for her.

"Fort Knox is child's play, but if that analogy works for you, then yes," she said, then smiled as a hostess came forward.

* * *

An hour later, coffee mugs and empty plates were scattered across the table, and she and Damian were still scanning traffic cam images. They'd spotted Smitty's car entering the neighborhood shortly after he'd purchased the gas and then started working back in time from that point in the hopes of being able to identify who might have entered the neighborhood with killer intentions. The going was slow as they had to run the plates of every car that passed through, but finally they had a hit. Forty-five minutes before Smitty visited Beekman, a car registered to a construction company that Kevin Farlow had once worked with passed through the intersection.

Now with a target on their radar, Naomi and Damian fast forwarded the videos and started looking at footage that would catch both cars leaving. They saw Smitty exiting the neighborhood less than ten minutes after he'd arrived. He didn't bother to stop for the red light before turning right and heading west. Fifteen minutes later, the car registered to the construction company followed; this time though, the camera caught the faces of the passengers and sure enough, Kevin Farlow was seated in the driver's seat. And the man next to him was the yet-to-be-identified second man Naomi had seen at Kate's pub.

"They're heading east, can we track them?" Damian asked, pointing to the car as it turned.

Silently, Naomi typed in a string of commands and, taking turns at the keyboard, they continued to track the car—traffic cam to traffic cam—as it left its easterly course and made its way south and then west toward Virginia. As it headed farther from the city, there were fewer cameras, and it took more and more trial and error to guess where the pair might be spotted next. But still, they kept at it.

The sun was just starting to rise when they came to a complete dead end; in a town just outside of Shenandoah National Park, the car passed through an intersection and then disappeared.

Damian cast her a look. They both knew that while the main entrances to the park had cameras, there were still several ways in—and out—that someone could use and stay undetected. Feeling disheartened but not ready to give up, Naomi split the screen on her computer, leaving the traffic camera running on the right, and pulled up a map of the road system inside the park on the left.

"I can pull the traffic cams from here, here, and here," she said, pointing out a few entrances to Damian. He leaned in to get a better look then abruptly straightened.

Reaching across, he hit a button on her keyboard and backed the video up a few minutes. Then he pressed play again. "Look," he said.

Naomi leaned over. "Oh my God," she said as Damian rewound the image and they watched again. Twenty minutes after first crossing through the intersection, Kevin Farlow and his companion passed through it again, this time heading the opposite way, back toward DC.

"Well, I think we have our general area," Damian said, sitting back and reaching his arms up to stretch.

Naomi nodded, "Assuming they needed a few minutes to dump the body, somewhere within seven to eight minutes from that light is where we need to look," she said.

Damian signaled the waitress for their check and glanced at his watch. "How do you feel about an early morning hike?"

She shot him a toothy grin. "Nothing ends an all-nighter quite like a hike."

* * *

With Damian at the wheel, they exited the Interstate and headed toward the town where they'd last seen Farlow and his buddy on camera. Naomi considered sending Jay a quick text, but hesitated given the early hour. She had no idea what time he had to get up or what time his meetings started and didn't want to wake him. Then again, if someone didn't want to be bothered by texts and left their phone on at night, well, they could hardly complain. Quickly, before they hit the last intersection where Farlow had been spotted and she'd have to pay attention to the road, she pulled out her phone and shot off a quick text.

104

"Went out last night. Long story, still out, but may be useful. Good luck with your meeting today. Kick ass and have fun."

She watched the screen to see if he'd start typing back. When he didn't, she slid it back into her pocket just as they crossed through the intersection.

"Got your Spidey sense working?" Damian asked.

"My Spidey sense begins and ends with a processor, but I'll do my best," she answered.

A half mile after the intersection, they encountered their first chance to turn off the main road. They debated, but then decided it was still too close to town to be a good option. Another mile farther, a single-lane road appeared on their right. Pausing at the intersection, they decided it was worth exploring for at least a mile.

A quarter mile in, they came upon a large campground with a few RVs scattered around the parking area—not an ideal spot to dump a body. Without a word, Damian turned the car around and they headed back to the main road. They continued on another mile until a dirt service road came into view. Damian slowed and pulled over.

Feeling a little slow after their all-nighter, Naomi opened her laptop and pulled up satellite imagery of the area—something she should have done before they'd even left the diner. Damian leaned over to look at the screen as she zoomed and refocused to find their exact location. Slowly, she shed the weight of her fatigue and adrenaline started teasing her system. The more she saw, the more she suspected they just might have their location.

"You have an excuse for why we might want to go for a walk down a service road that leads to an old quarry?" she asked, unable to keep the anticipation out of her voice.

Damian shrugged. "I have a friend who said the small pool of water attracts great wildlife," he offered.

"And everyone knows I'm a lover of wildlife," she finished.

"And so, what else would your good friend do when he decided you needed to take a little break from your busy schedule?"

"But take me for a walk to see some amazing wildlife," she said with a smile.

"Works for me," he said, opening his door and exiting. Naomi shut her computer down, slid it into her bag, then shoved the bag under her seat. After reaching for her jacket that she'd tossed into the back seat, she joined Damian.

Unlike Boston, it hadn't rained in the DC area beyond a drizzle in three weeks, and as they walked, Damian pointed out tire tracks here and there. They spotted at least two different kinds, but while they both knew the value of the potential evidence, neither were about to get overly excited.

Fifteen minutes in, they reached the old quarry. Unlike the iconic quarries shown in many movies and TV shows, this one wasn't a big, gaping hole in the ground. It was large, to be sure, but much shallower and with a gentle slope downward from one side to the other, much like a swimming pool. They'd come in at the "deep end" and before them lay a thirty foot drop to the floor of the pit where a pool of water had gathered.

They drew to a stop about ten feet from the lip of the cliff and scanned the area. They'd passed several danger signs posted but even so, Naomi was surprised the area hadn't been fenced off. On the outskirts of the Shenandoah Park and not too far from a campground, it seemed a precarious place to leave unattended.

"Ready?" Damian asked.

She sent him an arch look, "Who in their right mind is ever ready to find a body?"

Damian bobbed his head. "Fair enough, but are you ready to *look* for one?"

She took a deep breath and let it out with a cloud of fog, "As I'll ever be, I suppose."

Together, they moved closer to the edge of the drop and looked down. The ground fell away sharply, and Naomi felt a moment of vertigo wash over her. Damian reached over and wrapped his hand around her elbow.

"You okay?"

"Yes, heights just aren't my favorite," she answered.

"Well, it doesn't look like you'll need to be standing here long," he said, pointing to something poking up from the surface of the water.

"What is that?" she asked, taking a step closer and squinting in the sunlight; she hadn't thought to grab her sunglasses when they'd left the house in the dead of the night.

"Here," Damian said, pulling out a small pair of binoculars she hadn't noticed him slip into his back pocket. Silently she took them and brought them up to her eyes and into focus.

"It looks like the edge of a blanket," she said scanning the surface of the water. From where they stood, the pool itself seemed small. But bad things came in small packages, too.

"Is that a hand I see?" she asked, feeling her stomach swoop and churn with the thought.

"I think it is," Damian said. "The color caught my attention, but I can't see well enough to confirm. Not yet anyway," he said reaching for the binoculars.

Naomi gladly handed them back and stepped away from the cliff. She knew Beekman had likely been dead before being dumped, but that knowledge didn't make the image of him being discarded into the quarry any easier to handle.

"It's a hand," Damian confirmed a few minutes later. "I assume the rest of the body is wrapped up in that blanket, but we won't know until we call in the cavalry."

"Want me to do the honors?" Naomi asked, finding a big boulder to sit on as she pulled out her phone. Damian nodded but rather than join her, he started to make his way around the edge of the quarry. As she waited for her 911 call to be answered, she watched him walk toward the other side, perhaps to get a different view. Ideally, they would have called the FBI directly, but the case wasn't FBI jurisdiction, at least not yet, and so the proper channels needed to be followed.

A man answered her call, and though his voice wasn't soothing as she'd expected a 911 operator's to be, there was something kind of reassuring about his to the point questions and succinct delivery of instructions to stay put and to not go near the body. Not that he needed to worry about that.

She ended the call after providing her name and location and assuring the operator she didn't feel threatened or unsafe. The quarry wasn't far from the nearest town, but this part of the county was unincorporated and so the sheriff would be the one answering the call. How long that took would depend on where the nearest deputy in the county happened to be at that moment.

By some uncanny ability, Damian returned to where she sat less than two minutes before they saw a truck heading toward them.

"Are you going to lay into him for maybe rolling over those tire tracks we saw on the way in?" she asked as Damian stood sentinel and the vehicle came to a stop. When he didn't answer, she glanced at the truck then back at Damian, whose face had split into a huge smile.

"Holy shit, Washington, I'd heard you'd got out," he said, marching forward and unceremoniously enveloping the sheriff's deputy, a tall woman with jet black hair, and dark skin, in a hug.

"I should have known I'd find a piece of trouble like you out here, Rodriguez," she said with a laugh, returning the hug.

"Seriously, when did you get out?" Damian said stepping back.

The woman adjusted her jacket then slipped her hands into her pockets and out of the cold morning air. "A year ago. Spent some time down south unwinding with a cousin, finding my way, you know how it is. Then I came back up here about six months ago when my dad retired and couldn't stand the fact that a Washington wasn't in the department. There have been Washingtons in this sheriff's department since they allowed our people to join," she said deepening her voice for those last few words to, no doubt, mimic her father.

Naomi sat and watched as Damian and the deputy spent a few minutes catching up. She knew the woman hadn't been a Ranger, but Naomi also knew that for every mission Rangers, and really any special branch of the military, embarked on there were hundreds of people in vital support roles.

"Naomi, this is Eva Washington, she managed our stock of munitions for more than a few missions back in the day. Eva, this is Naomi DeMarco," Damian said, introducing the deputy as the two walked toward her.

Naomi rose from her boulder and reached for the woman's hand. She didn't miss the nearly black eyes assessing her. "Any relation to MacAllister's DeMarco? I'd heard he'd up and married some genius FBI agent with that name."

"She consults with the FBI," Naomi corrected. "And she's my cousin." Eva's eyes bounced speculatively between her and Damian, but after a beat, she turned toward the quarry.

"So, you going to tell me about this body you found? And while I'm sure there will be some official story about the two of you being out for a walk and just happening to come across it, I'd appreciate it if you'd not insult my intelligence."

"I don't know what you're talking about. Naomi loves unusual birds, and we'd heard this quarry was a good place to spot unique wildlife," Damian said.

Eva rolled her eyes then moved toward the edge of the cliff. Damian followed but Naomi opted to stay behind. Between not having much to offer and not loving heights, she figured she'd be better off forgoing another bout of vertigo.

Nearly three hours later, she and Damian found themselves standing at the end of the quarry opposite from where they'd started their morning. With no cliffs and just the land sloping away to the "deep end" before her, Naomi decided this location suited her better. Two more sheriff's trucks, an evidence team, and an ambulance all sat parked nearby, and the ten men and women who had occupied them were all either gathering evidence or waiting for the body to be pulled up.

Two men in waders had placed a tarp under the remains and were slowly bringing it out of the water when suddenly a shout went up by one. When several more followed, Naomi glanced at Damian to find him frowning at the hullabaloo as he watched the scene, his arms crossed and gaze fixed.

"You going down there?" Naomi asked. His brows dipped and his eyes narrowed, then he jogged away as his answer.

Leaning against the side of the truck nearest to her, Naomi contemplated sitting down on the ground but stopped herself knowing that if she sat down, she'd probably fall asleep. Resorting to social media to keep herself awake, she pulled out her phone only to find she'd missed a text from Jay.

"Will do, be safe, let me know when you can talk today," it said in response to the one she'd sent several hours ago.

She didn't know his schedule or if he'd have a break, but she shot off a text figuring he'd read it if he could. "Free now, but not sure for how long. Been a long night/day."

She'd barely hit send when her phone rang. "Hey," she said, hearing the smile in her own voice.

"Even your text sounded tired, how are you?"

She filled him in to the extent she could, keeping to the story she and Damian had agreed to regarding their presence near the quarry and knowing full well Jay would understand the subterfuge. She also knew full well he wouldn't go blabbing to the press or to other people. Just how she knew that, she wasn't entirely sure. But her instinct told her that he was as invested in seeing where their relationship might go as she was and to give it a real chance, they both seemed to respect that what they talked about, what they shared, would remain between the two of them.

"So, no birds, but you did find a body, imagine that," he said wryly.

"I know, we were shocked." Naomi felt a bubble of laughter—the tired hysterical kind—rising in her chest. To beat back the inappropriate emotion, she turned her attention to the crowd by the water. Still wrapped in a dark blanket, the body was now out and lying on the tarp ten feet from the water's edge. The medical examiner knelt beside it, pointing to certain things as her assistant stood over her shoulder taking notes.

"Naomi?"

With a start, she remembered Jay on the line. "Sorry, I got distracted. Did you say something?"

"I asked what your plans were tonight, after, well, after you're done doing what you're doing."

She straightened and frowned when she realized the two officials in waders were back in the water. Were they looking for evidence or something else?

"I'm not sure," she answered, distracted by the scene unfolding before her. "A nap, or very early night is definitely in store, but—" she cut herself off when it became clear just why the two men had gone back into the water. "Oh shit, I have to go, Jay," she said as she started walking toward Damian who stood beside Deputy Washington.

"Naomi? Is everything okay?"

She heard the genuine concern in his voice even as she kept moving toward the water. "I'm fine, Jay. There's no danger, I'm safe. But they just pulled a second body out of the water."

CHAPTER EIGHT

NAOMI CAUGHT Deputy Washington's eye as she approached, wanting to give the woman an opportunity to tell her to stay back. But when she turned her attention to the two men slowly guiding another body out of the water, Naomi came to stand beside them.

"I take it this is a surprise? And a simple 'yes' or 'no' will suffice," Deputy Washington added.

"Yes," Naomi and Damian both muttered.

Like the first body, the one they presumed to be Beekman, this one was also wrapped in a blanket. Although unlike the first, no body parts had worked their way free. The form itself was also a little taller and little thinner.

"I'm going to have to search the whole damn thing now," Washington said on a breath. And without taking her eyes from the second body the two men were now carrying, she pulled out her phone and began issuing orders for more deputies.

Not feeling overly useful, Naomi stood by as those around her did their jobs. Eventually the medical examiner gave the order to cut the blanket away from both bodies.

"With the bodies being in water, they worry about it falling apart if jostled too much, that's why they're cutting it. If this were the desert or even someone's basement—"

"No need to say more," she cut Damian off.

"It's not going to be pretty," he said.

"Violent death never is," Naomi conceded. And though she'd never been in this specific kind of situation, this body—these *bodies*—were not her first rodeo.

Starting at the feet and working her way up, the ME gently spread the sides of the blanket of the first victim pulled from the water. Naomi watched as a pair of bare feet were revealed, then bloated, naked calves. A few minutes later, a pair of red cargo shorts came into view and then the bottom hem of a blue shirt. The ME paused at waist level and carefully untangled the arm that had come free. When she finished and the appendage lay beside the body, she continued cutting the blanket to reveal a Captain America emblem on the blue shirt.

A gust of wind blew through the quarry and Naomi shivered. Tucking her chin into the collar of her jacket and hunching her shoulders, she balanced her weight on the balls of her feet, positioning herself to be able to turn away quickly should she need to.

Slowly the ME kept cutting and though Naomi knew the doctor was only taking precautions and following procedures, it almost felt as though she was taunting them. Annoyed at her own macabre antsy-ness, Naomi began to turn away only to freeze mid-turn.

"Naomi?" Damian asked beside her. Without answering she took a step closer; a step that would allow her to see the victim's neck more clearly. Damian moved in close as well, staying by her side.

"Oh my God," Naomi stuttered as her head snapped up and she took a few steps back, Damian catching her elbow.

"I know him," she said. Everyone and everything came to a complete halt.

"Naomi," she heard Damian warn her.

She spun to face him. *That's not Beekman*, she almost said out loud, but the flash in his eyes stopped her. It didn't stop her from saying the second part of what she'd intended. "His name is Carl Rogers, he's a white hat hacker from New York."

* * *

*D*amian's eyes shot to the form on the ground, but Naomi had no interest in seeing her friend lying there.

"Ms. DeMarco."

Naomi heard Deputy Washington's voice and knew the woman was waiting for an explanation. She took a few deep breaths and looked up.

"I recognize the birth mark on his neck. I've known him for over a decade, worked with him on several government projects. He has a wife who lives in New York City and a son at college at Cal Tech. His—" Naomi's voice broke as she raised a hand to her own neck. She cleared her throat. "His birthmark is unique, aside from its size, it's shaped like the state of Texas. He used to joke about it all the time. I haven't seen his face, but I can tell you it's him. His fingerprints will be in the system and —" She paused, pulling up information from the dredges of her mind. "And if he has his wedding ring on, it has his wife's name inscribed on the inside, Wendy, and the date of their marriage."

Deputy Washington looked over Naomi's shoulder toward the ME.

"He has a ring on, but I'm not going to be able to get it off until I have him back at the lab," the ME said, answering the unspoken question.

Washington's eyes returned to hers. "And this is a complete shock to you? Finding him here?" the deputy asked. Naomi gave a jerky nod. Washington's gaze turned to Damian who stood beside Naomi. The two held each other's eyes, then Damian gave a small nod. Deputy Washington pursed her lips.

"Okay, here's what we're going to do folks," she said, stepping away from Naomi and Damian. She began issuing orders, the first of which was to cut the blanket away from the second body to see if they could get an ID on it as well. By the time that task was done, reinforcements had arrived, and they were setting up to begin a grid search of the water. Thankfully, the quarry was no more than four feet deep at its deepest and so they didn't have to wait for divers.

Naomi and Damian confirmed that the second body pulled from the water was, in fact, Beekman, though they kept this information to themselves in order to stick to their original story of the discovery being accidental. Although, Naomi did see Damian lean in to say something to Deputy Washington, and she suspected he had suggested they look in the FBI records for an ID.

By early afternoon, Naomi was on her third cup of sheriff-station coffee. She took another sip as she waited in a hall outside the lobby—waited for Damian to join her so they could finally leave.

Once Beekman's body had been ID'd, the Bureau sent their agents racing down from DC and Damian was still sequestered in an office somewhere talking with them. With two agents killed in less than a week, in addition to Carl Rogers—an FBI consultant—Naomi knew they'd prioritize this investigation. She fully intended to continue her own—there were files and people she had access to that the investigating agents wouldn't —but having the firepower of the federal agency on this case which—with the death of Carl—just got a lot more complicated, could only help.

Naomi pulled her phone out of her pocket to check her messages. She'd texted Vivi an abbreviated version of the day's events as she and Damian had driven to the station, and though she wanted her cousin to truly take some time off, she also couldn't deny that she'd welcome Vivi's input. But she also sorely wanted to feel the comfort of family.

Her texting app popped open, and she spied a message from her cousin, but what caught her attention were the five messages from Jay. Not wanting her phone to go off while she'd been making her own official statement, she'd turned it to silent when they'd arrived and had missed them all. Knowing that she'd ended her call with him earlier in the day with the worst sort of cliffhanger, she wasn't surprised by the somewhat frantic tone of the messages and the two voicemails he'd left her.

Not knowing if he would be able to answer if she called, she sent him a text, but, like earlier, she'd barely hit send when her phone rang.

"Are you okay?" he said.

It flashed through her mind to just offer the standard "I'm fine," but the fear she heard in his voice stopped her. She lowered herself onto a chair and took a deep breath. "I'm fine, we're both fine, and I'm sorry I didn't call earlier. I was detained, and this is the first time I've really had a chance to talk."

She heard him taking a few deep breaths himself, and she admired the way he didn't just let his fear and anxiety explode into anger.

"Now that I know you are physically safe, how are you really? What happened?" he asked, his voice losing some of the strain.

"I think I'm a little in shock," she answered, hearing more honesty in her voice than she expected. Her hands started to shake as she talked—lack of sleep, too much caffeine, and an adrenaline rush would do that to a person. "I told you they found another body, it turned out to be someone else I know," she said then relayed what she knew the sheriff would be okay with her sharing, which was most of what she knew since she didn't know much about Carl's death. Yet.

At the end, silence fell for a beat then Jay spoke, "Jesus, what the hell did that Smitty guy get involved in?"

And wasn't that the question? "I wish I knew, but I can tell you I'm going to figure it out."

"People are dying around you, Naomi. Are you sure it's a good idea for you to keep looking?"

She almost smiled at that question; most men would have offered her their opinion that it *wasn't* a good idea. But because he'd asked and seemed to want to really hear her answer, she felt she had the freedom to answer honestly, with her own doubts and fears. Outside of her family, there were very few people in her life that made her feel that she could be herself; Jay was definitely earning himself a spot on that list.

"I'm not sure, but I feel like I don't have a choice. I don't plan to go gallivanting around anymore like we've been doing the past few days, but I can investigate how I investigate best, from behind a computer screen," she said.

Jay paused before he spoke again, "I know nothing is one hundred percent safe, but they got to that guy Beekman in his home. Is there anything you can do to protect against that? And Jesus, I never thought I'd be having a conversation like this."

She couldn't stop the laugh that bubbled out. "I'm sorry, I know you have your own stress right now, and I'm sorry I'm adding to it. I'd suggest that I'm not worth the trouble for you, that maybe you should just forget we met, but I'm tired and cranky and not feeling that selfless."

After a short pause, a chuckle rumbled over the line. "I'm glad you didn't suggest anything like that. But seriously, what will you do?"

"Smitty's memorial is in three days. I'll stay down here and attend that then head home. I have a few projects I need to get out of the way. Once I'm home, I'll be able to spend my time on figuring this whole thing out—if the FBI hasn't figured it out already, that is."

"You don't sound like you hold out a lot of hope that they will."

She bobbed her head even though he couldn't see. "I know things about Smitty the investigating agents don't, things they can't or won't be allowed to know unless someone cuts through the red tape and drastically changes clearance levels. I trust that they will do their best, I trust that they will do the leg work I don't want to do. And in the background, I'll be looking at the subtleties and nuances and feeding them what information I can."

"I'll admit, I don't completely understand what everything you just said means, but it sounds like you have a plan. Anything I can do to help?"

"You're doing it already. You're letting me talk, you're asking questions, and letting me sort and sift through everything that's happened in the past few days. I know it might sound trite, but it means a lot to me. We didn't meet that long ago, and not to freak you out or anything, but talking to you seems to help me tone down the anxiety I feel about all this and I appreciate it." Suddenly she felt uncomfortable and shifted in her seat as if physically moving would change things emotionally. She'd told the truth and had no interest in backing off of anything she'd said, but it was a big truth for not having known each other very long.

"And you have a cute butt," she added to lighten the mood.

He laughed but didn't let her off the hook. "There will be times in the next few days where I'll be totally off the grid, but other than those times, I will always take your call or answer your text. I'm here, use me. There isn't much else I can do, and I don't like that feeling so use me how you can. You'll be doing us both a favor."

"Deal," Naomi said. "On the condition that you don't let this distract you from the deal you're working on or stop you from having fun while you're doing it. I may be in a little bit of a shit storm right now, but don't you dare come in here with me. Go kick some ass, and when you do, bring some of the glory back to me to make me smile, to give me something to be happy about."

"That's a tall order," he said, but she heard him rising to the challenge in the tone of his voice.

"One I know you can fulfill. In fact, I have a sneaking suspicion you can fulfill a lot of my tall orders," she responded.

He groaned and she all but saw him letting his head fall back in frustration against whatever chair he was sitting in. "I know I promised you a date when this was all over, but maybe we can skip the date?"

Damian walked into the hallway just as she let out a laugh. He furrowed his brow at her but didn't stop walking toward her. "I thought I already made it clear that my expectations of a date were pretty low, just no dead bodies, please," she said.

"Please," Jay scoffed. "Keep those expectations high. I promise I'll deliver if it kills me." He paused and they both groaned. "Okay, worst choice of words, ever," he said.

"Yes, it was, but I like the sentiment. Now go kick ass, have fun, and tell me all about it tomorrow. I think after we get back to DC and I eat, I'm going to sleep until noon tomorrow," she said.

"I'll kick ass," he promised her. "And stay safe. Call me when you wake up. I'll be traveling tomorrow a bit, but otherwise, we have a break for the day."

She promised she'd call as soon as she felt human and then they hung up. Letting her hands fall to her lap, one holding her phone, the other her coffee, she rested her head against the wall and closed her eyes as fatigue washed through her.

"You really need to have higher expectations from a date," Damian said.

In response, she gave him the finger.

* * *

*N*aomi woke slowly, her head throbbing in a pulsing rhythm. She tried to will it to silence, then, with a grumble, she grabbed the blanket and rolled over in an attempt to turn her back on the effects of the night before.

She and Damian had finally staggered back to his apartment at four in the afternoon. Knowing if they went to sleep then, it would make for a bad night, they'd forced themselves to stay up, ordered take out Chinese and then, when that weird second wind hit—the one that bordered on hysteria—Damian had pulled out a bottle of Ardbeg and they'd knocked back more than a few. She'd like to say she'd fallen asleep gracefully after a few glasses, but she had vague memories of stumbling to her room and falling into bed. After that, there was nothing until now.

Taking some comfort in the warmth of the bed, she turned her head and looked at the clock, startled to see the morning had long passed and noon was fast approaching. Her eyes left the clock and traveled to her phone that lay plugged in on her bedside table. She considered texting Jay, then Vivi, but then quickly realized that both of them would probably call her back, and she was definitely not up to a conversation. In fact, about all she was up to was a glass of water, a couple of ibuprofens, and another nap. Her last thought before falling asleep again was that she'd call both Vivi and Jay as soon as she woke up.

Dusk was falling when she finally woke the second time. Knowing she'd regret sleeping through the day but feeling much more human, she rose, showered, dressed, and made her way to Damian's kitchen. Not normally an afternoon coffee drinker, she felt strange making a pot of coffee at nearly five in the evening, but her body seemed to be craving it, along with food.

Entranced by the drip of the liquid into the pot, Naomi started when she heard the key in the lock. She watched as Damian entered the apartment, looking far more chipper than he had a right to.

"They've linked Smitty and Beekman," he said without preamble as he dropped his keys in a bowl on the kitchen counter and swiped the pot out of the machine before it was full.

She glared at him, but he grinned and poured a cup before replacing the pot. Raising it to his lips, his grin broke into a smile, and then he shifted course and handed the cup to her. "You look like you need this more than I do."

She couldn't muster any indignity and instead just grabbed it, inhaled the scent deeply, then took a sip. When the hot liquid had made its way down her throat, she spoke, "What does that mean? Do they have any idea why Beekman ran a scan of Smitty's computer the day he died? Did they find anything?"

Damian shook his head. "Not yet, but they're working on it. At least now they understand that Smitty's death likely wasn't some random thing. I did find out that they are looking at Carl Rogers as a possible suspect for the disturbance in Smitty's department a couple of weeks ago. You know, the one you and Brian came in to investigate?" It was part statement part question, and Naomi found herself shaking her head before she'd even formulated a response.

"Not possible."

Damian's eyebrows shot up.

"Okay, technically, it is possible," she corrected. "He had the skill, but he wouldn't have done it."

Damian stared at her and stared some more. She let out a deep breath and tried to explain.

"As I said, he had the skill, but Carl Rogers was a man committed to king and country, so to speak. He and his wife were high school sweethearts, married at eighteen, parents at twenty, and by twenty-three, Carl had made a name for himself as one of the top IT security consultants in the world—not just the United States, but the world.

"I worked with him on several projects for the FBI, the CIA, the NSA, and every other alphabet agency you can think of. He wasn't righteous, but in our world, he was about as black and white as you can get in terms of what he would and wouldn't engage in," she said.

Damian poured himself a cup of coffee and gestured her toward his living room where he sank into a chair and she onto the couch.

"No one was going into detail about what happened other than to say that there was a tech issue. What was it exactly?" he asked.

Naomi wagged her head from side to side. "To be honest, I'm not entirely sure. There was a disturbance, but no actual attempt to hack the system. It felt to me a little like someone just wanted to see what would happen if they managed to get in."

"Why would they want to do that?" he asked.

She took a sip of her coffee before answering. "The best reason I can guess at would be that whoever did it is looking to do something bigger and was just gathering intel."

"The disturbance they set in motion is their version of electronic reconnaissance?" Damian said and Naomi nodded. "That sounds way more sinister than the talk around the office today."

"When we first discovered it, I raised the possibility, but no one seemed that interested in exploring it," Naomi said.

"If the higher ups had agreed with you that there was more to be concerned about, what would you have done differently?"

Naomi took a sip of her coffee and thought. "I would have tried to trace it back."

"Trace what though?"

"Whatever it was that caused the disruption. It was like some code had entered the system somewhere, made its way through, then self-destructed. The problem is the code that caused the issue could have been inserted at any time so tracing it back would have taken time."

"And let me guess, because there wasn't any actual breach of information, no one wanted to pay your exorbitant fees?"

"My fees are perfectly in line with the skill and experience I bring to the table, thank you very much. But in short, yes, you're right. Obviously there was a break in the system somewhere at some time for that bug, or worm, or whatever it was, to get in, but rather than trace it down, they asked me to just add a couple of security features to try and make sure it doesn't happen again."

"And did you?"

"Of course, but it will always happen again. Technology isn't stagnant, so the top of the line security today could be outdated tomorrow."

"Comforting thought."

"Ensures my job stability, that's for sure."

They sat in silence for a few minutes, both sipping their coffee. Finally, Damian rose from his seat. "So what are you going to do? I talked to Vivi today, by the way. She texted you a couple times and when she didn't hear back she got a little worried."

Naomi pulled a face, "Thanks, I woke up around noon but went right back to bed and I haven't looked at my phone since I got up the second time. I'll give her a call, probably call Jay too. I have no doubt I'll be up all night because I slept all day," she said. "Smitty's memorial is the day after tomorrow. Do you mind if I stay until then?"

Damian was happy to grant her request. Then they scrounged up some dinner as she called Vivi and filled her in. She also texted Jay to let him know that she was awake and would call him after she'd eaten.

Darkness had long since fallen when she climbed back into bed with her laptop and phone and dialed Jay.

"How'd it go yesterday?" she asked as soon as he answered.

She heard the smile in his voice. "It was fun, I know I shouldn't say that, but it was. And yes, we kicked ass."

"That's what I like to hear," she said with a small laugh. "Tell me about it, or what you can anyway." She knew a lot of business deals were hush hush until they were closed and, like the respect he'd given her, she fully intended to reciprocate and not pry.

"It's a franchise we've been gunning for for a long time. It's looking good, but we won't have a definitive outcome for a few more days," he said.

"Sounds exciting." It sounded like business to her, but she could tell how pleased Jay was feeling and she was happy for him.

"It is. It's something I've wanted for a long time and it's hard to believe it might happen. Though I don't want to tempt the fates by talking about it too much."

"It's weird how superstitious we can get, isn't it?" Naomi commented, thinking she was much the same way when it came to certain aspects of her work. When she was working a case, she'd learned not to keep things too close to the vest, knowing that people needed the information she uncovered. But in her own mind, the closer she got to successfully resolving a case, the more she tended to minimize the likelihood of that outcome so as not to tempt the fates, or what-have-you, to have a good laugh at her expense.

"We manage the intensity of a situation in whatever ways we need to. Now, enough about me, what about you? You didn't sleep all day did you?"

She let out a little humph and leaned back against the headboard of the bed. She proceeded to tell Jay about her lazy day and how she was no doubt going to pay for it that night. From there, the conversation meandered toward whiskey, which made her stomach churn a bit, though she was glad to hear they had similar tastes, then to Goo who was currently lying in bed with Jay, which he proved by snapping a picture of the retriever. With her head on his stomach, she'd deigned to open one eye for the picture but was clearly trying to sleep.

The conversation covered everything and nothing, and when they finally ended the call, it was close to ten. But as she knew would be the case, sleep wasn't even a hint on her horizon, and so instead of trying to convince herself otherwise, she powered up her laptop, got comfy against a couple of pillows, and hunkered down for a long night taking care of work that had piled up over the last two days.

CHAPTER NINE

JUST OVER A WEEK after she'd returned home from her ten-day trip to DC, Naomi once again stepped out of the elevator into her apartment. This time though, rather than going to the fifth floor, she'd gone directly to the fourth, turned left when she'd exited, and entered her bedroom. Full dark hadn't yet fallen and so she opted not to turn the lights on, the dim, subtleness of the light suiting her mood.

She kicked off her shoes as she dropped her bags beside the bed then slipped out of the black dress she'd worn to Smitty's memorial that had ended not three and a half hours ago. Wanting to rid herself of some of the sorrow, though knowing it to be impossible, she stepped into a hot shower and let the water soothe her. Feeling a bit like an automaton, she went through the motions of washing her hair and soaping her body, but all the while, her mind returned to the service.

She had expected to feel sad, she had expected to feel the loss. She hadn't expected to feel the complete devastation she'd experienced—was still experiencing—when she'd learned Smitty had had three children. Three foster children to be exact, though all three were grown now. She'd had no idea he had fostered kids, and while it was always hard to see the family of the deceased at funerals, the stories the now-adult children had told of their father had been heart wrenching and powerful. Joyful, too, in their own way, but hearing firsthand from the kids, two sons and a daughter, just what an impact their father had had, made the reality of losing him so much more than the loss of a colleague.

After climbing out of the shower, she pulled on her robe and turned the fireplace in her room on. Rather than climb into bed, she took a seat on the chaise and stared out the window to the inky blackness of the Charles River. Before today, she'd been keen to find out what had happened to Smitty. But after meeting his children, her determination had only grown stronger. Tonight, she would grieve, but tomorrow... tomorrow, she would take on the world if needed to find justice for him.

An hour later, Naomi had yet to move. She was just contemplating getting up and making some tea when her phone rang. Jay's number flashed up on the screen, and for the first time since she'd met him, seeing it didn't elicit her automatic smile. Not because her feelings for him had changed, but because tonight she simply felt too overwhelmed with emotion to be able to experience any more.

"Hey," she said as she answered, then immediately pulled the phone away from her ear as the sound of cheering and general ribaldry echoed across the line.

"Hold on," she heard Jay say. His words were followed by scuffling and the sound of a door opening and closing as he, presumably, tried to find somewhere quieter.

"Hey, sorry about that," he said as soon as the sounds faded.

"No problem, sounds like you guys closed the deal today then?" she asked.

He chuckled, "We did, there's just a little party going on right now."

She smiled then. "Sounds like it, sounds like you deserve a celebration. I know this was important to you."

"It was, it is, but I know your day was a little different from mine. How are you? How was the memorial? I know they are never easy..." he said, letting his voice trail off.

Naomi hadn't cried all day, not really. A few tears had seeped out while listening to Todd, Smitty's oldest son, talk about his dad, but other than that she'd held it in, thinking she, as a mere colleague, had very little reason to stake a claim on grief. But as soon as Jay's voice trailed off, she felt tears pooling in her eyes. Not wanting to rain on his parade, she quickly wiped them away with the sleeve of her robe before she spoke.

"It was," she stopped and cleared her throat willing herself to hold it together. "It was a nice memorial. A lot of people attended, several from the Bureau, of course, but lots of family and friends."

"Naomi," Jay said, his voice soft.

Just her name and the tears started again. "Hold on a second," she said, pressing the phone to her chest to hopefully muffle the sound of her sniffling as she tried to dry her eyes.

"Jay, look," she said, once she knew her voice wouldn't shake. "I'm not in a great place right now. I'll be better tomorrow, and I don't want to bring you down. I know you've worked hard to be in a position to celebrate tonight, and I want you to go do that. I'll be okay so please don't worry."

"Where are you?" he asked instead of responding to her comment.

"Home, why?"

"Where is home, exactly?"

She paused. "Jay, I don't want you to leave your party. I know this is a big deal for you, and I really look forward to hearing all about it when you can tell me, and I want you to join your colleagues in celebrating."

"Where is home, Naomi?"

She hesitated, not quite sure what to make of his tone. He hadn't sounded demanding or irritated just gentle but firm.

"Naomi?"

She let out a long exhale and told him. "But, Jay, seriously," she spoke quickly, "please don't come. Don't get me wrong, I want to see you again, but you deserve this night."

"There will be other parties, Naomi, trust me. I have a few things I need to wrap up before I leave, but I'll be there as soon as I can."

And then he hung up before she could protest any further. Recognizing a stubborn streak when it slapped her upside the head, she conceded that she'd have company that night. Rather than fight it, she texted him directions regarding which buzzer to press at which door when he arrived. When he responded with a quick "thank you," she set her phone on the table beside her, turned her attention to the darkness outside her picture window, and waited.

CHAPTER TEN

"Yo, Manny, are you and Liz leaving?" Jay asked as he walked out of the impromptu press conference. The press conference hadn't been a surprise, but he wished he hadn't been the one chosen to speak on behalf of his team. It had taken an extra twenty minutes that he could have used to be on his way to Naomi's.

Manny Rivera glanced at him in surprise. "We are, Liz is just saying goodbye to a couple of people. Why?"

"Um," Jay rubbed a hand over the back of his neck. He and Manny were close, but he hadn't yet mentioned Naomi to anyone and he knew, with his next request, questions would ensue. "Well, I was hoping you guys could give me a ride? It's not far from where you live."

Manny regarded him as his wife, Liz, joined them and slipped an arm through her husband's. "What's going on?" she asked.

"I was just asking if you guys could give me a ride. It's not a problem if you can't, I can take my car." Only parking on Beacon Hill was a nightmare, and more likely than not, he'd have to park blocks away, and he had no wish to be wandering the streets of Boston, especially not tonight.

"You want a ride?" Liz asked, more curious than confused.

"Does this have anything to do with all those texts you've been getting and sending and those phone calls I've seen you take?" Manny asked.

Two sets of brown eyes studied him, waiting for his response. There was no way he was getting out of this without telling them something.

"I'll tell you everything once we're in the car," he finally said with a pointed look around the room.

Liz grinned. "It's a deal."

The ride, which was no longer than fifteen minutes at that time of night, felt interminable with all the questions Liz and Manny asked. Jay was also certain Manny intentionally drew out the inquisition by slowing at a few yellow lights so that he'd have to stop before they turned red. But true to his word, he answered every question they asked covering everything from how he'd met Naomi to what his intentions were. He stumbled over an answer to the last one, and though his response felt unsatisfactory to him, Liz and Manny seemed very pleased with his inability to explain just what was happening between him and Naomi. He left them with a promise to set up a dinner with the four of them once things quieted down, and a few minutes later, he found himself standing in front of a five story mansion on Beacon Street—well six floors, if he counted the garden level.

Eyeing the behemoth as he approached, he wondered just how well government work paid—more than he knew, apparently. He pressed the buzzer to let him into the foyer as Naomi had instructed and a few seconds later an answering buzz, and the click of a lock, responded. After stepping into the vestibule and letting the door close behind him, a second door buzzed and unlocked. He passed through the double entry and continued on until he came to the elevator, which opened almost as soon as he stopped in front of it.

Stepping in, he looked for the buttons to push for a floor. He didn't find any obvious ones, but that didn't bother him too much since Naomi hadn't told him which floor to go to anyway. At this point, he was along for the ride in more ways than one.

As the elevator rose, he wondered what he'd find when the doors opened. Naomi of course, but in what state? He'd felt a sucker punch to the gut when he'd heard her trying to hide her tears from him. He hadn't given it a second thought when he'd made the decision to go to her. He wanted to comfort her, to be sure, but he also he wanted to be the one she felt she *could* come to when she needed comfort. And the only way to prove that was to be that person. He knew she wouldn't have begrudged him his party—it wasn't in her nature to deny him the celebration—but none of that mattered to him because his desire to be with her right now overrode everything else.

Not unaware that his actions that night *meant something*, he acknowledged them and recognized he'd need to better understand them at some point. But when the elevator doors opened, he knew that point would be a long way off.

Naomi stood before him wearing nothing but a robe and a wobbly smile. Her eyes met his, and they pooled with tears she was trying her hardest not to let fall. Her restraint broke him, and with no hesitation, he stepped into the room and took her in his arms. Sliding his hands into her hair, he tipped her head up to kiss her, and though he'd swear six ways to Sunday that he'd meant it to be nothing more than a kiss of comfort, the way Naomi poured her emotions into it turned it into something so much more.

He didn't know where he was going, but she wrapped an arm around his waist and pulled him, even as her other hand anchored on his shoulder. She walked backward and he followed her into a darkened room, lit only by the dancing flames of a gas fireplace. "Slow" wasn't a word Naomi seemed to want to let into the moment, and within minutes, her robe had dropped and his shirt had come off. He barely had time to appreciate the feel of her against his fingertips as he traced the lines of her body before they were on her bed, skin to skin.

"Please, Jay, please make it all go away if only for a little while," she whispered as he leaned over her, tracing kisses down her neck as a hand explored the dip of her waist.

He closed his eyes against the pain he heard in her voice. Gone was any desire to be out celebrating, gone was the ego and the satisfaction he'd reveled in just a few hours ago, gone was his intense focus on finally achieving what he'd been wanting for years. And in its place was just Naomi and his burning need to ease her sorrow, if only for a little while.

* * *

*J*ay woke alone in the big bed with a view of the Charles he hadn't seen in the darkness of the night before. In the silence of the apartment, he sensed Naomi nearby even if he didn't know exactly where. Propping himself up with a couple of pillows, he studied the view through the privacy blinds drawn across the big picture window—blinds that allowed him to see out but not others to see in.

He'd been impressed with the size of the home when he'd arrived last night, and as he lay there watching a few rowing sculls glide past on the glassy water, he realized that not only was the size of the home remarkable but its location made it even more so. There were only a handful of homes that sat so close to the Public Garden, but hers also had a view of the river. Once again, his mind pondered just what she did for the government.

Hearing a muffled curse from another room, Jay smiled. She had told him last night on the phone that she'd be better today, and by the sound of it, she hadn't lied. He had no doubt she sat somewhere in her apartment, laptop open, already working on finding Smitty's killer. Throwing the blankets back, he rose and found his boxers and T-shirt. He considered pulling on his jeans as well, but he didn't feel like getting fully dressed quite yet.

After a quick visit to the bathroom, he ventured out of the bedroom and into the hallway where he had first found Naomi when he'd arrived the night before. To his left lay a stairwell that rose up to another floor—a stairwell he hadn't noticed before—and in front of him were two doors, one directly before him and the other along the same wall as the elevator.

He heard another mumbled curse just in time to give him an idea of where Naomi had stashed herself, and he made his way forward, expecting to peek in the door and find her curled up on a couch with a laptop on her lap.

"Holy shit," the expletive escaped his mouth as the door swung open. Naomi, dressed in a robe, her hair pulled up into a loose ponytail, turned from where she stood and smiled at him.

"Surprised?" she said.

This was no cozy room he'd walked into, there were no couches and not a laptop in sight. Instead, the room held a bank of computers, he'd guess at least eight judging from what he could see, but what truly had him gawking was the wall opposite the computers. The entire space was, well, it looked to him like a projection screen covered with multiple images from various computer programs, but the resolution was more high definition-quality than a projection-quality. He stared, mesmerized by the separate images occupying the space that had to be thirty feet long by fifteen feet high. Filled with numbers, random words, and symbols, he hadn't a clue what it all meant, but watching them scroll and change, he felt a little like he'd stepped into a scene from *The Matrix*.

"Um, am I allowed in here?" he asked, wondering if state secrets were scrolling by in front of him.

She smiled and held out her hand. He stepped forward but rather than take her hand, he pulled her into an embrace and gave her a proper good morning kiss. When he drew back, he let his eyes stray to the screens opposite where they stood. "Is this one of those things where if you tell me you're going to have to kill me?"

She laughed and stepped out of his arms, but stayed close enough to touch. "What do you see?" she asked waving to the screen.

"Something that looks like it belongs in a movie. I seriously thought these types of rooms were made up for dramatic effect."

Another soft laugh escaped, and while he knew she'd needed to fall apart the night before—everyone needed to every now and then—he was glad to hear her humor and strength had returned.

"I designed the room myself, and if you are wondering, those are high definition screens on the wall, micro thin ones, but screens nonetheless. But that wasn't what I meant when I asked what you saw, I meant what do you see on the screens?"

He couldn't help himself, but he approached the wall, not because he felt he'd have a better understanding of what the screens contained but because the concept of micro thin screens held too much allure for a guy like him to resist.

"What do I see?" he repeated examining the edge of the wall where the screens hung. He leaned in and sure enough, he could see the edge of the device. "Can I touch it?" he asked. Naomi nodded and so he ran a finger along the seam, feeling where one screen connected to another, each section seemed to be about six feet long and five feet tall. Currently, there were four different images filling the fifteen screens.

Finally, he stepped back and let out a low whistle. "As far as what's scrolling," he said gesturing to the images before him, "It looks like Greek to me, or hieroglyphics, or whatever that saying is. I have no idea what you're looking at other than it looks like some sort of computer code. What I really see is the best room in the world to watch a baseball game if I can't be at the actual game." He paused and stepped back to give himself a better view of the entire wall. "Then again, this might be even better than being at the actual game," he modified.

He stared at the images scrolling and shifting before him, he had no idea what information they contained, but watching them was kind of hypnotic. After a long moment, he realized Naomi hadn't responded, and he turned to find her leaning over a computer typing something in. Something flashed on the screen, but her gaping robe caught his attention. She glanced up, noticed his focus, and smiled a smile that stirred certain parts of his anatomy.

She motioned for him to sit in one of the upholstered chairs in the room. She looked to be contemplating the chair beside him, but instead, he tugged her down and she came willingly onto his lap.

He slid a hand along her thigh as her robe fell away, but sensing something important had occurred to her, he didn't take it any further. "Talk to me, tell me what you think. I may not understand all that," he said, waving to the wall of images, "but I'm still a good person to bounce ideas off of."

She leaned forward and pressed her lips to his then, much to his dismay, rose from his lap and began pacing the room.

"Remember I told you about the small disruption that occurred in the department Smitty worked in? The one that happened just a few days before he disappeared?"

Jay nodded.

"Well, from the beginning I wondered if it was something like a fishing expedition. I still think that, but while I originally thought they might be fishing around for information on our *reaction* to security breach, I now think it was something much more than that," she said.

He frowned. "I don't follow."

Naomi pointed to three different screens. "Miami, Chicago, and New York," she started. "Each has its own financial analysis division, and over the course of the past five months, each has had a similar disruption as Smitty's DC office," she said.

"So, what happened in those offices?" he asked.

Naomi cocked her head to the side. "Nothing happened," she said after a pause. "Each department hired someone to come in and do a quick investigation and bolster its security and then nothing more."

"Then what happened in DC? What made it different?" he asked, not liking the sadness he now heard in her voice. Rising, he walked over to her and wrapped his arms around her waist from behind.

Naomi leaned into him but remained silent for a long time. And then she spoke, barely above a whisper. "I happened," she said.

She paused, took a shaky breath, then cleared her throat. "Remember when I mentioned that Smitty was kind of special?"

He nodded against her head and she continued. "Well, I think they were looking for someone like him all along. They might not have known who the specific agent was they were looking for, but I think they knew agents like Smitty existed, agents embedded in departments but with, well, additional secrets to keep. And when I added the extra security features to his system after the disturbance, I more or less put a neon sign on Smitty, pointing to where they should go."

He pulled her tighter against him. "You protected the information," he said softly, dropping a kiss on to her head.

"I did," she said, her voice filled with doubts. "But at what cost? And for how long?" she moved out of his embrace and toward the bank of images. "See this?" she said, pointing to one of the few static images.

"Yes, but I don't know what it is," he said, his eyes scanning the code.

"Three days after Smitty went missing, someone inserted this rogue line of code into his department's network."

"Not to sound flip, but it all looks the same to me."

At that, she gave him a soft smile, and he knew she was back to problem solving and no longer lingering on the questions of Smitty's death. Picking up a portable device from her desk, she typed in a few things. Instantly, a line of about fifteen characters glowed.

"Okay, I see it, but I don't know what it means."

"On its own, it doesn't mean anything, it's not the kind of code that will damage or compromise the security. But the fact that it was put there without triggering any of the security in place—and put there every day since it first showed up—is huge. It also doesn't help that that particular line of code is somewhat of a trademark of someone I know."

"Someone you know?" he asked.

She frowned and pondered the image. "Yes," she finally said. "My brother."

CHAPTER ELEVEN

"YOUR BROTHER," Jay repeated. That didn't sound too bad to him. "Why don't you just ask him?" he asked. She remained focused on the images scrolling and shifting on her wall. "Naomi?"

"Yes," she turned to face him, oblivious to his prior question. He repeated himself then waited.

"It's, well, it's hard to explain," she started. "I need coffee. Would you like some coffee?" she asked suddenly.

He didn't know if she was avoiding the subject because she couldn't talk about it or because she simply didn't want to. Regardless, he rose and followed her out of the room and up the stairs.

When he hit the landing on the top floor of the building, he couldn't help the low whistle that escaped. Naomi DeMarco wasn't as unassuming as she seemed. Or rather she was, but she certainly had, if not hidden depths, access to money somehow from somewhere.

"It used to be a single family home," Naomi said, in response to his reaction. "My brother and I modified it slightly. Okay, a little more than slightly," she added when he laughed. "The first floor, where our primary office space is, retains more of the original character, and believe it or not, so does my brother's apartment, which occupies the two floors below mine. But I prefer more open spaces, and so I did a few more renovations."

As she spoke, he followed her through a dining room at the front of the house and into a wide, spacious kitchen painted in warm tones. "Not to sound crude, but outside the tech million-aires we hear so much about, I didn't think the tech business was this lucrative," he said standing at one of the windows that fronted Beacon Street.

The trees had long lost their leaves due to the earlier storms, but today, the day was clear and the pale blue sky contrasted sharply with the red brick that made up many of the homes lining the street. Behind him, Naomi moved around the room, and the sounds of a one-cup coffee maker filled the silence. Below him, he watched people walking, bundled up against the chill in the air, jackets on, shoulders hunched, breath puffing in front of them.

"Ever heard the saying Boston Brahmin?" Naomi asked, coming to his side and offering him a cup. "Cream or sugar?"

He shook his head and took the mug. "Of course I have," he said, answering her first question.

"Well, my mom is one. I guess that makes me and Brian ones as well, but since my father is second generation Italian, it's a weird thing to contemplate."

"But just because she's from on old family doesn't mean money. A lot of old families have lost fortunes over time," he said, turning to watch her as she moved away to retrieve her own cup of coffee.

"Come," she said, gesturing with her head to the other room as she picked up her own mug. He followed her out, but they didn't stop in the dining room as he'd expected. Instead, they walked toward the back of the house, which opened into a huge living room that spanned the entire width of the building. Two fireplaces anchored each side wall, and behind the picture windows that framed the Charles River was a sun deck that also ran the width of the room. Flipping on the gas fire as she passed, Naomi led him to one of the conversation areas to their right. She sank onto the couch, and he took the seat on the opposite side. Pulling her feet onto his lap, he tucked a throw blanket around her legs then turned to face her.

"Well?" he said.

"Where to start? My mother or my brother?"

"Your mother, it will be a shorter story than your brother, I think," he answered.

She smiled. "That's true, and it's not a particularly exciting one. Her family made money generations ago in trade and shipping. Shipping mostly. They were smart and kept it. There were a few loose cannons along the way, but enough family around to keep them in line, so the fortune has grown and stayed mostly intact. My mother's father was an only child, so he inherited the entire estate, and my mom was also an only child. Brian and I grew up with our choice of silver spoons, if you will, although with a father from a working-class Italian family, staying grounded in the things that matter—like family and community —wasn't an option."

"How did your parents even meet?" he asked, intrigued despite knowing that the conversation about her brother was probably the more pressing of the two.

"My mother, who was raised and still lives in one of the few remaining single family homes on Marlborough Street, was on her way home with a date one night. The young man started to press his advantage, if you know what I mean. She was pushing him away when he grabbed her and shook her. My dad, a young cop at the time, happened to be walking by and put a stop to it. He sent the man on his way and took my mom, who was too shaken up to return home, to a coffee shop along Newbury Street. The rest, as they say, is history."

He smiled and reached under the blanket to rub her foot. "That's a sweet story. And are they still married?"

"Yes, and they still live in that house, the house Brian and I grew up in. It's only about five blocks from here. My dad is still ribbed endlessly by his blue collar family, but everyone loves my mom so it's all in good fun."

Jay took a sip of his coffee as the fan from the fireplace kicked in and the heat curled around them. "What about your brother? Why can't you ask him?" he asked, turning the conversation to the more pressing question.

Naomi looked toward the fireplace and the flames licking the glass. "There's this gig he and I trade off doing every year. Neither of us loves it, but it's important work, and this year is his year. But the thing is, it's a six week project and at an undisclosed location."

"Undisclosed location," Jay repeated, suddenly feeling like he'd stepped into an episode of *The X-Files*.

Naomi offered him a rueful grin. "I know, it sounds so Area-51ish doesn't it? But the truth is, it's just a bunch of hackers the government gathers together every year to test security systems of the various agencies. They put us up in some hole in the wall place, cut off our access to anything on the outside, and tell us to go to town."

"On hacking into government systems?"

"Sort of. I mean yes, but only for testing purposes, and the results are used to bolster security across multiple agencies. It's a lot of long days and generally nowhere near as fun as it sounds," she said with a wry quirk of her brow.

"Actually, none of it sounds very fun. It sounds like they more or less lock you in a room and don't let you out until they are satisfied."

"That's not far from the truth, but the ironic part is that the people who decide when they are 'satisfied' are nowhere near as knowledgeable as the people sitting in the room. It's kind of a weird setup, but I will admit a lot of good has come of it."

"Okay," he said, over the rim of his mug. "So, your brother is unreachable doing this testing thing, do you think he's testing you? Maybe taunting you a little by showing you he got through your security?"

Naomi wagged her head. "I thought about that, but if you were taunting your sister, would you do the same thing over and over again. I mean, if she didn't notice the first time, would you do the same thing a second or third?"

He thought then shook his head. "No, I'd escalate to make sure I got her attention."

"Exactly."

"So, you think someone is copying his signature? Who and why?" he asked.

Naomi nodded. "I do think it's someone else, someone mimicking him. But who and why I don't know."

Silence fell for several minutes as they both pondered the question and sipped their coffee. After a while he spoke, "In baseball, it's really hard to mimic someone else's style for any length of time. And I can't imagine doing it while also having to sneak around, and in this case, bypass all the security you put in place. Whoever they are, they probably know your brother well and have a will of steel," he said.

Judging by the way she pulled herself into a sitting position, tucked her legs under her, and stared into the fire, he suspected something had just kicked in and Naomi's brain was working faster than the fan on the fireplace.

Suddenly her eyes snapped open. "Oh, God," she said, jumping up. He reached out and snatched her mug from her hand before she dumped the rest of her drink on the carpet. "I need to..." She didn't finish her thought but instead rushed downstairs.

After depositing their cups in the kitchen, Jay followed her down. Walking into her "office" a few minutes later, he found her perched in front of two keyboards, her focus alternating between the two monitors in front of her and the images on the wall. His heart rate kicked up at her intensity. Whatever it was she was thinking, it wasn't good. His own eyes traveled to the wall, and he wondered just what he was seeing—global launch codes? A coded list of CIA operatives?

Suddenly, she stopped her typing and reached for the phone sitting beside her. There she hesitated before turning back to her computer where she slipped on a set of headphones and keyed in a few numbers.

She sat back in her chair and took a deep breath. But as soon as whoever was on the other line answered, she straightened again. "Mrs. Babson? It's Naomi DeMarco, we've met a few times. I'm a friend of Lucy's," she said.

She listened for a moment then continued. "I was wondering if you know where Lucy is? I have some work for her and I've tried calling but haven't heard back. Is she on one of her walkabouts by chance?"

Jay crossed his arms, fascinated with the myriad of expressions crossing Naomi's face, concern being the most prominent of them all. Finally, she nodded, "Okay, if you hear from her, will you let her know I called? She has my number." When Naomi ended the call, she removed her headphones and slumped back in the seat.

"What's wrong?" he asked.

Her gaze darted up, but she said nothing. After a beat, she picked up her phone. Pressing in a few numbers, she held the device to her ear.

"General Marsh, please," she said. "It's Naomi DeMarco."

He had no idea what ideas or thoughts or realizations were spinning inside her head, but when her eyes rose to meet his, he held her gaze.

"General Marsh? Hi, I'll cut to the chase. I need Brian sent home."

She listened to the person on the other end of the line, her eyes never leaving Jay's. "Yes, it's important," she said, the flat, certain tone in her voice nearly gave him the chills and definitely gave him some insight into just how serious she thought the situation was.

After another brief pause on her end, she offered a quick "thank you" and ended the call. Holding the phone in her hand, she tapped the back of it absentmindedly, her eyes on Jay's, yet not focused on him.

"Naomi? Can you tell me what's going on?"

Her finger stilled then resumed. "I'm not a hundred percent certain," she said, her attention back on him, "but I think someone has kidnapped Lucy James and is using her to hack deep into the FBI using the networks Smitty had access to."

* * *

"That's awfully specific," Jay said, and Naomi knew she likely sounded like a crazy lady to the man. He'd been such a good sport, listening to her talk about things he had very little interest in. Well, that wasn't an entirely true assessment, he was interested, but only because he was interested in her. And he probably didn't like bad things happening to good people like Smitty.

She glanced at the clock on the lower right side of her wall of screens. Glad that General Marsh had agreed to send Brian home, Naomi wondered how long it would be before he returned. The general had been willing to concede to her unusual request but would not go so far as to provide her any information other than to say he'd be home.

"Naomi?"

She brought her attention back around to Jay, who was

watching her expectantly. "Why don't you have a seat?" she said, moving in front of the desk. He studied her then returned to the seat he'd been in prior to their trip upstairs. Naomi began to walk. Brian called it pacing; she simply liked to think she was keeping her blood flowing. After a few circles around the room, she paused in front of Jay.

Despite everything else going on in her head, she spared a thought for how attractive he was. When he held out a hand, she didn't hesitate. It would be weird to walk through what was in her head without actually walking—as she normally did—but snuggling into his lap held a new appeal.

"Now talk, tell me what you can," Jay said, pulling up the side of her robe that had slipped down. Tucking it into place around her legs, he rested a hand on her thigh.

"You were right," she said. He frowned, and she continued. "There are very few people in the world who could get through the security I put on Smitty's network without raising any red flags, let alone do it in the time between Beekman's scan and when the code first showed up. Aside from my brother, there's really only one other person. One other person who would then leave that code embedded in the system," she said, waving toward the screen.

"The person you called about?" he asked.

She bobbed her head then studied the lines of code, absent-mindedly stroking her fingers across Jay's hand. "Her name is Lucy James. She's another white hat hacker. Crazy smart, super witty, drives my brother crazy, but overall an amazing person. We've worked together on a few projects, and while our specialty—mine and Brian's—is security related to network access, her specialty is security related to stored data."

"That seems like a big leap to make from her being *capable* of copying your brother to her being a kidnapping victim. Are you sure it's her?"

She started to nod then stopped. "I knew Lucy was on a

walkabout—something she does regularly—because I ran into her a few months ago and she mentioned it to me. That was her mom I just spoke to, and she said Lucy had called from the airport in Honolulu nearly two weeks ago to say she was headed home but then two days later, she called again to say she'd decided to take another trip, this time to walk part of the Appalachian Trail—Mrs. Babson hasn't heard from her since."

"And so you think Lucy is likely the most current hacker-victim they've lined up to execute their plan?"

"That's my best guess," Naomi nodded. "But you did get one thing wrong."

"What's that?"

"They may have Lucy, they may be using her. But one thing I know for certain is that Lucy will never be anyone's *victim.*"

* * *

"Why your brother?" Jay asked a few hours later as they stepped out of a very satisfying shower—Naomi hadn't wanted to be away from her office for long, but he always liked a good challenge, and he'd made it worth their time.

"Hm?" she said, drying her hair with a towel.

"Your brother. I understand that what's going on is important enough that you want him here, but it seems like more than that," he said.

He pulled on his boxers and acknowledged that at some point, he'd need to go home and attend to a few things in his own life. He needed clothes, and he wanted to see Goo. His boss had also left a few messages. He couldn't ignore his responsibilities forever, but for the first time since his teenage years, his job didn't hold his exclusive attention, and that realization was one he'd wanted to spend the day trying on, so to speak.

"Lucy and my brother don't always get along, but there is

something between them," Naomi said as she combed through her hair. "Not in a sexual way, not yet anyway. But a couple of years ago something happened to them. I don't know what it was but since then, they trust each other implicitly. Not only that, they seem to really get each other. If Lucy is sending messages to help us figure out what's going on, my brother would be the person she'd send them to, and he'll be the best person to figure them out."

Just then, an electronic bell rang. Naomi threw Jay a quick look of surprise, then, grabbing her robe as she left the bathroom, she hurried toward the foyer. Jay followed her as far as the bedroom where he paused to pull on his jeans and T-shirt. He'd just turned toward the door when he heard Naomi exclaim her brother's name. Jay glanced at the clock; it had been less than three hours since Naomi had made the call. Wherever Brian DeMarco had been it hadn't been far.

He walked through the bedroom and entered the foyer in time to see Naomi dragging her brother to her office. He paused, knowing that although she'd told him a lot, her brother's security clearance likely mirrored hers, and so what she might want to share with Brian may not be for Jay's ears. He started to head back into her bedroom but stopped when she called to him.

Turning back around, he entered the room to see both Naomi and her brother standing in front of the wall of screens. He smiled as he noted the likenesses. In looks, to be sure, as Brian had the same hair and build, though he was several inches taller than Naomi and his frame was more lean to Naomi's petite one; but also in their gestures. They both stood hip cocked, one arm wrapped around their waist, the other resting on top, heads tilted as they studied the images.

"Naomi?" he said.

She spun then smiled and held out a hand. "Brian, I want you to meet Jay, Jay this is my brother Brian."

The man in question turned and Jay noted his features were similar to Naomi's as well, including the brilliant green eyes.

"Jay?" Brian said, his eyes going to his sister then back to him.

"Jay Evans," Jay repeated and held out his hand as he came forward. Brian hesitated, his brow furrowed, but then he held out his hand.

"Nice to meet you, Jay," Brian said, tacking on his name at the end.

"I need to go get dressed. I'll be right back," Naomi said then disappeared, leaving Jay and her brother awkwardly staring at each other.

"She's glad you're back," Jay said.

A brow went up. "Been seeing my sister long, Jay?" he asked with a slight emphasis on his name again.

"We met at your cousin's pub while I was watching game seven of the American League championships."

At that, Brian's lips lifted into a smile. "She has no idea who you are, does she?"

Jay hid his grimace, thankful that Brian seemed more amused than worried. He shook his head. "She thinks I'm just a businessman who's been negotiating a deal with his team over the past week."

Brian snorted then turned his attention back to the screen.

"I'm gonna get so much mileage out of this," Naomi's brother muttered.

Jay caught a glimpse into the sibling relationship, and though he hadn't thought it any other way based on what Naomi had told him, it was clear the twins tormented each other in ways only those who love each other can. Jay was about to ask Brian what he thought of Naomi's theory when they heard her curse. Both men looked at each other then strode toward her room.

Naomi came out clad in yoga pants and oversized sweater and hopping on one foot as she tugged on a slipper.

"Problem, Nano?" Brian asked, sliding his hands into his pockets as his twin hopped about the foyer. Jay walked up to her and grabbed her outstretched arm to steady her. She flashed him a smile that turned to a grimace when she looked at her brother.

"Tonight is that charity event for the children's hospital that I promised Mom I'd go to. I completely forgot."

Jay had been to his fair share of black-tie events, even been invited to the one to which she referred, but he couldn't figure out why it would upset her so much. Brian, on the other hand, had started laughing—and not the funny "haha" kind of laugh either.

"I swear to God, Brian, I will call Mom and tell her you're home if you don't shut up." That sobered her brother up quick.

"You wouldn't," he said, his face no longer animated.

Naomi shot him a sickly smile. "I understand Millie Rossiter will be there. Her divorce is finally final."

Jay could swear Brian went pale. "I'm going to, go, to, uh, get back to things," Brian said pointing toward her office and scurrying away.

Naomi straightened, her slippers firmly in place, and crossed her arms. "I don't want to go tonight. This is more important," she said gesturing to the room Brian had just disappeared into. He caught a glance of a stubborn chin, something he hadn't seen in her before. Until now, he would have guessed her perennial cheery nature and charm was enough to get her whatever she wanted. Apparently, if that failed, there was a little stubbornness in there, too.

"Your brother needs to catch up on everything you've found," he said in an attempt to smooth things over. "And you said he's better positioned to figure out what Lucy is doing, or trying to do or say. So, will it really do any harm to step away for a few hours and give him the opportunity to dive in? I'll even go with you if you want me to," he offered.

Slowly her gaze turned away from the office and toward him. "It's a black-tie affair," she said.

He smiled. "Yes, I'm aware of that."

"It's kind of tedious."

"I'm aware of that, too."

She frowned. "You'd really go with me?"

"I'd really not mind seeing you dressed up. That would make the night worth it."

Slowly, her frown turned into a smile. "I bet you look amazing in a tux."

"Well you did say you like my ass. I hear there is something about a man in a suit," he grinned back.

She laughed. "Well, now that I've seen it in all its glory, I'm not sure seeing it any other way will be as satisfying. But I do agree, if a man wears a tux well, it's not a sorry sight."

"So, is it a date?"

She smiled. "It's a date."

* * *

*N*aomi exited her room wearing a roman style dress the same green as their eyes. It draped and clung the way it should, and though he was her brother and would never admit it out loud, she looked stunning. Her head was cocked to the side as she slid in her second earring, a subtle dangling diamond set their mother had given her when they'd graduated from high school.

A wave of guilt washed over him as he watched her. Smitty's death had shocked him, as had everything Naomi had told him since he'd walked through her door several hours ago. And the more time they'd spent culling through files and lines and lines of code, the more worried he'd grown. Not surprising, he agreed with Naomi's theory about Lucy. But he had an inkling Naomi had only skimmed the surface.

He wished he'd been here for her from the start. She shouldn't have been the only one to shoulder the initial investigation. He knew Damian had helped, and he sensed that even though Jay's expertise wasn't the same as theirs, he'd helped too. But he, himself, hadn't been there for her.

He was now, though. So, while she spent the evening dancing and making nice, he had every intention of finding Lucy, or at least figuring out how to find her, and getting to the bottom of whatever the hell was going on.

And then there was Lucy.

His stomach churned more than he wanted to admit at the thought of her being held captive. He didn't doubt Lucy's ability to take care of herself, but she'd experienced enough in her life that she didn't need whatever shit was happening to her right now. True to Lucy form, she was fighting back, sending him messages and clues, but the fact that she had to fight at all infuriated him.

The door to the elevator slid open, the bell having been what brought Naomi out in the first place, and Jay stepped out. Brian set aside his thoughts of Lucy and watched as Jay's attention darted to him, then traveled like a pilgrim to Naomi. Brian watched the man's gaze take in Naomi's appearance, her beauty to be sure, but Brian felt a little something relax in his chest when Jay only really smiled when his gaze met Naomi's and she smiled back.

"My shoes!" she said suddenly, then spun and turned back toward her room.

Jay cast him an amused look—only Naomi could forget her shoes—but then Brian fell serious.

"She needs to know who you are. Before you walk into the event tonight," he said.

Jay's smile faltered. "I know."

"I don't think you do," Brian countered. "We are part of a prominent family but the work we do is private," he said, "It's vital that we keep a low profile. We *can't* have people digging into our lives any more than what we give them in the public without jeopardizing the work we do. We don't *need* to work, but we are good at it, and what we do is important. She needs to know who you are in order to protect who she is," Brian finished. He held Jay's gaze and saw the corners of the man's mouth tighten and his jaw clench. He knew his speech had probably irritated him, but he also knew that if his sister was truly interested in the man before him, which she appeared to be, then Jay wasn't a thoughtless man.

After a moment, Jay gave a curt nod just as Naomi returned to join them. "Ready?" she said, pulling a black wrap around her shoulders.

Jay held out his hand and Brian watched as his sister slipped hers into it like they'd been doing this for years. Neither of the two people in front of him seemed to notice the easy familiarity. On one hand, he was glad of it—Naomi had had a number of relationships throughout the years, but none appeared so *easy* as he saw her now. On the other hand, who Jay was and what he did would throw a wrench in the game—not an insurmountable wrench, but a wrench nonetheless.

Brian stepped forward and kissed his sister on the cheek, surprising her into a smile.

"Have fun, kids," he said.

She rolled her eyes at him as Jay called the elevator. "It's your turn next year," she said. "And I'm only going for a few hours to make Mom happy. When I get back, we'll need to figure out what to do about..."she gestured toward her office as Jay ushered her into the elevator.

"I'll be here," he said as the elevator doors slid shut.

As he stood alone in the foyer, he wasn't about to call a justice of the peace, but, for the first time in his life, he contemplated the fact that it wouldn't always be just the two of them.

CHAPTER TWELVE

"OH, YOU GOT A CAR!" Naomi exclaimed as they exited her building and she spotted the limo waiting for them.

"I did. I figured it would be easier than driving," he said. Gesturing to the driver to stay behind the wheel, he opened the door for her himself. Naomi slid gracefully inside and he followed, pulling the door shut behind them.

"This feels weird," she said.

"Which part? The limo, going out, something else?"

Naomi relaxed back into the corner of the seat and faced him. "Going out to this fancy affair when my brother is home trying to figure out if a friend of ours has been kidnapped. I couldn't do anything to stop Smitty being killed, but now that I might be able to prevent something bad happening to Lucy, I feel like I should be doing that. Not getting dressed up and going dancing," she said gesturing to their fancy clothes.

He reached down and pulled her legs onto his lap. He smoothed out her dress with one hand, while the other massaged her calf. "You wanted him here because of his relationship with Lucy. Now you need to give him time to leverage that."

Naomi gave him a look that told him she agreed but still didn't like it. He doubted she'd like what he had to tell her next too, but as they made their way through the evening traffic, Jay knew he had to bite the bullet.

Hitting the intercom button, he spoke, "Rob?"

"Yes, sir?" answered the driver.

"Sometime before we reach our destination, can you pull over for a few minutes?"

"Of course, sir," the driver answered.

Naomi arched a brow at him, but he said nothing as he switched the intercom off. He felt more nervous than he had in the recent past and given what had happened in the recent past, that was saying a lot.

Finally, Rob pulled over on a small side street not far from the museum where the charity event was being held.

"Do I need to be worried?" Naomi asked. Her voice held more curiosity than concern, and it gave him the push he needed.

He took a deep breath. "There is something I need to tell you, and though I'm going to preface it with saying that I've never lied to you, I do know there is such a thing as a lie of omission."

He glanced over and met her gaze. Her green eyes had taken on the look she got when she began to assess something, but she hadn't pulled her legs off his lap yet. "My full name is Jason Evans Greene. My mom and sister and a few friends call me Jay, but most people call me Jason."

Confusion flashed in her eyes, no doubt as she wondered why his full name was important, then her brow furrowed.

"You mean Jason Evans Greene like the…" her voice trailed off and he saw the recognition in her eyes. "No, not *like* the star pitcher from the New England Rebels, *the* star pitcher from the New England Rebels, the one who just led the team to a four-game sweep of the World Series?"

She started to sit up, but he held her still, wrapping a hand around one of her ankles and the other around her knee. "I pitched some good games, that's true, but winning and losing in baseball is a team effort. It wouldn't have mattered how well I pitched if the line-up hadn't come through with the batting."

A single eyebrow went up. "But yes," he continued. "That's me."

He held her gaze and noted that for as animated as Naomi typically was, she had a remarkable ability to hide her thoughts when she wanted.

Finally, after a long, silent moment, she looked away. "I see," she said. "Well, that complicates things."

His heart started thudding in his chest. "I know it sounds like a cliché, I know it *is* a cliché, but when I met you and you had no idea who I was, it felt like the first time in years I could really get to know someone."

She turned her attention back to him and her eyes searched his face. She offered him a small smile. "You have it wrong there," she said. "I knew who you were, I knew you were a man who loved his dog, teased his sister, brought his mom flowers. I knew you were a man who seemed kind and interesting and not intimidated by me or the work I do. I knew you were a man who didn't drink and drive, and a man who wanted to do the right thing when we found Smitty. What I didn't know was what you did for a living. I'm not crazy enough to think that what you do doesn't form part of who you are, that's impossible for those of us who care about our work, but I also know it's not *all* that you are."

Never in his life had Jay struggled so much to *not* pull a woman into his arms. He wanted to. Desperately. But if he did, whatever they started wouldn't stop. And if the night was important enough for Naomi to take a break from hunting a potential murdering kidnapper, it certainly couldn't be missed because he wanted to take her home and worship her six ways to Sunday.

He let his head fall back against the seat and took a few deep breaths before he spoke. "Your brother said I needed to tell you before we arrive."

"Hm, he was right about that," she said. "I don't have time to come up with a proper plan, and so I think the best thing would be to have Rob drop me at a side entrance and you go in the main entrance."

His head shot up and he looked at her. "No, why don't I go in the side entrance and you can arrive the way your parents would expect?"

She smiled. "Because having the pitcher from the Rebs show up tonight will be a huge coup for my mom and the board of the hospital who have put so much work into the event. I don't want to take that away from them by having you slink in. If I slink in, no one will notice."

"Now that you know who I am, you want to use me?" he asked, his lips tipping into a grin. How like Naomi to just simply move on.

"We are not put on this earth to take up space. Since I will no longer be able to use you for myself and I'll have to ogle you from afar, I figure you should at least be useful to someone else."

He laughed then hit the intercom and told Rob the new plan. Once the intercom was off, he slid Naomi's legs from his lap and pulled her closer. "Are you sure it has to be this way? That we can't show up together? Because, selfishly, it means I have to ogle you from afar, too," he said, tracing his fingers from her shoulder down her bare arm. "And *afar* couldn't be more opposite from where I really want to be."

A small laugh escaped Naomi's lips as she leaned forward and kissed him. He'd have to be sure to wipe the lipstick off before he exited the limo, but he'd take the trouble of traveling to Timbuktu and back to kiss Naomi.

Finally, she drew back and reluctantly he let her go. She sighed, expressing perfectly his own sentiment.

"Unfortunately, it does have to be this way. At least tonight. When things quiet down and your life gets a little bit back to normal, or as normal as it gets, we'll figure out then when or if we want to go public, and if so, how we'll manage it."

"When," he said. When she shot him a look, he clarified. "You said 'when or if' we want to go public. There's no 'if' about it, Naomi. I just want to be clear about that. I get that we'll have to think about the how and the when, but those are the only questions in my mind."

She smiled again then leaned forward and placed a by comparison, chaste kiss on his lips. "If we can figure out how to stop a lunatic who's kidnapping and killing hackers I'm pretty sure we can figure almost anything else out." He gave her hand a squeeze in response. "Although there is one thing that might be a bit of a stumbling block," she said, her smile widening.

"What's that?"

"My lipstick is lip stain. It's going to be hell getting it off of you without any make-up remover."

* * *

*N*aomi had called her mom and asked to have security meet her at one of the side doors so she could slip into the museum, but still, Jay asked Rob to stay parked until he saw her safely inside the building. He hated not being able to walk into the event with her, hated the fact that he was going to be there with her and yet not with her at the same time. He thought about slipping in through the side door with her, but she'd been right—the press would have a field day with him and given what he'd just dumped on her, helping the charity, and her mom, was the least he could do.

He exited the limo much to the surprise of the few photographers present; instantly flashes went off, questions flew at him, and a smile appeared on his face. Known for his congeniality and his friendliness with the press, he did what they expected, but with Naomi in mind, he made a point of talking about the importance of the event and the impact of the hospital on the lives of so many children.

He didn't actually know how important the gala was, but at least the second part of his comments wasn't a stretch to talk about. Manny and Liz's youngest daughter had had four heart surgeries by the time she'd turned two, and he'd spent many a night walking the halls with Manny. Now a happy and healthy five-year-old, Rowena reminded him every time he saw her of just how important the hospital was to so many families.

The shouting of the reporters and the flash of the cameras abruptly cut off as he finally stepped inside the elegant building and the doors closed behind him. Vases of flowers as tall as he graced the entryway, waiters in tuxedos moved through the crowd carrying trays of champagne and small bites, and all around him, paintings looked down on the goings on below. His eyes lingered on the image of a man, his long ebony hair falling from beneath a black hat. The dark tones gave the painting an almost foreboding feeling, and Jay wondered what the subject had been thinking as he'd sat for the portrait. His thoughts had just started to create a story when Liz appeared at his side and slipped her arm through his, and Manny came up on his other side.

"And what on earth are you doing here?" she demanded, planting a kiss on his cheek. Jay was fairly certain she just barely refrained from planting her hands on her hips.

Instead of answering, he nodded to where he'd spotted Naomi chatting with, if he wasn't mistaken, a state representative. The young man, well, not so young but probably within a few years of his own thirty-seven, was smiling down at Naomi and listening intently to whatever she happened to be saying.

"You're scowling," Manny said.

"That's Naomi," he said. Manny snorted and Liz turned her full attention to the situation. All three of them watched Naomi for a few seconds before Liz tugged his arm and stepped in front of him, creating a small circle of just the three of them.

"You didn't tell me she was a Winchester," Liz said, mildly accusing.

"A what?" he asked. "Her last name is DeMarco."

"Yes, but her mother, the older woman standing to her left, is Collette DeMarco nee Winchester. President of the board of trustees and matriarch of one of Boston's oldest, and wealthiest, families," Liz said. Manny's snort had turned into a real laugh. Jay glared at him.

"She mentioned something about Boston Brahmin, and I knew she came from a wealthy family, but we didn't really get into it." The three of them glanced over again and Naomi looked up in the moment. Their eyes held, then her attention jumped to Manny then Liz, a small smile flitted on her lips before her mother said something that caught her attention.

"I want to know why you're here with us and she's not." Manny said, still laughing. "Did she find out who you are and refuse to be seen with you?"

Jay glared at his best friend again.

"Stop that," Liz said to her husband, though Jay didn't miss the amusement in her expression. "Clearly she's interested in Jay judging by that look, but I have to admit, I'm curious, too."

Both sets of eyes bored into him and he felt like he'd been cornered by Mom and Dad, who were not so patiently waiting to hear his excuse. He grumbled something then snagged a glass of champagne from a passing waiter and told them the rest of the story.

Both Manny and Liz were doing their best to hide their laughter when he finished; Liz was doing admirably well but

Manny's shoulders were shaking with restraint and his eyes were watering.

"The irony is too much," Manny finally managed to say before suppressing another laugh. "After all those times you gave me shit for falling for Liz—"

Liz shot him a look.

"You were too good for him," Jay quickly responded. "When he finally convinced you to give him a shot, he turned into a peacock. It was annoying"

Liz looked at her husband, her lips hinting at an indulgent smile.

Manny shrugged. "It's probably true. I probably was annoying, but I don't care. At least she knew who I was." He slipped his arm around his wife and pulled her close, dropping a kiss on the top of her head.

"You're the face of the Rebs," Manny continued. "And yet you found probably the only person in Boston who had no idea who you are, and not only that, but just by being *you*, you get in your own way of being with her. This is going to be fun."

"It's not fun," Jay snapped back as the young representative put his hand on Naomi's shoulder and leaned in to say something.

Liz sighed. "It is kind of fun, but how do you feel about meeting Quinten Longmore, our newest member of the state legislature, and the man who currently has his hand on Naomi? I'll take you if you promise to behave," Liz said, shooting him a pointed look.

"I always behave. I'm the face of the Rebs, remember?" he flashed her a toothy smile. Liz regarded him skeptically then nodded and, with her hand in her husband's, the three made their way toward Naomi.

Waylaid a number of times as they crossed the gallery, the three finally arrived just as Quinten Longmore said something funny and the whole group laughed. The laughter stopped abruptly when the representative saw who had joined them.

"Oh, wow," he said, sounding more like a fourteen-year-old than an elected official. "Quinten Longmore," he said holding out his hand "and of course, I know who you both are. That was a hell of a Series."

"Quinten, I'd like to introduce you to my husband, Manny Rivera, and of course this is Jason Greene," Liz said. "And Manny, Jay, this is Collette DeMarco, the president of our board, her husband Anthony, and Wilton Denton, another board member. And I don't believe we've met," Liz added turning toward Naomi.

Clearly Naomi's parents were aware of the situation, too because he saw the same dance of mischief in their eyes that he often saw in Naomi's, although one set was a brilliant blue and the other a dark brown.

"Liz," Mrs. DeMarco spoke, "this is our daughter, Naomi. I don't usually get her to attend my events, but I extracted her promise to attend this one in lieu of a birthday gift this year."

"Naomi, it's lovely to meet you," Liz said then moved across the group to position herself beside Naomi and leaving the five men standing in a row. Not surprisingly, the talk turned to baseball and the Series the Rebels had swept, winning game four and the Series just the day before. Jay attended the conversation but couldn't stop his eyes from skating to Naomi as she spoke with her mom and Liz.

He hadn't mentioned Naomi's last name to Liz and Manny the night before, and though he often commented on what a small world it was, he hadn't thought it would be this small. Liz and Collette were obviously well acquainted as Liz had joined the board of the hospital two years earlier, and Naomi seemed to slip comfortably into conversation with his best friend's wife. He also saw where Naomi got her looks from. Petite like her mother, they also shared high cheek bones, round eyes, a mouth a little wider than perfect proportions would suggest, although he couldn't imagine Naomi any other way. They differed in hair color with Mrs. DeMarco a golden white, the way blond women get rather than going gray, and in skin tone with Naomi's fair skin carrying undertones of Mediterranean warmth from her father's side of the family.

"Let's go get a beer," Anthony DeMarco said, clapping a hand on Jay's shoulder and bringing him out of his reverie regarding the mother and daughter pair standing opposite him. His eyes landed on Naomi, who very subtly winked at him, before he turned to face her father.

"Yes, why don't you go do that? I need to drag Naomi off to say hello to Jane Winthrop," Collette DeMarco said.

"And I see our governor has just arrived," Quinten interjected.

"I have a few things to check on," Liz commented. And within mere seconds, everyone had said their "nice to meet yous" and "goodbyes," and he stood there alone with Naomi's father.

"You look like you could use a beer, son," he said.

Jay looked at the still full glass of champagne in his hand. He didn't tend to drink, and he almost never drank champagne. Setting the glass on the tray of a passing waiter, he nodded to Naomi's dad.

"A beer would be a little more my style, thanks." The two turned toward one of the bars set up at the end of the gallery.

"So, you're dating my daughter?" Mr. DeMarco asked as they wound their way through the crowd. He'd spoken softly enough that no one but Jay could have heard, but still, Jay looked around before answering.

"Yes," he said definitively.

"And you were with her the night her colleague was found?"

Jay nodded as he sidestepped a large party gathered around one of the paintings.

"You must have been happy to keep your name out of the paper that night," Mr. DeMarco said.

That comment brought Jay to a halt; Naomi's dad came to a stop beside him. "A man died, Mr. DeMarco," Jay said. "I wouldn't have cared in the least if my name had been brought into it. I was thankful though that Naomi's stayed out of it, given her connection to Smitty."

Mr. DeMarco studied him then nodded and gestured to the bar. "Let me buy you a drink," he said. Jay's eyes went to the no cash bar then back to Mr. DeMarco who smiled. "My treat."

* * *

*N*aomi fidgeted with her clutch. She'd felt her phone vibrate in the small bag but knew if she brought it out, her mother would *Not Be Pleased*. Still, she suspected the message would be from Brian, and if so, she needed to answer it. Glancing up at Jay, who sat two tables away with Manny and Liz, an emotion—part desire, part annoyance, and part frustration—rolled through her. She wanted to be with him, to be sitting beside him and getting to know his friends. But instead, she was relegated to sitting with her parents and admiring the way his tux fit.

With a sigh, she scooted her chair back and excused herself. Dinner had just been served, but her stomach was twisted into too many knots to eat anyway. Without looking back, she made her way not toward the restroom, but to one of the quiet upper galleries. A few minutes alone to regain her cool and read Brian's message would give her something to think about other than Jay.

Her phone buzzed again. Taking a seat on a small settee set against a wall, she pulled it out. With the muted din of the gala below her, she read the first message, which was, as predicted, from Brian.

"I have an idea. I know you can't rush out, but as soon as you can, do. I'm calling in reinforcements."

"What reinforcements?" she typed back.

A few minutes later, a response popped up. "Can't text, working on something, just come when you can." Annoyance lanced through her at his vague response, but she reminded herself it wasn't his fault she hadn't been able to reply right away.

Closing the string, she saw another message, this one from Jay. "Everything okay?"

She smiled. "Yes, just anxious to get home," she typed.

"Can we leave soon?"

She smiled at his question. "I can leave once the dancing starts. You can leave whenever you want though." He wasn't the one who'd made the promise to attend.

"Not without you," came his quick reply. "What are my chances of getting an invite for a sleepover?"

She laughed. "Pretty good so long as you can convince me Goo won't suffer. I don't want to make her jealous."

A minute passed and then a picture came through. Goo was staring at the camera, her tongue lolling to the side. Beside her a dark-haired young woman with the same bright blue eyes as Jay had her arm looped around the retriever—both appeared to be smiling, maybe even laughing.

"She's having an overnight with my sister. I wasn't sure what time I'd get back tonight so I asked Allie to take her. They're having a girls' night. I think Allie might have done Goo's nails."

At that, Naomi took a closer look, and sure enough, she saw a hint of pink on one of Goo's toes.

"Then consider yourself invited, though I don't know how late Brian and I will be up."

"I'll take it. I'd come find you now, but that lipstick was a bitch to get off with the water and face wipes in the limo."

She laughed again, feeling the tension in her stomach easing just a bit. "Just another hour or so," she said, then ended the conversation with an emoji of a pair of bright red lips. Slipping her phone into her clutch, she leaned back against the cool wall behind her and closed her eyes. She'd like nothing more than to be home, working on finding Lucy with Brian in one room and Jay in the other. She didn't know how she'd juggle the two, but that was just one more thing she'd have to add to the metaphorical "things to figure out" bucket. That bucket was getting a little full with Jay's revelation earlier in the evening, but given some of the things she'd had to figure out in the past, she didn't doubt for a minute that if they wanted to, they'd find a way for this as well.

* * *

"Mom," Naomi said as she walked up to the woman in question. "I've been traveling almost nonstop for more than two weeks, all that's left of the evening is dancing, and I really don't feel like dancing tonight. But I made you a promise, and I want to make sure if I head home now, you'll consider it fulfilled?"

"Yes, it's fine. Go home, I'm sure more interesting things await you there than here."

Naomi's head drew back. Collette grinned. "He seems like a nice man and he has an adorable dog, too." Naomi didn't quite know where to go with that statement; when had Jay shown her mom a picture of Goo?

Her phone vibrated in her purse, and thankful for the distraction, she quickly pulled the device out and read the text from Jay. "Rob will pick me up out front in ten minutes and then we'll come to the side entrance for you right after. Do not wait outside if we're not there when you get there. Stay inside. Please."

She liked that he'd tacked on a "please," and she texted him back a goofy thumbs up. Across the room, she saw him shake his head and smile as he slid his phone back into his pocket. Ten minutes later, she was slipping from the room, having said her goodbyes to her parents and ghosted.

A few minutes later Naomi was at the side entrance where Rob and Jay were waiting for her. Less than two minutes after that, she was snuggled up against Jay as they traveled the streets of Boston back toward her Beacon Hill home.

They said very little along the way, content to just be able to be in each other's company, but five minutes from home, she texted Brian to let him know they were on their way. He replied immediately saying that he'd moved down to his office and that she should come down as soon as she changed.

"Soon" was a relative term, and though they didn't dawdle, it seemed Jay had made a study of her dress all night and had a few theories on how best to remove it that he wanted to test. Then Naomi felt the need to wash all the product out of her hair and so a shower ensued. Forty minutes after arriving at Beacon Street, they were back in the elevator and headed down a floor to Brian's office.

The door slid open, and Naomi stepped out followed by Jay. Having changed into a pair of leggings and sweatshirt, she felt ready to take on whatever Brian had found.

Turning right out of the elevator, she led Jay to one of the two doors that both opened to rooms fronting Beacon Street. Unlike the airy spaces in her apartment, Brian preferred rooms with purposes and so, rather than being one big office and a laundry room like hers, this section of his apartment contained a large-ish office, a TV room, and a guest room. On the back-side of the building, under her master bedroom, he had his bedroom as well as another guest room.

"I'm not sure how long you'll be able to stay," Naomi said, pausing outside the office door.

Jay shrugged. "It's fine, don't worry about me. If you need me to leave, I'll head back to your place."

"Nano." The door to the guest room flew open before she could respond to Jay, and rather than her brother greeting her, Damian stood there.

"Ugh, no one calls me that but Brian," she said and pushed past him into the office.

"I know, that's why I did it, of course. Are you going to introduce me?" he asked, her attention immediately having gone to the myriad of screens her brother had up and running. Unlike her floor-to-ceiling version, Brian had six monitors placed along one wall but at different heights and depths. Brian claimed it helped him track information better, but it always felt a bit disorienting to Naomi whenever she first walked into the room.

"Jay, this is Damian. Damian, Jay," she said her eyes scanning one screen that had caught her focus.

"Jay," she heard Damian say. "You've got to be fucking kidding me, Naomi."

She straightened and looked at him. "What?"

"You're dating Jason Greene and you didn't bother to tell me?" She stared at him, unclear what the issue was, and said nothing. "Oh, wait, don't even tell me," he continued as he turned to Jay. "She didn't even know who you were did she?"

Jay glanced at her then shook his head. In response, Damian pulled out his phone, tapped in a few keys and brought up a picture.

"Who is this Naomi?"

She frowned at him, but glanced at the picture on the device. "That's Grace Hopper," she said then turned back to data she'd been studying.

But out of the corner of her eye, she saw Damian show Jay the picture, Jay shook his head, not recognizing the woman.

"She recognizes someone who's been dead for more than

twenty-five years, and a computer scientist at that, but not one of the greatest pitchers of modern times." Damian shook his head in dismay. "That's one hell of a Series you and the Rebs just won."

"Thanks, team effort," Jay said.

"Are you sure you want to date her?" Damian asked Jay. "There's something not quite right with both of them," he said gesturing to the twins. "Vivi, too, come to think of it. Then again, between your athletic prowess and her super genius, if you guys ever have kids they'll probably turn out to be some sort of mutant superhero species."

"Is there a reason you're here, Damian?" Naomi interjected, saving Jay from being tormented by him any longer.

"I called him," Brian said, speaking for the first time. "We need someone on the inside and, well." He paused then shrugged. "He's our go-to guy."

Damian flashed her and Jay a smile. "Lucky me."

"Talk to me," she said to her brother as she gestured for Jay to have a seat in one of the upholstered chairs scattered around the room. She moved up behind Brian to better see what he might be looking at.

"What do you think of that?" he asked, pointing to a screen.

Naomi leaned down to get a closer look. "She's already extracted a file," she said, pointing to several lines of code on the screen in front of her.

"She has," again Brian confirmed, as the file in question popped open on his screen. "Although it's one from the department, not one of Smitty's special ones."

"Uh, Brian, we have a civilian in here," Damian reminded them all. Brian looked at Naomi then at Jay who was lounging in a chair, an ankle resting on his knee. "I can leave," Jay offered.

"Or you can understand that if a word of this gets out we can make your bank accounts disappear," Brian countered.

"Brian!" Naomi said.

"Fair enough," Jay said. The two men eyed each other, then Brian glanced at Damian, who did not look happy. He also didn't look surprised and, after a beat, just lifted his eyes and shook his head as if he knew he shouldn't have expected any different.

"So, the file?" Naomi said.

"Low level embezzler. Embezzled a couple of million from a small insurance company in the aftermath of Katrina," Brian said.

"Was he caught?" she asked.

Brian nodded. "He's serving eight years in prison," he said.

"That's an odd file to pull given what else she should be able to gain access to," she said then frowned. "Come to think of it, that's an odd file to even be in there."

"Why's that?" Jay asked. "If that guy's an embezzler why's it weird that it's part of that department?"

"The file she copied is a closed case and sits with files of people who have embezzled tens and even hundreds of millions of dollars, most which are ongoing and open investigations," Naomi said as she frowned. "Why go for such a small, closed case?"

"My guess is that whoever has Lucy told her to pull a test file to see what would happen, see if she could do it without raising any alarms." Brian said. "And I think she pulled this specific file for *that* reason," he said pointing the screen on the opposite side of the room.

"Madison, Athens, Union Point, and Stephens?" Naomi said, reading the list out loud.

"They're all in Georgia," Jay said. "If you were to draw lines between them they form a sort of square."

All three heads swiveled to him. "That's right, you're from Georgia, aren't you?" Damian asked after a beat.

"Born and raised in that area," Jay confirmed.

The strange coincidence threw Naomi off for a few disorienting seconds, but then she turned back to the monitors. "How did you get from here," she said pointing to the file highlighted on one screen, "to here?" she asked moving her finger to the list of locations.

"Anton Petrov, the man who owned the business that was embezzled from, has a home base in *Athens*, Greece. The man who embezzled from him is named Harold *Madison*. The woman who ran the operation was named Natalie *Stephens*, and look at the name of the company," Brian answered succinctly.

"Union Insurance," Naomi read it off. "If this is a clue as to where Lucy is being kept how in the hell did she find a single file with enough coincidences to give us a general location?"

Brian grinned. "I'm not sure she did. I pulled up a back-up file from three weeks ago, and at that time, the woman running the operation was named Natalia Stepov. The other three are still accurate."

"Okay," Naomi said, still pondering the data. "Do we assume she's in that area? And if so, how do we find her?" she asked.

"And I hate to interrupt, but are you sure she was even taken?" Jay piped in.

Brian let out a long exhale. "She's definitely been taken, but sorting out how and who is one of the reasons I called Damian in. I need to focus on the computer stuff. She's talking to me and I need to figure out how to keep listening without raising any flags. Damian has started tracking everything else, like her last known movements, her credit cards, phone usage, those sorts of the things,"

"All we know now is that she returned from her walkabout in New Zealand, flew through Honolulu, and then disappeared," Damian said.

"Her mother said she received a call from her saying she decided to hike some of the Appalachian Trail," Naomi said.

"There's been no activity on her phone since she landed in

Hawaii, but I'll run a backward trace on her mom's phone," Damian said.

Silence reigned then Naomi spoke, her voice sharp with frustration. "So what now?"

Damian eyed the twins then slowly grinned. "We go to Georgia to find Lucy," he said.

"What?" Naomi said. "That's a needle in the haystack."

"No," Brian said, his eyes fixed on his computer. Naomi turned to give Damian a smug look, but Brian's next words cut her off.

"Naomi goes to Georgia to find Lucy," he said. "Everyone else stays here."

CHAPTER THIRTEEN

"No," both Damian and Jay spoke at the same time. Startled at the strength of the response, it took Naomi a few seconds to process it.

Her eyes narrowed on both of them. "And just why shouldn't I go to Georgia?" She didn't want to go because she thought her efforts would be better spent with her brother, but it sounded suspiciously like Damian and Jay didn't want her to go for unreasonable macho reasons.

"Because it's dangerous," Jay barked, sitting up straighter in his chair. "Jesus, they've already killed three people, Naomi."

"And I'm the only actual field agent here," Damian said.

"But I need you to be running the investigation into Lucy's disappearance and I need to stay focused on this," he said waving toward his computers. "Which just leaves Naomi."

"Or any other agent I bring in," Damian snapped back.

"With someone on the inside do you really think that's a good idea, Damian? Even if you do, I don't," Brian said. "Given the way they tested the Miami, New York, and Chicago offices before hitting gold with the DC office, the way they involved Corbin Beekman, and the speed with which they picked up

Lucy, you *know* it's someone higher up on the food chain." The room fell quiet with the enormity of his statement.

"The FBI is officially investigating the deaths of Smitty, Carl Rogers, and Beekman," Brian continued. "And it's probably best to let whoever is behind this think that that investigation is the extent of what is going on. If you bring in someone else to help us, there's a high probability that the insider will know there's a second investigation going on. With three people already dead, I don't want to corner the bear and risk Lucy. I know none of you do either." With a look, he challenged anyone to contradict him.

Damian jammed his hands on his hips and glared at the floor. Naomi risked a glance at Jay, who was glowering from his seat. The tension in the room crept up as the seconds ticked by; finally Jay spoke.

"If you're going, I'm going," he said.

Naomi blinked at him. "You can't just take off. You just won the World Series. You have press conferences and a parade or something, don't you?"

He smiled. "I do have a parade. It's tomorrow, by the way."

She shot him an apologetic look—despite only having found out what he did for a living less than seven hours ago, she still felt like she should have known when the parade honoring him and his team was scheduled.

She mumbled something about watching it on TV, but he cut her off. "Press conferences are all morning, the parade starts at two. It will be over by three-thirty, and then there is a reception. We can be out of here by six. I'll charter a flight so we don't have to fly separately in order to not be seen together."

She waved him off. "I have a cousin who can fly us down. I'm not concerned about that, but how would we move around without calling too much attention to ourselves?" She still wasn't convinced going to Georgia was the best use of her time but opted to trust her brother.

"We'll hide in plain sight," Jay said rising from his seat. "A couple of high schools in the area have reached out to me a few times asking if I would come down and give some clinics to their young players. I've never had the time before, but now is as good a time as any. Damian can travel with us, we'll tell everyone you two are my support staff, no one will bat an eye. That is, of course," he said turning to Damian, "if you can run your investigation stuff Brian needs from the road?"

Damian took a several seconds to ponder the idea, but even if he hadn't taken the time, Naomi knew both Brian and Damian would go for it—Damian would continue to focus where Brian needed him to focus, but he could still be in the area if she and Jay encountered any danger.

After a few moments, Damian looked up and one by one met everyone's eyes. Finally, he nodded.

"We'll leave tomorrow, then."

* * *

"*H*ave you been able to reach her yet?" Naomi asked through the audio system that connected her to her brother one floor below. Both in their respective offices, they'd developed an approach to finding Lucy and were working furiously.

"You asked an hour ago, Nano. I've left a few signs she'll recognize, but I haven't heard anything. I don't know if that's because she's not in the system right now, or she's not seeing them, or she's seeing them but can't respond," he replied patiently. Or so he sounded. Naomi knew from vast experience that the more worked up her brother got on the inside, the calmer he got on the outside.

She sighed and muted her connection to him. She had no idea what had happened between him and Lucy several years ago, but she could feel her brother's anxiety. It wasn't just his preternatural calm that belied his state; as cliché as it was, as his twin, she could *feel* it.

Naomi's attention focused on the image currently before her, lines crisscrossing her screen in a dizzying pattern. She and Brian had divided their approach to finding Lucy, and while Brian was tasked with finding a way to communicate with her, Naomi's job involved trying to find a way to narrow down her geographic location. Lucy had given them an area to look in, but that area, though not densely populated, wasn't small.

Her eyes were tracing the lines of communication towers in the region of Georgia where she would soon travel when her phone rang. Glancing down, Kate's name popped up.

"Hey," she said answering the call.

"You're not at the parade," Kate said. "I thought you and *Jay* hit it off the other day."

"You *knew* who he was?" Naomi asked. It was hard to get too worked up about it, especially now, but still, her cousin might have said *something*.

"Of course I did," Kate answered. "But it was fun knowing something you didn't for once. Besides, I knew you wouldn't really care, so why did it matter."

In some ways, Kate was right, it didn't really matter. In others, it really did, but she and Jay would figure that out eventually.

"No, I'm not at the parade, and you know why. Though I do have it streaming on one of my computers," Naomi said as she looked at the screen in question. Just then, the camera flashed on the car carrying Manny and Jay. Perched on the top of the seat of some sort of classic convertible, Naomi watched as Jay leaned over and said something to Manny, making them both laugh even as they continued to wave to the crowds who lined the streets. He'd left her earlier in the morning than she would have liked, but given what she had on her plate for the day and what he had on his—not just the parade but working with his agent and publicist to organize the impromptu clinics with the high school kids—they had a lot to accomplish before her cousin Luca, Kate's brother, flew them to Georgia that evening.

"That man looks good in a suit," Kate said, obviously watching the parade herself. Naomi murmured her agreement, he looked good in just about anything as far as she was concerned. But even so, what made her smile, what made her heart warm, wasn't the way his clothes fit his body, but the way the laugh lines around his blue eyes creased and his smile flashed when Manny said something in return.

Silence fell on the line as both women watched, then Kate spoke. "I heard Luca is flying you out tonight? He wouldn't say where, but you'll be safe? I assume this has to do with what happened the other night?"

"Why don't you tack on a few more questions, I don't think you covered everything."

"You are such a brat," her cousin shot back. Naomi let out a small laugh, then filled her cousin in to the extent she could. Although based on the questions flying at her, Kate was more interested in her relationship with Jay than anything else.

"So other than being nosey, is there a reason you called?" Naomi asked when she finished her brief summary.

Kate hesitated before answering. "Actually, yes. There was an agent in last night asking questions. I would have called you then, but it was really busy with the Halloween crowd, and then by the time I had a moment to catch my breath, it was so late. But anyway, her name was Jacinda Brown. She asked all the same questions the first pair of agents asked, the ones that came the day after you found your colleague, but there was..." Kate paused. "I don't know, maybe I'm being too judgy, but there was something about her I didn't like. She asked about the CCTV files, which I thought was weird since the FBI already has them, and she asked me a few times if there was anyone in the bar that night that caught my attention."

Naomi hit a few keys, her attention split between the map in front of her, the parade, and her cousin. "I assume you said nothing?"

"I played the 'I'm too busy to notice everyone' card and coupled it with the 'it's tourist season, we get a lot of different people' card. She seemed annoyed, but there wasn't much she could do. She left a few minutes after. Again, it could be nothing, but I wanted you to know."

"Thanks, I don't know the intricacies of how the FBI runs their homicide investigations, but I'll run this by Damian and he can look into it."

Kate admonished her to stay safe then they ended the call. Naomi returned her attention to the lines that marked communication relay towers. A wave of dissatisfaction washed over her. Her goal was to try to narrow it down to a tower or two to monitor for signs of Lucy's activities. But the bigger towns in the region would have underground fiber optic internet connections, so studying relay towers and satellite connections could prove worthless. Rising from her seat, she began to walk to her office, a thought niggling in her mind.

Approaching the screen that showed a map of the area Brian had identified, Naomi studied it. Damian had traced the call Lucy had made to her mother and confirmed it had originated in Athens. He was still working on figuring out how she'd gotten from Honolulu to Athens, but at least with his confirmation, they felt more confident in their interpretation of the clues Brian had found.

Naomi's gaze lingered on the private airstrip just outside of Athens. It was conceivable that Lucy might have recognized Athens if they'd landed there, but how had she known about the other towns? Madison, Stephens, and Union Point, along with Athens, roughly formed a square area. There was no reason why anyone would pass through all four towns unless they were driving in a circle, or circling Oconee National Forest, the national park that sat almost right in the middle of their target area.

She strode back to her desk and hit the unmute button on her computer. "Brian?"

"Still no word," he replied, his voice sharp.

"Does Lucy have any ties to Georgia?"

"No," came his quick reply. "Not that I know of. Why?"

"I'm just thinking about how she came to identify those four towns. Athens is a pretty big town, and Madison is historic and so sort of well-known in the area, but the other two are really small. Even if she knew she landed in Athens, there's no way she'd know about the other three towns unless she saw them. And I think she did see them and not on a map," Naomi said.

"You think they're moving her from place to place," Brian said. She heard a hitch of excitement in his voice.

"Or she's mobile in general, like an RV or mobile tech van," she said. "If they are moving her, it would help explain the sporadic timing of her incursions into the system and maybe why she hasn't responded to you yet," Naomi added, warming up to the idea. She paused, her attention fixed on the map.

"What are you thinking?" Brian asked into the silence.

"I'm thinking that if they are moving her from location to location then we might be able to run searches to look for common property owners in each town. Or, alternatively online rental sites in the area. I don't want to discount the possibility of an RV or something like that though, too."

"Why didn't I think of that?" Brian grumbled even as she heard him typing in some keys.

"What are you taking?" she asked, moving back to her seat.

"I'll take the common property owners. You search the online rental sites and RV rentals."

"Will do," she said.

"You're the best," her brother replied, already distracted by his new line of investigation. She listened to him typing, knowing he'd forgotten to mute his line. She could feel his intensity through the connection.

"Brian?"

"Yeah," he said, distracted.

"We'll find her," she said. "You know we will."

His typing paused and he let out a deep breath. "I know, and I have to believe we'll find her in time. But even so, while I wouldn't wish what's happening on anyone, I hate even more that it's happening to her."

Naomi knew there was nothing to say to make it better, not for Brian and not for Lucy. So, without another word, she hit the mute button and went back to work, more focused than ever.

* * *

The plane hit a small pocket of air, and Naomi glanced up from her computer to keep an eye on the mug of coffee Jay had placed before her a few minutes earlier. Her gaze then traveled to Jay, who sat across the aisle at one end of the couch, his own computer open on his lap, a phone to his ear, and Goo curled up at his feet. She smiled at the retriever and thanked the wonders of private air travel that let her come along.

"There's definitely something hinky about Agent Jacinda Brown," Damian said. With his attention focused on his own computer, he'd spoken without looking up. "I can't quite put my finger on it though."

"Meaning?" Naomi asked, as Jay laughed at something his publicist must have said. Goo raised her head, glanced at Jay, then sank back to sleep.

"The agents that started the investigation were based out of the Boston field office, but Agent Brown is out of the DC field office, my office," he said.

"You've never met her?"

Damian shook his head. "She just transferred in from Miami about a month or so ago, and while she *is* an agent, I can't quite figure out where she came from or what unit she transferred into, though I know it wasn't mine."

"How can you not know?" Naomi asked. Viewing the question as a challenge, she minimized her current screen that had been culling through property rental data, and pulled up a new secure browser. Typing in her credentials, she logged onto the FBI network and began her own search.

"It looks like she was a bit of a jack-of-all-trades in Miami, which may have got her noticed in DC, but again, that's unusual, and I can't find any confirmation," Damian said.

Naomi paused, quickly sorting through the best way to approach the problem. When she landed on a process, she began to key in code, and within a few minutes, her device was running an automated search. Sitting back in her seat, she watched the files scroll across her screen at breakneck speed.

"We're all set," Jay said from across the aisle as he closed his laptop. "The day after tomorrow, I have an impromptu clinic for the high school players in Athens then four days off followed by a two day clinic in Madison. The other two towns are too small to be able to organize anything without it seeming odd, and I figured five hours of coaching each day then the rest of the day off should give us plenty of time to be mobile."

"Isn't Madison small too?" Naomi asked.

Jay nodded. "But it's still about three times bigger than Stephens or Union Point, and it's just off Interstate 20 so tends to be a central meeting area. Their high school coach is 'beyond thrilled,'" he said, making air quotes, "and he'll be coordinating to invite players from a couple of the other local high schools, too."

"You're a man in demand," Naomi said with a grin. "I can understand that."

"You don't have to demand anything, you don't even need to ask," he said, one side of his mouth cocking up as he held out his hand for her. Naomi grabbed her computer and happily joined him, dropping a kiss on his lips before settling in beside him, her device on her lap. Goo opened an eye, thumped her tail, then went back to sleep, clearly an experienced air traveler.

"Get a room, you two," Damian said from behind his screen.

"I guess you're already over the fact that you're now hanging out with one of the greatest pitchers in modern history," Jay teased, repeating Damian's earlier words.

"The polish wears off pretty quick, especially when you spend most of your time mooning over Naomi."

"I think he's jealous," Naomi said, smiling at the conversation even as her eyes tracked her computer's progress. "He'd like you more if it was just you two having a beer and you were sharing your glory days with him."

Damian flashed her a middle finger salute, but never took his eyes from his computer. "Well, well, well," he said, suddenly straightening as something on his screen caught his attention.

Naomi was about to ask what he'd found when a notice popped up on her screen, indicating her own search had finished. Forty-seven files for her to review. She scanned the names, none looked familiar, but she knew she'd find a pattern once she started looking.

She glanced up to find Jay and Damian watching her. "You first?" she said to Damian.

He nodded. "I put my own search into Jacinda Brown on hold when I knew you were taking it up," he said with a gesture of his head toward her computer. "You didn't say anything about doing that, but since you can't resist a challenge I figured you did. And you did, didn't you?"

Tucked up against Jay, he chuckled in her ear, clearly having seen her screen. "She did," he answered.

Damian shook his head and continued. "So, I started to look

into how these people could have gotten Lucy from Honolulu to Georgia, and yes, I am assuming she was picked up in Honolulu and didn't come to Georgia on her own and *then* get picked up."

"So, what did you find?"

"There are two likely possibilities. One is a flight that made five stops between Honolulu and Atlanta, and the second isn't a single plane but four different planes that, if taken in sequence, could have made the trip."

"The use of multiple planes would be a better way to cover your tracks and harder to track. Do you have any information on who was on board the flights?" Naomi asked.

Damian shot her a look. "Actually..."

She sighed. "Of course I can find out. Just give me the names of the airfields, the times, and the call numbers of the planes."

She felt Jay draw away to look at her. "You're not going to do anything illegal are you? Aside from it maybe being dangerous, isn't there a fruit of the poison tree kind of thing when it comes to evidence?"

"Are you a *Law and Order* fan by any chance?" she asked, a smile teasing at her lips.

Damian snorted.

Jay grunted and looked away.

She poked him in the ribs.

"Fine, I'm a *Castle* fan. I love that show," he said.

Damian laughed and Naomi leaned up and kissed his cheek.

"To be fair, you're not wrong," Damian said. "But Naomi has different kinds of access to networks and businesses that I don't."

"And I like how you make it sound not sketchy at all, Damian," Naomi laughed. She turned to Jay and clarified. "I do have access that Damian doesn't, and while what Damian has asked me to do is technically and legally *legal*. Ethically it's questionable, but ethically, I don't care right now. And yes, I know that makes me sound a little like I'm playing a demigod or worse, an autocrat, but as you've pointed out more than once, three people have died. I don't want anyone else to die, and I also promised my brother we'd find Lucy, and I'd *really* like to find her alive."

"That sounds ethical enough for me," Jay said, though Naomi didn't miss the hint of something not quite doubt but maybe uncertainty in his voice. She sat up to give him some space. They'd become so comfortable together in just two days, but she needed to remind herself that while she may feel some certainty about him—not planning-a-wedding kind of certainty, but more a he's-a-solid-person kind of certainty—he might not necessarily feel the same and might need more time, especially considering everything she was exposing him to with her work. But to her surprise, he pulled her back against his side and draped his arm around her shoulders.

"Time does not mean distance," he said quietly as if reading her mind. Damian, in a rare burst of consideration, returned his attention to his computer as Naomi studied Jay. "Don't worry about it, Naomi," he continued. "I don't always understand what you do, but that's all it is. If I have an issue, a real issue, I'll let you know. The rest I'll sort through." She studied his eyes; his gaze didn't waver from hers. Finally, she nodded, turned her head, and rested it against his shoulder.

"If your moment is over, I'd like to know what you found, Naomi," Damian said, darting a cautious glance in their direction.

"I have access to your pension fund, Rodriguez," she reminded him even as she sat up to better read her screen.

"As if I haven't heard that before. You're going to have to come up with something new," he retorted, turning in his seat to face them.

"How about I make your Netflix account public?" she said, quickly sorting through the files her computer had flagged as

THROUGH THE NIGHT

she spoke. When Damian didn't respond, she looked up to find his troubled gaze on her.

"What?" she said.

He frowned. "You don't really have access to that do you?"

"What I *have* and what I can *get*, are two very different things, and now you've made me curious."

His eyes narrowed. She grinned.

"Time to break it up, kids," Jay said. "Why don't you tell the nice FBI agent what you found?" he said, nudging her.

She slid him a party-pooper look but dutifully returned to the issue at hand. "What I have is a list of forty-seven cases that Jacinda Brown contributed to."

Damian frowned again. "I looked up her case load. I found a hundred and twenty-two cases."

"A hundred and twenty-two cases that she either led or her unit did. I figured you'd find those, so I didn't bother looking at them. My search brought up all the cases she consulted on or contributed to but didn't lead. Did you know she was JAG before joining the FBI?" Naomi asked.

Damian shook his head. "A lawyer?"

"No. She was an investigator for them, too. Not Naval Investigations, but an investigator for JAG," she clarified, drawing the line between those that investigated crimes and the investigators who were hired by the lawyers once a person had been charged.

"Why didn't that show up in my background search? I saw she was Navy, but not that," he asked.

"Because it's not in her file, but it is in the case files of the attorneys she worked for."

Damian sat back in his chair as the plane hit another air pocket. Naomi eyed the coffee, no doubt now cold, that she'd left on the table. Rising from her seat, she reached for the cup.

"Does that mean anything?" Jay asked.

"Maybe, but maybe not," Naomi said over her shoulder as

she walked to the galley kitchen to dump the drink and put the mug in the wash rack. "That's why I said I wasn't sure what I had. It's interesting that she was an investigator before joining the FBI, and it's interesting that she's consulted on so many cases that were not her own or her unit's, but I don't know what it means yet. When we get to Georgia, I'll review the actual files and see if I can find any connections."

"And when are you going to look into the airfields?" Damian asked, handing her a piece of paper as she walked back to her seat. Glancing at it, she recognized the data she'd asked for scrawled in Damian's tidy hand.

"And when are you going to sleep?" Jay asked. Naomi didn't miss the displeased expression Jay shot Damian.

"When she's dead?" Damian joked. Or tried to.

"Not funny, Rodriguez. Not even a little bit," Jay said, tugging her back down beside him as if he needed to be sure she was alive and well.

Damian had the grace to concede. "You're right, it wasn't funny. Sorry, Nano," he said. "In all seriousness," he continued before she could say anything, "Jay is right. We have a lot on our plate and starting tomorrow, we're going to be driving all over Greene County, Georgia looking for a kidnapped hacker and a killer. I do think a good night's sleep is in order," Damian said. "We're not any good to anyone, especially not Lucy, if we go bumbling about."

Naomi stared at Damian. She'd known him for several years and not once had he been solicitous. Oh, he'd never been uncaring, but when they were in their respective work modes, he was just as single-minded as she.

Thankfully, she was saved from a response when the plane dipped and they began their decent. Being in a small plane, she knew the process would be much faster than the standard thirty-minutes it took in a commercial flight and sure enough, Luca's voice came over the intercom.

"Fifteen minutes to landing. Buckle up."

"A man of few words," Jay said, reaching for his seatbelt. Naomi and Damian shut their laptops down and she stood to slide hers into her bag that sat beside the chair she'd vacated earlier. The plane dipped again and she stumbled. Jay caught her and pulled her onto his lap.

She stiffened as the plane bounced a bit, then she took a breath and snuggled in.

"You need to put your seatbelt on," Jay said, one hand around her waist the other resting on her hip.

"If we crash the seatbelt isn't going to help," Naomi pointed out.

"Statistically, if there is a bad landing, not a crash, but a problem at landing—"

"Shut up, Damian," Jay said, sliding Naomi into the seat beside him. A seat with a seatbelt which she dutifully fastened.

No one spoke the last ten minutes of the flight, and when Luca finally killed the engines at the private airfield just outside of Athens, the silence vibrated around them. The reality of what lay before her—before them—settled on her shoulders. Not that it hadn't been *real* before, it didn't get more real than finding three bodies, but this felt like a precipice. And judging by the way both Damian and Jay hesitated, they felt the tension—the expectation—too.

Suddenly the cockpit door flew open and Luca stepped out. Her cousin—one of the most imposing of her relatives—eyed them all.

"Well?" he said. "Are you going to get off or are you coming back with me?" Luca had never inherited the DeMarco charm, but four tours in the Middle East as a pilot had washed away what little he'd ever possessed.

"We're getting off," Jay said, unbuckling his belt and standing. Naomi did the same and Goo popped up and stood beside them, tail wagging. A few minutes later, they were standing on the tarmac. Not as biting as Boston, the night was still cool, and the scent of recent rain lingered in the air. Luca had given her a perfunctory kiss on the cheek as she'd left the plane then, as soon as they'd disembarked, he'd rolled up the stairs—so to speak—and re-started the engines.

"Um, I hadn't thought to ask, but did we make arrangements to stay somewhere? Or for a rental car?" Damian asked as the plane taxied back down the runaway.

"We did," Jay said, hitching his duffel bag on his shoulder and gripping his bat bag in his hand. Goo started to dance around.

"We did?" Naomi asked.

Jay nodded and started walking toward the nearest hangar. Naomi glanced at Damian, and they both followed. After a few strides, a black pick-up truck, the kind with the extended cab and big tires, came into view. At the sight of the truck, Goo took off toward it.

"Yours?" Damian asked.

"Mine," Jay confirmed, and Naomi heard the smile in his voice.

"And where are we staying?" Damian asked.

Jay paused and looked back at them. As he did, a smile split across his face. "At my mom's, of course."

CHAPTER FOURTEEN

"Your mom's?" Naomi asked as Jay helped her into the passenger seat. He knew he'd shocked her. She was one of the smartest people he'd ever met, and it was kind of fun surprising her. Not to mention, seeing her just a little less than confident was kind of endearing. Especially when she picked up the huge bouquet of flowers he'd had left on the seat to bring to his mom.

"Yep," he said as he shut the door then tossed their bags onto the seat behind her, Damian having already staked a claim on the seat behind the driver with Goo perched beside him in the middle. He walked around to the driver's side and climbed in. "I figured it's private and better for our purposes than a hotel. And I wanted to see my mom." He grinned as he turned the key in the ignition and the truck roared to life.

"Nice, I bet your mom has a nice house. I bet you bought her a nice pad didn't you?" Damian asked from the back seat, sounding like a twelve-year-old.

"I did. It's not a huge place, she didn't want anything big, but it's a historic farmhouse that we had redone. It sits on five acres with a stream and lots of live oaks. I built a smaller guesthouse in the back. I usually stay there but you can take it this time, Damian. Naomi and I can stay at the main house."

"Nice," Damian said at the same time Naomi spoke.

"There are enough rooms for us?" she asked, her fingers lightly picking at the ribbon tied around the bouquet of assorted wildflowers.

"Rooms?" Jay asked and then it dawned on him what she was thinking. "We're sharing *a* room, Naomi, and yes, she has *a* room for us."

Naomi stared at him, then shook her head and turned away. "I'm not sharing a room with you in your mother's house," she said.

"We're in our thirties, I'm pretty sure she knows we're having sex."

"Seriously, guys?" Damian piped up from the back seat.

"But we don't have to rub it in her face," Naomi countered. She held up a hand to forestall what he was about to say. "It's not happening," she said. "Not right now. If that means we need to get a hotel room, then we'll get a hotel room; unless there are two guest rooms?"

Jay remained silent as he turned onto the Perimeter Highway and began heading toward Route 441 south of the city. He wasn't sure where Naomi's hesitance came from, and he nearly asked her if she would feel the same way if they were married. But he stopped himself. First, because he knew the answer to that; no, she wouldn't feel the same way. And second, he'd shocked himself into silence when he'd realized the "M" word had nearly fallen from his tongue without a second thought. It would have been spoken in jest of course, but then he wasn't entirely certain that the question would have come out as "*If* we were married would you still feel the same way?" No, he had a sneaking suspicion that what he might have actually said would have been more along the lines of, "Will you feel this way *when* we're married?"

It was too soon for any of that. Too soon for even the hint of any of that. But he still didn't want to sleep in separate rooms— even if his mom had two guest rooms, which she did.

"Damian?" he said glancing in the rearview mirror. The agent had been looking out the window, but he looked up and met Jay's gaze in the reflection.

"Yeah?"

"How do you feel about sleeping in the main house? My mom is great, she'll leave you be."

Damian lifted a shoulder. "Sure, I don't mind."

"There," he said taking his eyes off the road to look at Naomi. "Problem solved. Damian will stay in the main house, and we'll take the guest house." He returned his attention to the road. "And before you protest, it's two bedrooms, so you can pretend we're not sleeping in the same room. It's also where I usually sleep when I stay with her so you're not causing any rifts or changes."

He felt Naomi's eyes on him as he turned his attention back to the road. Athens was a college town, but the Perimeter Highway this time of night was more or less empty. She rotated in her seat, no doubt to check on Damian, but a glance in the mirror told him Damian had already checked out of the conversation and was back to staring out the window.

Finally, Naomi spoke. "Okay, fine," she said.

He reached over and took her hand. "It will be fine, you'll see."

She gave him a skeptical smile but didn't contradict him. Instead, she laid a hand on the flowers. "Where did these come from and who left your truck?"

"Kara and Bill Watson. Kara and I went to high school together. She was one of the few people who believed in me. Really one of the few true friends I had. Anyway, I'm a loyal kind of guy. She owns a flower shop now, and I have her deliver flowers to my mom almost every week. I asked her to make up a bouquet for today since I always bring my mom flowers when I see her, too. Bill, Kara's husband, is a groundskeeper and works mostly at a couple of the bigger farms in the area, but he also works for me on my mom's place. She loves the space, and while she's still able to do a lot of gardening around the house, he takes care of the rest of the land and helps her with some of the bigger things. He also maintains my truck for me while I'm not around."

Naomi murmured something about the arrangement lying in her lap then fell silent. He navigated them off the Perimeter Highway and onto Route 441 heading south. "Have you found anything on the rental properties yet?" he asked.

Naomi started to shake her head then stopped. "Athens has a number of short-term rentals, and Madison has a few as well. There are far fewer near Union Point and none that I could find so far near Stephens," she said.

"Yeah, Stephens is the weird one," Jay said, beginning to mull over something that had been percolating in his mind.

"It's definitely the most out of the way," Naomi agreed. "It's about the same size as Union Point, but Union Point seems to have better access to the forest; at least that's how it appears based on what I'm seeing on the rentals sites." She stroked the petal of one of the flowers as she spoke.

"It does, to a certain extent. So then how'd Lucy learn about Stephens?" he asked.

"We assume driving around," Naomi answered, laying her hand gently on the bouquet so as to keep it firmly on her lap. "We're still working on the theory that she's either in an RV of some sort or she's being moved between rental houses. Ah," she said, catching on, "you think the fact that she knows about Stephens at all tends to tip the balance toward the van/RV theory because there aren't really any rentals in that area?"

He inclined his head, not quite a nod. "There are a number of campgrounds where an RV wouldn't look out of place, especially around the National Forest. And when I think about that versus having to find a rental that is remote enough to keep someone prisoner but still be a short-term rental in each of those locations? Well, I don't really see it happening. I suppose they could have picked up several longer-term rentals, but even those would be hard to come by in some of the towns we're looking at."

"Not to mention if these towns are anything like Windsor, if a house *was* taken as a long-term rental and no one moved in, people would probably talk," Naomi added.

Jay nodded. "People would definitely talk. Not in Athens, but in the other three locations, for sure."

"So maybe we should be looking for campgrounds?" she asked.

"Yeah, it might be worth checking campgrounds. There are several around here that are private, so you'll probably want to dig into business licenses as well because many of them won't advertise." She pulled out her phone and began texting Brian before he'd even finished speaking.

The road had changed to a two-lane road rather than a highway as it wound its way gently south. He didn't have to see the land to know it, and though he now considered Boston his home, this part of the country had locked itself into his DNA somehow. He even heard a little hint of drawl creeping back into his voice.

Taking the next exit, he headed east on an even smaller two-lane road. This one curved more than the highway, and the trees encroached along its banks in smatters of starts and stops with breaks of wide open fields visible in the gaps.

"At the risk of sounding like a seven-year-old, how much farther?" Naomi asked.

He smiled and reached for her hand again. "Less than five minutes." He felt her hand twitch in his, but she said nothing more. She remained silent when he made a turn onto an even smaller road then another turn onto a dirt driveway. In the dark, the area looked more secluded than it was, and though his mother couldn't see any of her neighbors, the area was littered with five- and ten-acre estates.

The drive smoothed out, and his tires crunched the ground as the dirt turned into a gravel drive. A few seconds later, his mom's house came into view. The two-story pale yellow home gleamed in the dim moonlight. Glowing lights illuminated the wide porch that extended along the front of the house and wrapped around both sides. Dark green shutters punctuated the evenly spaced windows, each of which was trimmed in white.

"It's lovely," Naomi said leaning forward to get a better look through the windshield.

"In the morning, you'll see the gardens, that's her true love and it shows," Jay said, not hiding the bit of pride he felt at being able to provide the opportunity for his mom to do something she loved. She'd been a teacher her entire career and also a single mom with two kids—she'd worked damn hard to make sure they had a roof over their heads, food on the table, and clothes on their backs.

There were many months Jay remembered it being touch and go as to whether all three of those things could be accomplished. And the fact that she'd never hidden her struggles from him, not after he'd reached the age when he could understand them, made him appreciate her even more. She had never complained or sought sympathy but had always just laid out the facts, and together they'd worked to find solutions. Sometimes that meant getting a little extra food from the food bank or clothes from the donations brought to their local church, but she—and they—had always just figured it out.

But now, now he liked that the most pressing thing his mom had to think about was which flowers to prune or plant. That wasn't to say she didn't think about other things—she volunteered her time at the same food bank that she had once frequented and still helped coordinate the clothing closet at the church—but she didn't *have* to do any of these, and that alone was the one of the highlights of his career.

"Over there is the guesthouse," he said pulling the truck to a stop in the drive and pointing to where a faint glow could be seen through the trees. "We'll pop in, see my mom, say hi, then come back for our bags," he said.

The three of them slid from their seats, Goo bounding out after Damian and taking off into the night. Naomi handed Jay the bouquet when they met in front of the truck. "Do we need to worry about her?" Naomi asked pointing to where the retriever had disappeared to.

Jay shook his head. "She knows where she is. She'll go to the bathroom, take a couple laps around the house then show up at the back door for the treat my mom always has for her."

The front door opened before them and his mom stepped out. With a smile, he bounded up the five stairs and enveloped her in a hug. "I can't believe you're here," she said. "Shouldn't you be out celebrating or doing whatever it is you do to celebrate what you just did?"

"Team effort, Mom. I didn't win the series on my own," he said pulling back and handing her the flowers. The large bouquet made her laugh and she wrapped an arm around it, holding it against her chest as she pointedly looked behind him.

"Mom, this is Naomi DeMarco," he said, gesturing Naomi up the stairs. "Naomi, this is my mom, Margaret Greene."

"Mrs. Greene, it's nice to meet you," Naomi said holding her hand out.

"Margaret, please. I had enough with the 'Mrs. Greene' when I was a teacher," his mom replied with a smile.

"And this is Damian Rodriguez," Jay said, introducing the agent who stepped up and extended his hand as well.

"It's a beautiful place, Margaret. Is that a gentian?" he asked pointing toward the baskets hanging from the porch railing.

His mother beamed. "It is. A friend rescued it from a creek earlier this year when they were doing some development. I've been maintaining it here and hope to plant it in the spring out along the back yard, near the tree line."

"South facing?" he asked.

She shook her head, "No, it's east facing so some filtered morning sun. It's also along the small brook that runs through the property."

Damian eyed the plant then nodded. "I bet it will like it there."

His mom laughed and Jay glanced at Naomi who seemed as surprised as he by this glimpse into Damian.

"Come in, come in," Margaret said, stepping back from the door and ushering the three of them into a center foyer. Jay entered first and led them straight back into the kitchen, bypassing the sitting room and formal dining room on the right because if he knew his mom...

"Ah, cookies," he said, heading straight for the plate. "And snickerdoodles, my favorite." He grinned, grabbed two, then took a massive bite from one.

"Jason Evans Greene," his mother's voice came from behind him. "You mind your manners and offer our guests some before you clean off the plate."

"You have another plate stashed somewhere, I know you do," he teased, because she always had another plate stashed some- where. "But Naomi, Damian, would you like a cookie?" he offered holding out the plate.

"I can make coffee or tea too," Margaret said, having laid the flowers down on the granite counter and begun searching for a vase.

"Or milk," Jay added, walking to the fridge.

"Or milk," she agreed, straightening up with a vase in hand.

"Tea would be good, if it's not too difficult?" Naomi said. "I can make it myself if you want to get those flowers arranged?"

"That would be great, dear," his mom answered, taking it in stride that he'd brought a woman home with him. Granted it wasn't a usual kind of family visit, but his mother wasn't fooled by the situation, especially as he'd never brought a woman home before. Ever.

"Kettle is on the stove. Water is from the well so good from the tap. Mugs are to the left of the cooktop and tea is in the drawer just below. Jay can help with cream or sugar if you like," she said, making everyone feel instantly at home the way she always did; including Goo who, as predicted, showed up at the back door, letting out a little bark to alert everyone that she was now ready to come in and get her treat.

Thirty minutes later, he watched Naomi stifle a yawn and realized that although he'd been riding a high of playing, and then winning, the Series, she'd been working a lot of late nights and early mornings. Making his excuses to his mom, he hustled her out of the house and led her down the gently lit path to the guesthouse. Goo, having opted to stay with his mom—and her treats—remained at the house.

"Our bags," Naomi said when they stepped inside the cottage.

"You settle in, I'll get them," he said. He gave her a quick tour, mostly just pointing out the rooms from where they stood, then turned to retrieve their belongings from the truck. He'd just hefted his bat bag over his shoulder when he heard the front door of his mom's house open. Turning, he saw Damian jogging down the steps.

Jay stood aside as the agent collected his own bags. "You all set?"

Damian slung a black duffle bag over his shoulder and reached in for a rectangular hard-shelled case. "Yep. Mags has me set up in the back room. Not the room your sister uses but the other one," he answered.

"Mags?" Jay said, a smile quirking his lips.

"Your mom's too vibrant to be a 'Margaret' but we decided 'Mags' fits," Damian responded his hip resting against the now closed door of the truck. "Make sure Naomi sleeps tonight," Damian said suddenly, all hint of fun gone from his voice.

Jay studied the man before him then nodded. "She does look tired," he said.

"And she'll keep going unless someone stops her or she drops, literally," Damian said.

Jay's eyebrow went up in question.

"I worked a case with her last year, a human trafficking case. They were using the internet to both find and sell kids. Hidden underneath all her good cheer and seemingly happy-go-lucky charm, Naomi is one of the toughest people I know and one of the most sensitive. The case was one of the worst I've ever worked, and it absolutely wrecked her.

"Those last few days I wasn't paying much attention, but when we finally cut the head off the ring and found the kids we could, she very literally collapsed at her desk," he said, shifting his bag to his other shoulder.

"Another agent took her to the hospital where she was admitted for dehydration, fatigue, and of all things, lack of nourishment. When we pieced things together, we realized she hadn't eaten, drank anything more than coffee, or slept for nearly four straight days," he said with a shake of his head.

"That's the kind of person she is when she's involved. It's not always like that, most of the time she's pretty good at taking care of herself. But when she's involved—and she's definitely involved in this case because Lucy is a friend—she doesn't—" He paused, looking for the right phrasing. "Well, she doesn't prioritize herself. That whole 'put your mask on first so you're alive to help someone else' sort of gets lost with her."

Jay glanced back in the direction of the guesthouse, only a faint light glowing through the trees giving any sign of its presence. "She's probably on her computer already, isn't she?" It was the one bag she'd brought in from the truck with her.

"If you've left her alone for more than a minute, she's on her computer already," Damian said with a chuckle as he pushed himself off the truck. "I'm going to bed, but I'll be up early. I may go for a run if you want to join me unless you're taking a break?"

Jay nodded, "There's a nice five-mile loop from here. Six-thirty?" he suggested. Damian nodded then disappeared back into the house. Jay picked up his duffel then reached for Naomi's bag. He didn't have to think hard about what he'd find when he reentered the guest house. But as he walked back, he developed a plan to make sure she took care of herself for the next few days—or at least allowed him to take care of her. His team had just come off one of the most perfect seasons in the history of baseball. They'd swept the division championships and then the Series; that kind of season took a little luck and a lot of planning.

Dealing with Naomi couldn't be much harder than that.

Right?

* * *

*N*aomi could not believe this was happening to her. The heels of Jay's shoes popped in and out of her vision as they traveled the packed dirt path from the guest house to his mom's. Flung over his shoulder, like little more than a sack of potatoes, she decided to suffer the humiliation in silence—after her initial shriek of protest of course. And, yes, that was one more thing she couldn't believe had happened. She was pretty sure that the last time she'd shrieked she'd been seven.

"Good lord, Jason," Margaret called from the porch. "What on earth are you doing? Put her down this instant."

Naomi smiled to herself, liking Jay's mom even more. With a scrabble of nails, Goo came bounding into the picture, dancing around her and Jay.

"Sorry, Mom, I can't do that until I'm in the house."

"No, you will do that right now or there will be no breakfast for you," Margaret shot back. All Naomi could see was a pretty nice view of Jay's behind, but she pictured Margaret standing on the porch with her hands on her hips, glaring at her son.

"She wouldn't stop working. She needs to eat," he said. Naomi could hear the beginnings of concern in his voice. The fact that his mom scared him maybe just a little bit was kind of sweet.

"*She* is right there and can hear you," Margaret said. "Stop speaking about her as if she isn't here. *And she* is also a grown woman who can decide whether she wants to eat or not. *And*," Margaret continued, clearly on a roll, "if you were so concerned about her eating, why didn't you just come get her some food? My plates will travel as well as anything. Honestly, Jason, Naomi is not one of your teammates, you are not the captain, you do not get to make this game plan on your own. Now put her down."

Jay paused, then after a beat, he slid her gently to the ground, steadied her with his hands on her hips and stepped away. Goo pressed into her leg, and Naomi dropped a hand to her soft head.

"Sorry?" he said.

Behind her, Margaret made some sort sound of disgruntlement. "Naomi, come inside, it won't take but a minute to make you a plate to take back if that's what you like." The sound of the screen door closing behind her punctuated the statement.

Jay shoved his hands in his pockets, and though he didn't look entirely repentant, he did look like maybe his mom had given him something to think about. "I forgive you," Naomi said with a grin as she went up on her toes and kissed his cheek. "But only because the humiliation was tempered by the fact that I had a nice view while being slung around."

Jay rolled his eyes but smiled, then he captured her face between his hands and drew her back for a much longer kiss. When they parted, he looped an arm around her shoulder and walked with her up the stairs and into the kitchen, Goo following behind.

"Here, dear," Margaret said, handing Naomi a plate as she walked in the door. "Of course you are welcome to stay and eat at the table," she said with a gesture toward where Damian sat with a cup of coffee in front of him and his own plate piled with biscuits, eggs, and sausages.

"Actually, now that I'm here, there is something I was hoping you might be able to help me with," Naomi responded, taking the plate and beginning to help herself to the breakfast buffet Margaret had laid out.

"Of course, anything," she said as she filled a mug with coffee then wrapped her hands around it.

"You'll join us?" Naomi asked, setting her plate down as Jay went to pour them some coffee. She'd had a cup already when Jay had gone out for his run, but today was easily going to be a three-to-four cup day—especially considering she'd stayed up late the night before adding some additional security to Margaret's Wi-Fi network.

Margaret took a seat beside her at the round table. "What can I help you with?"

Naomi pulled a list from her pocket. "These are the campgrounds in the area that have business permits on file. I don't know about down here, but I do know that in some other states I've traveled to, there are often a few folks here and there who don't so much as operate a campground but offer to let friends, and friends of friends—you know what I mean—stay there. There won't be any record of *those* places, so I was hoping you could take a look at the list and then see if you know of any we missed."

Naomi handed her the list and Margaret sipped her coffee as she perused the names. "Hm, interesting that this one still has a permit," she said pointing to the second business on the list, Coopers Campground. "Raymond Cooper died two years ago, and as far as I know, his daughter Kacey has no interest in opening it back up. She moved to Savannah about ten years ago and comes back every now and then, but doesn't live here."

Jay reached for the list but when his mother shot him a look that said she was not done yet, he let out a dramatic sigh, scraped his chair back, and moved to read over her shoulder.

"So, the land is just sitting there?" he asked.

His mother nodded. "And the home."

Naomi looked up at Jay for an explanation. He shook his head. "It's a big piece of land, about 400 acres or so, between Madison and the National Forest. The house isn't much, but I'm surprised some developer hasn't picked it up."

Naomi glanced at Damian, who was writing something down, most likely a note to look into Kacey Cooper and why she'd file a permit for a business that didn't exist. "I'll send you a copy of the permit, Damian," Naomi said. "Brian sent the list this morning, but he also sent images of the permits themselves."

He nodded then shoved another biscuit into his mouth.

"What about the others?" Naomi asked, turning her attention back to Margaret, who was frowning.

"Here's one that shut down last year, but it might have been after they filed that year's permit, so it may not be as unusual as the Coopers' situation," she said, pointing to another name. Naomi read it off for Damian who made another note.

"The rest are all functioning as far as I know, but the Lesley place is less of a campground now and more of just a hunting ground. Oh, there's camping there, but only so far as folks are there to hunt," Margaret continued.

"And are there any *not* on the list?" Naomi prompted.

Margaret turned and looked over her shoulder at her son, the two held eye contact for a moment as if trying to pull up their collective memory.

"The Anderson place," Jay said.

Margaret shook her head. "They used to allow camping when you were growing up, but they sold off most of their land to a couple from Atlanta who built an inn on it. Lovely place, especially for events and weddings." Margaret lowered her eyes back to the list as she spoke so it was hard for Naomi to gauge if she'd been dropping a hint or not. Although Naomi was fairly certain no sane mother would be doing any such thing like hint at a wedding after only three weeks of dating, so she decided to assume Margaret had just meant it as an offhand comment.

"There's the Mays' place, over near Stephens," she said suddenly.

"Oh yeah, I remember that place," Jay said with a smile. "It had a small pond on it that we'd sneak to at night and swim in."

"Bless your heart it's a miracle you lived," his mother muttered with a shake of her head. "The May family is less than hospitable. And there are alligators." She shared an exasperated look with Naomi as she rose and began loading the dishwasher.

Jay opened his mouth to say something, but Naomi silenced him by rising and giving him a quick kiss. "I'm sure you were perfect, dear," she said with a grin. Jay's eyes narrowed and Damian snickered, but Naomi moved away to help Margaret with the clean-up.

"I'll get that," Jay said, on yet another sigh. "Mom you cooked, I'll clean. Naomi and Damian, well, you have FBI-ish things to do."

Damian rose, picking up his plate. "I want to take a look at some of these campgrounds, if you don't mind. Can I borrow your truck, or can you take me to a rental agency?"

"I'd like to see them too so that when I run the satellite imagery I'll know what to zero in on," Naomi said, handing Jay a plate.

"Why don't I finish cleaning up the kitchen, make a few calls, and then I can chauffer you around?" Jay offered. "The roads aren't tricky but there are a few here and there that are really only used by locals."

"And by 'locals' he means teenagers out doing things they shouldn't," Margaret interjected.

"And such knowledge may now benefit the FBI," Jay retorted with a grin. "You should be glad I spent all those summer nights driving around. I'm aiding an FBI investigation now."

Margaret shook her head, then leaned in and gave her son a peck on the cheek. "You're lucky I love you, dear. Now go have, well, not fun, but I supposed I should say a *productive* day," she said, then sailed out of the kitchen as the remaining three called out thank yous.

"You sure you want to drive us around?" Damian asked doubtfully.

"It's been a while since I've had a chance to take some back roads, if you know what I mean. I do need to stop by the organization in Athens that's coordinating the clinic tomorrow, but that shouldn't take more than twenty minutes. If we head south from here, then loop east toward Union Point, then north toward Stephens, we can finish the loop by heading west into Athens and then home again. If we do that, we'll be able to hit all those spots, including the Mays' property."

Naomi glanced at Damian. He didn't usually like giving up control of the driving, but he surprised her by nodding in agreement.

"We leave in forty-five minutes?" Damian asked.

"Make it an hour," Naomi countered. "I need to shower, and

I want to get a program running to cross-reference all those cases Agent Brown was involved in and see if I can find any patterns. I don't know if it will help find Lucy, but it can't hurt."

Damian nodded. "I'll see you out front in an hour," he said then turned and headed upstairs.

Naomi eyed Jay, not wanting to leave him to do all the clean-up but really wanting to get back to her work.

"Go," Jay said, reaching for a sponge and turning on the hot water. "The sooner you get started on whatever it is you need to do, the better chance we have of actually leaving in an hour."

She grinned, pulled him down for a deep kiss, even as he held the sponge in one hand and a dish in the other. "I'll be ready in an hour," she said when she pulled away. Then she darted out of the main house and jogged to the guesthouse.

CHAPTER FIFTEEN

PRECISELY AN HOUR LATER, Jay opened the passenger door for her as Damian climbed in behind the driver's seat. She hadn't bothered to put her laptop in its bag and so climbing in with her open computer in one hand, her bag draped over her shoulder, and a coffee cup in her other hand was a bit awkward. Until Jay simply picked her up and set her on the seat. Damian snickered.

"If you ever tell Brian or Vivi about that you are a dead man," she snapped at the agent.

"It's really hard to take you seriously when you can't even get into a vehicle without help, pixie," he retorted.

Naomi opened her mouth to snap back but Jay cut her off.

"Children," he said, with a long-suffering sigh as he climbed into his seat. She started to protest but Jay shot her a look. "Where to first?" he asked, cutting her off.

She let out a huff and turned to the map she'd pulled up on her laptop. "This one I think," she said, rotating the screen toward him and pointing to a spot. He nodded and started the engine.

"Are you two going to behave?" he asked, backing the car into a three point turn and heading out the drive. "And don't start with the bank account stuff again, Naomi, we all know you can make our savings, or pensions as the case may be, disappear."

Damian snickered again and she turned to glare at him.

"And Damian, I'd be careful if I were you. I know about Charlotte and I know about some pictures Naomi has. You may not want to taunt the bear," Jay said. Damian's eyes narrowed into little slits as he glared right back at her.

"Pixies can be vicious little creatures," Naomi added with a grin.

"You are such a pain in my ass," he finally said, turning his attention to the window.

"Right back at ya," Naomi said, refocusing her own attention back on her laptop. "But bless your heart, it's a good thing I love you."

Jay laughed. "Not quite the way to blend those two sayings, but we get the point."

They turned back onto Highway 441 and headed toward Madison and the first of seven campgrounds on their list—eight including the Mays' property Margaret had mentioned. Naomi divided her attention between her laptop and watching the surroundings as Jay drove. She was running a facial recognition program on the CCTV feeds she'd collected from the airfields Damian had identified, looking for Lucy. Naomi suspected she might also find Kevin Farlow or the second mystery man or maybe even Agent Brown on the footage, but Lucy was the only one she knew for certain to look for.

Lost in the data, she barely registered the quaint little town they passed through as she viewed the footage. A few minutes later, they pulled onto a dirt road, hitting a deep rut.

"Dammit!" Naomi exclaimed.

"That was a bit dramatic," Damian said. "It was just a rut, not sure what you expect from dirt roads."

Rather than snap back, she turned around and handed

Damian her laptop. She watched as his eyes scanned the screen then narrowed in on the same thing she'd noticed.

"What the hell? Who is this guy?" he said.

She let out a growl of frustration and snatched her laptop back. "I don't know, and it's killing me. At least now we know how Lucy got from Honolulu to Athens." She glared at the image on her screen as if it were its fault that the man she had yet to identify—the man who'd been with Kevin Farlow the night Smitty had been killed—had the gall to be one of the three-member team that appeared to have kidnapped Lucy. It was there, right in front of her, Lucy James walking with Naomi's unidentified man beside her, trailed by two others.

"How did they get her from there to here?" Damian asked.

"They took multiple planes and traveled over several days," Naomi said, her eyes not straying from the screen.

"Good, assuming each plane was rented under a different name or is owned by different people, we'll have more evidence than the single plane option we discussed."

Naomi knew Damian's observation to be true, but rather than answer, she focused on the man she had yet to identify and barely noticed when Jay pulled the truck to a stop.

"First stop, Lawsons' Campground," he said. Naomi glanced up to see a closed gate with a sign hanging from it. Printed along the bottom was a phone number and directions to call if one had reservations.

"What do we do from here?" Jay asked.

"I'm going for a little walk. If anyone stops by, you two start making out or something," Damian said.

"What?" Jay asked, confused.

"Bring me pictures?" Naomi said.

"Always," Damian said as he opened the door and hopped down. Naomi and Jay watched him vault over the fence with a grace that shouldn't surprise her but did.

"He's trespassing," Jay said, not sounding overly concerned

about the law but more about Damian's safety, which his next comment confirmed. "He does realize it's hunting season and people take gun ownership and property rights very seriously down here. I mean, we're not Texas or anything, but..."

"He'll be fine," Naomi said, letting her mind absorb their surroundings.

"Until he's not," Jay said. "The Lawsons are pretty lax. Damian shouldn't have any problems here. But there are a few of the other places where that might not be the case."

Naomi heard the words, and even believed them—Jay would certainly know better than she about any dangers Damian might encounter. But there was little she could do about it, so she turned back to her computer.

Sooner than she expected, Damian strolled back through the trees and vaulted back over the gate. She hadn't thought he'd find a smoking gun, or in this case the RV or whatever vehicle they now believed was being used to transport Lucy, but all the same, she felt a bit deflated when he gave a quick shake of his head as he walked toward the truck.

"I just sent you some photos, but it looks like no one is, or has been, here in a while," he said climbing back into his seat.

"You do know it's hunting season," Jay said, firing up the engine and turning around.

Damian looked unimpressed. "Nope."

"And there are a couple of properties I recommend not tres-passing on if you value your manhood."

"Is it trespassing if it's a business?" he asked. "I mean, I know it could be, but how do they expect people to decide if they want to camp at a particular place if they can't check it out without the risk of getting shot?"

Jay turned the truck back toward Highway 20 then pulled over. "I forgot to ask which one is next," he said, looking at Naomi and ignoring Damian's mostly philosophical question.

"Here, then here, then here." Naomi showed him the route

she'd mapped out. "I think this is the May place?" she pointed to a spot on the map. Jay nodded. "Then we can hit the rest in this order," she said, pointing out the remaining campgrounds.

"Got it," Jay said then pulled back out onto the road. Naomi glanced behind her to find Damian staring out the window. Leaving him to his musings, she pulled up the footage where she'd spotted Lucy and sent it to Brian. She hadn't heard from him since they'd left the night before, and she wondered if he'd gotten any sleep. Monitoring the system Lucy had already infiltrated was going to be a twenty-four/seven job but it was also the best way, the only way, to get any real time evidence. And to let her know she wasn't alone.

A moment later, just as they passed over Lake Oconee, a response showed up in her inbox.

"Who's the guy?" Brian asked.

She opened a secure chat window to respond. "Hell if I know. I've run him through every system I know, and I still don't have an ID. I'm starting to take this as a personal challenge."

"Every system?" her brother wrote.

"Yes." She refrained from pointing out that when she said "every system" she meant every system, not every system but a few. Her brother's tolerance for sarcasm had fled once he'd learned about Lucy.

"John Taylor's record was breached early this morning," he wrote, abruptly changing the subject.

Naomi racked her brain then frowned. "Shit, she's in the system, isn't she?" Taylor's file was one of Smitty's secret files.

"Yes, she is," Brian confirmed.

"Where is Taylor now?"

"Living the life on Curacao."

"Any reason his file was targeted?" Taylor was pretty small time when it came to the special files Smitty had. He was just a guy who embezzled some money from another rich, but ethically challenged, guy and now lived the life of Riley on a Caribbean island. Okay, he was a little more than that, but not much.

"Working on that," Brian wrote. Naomi bit her lip as she tried to puzzle out why Taylor.

"Everything okay?" Jay asked, reaching over and rubbing her neck. She tilted her head to give him better access.

"I'll feel better when this is over," she said. Taylor might be small potatoes, but he still had value to the FBI.

"Do you think she knows you're there?" Naomi asked returning to the chat with her brother.

"Yes."

Naomi expected more and it was on the tip of her tongue to ask, but something held her back.

"Let me know if you need me to do anything more, anything different," she wrote instead.

"Thanks. I know you're working on figuring out who that guy is. I think he could be the key."

"Will do. I'll call you tonight unless we find anything game changing."

"Thanks, and I'll keep you posted if I hear anything from her that I can pass on."

Naomi paused at the interesting wording. Was her brother getting information from Lucy he couldn't pass on? Rather than ask, she typed in that she loved him then closed the window and, taking a cue from Damian, turned and stared out the window. She needed to figure out how to identify her mystery man—it was a longshot but maybe if she identified him, they might be able to tie him to the area, which might then help them find Lucy.

The scenery flew by her, and though she felt a passing acknowledgment of its beauty, none of it really sank in. She was still pondering how to go about identifying the man when they bumped onto another dirt road.

This campground was open and they were able to drive in and check it out; seeing nothing but a couple of local pick-up trucks, they continued on their way toward Union Point.

"Are you looking into the plane information I sent you? The planes that were used to transport Lucy?" Naomi asked a little more sharply than intended.

Damian raised an eyebrow at her.

"Sorry, I'm getting more annoyed by the minute that I can't identify that guy," she said with a sigh.

Damian acknowledged her apology with small smile. "I sent the info to an analyst I know. He's FBI, but formerly with the SEAL teams and only joined a few months ago, so I trust him. If there's a connection between the plane rentals he'll find it," he said. "Maybe the guy had plastic surgery," Damian suggested switching topics back to the mystery man.

"Thought of that," she said, pulling up an image of him again. "We ran his prints from the glasses at my cousin's and unless he changed his fingerprints too, he's not in the system."

"How is that even possible? They fingerprint when you travel, you're fingerprinted for driver's licenses in many places, not to mention all the devices using fingerprinting now. Can you just tap into those? It just seems almost impossible that there isn't some sort of hint of who he is," Jay said.

Something in Jay's words caught in Naomi's mind, and her body stilled the way it often did when she wanted to let a tendril of thought seep into her mind and take hold. She didn't know specifically what it was that he'd said which had triggered something inside her mind, but she knew enough about herself to know *something* important had just been expressed.

"Naomi?" Jay said, a hint of worry in his voice.

She held up a hand to silence him.

He eyed her for a beat then returned his attention to the road.

"Oh my God," she said whipping her attention back to her computer as Jay took another turn.

"Naomi?" Jay said again, sounding a bit more uncertain.

"Just let her do her thing, she'll tell us when she can," Damian said, and then they were blessedly silent.

She absorbed the bumps and turns as the truck continued to travel the back roads of Greene County, but her eyes stayed glued to the screen, and her fingers flew across the keyboard. She had no idea how much time had passed when she finally looked up. And grinned.

But that grin faltered when she took in her surroundings. "Where are we?"

"We're close to Stephens. You've been focused on your computer, and we've already seen four more campgrounds," Jay answered.

She turned to look at Damian. "Did I miss anything?"

He gave her a wry look. "Despite being dead to the world, do you think I would have let you miss anything important?"

He had a point, he wouldn't. Naomi nodded.

"So, what did you find? Do you have an ID?"

"Not yet, but I know how to get one. Something Jay said about it being nearly impossible to stay out of the system made me think that really, the only two kinds of people who *aren't* in the system—excluding kids who often won't have fingerprints in any database—are those who live off the grid and those who have been erased from the grid."

"Shit," Damian said. "He was erased, wasn't he?"

Naomi nodded.

"How? That is a monumental feat," he said.

"You forget who they're kidnapping," she said.

"Carl Rogers," Damian said.

Naomi nodded. "He'd definitely have the skill to do it."

"So how are you going to find him if Rogers was good enough to clean the man from the system."

"Carl would have had to start somewhere. I hacked into his account to see what he accessed in the days before he died. Not surprisingly, and I can't believe I didn't think of this earlier, he left a bread crumb trail just like Lucy is doing. Nothing a moderately trained eye would catch, but something I did when I finally started looking."

"So, what now?" Jay asked.

"I'm creating a list of all the systems and files Carl accessed," she said. "Based on that, I should be able to figure out dates and locations of any travel our target might have taken. We can then cross reference that information with any crimes committed in those locations."

"And then we can call the locals and see if they have information in *their* systems," Damian said with a grin. "Thank God for substandard IT."

At Jay's confused look, Naomi explained. "Some local jurisdictions, even some local airports internationally, aren't hooked up into federal or international databases."

"And if they aren't feeding into those systems, Rogers couldn't have completely wiped out his existence," Jay finished.

"Exactly," Naomi said with a smile. "We'll use the information Carl *did* erase to find the places he *could not* have erased." They didn't have him yet, but now that she was into Carl's account, she knew she'd have him soon. "So, what now?" she asked looking around her.

Jay inhaled deeply and let it out slowly. "Now I call the May family and ask if we can access their property. The concept of southern hospitality isn't one they embrace."

CHAPTER SIXTEEN

JAY TOOK a deep breath and lied to Mr. Roland May about his reasons for wanting to visit. Over the years, he'd become adept at masking emotions and thoughts—it was hard to be a professional baseball player if your emotions were out there for everyone to see—but even so, outright lying didn't come easy to him. Thankfully, Roland didn't seem to like being on the phone, and after telling the older man that Kara and Bill Watson had recommended his campground, Jay didn't have to say much more—Roland simply told him to be there in fifteen minutes then hung up.

His relief was short lived, though, when Roland met them at the gate carrying a shotgun slung over his shoulder. Jay heard Damian shift in the seat behind him, but with her head still buried in her computer, he was fairly certain Naomi hadn't even noticed.

"Don't mention you're FBI," Jay warned Damian as he rolled closer to the owner. Roland and his wife Kathy begrudgingly accepted that the civil war had ended, but always made no bones about believing the wrong side had won. And since the wrong side had won, the existing government was at best corrupt and at worst, illegitimate.

"I plan to be silent as a church mouse back here," Damian answered.

Jay rolled the window down as he came to a stop and Roland approached the truck. In his early seventies, the man still stood tall, over six feet, and wearing overalls, a flannel shirt, work boots, and a scowl, he did not look like anyone Jay would want to cross.

"Jason Greene, you're that baseball player, aren't you?" Roland said.

"Yes, sir," Jay said, keeping his answer short as he had no idea what Roland thought about his profession and didn't want to say the wrong thing.

"And how do you know Bill?"

"Kara and I went to high school together. Bill works on my mom's property."

Roland eyed him for a good long time then his attention drifted to Damian in the back seat. His attention lingered there before shifting to Naomi who'd finally pried herself away from her laptop.

Roland's eyes narrowed, and though Jay didn't look over his shoulder at Naomi, he knew she gazed at the man with a frankness and confidence their host wouldn't appreciate from a woman. He couldn't tell her to drop her gaze, but he did flash a look at Damian, who seemed to grasp the issue, and he cleared his throat much louder than needed, drawing Roland's attention back to him.

"If it's a problem, you don't have to let us in," Jay said, knowing nonchalance was the only way to deal with a man like Roland May.

"What do you want to see it for?" the man all but grunted.

"I'm looking for a private place to hold an event for a small group of friends, maybe do a little hunting and fishing for a few days." That was as far as Jay could go without starting to ramble on and sound like the liar he was.

Finally, after what seemed like an age had passed, Roland stepped back. "About a quarter mile in, you'll see the spot we allow certain folks to use," he said. "Stay on the road and be back here in fifteen minutes."

"And don't let the gate slam you on your ass on your way out," Naomi muttered, thankfully quiet enough that Roland didn't hear. Even so, Jay shot her a warning glare as he rolled his window back up and passed through the gate Roland had opened.

"How do people find out about this place?" Naomi asked as they crawled up the quarter mile road. "It's not a business, clearly they don't advertise, and he isn't even very friendly, so I have a hard time believing he or his wife are talking it up at the local coffee shop."

"If you've lived around here long enough you'd hear about it," Jay said as they crawled along the dirt road.

"Stop here," Damian said suddenly. The parking and camping area had just come into sight alongside the rather picturesque pond he'd mentioned earlier. With its rolling green hills in the distance, weeping willows on the banks of the pond, and lilies scattered about the water's edge, the beauty of the location stood in stark contrast to the man who owned it.

"Stay here," Damian said, hopping out of the truck and walking toward the parking area. A single wood pole rose from the ground with an electrical conduit attached, a couple of tables were scattered nearby, but other than that, there was nothing but nature.

"He does not need to tell me that twice," Naomi said, then reached for her laptop and flipped it open again.

"Having any luck?" he asked, not entirely sure what she was working on at that precise moment.

"Hm, I don't know," she said, surprising him by turning the

screen a bit so he could see several lists. "I have a program scanning Carl Rogers' system, and I should have some result within the hour. After that, we'll need to do some old-fashioned police work and talk to people. But while that's running in the background, I'm also looking at Agent Brown's files. I'm not sure if it will tell us anything relevant to finding Lucy or to the case..." Her voice trailed off as they both scanned the list.

"Is it common for agents to travel this much?" he asked, pointing to a list of cities where Agent Brown had worked a case, a list ranging from Albuquerque to Zion and everything in between.

Naomi rotated the screen back toward her and frowned. "It isn't unusual for an agent to travel depending on the unit they are a part of or if they are a specialist in their field. But what's weird about what you noticed is that there doesn't appear to be any reason for *Agent Brown* to travel so much. She isn't a specialist, or at least it's not in her record, and she isn't with one of the units that tends to travel a lot." She paused and studied the list again.

Staring at her staring at the list, Jay felt something shift in his chest. He'd known from the first night he'd met Naomi that she was someone he wanted to know. Now, watching her, he knew that whatever it was between them was much more, or could be much more, than just that initial attraction and curiosity. Smart, funny, and yes, even a little intense and maybe not quite as socially adept as he, Naomi intrigued him in a way no other ever had and Jay had no trouble picturing them many years from now, sitting on some front porch laughing about something. Maybe watching grandkids cavort on the lawn.

The thought was both an easy one and a distant one, almost a gentle whisper of a memory to come. And for some reason—a reason he didn't feel like exploring—the possibility didn't raise any panic or even discomfort. It was just there, floating through his mind.

"You okay?" Naomi asked, bringing him back to the truck and their purpose for the day.

Her head was tilted, and she was studying him; a strand of her hair had slipped out from behind her ear. Reaching up to tuck it back, he used that as an excuse to tug her closer and leaned in for a kiss. He felt her response to the soles of his feet, and though he wanted nothing more than to pull her onto his lap and hold her, he forced himself to stop and pull away.

"You were saying?" he asked as he brushed his thumb over her lip then sat back just as Damian returned to the truck.

"I was saying?" Naomi repeated.

"You were about to say something about Agent Brown's travel, I believe," Jay said as Damian climbed back into the car.

"Hold that thought," Damian said as he handed Naomi his phone.

Jay watched a myriad of emotions play across her face from curiosity to recognition to anger. "They were here," she said, turning the phone for him to see an image of a tire track. A very deep tire track, the kind of imprint a large RV or camper would leave.

"Did you get the measurements?" Naomi asked, handing the phone back to Damian. The agent nodded as Jay started the truck and turned around.

"I just sent it to the same analyst I sent the plane data to. He'll probably be able to give us the make and model of the RV by the end of the day. It might not be them, but..." Damian let the possibility hang.

"How the hell did they even find this place?" Naomi asked, obviously ignoring the possibility that it *hadn't* been them. They approached the gate, and Roland stood to the side of the driveway holding it open. This time, Jay didn't stop but rather raised his palm from the steering wheel in a one-hand wave and kept going.

"I think it just confirms what we're already thinking;

someone who is part of this operation is either from this area or has ties here," Damian said.

"Can you find out?" Jay asked, gesturing vaguely at Naomi's computer as he turned back onto the local road heading northwest toward Athens. It seemed a monumental task, but he had yet to see Naomi fazed about anything when it came to computers.

"It's easy enough to identify agents who were born or raised in the area and even those who have lived here at one time or another," she answered. "But finding ones with ties to the area that aren't their own would take a while." But even with that qualifier, her fingers were already flying across the keyboard.

"Does Agent Brown have ties to the area?" Damian asked. Jay glanced at the agent in the back seat, he was staring out the window as he spoke, his hands resting in his lap. Despite all the taunts and good-natured insults that flew between him and Naomi, Jay didn't doubt Damian was a man to be reckoned with, the kind of guy he'd want on his team, so to speak.

"Just a minute," Naomi answered, and the cab fell silent as Jay navigated the country roads. They had one more campground to visit, but first he planned to take the two for lunch. After that, they'd drive to Athens for his appointment with the clinic organizers then hit the last campground on their way back to his mom's house.

"Did you like growing up here?" Damian asked out of the blue.

"Not really, no," Jay said, surprising himself with his prompt honesty. Usually he hemmed and hawed when asked about his childhood. He didn't want to insult the people and the area where his mom still lived, but the truth was, growing up poor with a single mom and an ethnically mixed half-sister hadn't been a storybook tale in this part of the South. Baseball had been his refuge, and so other than praising the two coaches who had guided him throughout his high school career and given him a positive place to focus, he tended to avoid talking about his childhood.

Damian grunted some sort of response, and Jay felt Naomi's gaze flit to him from her screen, but neither one asked any further questions. While he thought Damian probably wasn't all that interested in the details, he suspected Naomi was simply holding off on asking rather than forgoing it altogether.

With his tales of woe, at least he might be able to drag her from her computer tonight. Maybe.

And maybe if he could get her away from her computer, he could convince her to have their conversation in bed. Not for sex, although he wouldn't be averse to that, but because if he could get her to lie down and get cozy at a reasonable hour, he might have a better chance of getting her to get a decent night's sleep, too.

He didn't stop the laugh that barked out of him. Both Naomi and Damian looked up sharply, but he just shook his head at them and chuckled. Damian's brows went up, but then he turned his attention back to the window. Naomi's eyes lingered, then something on her screen caught her attention and she dropped her gaze.

Never in his life had he plotted to use *talking* as a way to get a woman to sleep. His career and experience had taught him to be cautious about how much of his private life he shared. But now it seemed he'd happily throw it out there if it would help Naomi get some *sleep*. If he'd had any doubts about what was growing between them before, they were promptly decimated by this realization.

"Okay, I have the program running to check the HR files in Quantico. Of course, it won't check all employees of the Bureau, but it will check nearly all of them, and that should give us a good start. Now, as to Agent Brown..." She let her voice trail off as she looked to be pulling up a file.

"You were about to say something to Jay about her when I got back in the truck," Damian said.

"Hm," she said, her eyes on her computer. "Yeah, he asked if it was normal for an agent to travel as much as she does. She was part of the anti-terrorism team in Miami for about a year and would have traveled then, but other than that she seems to float around a lot, which says one of two things to me, either she's not very good at her job and they are passing her around—although I'm not finding any employment reports to support that—"

"Or she's counter intelligence," Damian said, finishing Naomi's sentence.

"And I'm not finding anything to support that either," she said. "Although I wouldn't unless I dig deeper."

"Dig deeper," Damian said, his voice sounding even harsher in its surety.

Jay saw Naomi turn and look at Damian over the seat. He could see the concern on her face at Damian's tone. He didn't know for certain, but he'd bet that the idea that someone within the FBI was a part of the death of three people was driving the agent's determination.

"What else?" Damian said.

Naomi refocused on her computer and looked poised to answer, although Jay didn't know how much "else" she could be doing and doing functionally. She was already digging into Agent Brown, the entire FBI HR system, Carl Rogers' computer system, and—

"I've got financials running on Beekman to see if he was paid anything for his work. My guess is that whoever contacted him appealed to his desire to be an agent and probably used that as a driver to get him to do what they wanted rather than payment," she started.

"Meaning they tricked him," Damian said.

"That's my guess," Naomi said, "But in case I'm wrong, he

wasn't dumb, naïve perhaps, but not dumb. If he was going to be paid for his work, chances are he would have demanded some up front, so I'm looking into that. Also, now that we know that the RV or whatever it is we think they might have Lucy in was probably at the Mays' place, I've also started calling up the satellite imagery of the area. Once I get that, I'll see if we can locate and track the vehicle." Her gaze came up when she finished speaking, and Jay was pretty sure this was the first time she'd actually taken in the rural landscape. Although now that they were on the outskirts of Athens, more and more homes could be seen.

"Where are we going?" she asked.

"Lunch," Jay said.

Silence greeted his pronouncement. He glanced at Damian, and even though the man had told him to make sure Naomi ate and slept, he didn't look much like a man who had any interest in interrupting his investigation. "We're going to lunch and then we're going to stop by the clinic organizer's office and then we will continue our sojourn across the county," Jay said with emphasis. Naomi frowned and Damian's eyes narrowed but neither said anything.

Feeling a little annoyed that his efforts at hospitality weren't being appreciated, he decided to ignore the two. After a beat, Damian went back to staring out the window and Naomi once again got sucked back into her computer when something flashed on the screen.

"Agent Brown has no known ties to this area," she said. "She worked a case in Atlanta a few years ago, a hate crime murder of a young man, but no other ties."

Damian didn't respond for a long moment, then he asked, "Who would know about you all?"

Naomi's head came up. "I beg your pardon?"

"We think there is someone on the inside running this, or at least influencing it. I can't imagine there are very many people in the Bureau who would know Beekman, Carl Rogers, *and* Lucy James. But obviously someone does, who could that be?"

"Maybe that's something you could put your analyst on, Damian?" Jay asked, thinking Naomi already had enough on her plate. They'd come to a stop at a stop sign, and he met and held Damian's gaze in his rearview mirror. The agent seemed to get the message.

"Not my analyst," Damian conceded. "But maybe it's something Brian can do as he'll be more familiar with how consultants like Lucy and Carl work. It might also give him something to do while he's waiting for Lucy to come online. I'll give him a call when we stop for lunch," he said.

Jay gave a small nod, acknowledging Damian's concession then turned right and started heading toward his favorite diner, a place that had been like a second—well, third, after the baseball field—home to him growing up.

"Ask him to reach out to a few other folks, too to see if anyone has been contacted to do any of this work," Naomi said. "Have him look at Jason Moran first."

"Isn't he the guy who helped during the investigation into the murder of Carly's mother and uncle?" Damian asked.

"He is," Naomi said with a sour look. "I still don't like him."

Jay almost chuckled at her comment, for as intelligent as Naomi was, she wasn't above sounding a little like a petulant child.

"Carly?" Jay asked.

"She's a friend who lives in Windsor, where my cousin Vivi lives. Her mom was killed when Carly was a kid, but the case remained unsolved until a couple of years ago."

"And Jason Moran helped with that?" he clarified.

It looked like it pained her to admit it, but Naomi nodded. "He's still slimy," she added under her breath.

Jay chuckled at her tone, but rather than discuss Jason Moran's ethics any more, he pulled into a parking lot.

"Lunch," he said. "It's my favorite place. Everything you ever wanted to know about Southern cooking you learn or try here." He grinned at them both.

"So, you're saying my cholesterol level—the bad one—is going to double before the end of the meal?" Damian said as the three exited the truck.

"Yep," Jay said, happily. "And you're going to love every minute of it."

CHAPTER SEVENTEEN

NAOMI EYED Maisy's Diner skeptically. Not that she doubted Jay about the quality of the food, but her stomach still hadn't settled from breakfast. She knew Damian thought she stopped eating during investigations because she got too caught up to remember, but the reality was, her stomach tended to tie itself in knots when she was on a case. So much so that eating never appealed to her, and when she did eat, it never settled well. Which, in turn made her even *less* interested in food.

"You'll love it, I promise," Jay said coming to a stop beside her.

"I'm sure it's great," she replied, watching Damian stride toward the front door with all the enthusiasm of a kid headed into a candy store.

She felt Jay's attention on her, but she didn't want to disappoint him, and so she smiled and grabbed his hand. "Let's go," she said pulling him forward.

He stayed put and she jerked back. Turning to face him, she raised her eyebrows in question.

"You okay?" he asked.

"Of course." She said. "I'm fine," she added more firmly.

He cocked his head and studied her. "I don't think you are."

"I am," she assured him, wondering if he, too was thinking of all those stupid memes that told men to be afraid when a woman said she was fine. She hated those memes and always felt that if a woman said she was fine when she wasn't that was her shit to deal with. And this was her shit to deal with—she wasn't fine, but it had nothing to do with Jay, and she had no interest in dampening his obvious excitement for lunch.

"You didn't eat much at breakfast," he said.

She wagged her head. "I'm not much of an eater on the best of days," she said.

He studied her then nodded as if coming to a conclusion about something. "Maisy always has a great chicken soup on the menu," he said, ushering her toward the door. "She also makes a mean grilled cheese and tomato soup. I used to come here before games when I was a kid, especially the big games, and she'd feed me one of those two things." He opened the door as he made that last comment, and a loud, husky voice called out even before the door swung shut behind them.

"Well, well, well, if it ain't the big in his britches, Series ring wearing, most valuable player, then I ain't Maisy Hamilton," a whipcord thin woman bellowed from behind the counter.

"You got it wrong Miss Maisy. The only time I was big in my britches was when you were feeding me all that pie," Jay shot back, striding forward and wrapping the woman, who'd come around from behind the counter, in a huge hug. Almost as tall as Jay, Maisy Hamilton all but disappeared in the embrace she was so thin.

The hug lasted for a good long while, the kind of hug a mother gives her babies when she hasn't seen them in a while. Finally, Maisy stepped back, and Naomi was completely charmed watching the woman struggle to blink back tears at seeing Jay again.

"It's about time you came for some of my food, Jay," she said.

A look of regret flashed across Jay's face at the subtle rebuke. Naomi didn't know how long it had been since he'd been back, or since he'd last seen this woman who obviously meant something to him, but clearly it had been too long.

"But you're here now," she continued. "And where are my manners? Are you going to introduce me to your friends?" She stepped away from Jay and reached up to check on her hair, which was wound in a tight bun on the top of her head.

Jay gave her another quick, one-armed hug then stepped back. "Damian," he said, drawing the man's attention away from the pies in the pie case. "This is Miss Maisy Hamilton. Miss Maisy, this is Damian Rodriguez." Damian stepped forward and shook the woman's hand.

"It's nice to meet you ma'am," he said.

Maisy smiled. "A northern boy with manners. Will wonders never cease?"

"Stop that, Miss Maisy," Jay admonished with a grin. "They aren't all bad."

"I suspect some are rather good," she said turning her attention to Naomi.

"This is Naomi DeMarco, Naomi, Miss Maisy," Jay said.

"It's nice to meet you," Naomi said, the bones of Miss Maisy's hand feeling frail and sharp in her palm as she shook it.

"Another northerner," Maisy said, speculation thick in her voice.

"Yes, ma'am," Naomi said.

"And you're here with my Jay?" Maisy asked.

Jay started to put his arm around her shoulder, but she stopped him with a quick look. "Yes, ma'am," Naomi answered, holding the woman's frank gaze.

Maisy studied her, then she nodded, not so much in approval but in acceptance of something she might approve of later. "Y'all need to sit down, I'll bring you some food. I just closed for lunch, but I'm always open for my Jay."

Jay motioned them toward a large booth against the back wall. By the time they'd settled into their seats, Maisy was already back with tea—sweet tea Naomi discovered after her first sip.

"Lunch will be out in a minute. I'll let you be for now, but I expect you to come back for a good sit down," she said to Jay with a pointed look.

"Yes, ma'am," he said. "We'll be here for at least five days."

"A long stay then," Miss Maisy said, her eyes flickering to the Yankees at the table. Her gaze lingered on Naomi, then Maisy turned and disappeared into the kitchen.

"She's definitely withholding judgment on us," Naomi said once the woman was out of earshot.

Damian snorted. "Not me, she loves me. She's just withholding judgment on you," he said, then took a sip of tea.

"You know how much you suck, right?" Naomi said. And then when he got that stupid look on his face that men got when they were about to turn a normal conversation into something deviant she cut him off by flicking her straw at him.

He started as a few drops of tea shot across the table and hit him in the face. "You did not just do that," he said even as he wiped his forehead and cheek.

She gave him a toothy smile then turned to Jay. "I left my computer in the truck," she said, suddenly feeling like she needed it like a security blanket. Tucked behind the screen of her computer, she felt cozy and comfortable. She did *not* feel twitchy, judged, and annoyed. Well, not usually.

Beneath the table, Jay grabbed her hand and rubbed his thumb across her palm in a soothing circular gesture. "Miss Maisy doesn't allow computers in her diner, but you can use your phone if you need to."

His comment was meant to comfort, but instead, it made her feel just a little vulnerable by exposing her reliance on the device. "It's fine," she grumbled, taking another sip of her tea, feeling oddly out of sorts.

"Damian, weren't you going to call Brian about looking into the link between Carl, Lucy, and Beekman?" Jay asked. Damian sat back in his seat as his attention bounced between them. When Damian's gaze met Jay's, some form of communication happened between the two men, then Damian straightened and slid from his seat.

"What's going on, Naomi?" Jay asked when Damian was out of earshot.

Her first inclination was to say "nothing," but hadn't she just been thinking about how annoying it was when people didn't own their own shit? She *was* feeling antsy, and it was making her mean—not her usual state.

She took a deep breath and let it out slowly. "I've never had anyone pull me away from an investigation like you have. This is a first for me, and I recognize I'm not handling it well."

To his credit, he said nothing, just waited for her to continue, which, after a long moment, she did; toying with the paper napkin in front of her with her free hand as she spoke. "I don't do these kinds of investigations very often," she said. "I've done maybe one or two a year since Brian and I started our business. Usually we're testing systems, building them, that kind of thing. So, these situations aren't, well, they aren't *common* for me like they are for Damian." She paused and let memories of past cases wash over her. She had no idea how people like Damian managed to stay sane. Even with the relatively few cases she *had* worked on, she still sometimes had a hard time sleeping at night.

"I've found, over the years, that my way of coping with the stress of the situation is to just keep working. The more I work, the chances are the faster the case will close, and then I can be back to what I normally do." She offered him a wayward smile and what she knew was flawed logic.

"But I'm not letting you do that," Jay said.

She squeezed his hand. "No, you're not, but you're not doing anything *wrong* either. I do need to eat, if only just a little, and I *know* it's a good idea to sometimes just take a break and walk away. But I find that each time I do, I start thinking about Smitty and Beekman and Carl and all their families and what they've all lost over the past few weeks. And then I start thinking about Lucy, my friend, and start to see her with a bullet in her head or her body bloated from being dumped in some lake somewhere, and the only thing I want to do is run and get my computer and start working. And then when I can't," she held up her hand in a one arm shrug. "I, well, you see what it does to me. I'll try to be nicer, more reasonable," she finished, glad to have spoken what felt like the truth, even though it didn't reduce her desire to be back on her computer. She didn't think that feeling would ever go away but she did need to figure out how to manage it.

Jay brought her hand to his lips and kissed her palm. "I know what it's like to feel anxious and to feel that the weight of something is all on your shoulders even when you know it's not. But even so, I've never experienced it when someone's life was in the balance. No one was going to die if I lost a game—they might act like it, but as you pointed out that first night we met, at the end of the day, it's just a game. And so, I won't pretend to know how you feel, or pretend that any of the techniques I use to keep me calm when I need to stay calm will help, but I can promise you I can keep this meal, and all the others, short. I can promise you that in all this chaos, in all this stress, I will try to only do things that actually make things easier for you not harder. I'm not sure what else I can do, but I'm pretty good at reading people, so I'll just promise you that I'll try to help you figure this out."

Naomi blinked. Several times. Not that she was trying to

stop the sudden press of tears that seemed to pop up, uncomfortably. No, the sun was just bright through the window.

Jay offered her a soft smile then brushed a thumb under her right eye. Leaning in, he pressed a gentle kiss to her cheek, then sat back and let go of her hand. "Why don't you check your phone while I go chat with Miss Maisy about our lunch?" He slid from the seat as he spoke, and she was pretty sure the smile she gave in return was just a touch watery. It seemed her emotions were one more thing she lost control over during an investigation along with her appetite.

Jay had just disappeared into the kitchen when Damian came back inside and returned to the booth. He froze for just a split second when he looked at her, no doubt reading her expression. Like Jay, Damian seemed to be annoyingly good at that. But thankfully, he opted not to say anything and instead took a sip of tea as he slid his phone in front of her. On the screen she read the probable make and model of the RV they were now looking for; information Damian's analyst had gathered. It wasn't a guarantee that if they found it, they'd find Lucy, but it was currently their best lead.

"Any chance he pulled a license plate or could identify the color?" she asked, only somewhat tongue-in-cheek.

"Not yet, but you don't have to run the satellite images, he'll do it. I figured it would take something off your plate, and it's really his kind of thing."

"Who is this mystery analyst?" she asked sliding the phone back over to Damian. "Do Brian and I need to poach him? That was fast." She nodded to his phone.

"His name is Russ Harris; he was in BUD/S training when there was a fluke accident. I don't know all the details, but it had to do with some sort of water drop and equipment failure. It ended his chance at becoming a SEAL. They liked him, though, so kept him as part of their support team, and he ran their target location unit for several years. He just got out last year, took a few months off, and then joined the Bureau about four months ago. I'd say don't even think of poaching him, but the truth is, I think he's going to be bored pretty soon."

"Hm, maybe I'll see about taking him to lunch next time I'm in DC," she said. "Did Brian have any updates?" she asked.

Damian started to shake his head then stopped. "Nothing he could pinpoint. Lucy is communicating with him, so that's good, but it's the kind of communication that is the equivalent of one letter at a time—at least that's how he described it to me. He's doing what he can to try to pinpoint her location, but he said he'll also look into any connection between her and the three victims."

Naomi nodded then, her attention caught on the kitchen door as it swung open and Jay walked out carrying two plates; Maisy followed carrying three. They set down plates of fried chicken, okra, biscuits, mashed potatoes, and green beans. Then, before Naomi and Damian could say anything, both Jay and Maisy turned and walked back into the kitchen. They reappeared thirty seconds later carrying plates, silverware, and what looked like a bowl.

"Jay said you needed something like this today," Maisy said, sliding the bowl of steaming chicken soup in front of her. The woman's voice had softened a touch, and Naomi wondered what Jay had said to her while the two had been alone.

"Thank you," Naomi said, touched at the gesture. "I hope it wasn't too much trouble?"

Maisy waved her off, "The only trouble would be if I couldn't feed you. Now eat y'all, I know you have some important things to do while you're visiting. But don't think you're getting out of here without a piece of pie, young man," she said turning to Damian.

"I wouldn't dream of it, Miss Maisy. That pecan pie looked something special," he said with a grin.

She gave a sharp nod. "I'll wrap you up a whole one and you

can take it home. It's Margaret's favorite, too," she said looking at Jay who nodded. "Now eat, and eat fast so I can start my dinner prep," she added before striding away. Naomi was pretty sure the woman had said that just to give them an excuse to hurry. And hurry they did.

Twenty-five minutes later, they were back in Jay's truck pulling out of the drive, a warm pecan pie in a box on the back seat beside Damian. If he'd had a fork, it would have been gone by now, but thankfully Miss Maisy had the foresight to "forget" to pack that utensil. Although if they stayed in the car much longer Naomi wouldn't make any promises about the pie making it to Margaret's intact.

With her computer perched on her lap, she began culling through the FBI HR files to see if she could narrow down which agents, if any, had ties to the area. She was so lost in her search, she didn't even realize they'd driven through most of Athens, and Jay was already pulling into the parking lot near the University ballfield; the ballfield where he would host the first of his two clinics.

"Be good," was all he said before he slid from his seat and left her and Damian to their own devices. She didn't know what Damian was up to but trusted he was up to something other than stealing bites of the pie.

"Hm, that's interesting," he said after who knew how much time had passed.

"What's that?" she asked, her eyes not straying from the program on computer.

"John Taylor died," he said.

Naomi raised her head but didn't immediately respond, after a moment, she spoke. "John Taylor, the singer from Duran Duran? We're trying to track down a murderer, and you're reading infotainment?"

A beat passed. "I have no idea who you are talking about, but

I'm talking about a different John Taylor," he said. "He was suspected of embezzling—"

"Oh, my God," Naomi said, whirling in her seat. "Of course you're talking about John Taylor." She paused then slumped back in her seat. "I think I'm going to be sick."

"Uh, you didn't eat enough to be sick, so really, I would recommend trying to skip that if you can."

"Lucy hacked John Taylor's file early this morning," she said. "Brian mentioned it to me earlier."

Damian stared at her. "Shit."

"Uh, yeah," she agreed.

"Have any other files been hacked?" he asked at the same time she asked, "How did you find out he'd died?"

They eyed each other, then Naomi nodded. "I'll go first," she said. "I only know what Brian told me, but to the best of my knowledge, Taylor's file is the only one that's been compromised."

"We need to move all those files," Damian said.

Naomi rolled her eyes. "No, we don't because we've already moved them. Mostly. And how do you even know about those files?" she asked. "They aren't common knowledge, not even within the FBI."

"Mostly?" he said, ignoring her question.

"We actually want to catch these people, and the best chance we have at doing that is to keep them on trails we create for them. So yes, we moved them, but we didn't *remove* them," she said. "Now tell me how do you even know about those files? I know you don't have access to them. Technically, you're not even supposed to know they exist," she pointed out trying to find out just how much Damian knew without revealing everything she knew. Taylor's file, along with several others, were one of the FBI's dirty little secrets that Smitty protected. And though she and Brian hadn't withheld the fact that Smitty was more than just a regular forensic accountant, she knew she'd never mentioned the specifics of what was in those files.

Damian turned his attention to look out the window. "Three years ago, I was working a case and we needed information about a man who was a senior executive at a hedge fund. We suspected him of laundering money for terrorist organizations but the fund he worked for wasn't interested in talking to us without a warrant. At least not until I was able to offer them the location of Marsha Moore, a woman who had embezzled about six million dollars from them the year before," he said. "Once I provided them her whereabouts, they were more than happy to provide me the information I needed."

"What happened to Marsha?" Naomi asked.

He shot her a look. "She's not dead somewhere like John Taylor, I'll tell you that much," he said.

She sighed, trying not to let his defensiveness get to her. "How did you make the leap from you getting access to Marsha's information to knowing Smitty was the keeper of that kind of information?"

He snorted. "Come on, Naomi, that kind of information doesn't just pop up out of the blue when I need it. If it was there when I needed it's because it was there all along. And then when you started putting pieces together for me, it didn't take a genius to figure out Smitty was more than meets the eye, or dossier as the case may be. Besides," he continued, "It's a common tactic; hide the diamond in the gold kind of thing. We used to do it all the time in Afghanistan, carry something valuable enough to distract insurgents if anything happened, which would then allow us to protect whatever the real item was that we were trying to transport. At some point, in some training somewhere, we were told to look for the truth in the lie, but in these cases, you look for the truth in the truth."

"So, his regular files, the case files, are the first 'truth,' and the information on people like Marsha and John Taylor—people who become bargaining chips for the government—are the second truth?" she asked.

He shrugged as if it were obvious. "So, I know you've been lollygagging around since the night Smitty died," he said, returning to the earlier topic. "Out of curiosity, just when did you have the time to move all those files?" he asked.

She shot him a look, not amused by his sarcasm. "I started the night Jay and I found Smitty and then plugged away at it over the next few days. The files on people like John Taylor and Marsha Moore are scattered to the winds for all intents and purposes, but not so scattered that Lucy wouldn't be able to find them."

"But you didn't even know Lucy was going to be roped into this that night," he pointed out.

"Didn't matter," she said. "You're right in that I wasn't certain what was going on that first night, but since they had gone to the trouble of scanning Smitty's computer, I knew it couldn't be good. Then I figured on the off chance they *were* after those files, then whoever it was would either be someone smart enough to figure out the transfer protocols and follow my trail, or it would be someone without the skills to find them, in which case, we wouldn't have to worry."

"Your mind is a scary place."

She smiled. "You have no idea. And now it's your turn," she said.

"My what?" he responded.

"How did you find out John Taylor died?" she repeated her earlier question.

"He was murdered, by the way," he said.

Naomi swallowed. "I figured"

"When I found out about Smitty and made an educated guess about the files he probably had access to, I had Russ set up some alerts for a few people. Hey, look at your man," Damian said abruptly changing the subject with a nod toward the building Jay had walked into earlier. Naomi turned to see Jay emerge surrounded by a group that looked to include a few reporters and a photographer. Jay was smiling and talking about something as he gestured with his hands. Everyone appeared to be hanging on his every word.

"He looks like he's enjoying himself," Damian commented.

"Brian mentioned he's never been one to shy away from media attention," Naomi said, watching the group fawn all over Jay.

"Is that going to be a problem?" Damian asked.

A camera flashed, and Jay grinned. It flashed again. "I don't know, I really don't," she answered honestly. "But I wouldn't want him to give that up—not that he even could. He's worked hard to get where he is, and he deserves to revel in it in whatever way he likes."

In silence, they watched the group walk toward the baseball field where the actual clinic would be held the following day. Just before they disappeared through one of the gates, Jay turned and caught her gaze—a moment so short no one would even notice or think it anything other than him checking on his truck. Naomi smiled and thought she caught a glimpse of one in return; one just for her.

"If you can figure out how to hack into the black op files at the CIA then you and Jay can figure this thing out," Damian said.

She whipped around at that statement, "How could you possibly know…" Her surprise turned to a scowl. "You didn't know, did you?"

Damian grinned. "I do now."

Naomi glared at him then giving up the ghost she grinned, shook her head, and went back to her computer.

CHAPTER EIGHTEEN

"JOHN TAYLOR'S ACCOUNTS WERE WIPED," Naomi said to Damian as she took a sip of the wine Jay had brought her. Night had fallen hours ago, and the three of them had retired to the guest-house after they'd eaten dinner, which had consisted mostly of Miss Maisy's pecan pie. Jay had sequestered himself in one of the bedrooms to plan out his clinic schedule while she and Damian had set up on the small kitchen table and continued putting the pieces of the puzzle together.

Russ had sorted through satellite images of the area and found several that included an RV they believed could be the one they were looking for. He was in the process of watching and analyzing more images as they came in, hoping to identify its current location, or barring that, some information about where it might be heading.

In addition to the RV search, he had tracked the names of the companies that had rented two of the three planes that had transported Lucy across the country to Georgia, and he was cross checking them against each other and potential players in this unfolding situation.

Brian was still tracking Lucy while simultaneously trying to figure out who at the FBI might be the connection between the hackers, and Naomi herself was culling through Carl Rogers' last movements—those on his computer anyway—and digging into the death of John Taylor.

"What?" Damian asked looking up from where he was going through some of the FBI HR files Naomi had forwarded to him in the hopes of narrowing down the list of people within the Bureau with ties to the area.

"John Taylor, the embezzler who was murdered today?" She waited to see Damian's mind shift from his current task to their earlier conversation, and when he nodded, she continued. "His accounts, the ones that held the money he stole, well, they were wiped out today."

Damian's lips flattened. "The only person who would have motive for killing Taylor and stealing the money is the man he stole the money from in the first place. Do you have any leads on that?"

"I'm working on it. He originally embezzled it from Coastal Developments, a small group headquartered in Miami with ties to some rather sketchy characters. I don't think Taylor realized who he was stealing from," she added, almost feeling sorry for the man. Almost.

"Anything I can do?" Damian offered.

Naomi started to shake her head then stopped herself. "It feels like we're all over the place, but I can't imagine *not* following up on any of our lines of inquiry. Is this normal?" she asked.

Before Damian could answer, the bedroom door swung open behind her. Turning, Naomi smiled at the sight of Jay, hair damp, wearing a pair of jeans and a Rebels T-shirt. A totally unprofessional wave of lust rolled over her and for a half a second, she considered throwing Damian out and having her way with Jay. He grinned, as if reading her mind, but rather than encouraging her, he came forward and dropped a kiss on her forehead. And then another on her lips.

"Seriously, guys," Damian said.

Jay pulled back just enough to hold her gaze then smiled and straightened, leaving his hand to rest on the nape of her neck as he gently fingered the fine hairs.

"My mom texted and can't sleep. I thought I'd go over and keep her and Goo company for a little while since I didn't get to spend much time with either today," he said, now rubbing Naomi's neck. She was quickly realizing that one of the side benefits of dating a professional pitcher was that he was very good with his hands.

"I'll be back in about an hour and will head to bed then. If at all possible, I'd recommend you two hit the sack at the same time. Tomorrow will be a long day," he said. And it would be. The clinic was scheduled to run from eight until one with an autograph and photo session after. The clinic itself would be closed to the public as Jay hadn't wanted the kids distracted by —or feeling pressured by—any watching crowds, but the photo op session would be open to the public as well as parents of the participants attending and a couple of reporters.

Damian and Naomi had debated whether to attend or not. Ultimately, Naomi had decided that she wanted to watch Jay in action, and there was no reason they couldn't sit in the announcers' box and watch and work at the same time. The look of pleasure that had shown in Jay's eyes when she'd said she wanted to attend was something she'd hold dear. She hadn't realized how important the clinic was to him. She'd thought it was something he'd just done to give them all a cover story, but with that look, she knew that it was more than that. And she was looking forward to seeing this part, this very huge part, of his life.

"Yeah, I'll be done for in about an hour," Damian said. "I'll head back to the house when you get back. Because God knows

I don't want to be anywhere around you two when it's bedtime. Daytime is bad enough."

"You're just jealous," Naomi said at the same time that Jay laughed and said, "If the time of day is what dictates your activity, then maybe that's your problem with Charlotte."

Naomi almost snorted out the sip of wine she'd just taken.

"Fuck you, Greene," Damian said obviously well past his hero worship of the baseball player. "And I swear to God if you say anything," he said spearing Naomi with a look of daggers, "I will tell Ian about Dave Gregory."

"What...how..." she sputtered.

"Who's Dave Gregory?" Jay asked.

"No one," both she and Damian said at the same time.

An awkward silence fell across the room. Jay's fingers still lingered on her neck then they inched their way up into her hair. She leaned back into his touch and found herself looking into his eyes. His questioning eyes. To his credit, he seemed more curious than concerned, but curious nonetheless.

She sighed. "I'll tell you later," she conceded.

He quirked a brow, then bent and dropped one more kiss on her lips.

"So much to look forward to tonight," he said. "You kids have fun saving the world. I'll see you in an hour or so."

Naomi watched the door close behind him then she turned to Damian. "How in the hell do you know about Dave?"

"I visited while you were both at Vivi and Ian's remember? It was when Charlotte and I were together, so she and I were staying with Matty and Dash, but Dave and I went on a couple of hikes, it wasn't hard to figure out what was going on."

"You can't ever say anything to Ian," she said. "It was so important to him that he was able to help Dave. You and Dave saved Ian's life, and though I know neither of you ever thought of it that way, he always felt he owed you guys so much. You, well, you adjusted to civilian life and didn't seem to need anything more than friendship, but Dave needed more, and it was important to Ian that he was able to help. I don't want to take that away from him."

"I agree Dave's time in Windsor was just as good for Ian as it was for Dave," Damian said, but then, much to her dismay he didn't make any promises. Instead, he took the conversation back to the more pressing topic at hand. "I think this feels like we're all over the place because in normal circumstances, we'd have a team double the number of our current team of four; plus, we'd have administrative help," he said. "You wouldn't be doing so many things."

There was truth to his statement, she knew. But it didn't help her bring any order to their process, a process that she felt was on the verge of spiraling into chaos. She looked at Damian, ready to point this out, then stopped short. The reason they were on their own was because someone in the Bureau—his Bureau—was dirty. And judging by the hard glint in Damian's eye, that fact was one he was taking personally.

"We'll find Lucy," she said with a definitive nod. "And once we've found Lucy then we'll find whoever is behind this."

Damian's gaze narrowed on her, but she knew his anger wasn't directed at her. He gave a sharp nod. "And when we do, I promise you, they're done," Damian finished.

* * *

*N*aomi looked up from her computer screen to see Jay in a serious conversation with a kid who watched him raptly. The young man was about Jay's height but hadn't yet filled out. Surrounding the two were three other young men, also listening to Jay as he gave an instruction, drawing his arm back, and balancing on one leg, bouncing up and down as if to demonstrate something though Naomi didn't know what.

"He's good with the kids," Damian said from beside her. They were seated in the announcers' box behind home plate with a view of the field. About forty kids were dressed in their high school uniforms, and despite coming from different schools, and it being the off season for high school baseball, they were all running drills as if they'd played together all summer.

"Doesn't surprise me," Naomi said dropping her eyes back down to her computer screen. "He loves the game. I know that doesn't always mean someone will make a good teacher, but I think because baseball was his refuge growing up, it's important to him to share it in a way that the kids can connect to and use."

"What do you mean, his refuge? You make it sound like he had a shitty childhood. Mags is amazing. I bet she was a great mom to have while he was growing up," Damian said as his fingers began to move over his own keyboard.

She knew that he was expecting more satellite images from Russ any minute; and she had to admit, she was not so patiently waiting for them too. Stealing a glance at his computer, she answered. "Not my story to tell, but you're right, Margaret is an amazing woman," she said.

She stared at her computer for a few seconds more then suddenly bolted from her seat, the legs of the chair scraping on cement floor. "Screw this," she said as she began to pace. Unbidden her eyes went back to the field. Assistant coaches were rotating kids through different drills Jay had set up. Every thirty minutes a new group of four boys would get to work directly with the star Rebels pitcher. Though she knew it was impossible, it seemed as if Jay sensed her frustration and glanced up.

"Problem, pixie?" Damian asked.

She turned and glared at Damian. "Don't call me that," she said. Then she took a deep breath, followed by a long exhale, and retook her seat. She needed to pull it together. Minimizing the program running on Carl's hack job, she opened another. "Yes, there is a problem. I know that just last night we talked about why we need to focus on all the pieces of the pie, but I don't think I can. I think I need to let some of them go and focus only on what's important right now and that's finding Lucy," she said.

Culling through Carl's code and realizing that he'd basically left her an accounting of his own death in the trail he'd left had filled her with an even more heightened sense of urgency. Finding out who in the FBI might be behind all this and what their end game was were things they could figure out *after* Lucy was safe.

Damian pulled his phone out of his pocket as it beeped with an incoming text.

"Is that Russ?" she asked, leaning over to look at his phone screen.

She knew he hated it when people read over his shoulder, but she ignored the look he gave her and read the name. "Why's Margaret texting you?"

He pulled his phone away from her prying eyes. "I don't know, maybe because she likes me and wants me to bring back another pie," he said as he opened the message and read. "Or maybe she remembered another campground," he said holding the phone out for Naomi to read the screen.

"The Robinson farm, off of route fifteen, near the National Forest," she read. Glancing at her watch, she added, "Jay has an hour left of the clinic then the meet and greet. We can go after."

But Damian was already rising from his seat. "There's a rental car place not far from here. I'll pick one up then meet you guys back at Jay's later."

Naomi frowned; she didn't like the idea of him going off on his own. She wasn't entirely sure what she could do to protect him if the need arose, but at least he'd have someone with him if something went wrong. "I don't think that's a good idea," she said.

"It's fine," he responded. "I want to get a better lay of the land anyway. We did a fair bit of driving yesterday, but I want to check out a few things on my own."

"I don't think you should go anywhere without telling someone, like me or Russ, where you are," she said, starting to feel a little alarmed. "Seriously, Damian. Aside from the fact we *know* these people have killed at least three people, there may also be more folks like the Mays who won't take kindly to you snooping around."

Damian tugged on his jacket as he picked up his computer bag. "I'll let one or the other of you know. Besides, Russ can always track me through my phone if needed. Hell, don't pretend you can't track me if you need to, but," he held up a hand to forestall her protest that that wasn't the point, though she *could* track him if needed, "I will let you both know where I am and where I might be going. Just in case."

She'd have to take it because it was all she was going to get, and he was already halfway out the door. "Be safe," she called out.

"Always," he answered. "I'll meet you back at Margaret's no later than four. And if you can pick up another one of Maisy's pies, we'd both appreciate it." Then, with a cheeky grin flashed in her direction, he was gone.

Naomi tried to quiet the unease fluttering in her stomach after Damian's departure, and she turned back to see Jay working with a new group of four boys. Arms folded across his chest, Jay stood watching one of the boys pitch. She could all but feel his assessing gaze on the young man as he decided what he would teach him in their short time together.

Her computer beeped alerting her to an incoming message, and she saw an IM from Brian pop up. "Call me when you can," it said. Reaching for her phone, she hit his contact and heard the ring. Before the first ring even finished, he answered.

"I think they are using satellite rather than data," he said without preamble.

"Have you started identifying the satellite?" she asked. Not many people had access to mobile satellite internet like she did —satellite *phones* were fairly easily accessible, but satellite phones weren't like cellular phones and in general, did not transmit internet data or create an internet hotspot. If Lucy was using satellite access to hack into the FBI systems then that all but confirmed that someone from the Bureau, or somewhere in the government, was involved.

"Of course. Lucy just dropped the lead this morning, I've pulled up what's in the area that might be reachable for her and started looking at the traffic. There are twelve possibilities," Brian said.

"How is she?" Naomi asked.

Brian hesitated. "I don't know. I can tell she's getting closer to another file, but I can also see that she's trying to drag her feet on it, too. I just don't want her to go so slowly that they start to think she's not worth the effort."

"She won't let that happen," Naomi said quickly. "She'll be able to figure out just how long she can draw things out. Safely." She winced at the forced confidence she'd injected into that last word, knowing her brother would hear it.

Again, Brian paused, then he let out a long breath. "I hope so."

Naomi's heart ached for the uncertainty she heard in her normally-upbeat brother. Someday she'd find out just what was between Lucy and him, but for now, she needed to focus on finding Lucy so she could actually *have* that conversation.

She watched Jay work as she updated Brian with her new strategy of just letting everything else go but finding that elusive RV. He agreed that everything else could wait until Lucy was safe. Once they had her back, they could pick up all the other lines of inquiry and put a stop to the information bleed.

Naomi also filled Brian in on Russ's role—scanning traffic cams and satellite images hoping to get a glimpse of the RV—and told her brother she'd be doubling up on this task for the time being. Between that and his focus on the satellite connection, they hoped to potentially, narrow down, and maybe even pinpoint, Lucy's location.

With all of them now focused solely on finding Lucy, Naomi felt a weight lift from her shoulders. In the eyes of the FBI, an agency often more interested in protecting their secrets than their people, the decision might not be looked upon favorably. But there was no doubt in Naomi's mind they'd made the right one.

Feeling a renewed sense of purpose, she ended her call with her brother and started pulling up satellite images.

* * *

"*Y*ou ready?" Jay asked walking into the announcers' box. "Where's Damian?" he asked when he noticed the man was missing. He couldn't have gone far, he didn't have a car, but still, Jay didn't like the idea of Naomi being alone. It was unlikely she'd be the next kidnapping target since the people behind the entire situation still had Lucy James, but he didn't think it worth taking any risks.

Naomi raised her head from her computer and gave him an owlish look. "You're done?" she asked glancing at the time on her phone. "Oh, you're done. How did it go? The kids looked excited," she said standing and stretching her petite body by raising her arms overhead.

He stepped forward and slid his hands around her waist under the hem of her shirt and pulled her toward him.

"Hello," he said, dipping down for a kiss.

"Hello to you, too," she said against his lips, her fingers splayed across his chest. They inched up and curled around his neck.

"I missed you," he said.

She laughed softly and pulled away, but only a touch. "You did not," she said, not sounding the least offended. "You were too busy focusing on those kids. How did it go?" she repeated her question.

He let her pull back but kept his hands at her waist, her soft skin under his fingertips. "Great, it was a good group of boys. Focused, respectful, wanting to learn. They asked a lot of good questions. Some were more talented than others, some worked harder than others, but all in all, I think it went well. Now what about my question. Where's Damian?"

She stepped out of his arms, telling him about the text from his mom as she gathered her things. "Damian checked in about an hour ago and was on his way," she said. "He wants to drive around a bit, too and said he'll just meet us back at home." She shrugged into her jacket as she spoke. He held his hand out for her computer bag. She eyed him, as if debating whether or not she wanted to let go of it, but after a beat, she handed it over.

"I'll call him once we're on the road and check in again. I don't like him going off on his own," she said as they left the room and began making their way to his truck.

"The Robinson farm has been abandoned for a few years," he said. "I'm surprised my mom thought of it." Knowing she'd only protest, he opted to drop the issue of Damian leaving her alone and instead, he just reached for her hand as they started down the stairs.

"Abandoned as in nobody lives there and they wouldn't be allowing people to camp anymore, or abandoned as in that nobody is living there but people still camp?" she asked as they hit the landing and walked out into the soft fall sunshine.

Jay wagged his head back and forth. "I'm not sure," he said.

"There's no one there to *allow* any camping, but I don't know if people are trespassing and using it, or if maybe the family has given standing permission to some." He opened the passenger door of his truck and placed Naomi's bag inside. Once she'd climbed in, he closed it and went around to the driver's side.

"I pulled up images of the property and it doesn't look like anyone is there, or at least there weren't any cars, and certainly not an RV. I suppose one could have been parked in the barn," she said once he'd seated himself. "The image I checked was from about two hours ago."

He had a moment's disorientation at that comment. He was now dating a woman who could call upon government owned satellites any time she wished. Life was definitely different with Naomi DeMarco a part of it.

"Did you eat lunch?" he asked, pulling out of the parking lot. "We can grab some sandwiches to take back, if you're hungry." He'd been fed by the committee who'd put the clinic together, but he doubted Naomi had bothered to eat, especially if Damian hadn't been there to remind her.

"Damian—" She cut herself off when her phone rang, interrupting whatever she'd been about to say. He watched her glance at the name then quickly hit the answer button.

"Russ?" she answered. "What do you mean you can't find him?" she said. He didn't need to hear the words to hear the panic creeping into her tone. On instinct, he headed directly for Route 15 and toward the Robinson place.

"He called when he arrived, but you haven't heard from him since?" she said. "And did you track his phone? Sorry, of course you did, and there's nothing?" She waited for Russ to say something before speaking again. "No, the closest satellite should be within range in…" She paused as she looked at the clock on his dash. "It should be in range in about eight minutes. Pull up the image as soon as you can and call me. We'll head down there now."

She ended the call and turned toward him. "We need to—"

"We're already headed in that direction. I know exactly where it is," Jay said, relieved that while he couldn't do much to help her, he could at least do this.

She stared at him then set her phone beside her and twined her fingers together. Reaching over, he unwound them and laced his free hand with one of hers. "He'll be okay," he said, hoping it was true. "Is it possible he's out of range or turned his phone off?"

Her hand gripped his in a surprisingly strong hold. "It's possible he turned it off, though I don't know why he would. If he were in a situation where he didn't want to be interrupted, he could have just silenced it. As for being out of range, the tracking system Russ has on his phone isn't based on cell coverage. So assuming it's on, even if he were lost at sea, we should be able to locate him."

He didn't know what more to say, so he simply held her hand and navigated them out of Athens and toward the Robinson property. Seven minutes after hanging up with Russ, Naomi started fingering her phone, no doubt waiting for the call and information on what the satellite might show them. When nine minutes had passed and he had just exited highway 441 onto 15, she was holding the phone staring at it. He could feel the tension in her body as her attention darted between the road and her phone. She flinched when it suddenly rang, startling him as well, but even so, he didn't let go of her hand.

To his surprise, instead of just taking the call, she put it on speaker. "Russ, I'm with Jay Greene and he's driving us to the Robinson place, I figured whatever you tell me, he should hear, too since we're in this together."

"Jay Greene, like Jason Greene, the pitcher? I bet you get that a lot," Russ said.

Naomi shot Jay a look.

"Um, yeah, I get that a lot," he said, hoping it was the right answer to move Russ along to the topic Naomi wanted to hear.

"So, the images," Naomi prompted.

"There's still no one there," he said.

Naomi frowned. "Has he been and gone?" she asked.

"It's hard to say since I can't track him, but I did do a comparison of the images you pulled up from a couple of hours ago and the ones that just came in and there has been traffic on the driveway leading up to both the house and the barn," Russ said.

"Can you tell what kind of traffic?"

"Not really. It's hard to tell if the deeper tracks I see come from the weight of two vehicles or just one, and there is so much overlap that it's hard to decipher which tracks belong to which vehicle. And before you ask, yes, I'm running photo enhancements and working on it. It might just take a little while —not long, but longer than a few minutes."

"Can you tell how many cars?"

"At least two, maybe three," he said. "I'm leaning toward three, but I won't be able to say definitively until I can enhance the images properly."

"But all vehicles are gone now?" she clarified, glancing at Jay.

"Well, they're out of sight. There are some heavily wooded areas around the property and a barn as well. I don't see any tracks going *into* the woods, so unless those were disguised somehow, I'd say it's unlikely any vehicles were moved in that direction. But there are all sorts of tracks around the barn. I can't tell which direction they're all going though yet."

Naomi seemed to ponder this, then she nodded to no one in particular. "You are tracking my phone right?"

"Yes, I assume your brother is, too?" Russ asked.

"He is, he is also tracking Jay's." She threw Jay an apologetic look that said she'd explain later. Her revelation came as a surprise, not an entirely pleasant one, but given the circumstances, he didn't think it was an unwise decision.

"I also have a GPS device I'll slip into my pocket when we get there." She'd said the words casually, but they still made his stomach roil. The only reason she'd be concerned about having a plan C—her phone being plan A and his, Plan B—was if she were truly concerned about something happening to them that would lead to them either being separated from their phones or the phones being disabled.

"Good, I'll ping your brother and keep in touch. You'll let me know as soon as you can?" Russ said.

"Yes, as soon as we know anything," she promised then ended the call. "How far out are we?" she asked him.

"About five minutes from the entrance to the property. The driveway is fairly long and a bit winding, it will probably take another minute or two to reach the house and barn."

He heard her take a few deep breaths.

"We don't have to do this," he said. "We can call local police."

"And say what? That we think a federal agent might have been trespassing on the Robinson property and we can't find him anymore?" she said, more than asked. "As appealing as it sounds to have someone else do this, I don't think it's a good idea."

And put like that, it probably wasn't. He doubted the trespassing thing would be an issue, it would be easy enough to explain that Damian hadn't known the place was abandoned and had simply gone to the house to talk to the owners. But the other piece—the piece about him being missing—would be a bit harder. Damian was a grown man, and he'd been out of communication for just over an hour. They'd be laughed at if they tried to rouse any help. Well, *he* might not be laughed at, the locals would probably offer at least some cursory help because of who he was, but he knew they wouldn't take anything he and Naomi said seriously.

Jay grimaced. "You're right. But we stick together," he insisted.

"You'll get no argument from me there," she said.

"Good, because we're here," he said, pulling to a stop at the entrance to the property. Both of them leaned forward a touch to look out the window. Through years of neglect, the weeds had grown over the gravel drive and trees looked to be making a play to take over that same space. All in all, if he hadn't known where the Robinson place was, hadn't been there a few times as a kid, he probably would have overlooked this road.

As it was, he and Naomi both stared at it before he spoke.

"You ready?" he said finally, squeezing her hand.

"As I'll ever be," she all but whispered.

CHAPTER NINETEEN

SLOWLY, Jay pulled forward onto the drive, following the recent tracks made by Damian and who knew who else. Soon they rounded a bend in the drive and, with the vegetation closing in behind them, he knew they were now invisible from the main road—a simple yet disquieting thought.

Another few moments of silence passed when the house finally came into view. He'd let go of Naomi's hand and was now navigating the pothole-filled drive with both hands on the steering wheel. Beside him, Naomi clutched her phone. From the corner of his eye, he could see her scanning the area. He pulled to a stop more or less right in front of the old, white farmhouse. They both eyed the decrepit structure, its collapsing porch, the weeds growing up between the cracks, and the broken windows.

"I think you should park over there," Naomi said pointing to a small clearing about a hundred yards from the house, near an old, wooden barn. Jay followed her request and guided his truck to the opening. When he stopped at a spot he'd randomly chosen, he killed the engine and they both slid from their seats.

The sound of the truck doors shutting echoed across the

opening, and he came to stand beside Naomi who was eying several tire tracks. Pulling out her phone, she took a few pictures then texted them off to Russ.

"House or barn first?" he asked when she met his eye.

She'd pulled her hair up into a ponytail and a gust of wind whipped it around her neck. She shivered, tugging her light-weight jacket tighter around her. "Barn," she said, looking around. "It looks easier to search. We can get that out of the way then look at the house."

He nodded then reached for her hand as they walked toward the simple structure. He hadn't been kidding when he'd said they would stick together. He had no intention, barring any unforeseen problems, of letting her go.

His senses on as high alert as hers, they both continually scanned the area as they closed the fifty yards to the wide open door of the unpainted barn. Rectangular in shape with one big sliding door and one cavernous space inside, it was the kind of straightforward construction common in the area.

They approached the open door from the side, and taking his cue from Naomi, he paused and listened. The only sounds he could hear were the rustling of the trees in the breeze that had picked up and the occasional sound of a tractor nearby when the wind carried it just right. With a gentle squeeze of his hand, Naomi let him know she was going to move to the door. Tugging her back, he silently insisted he precede her. She glared at him, but he ignored her. They didn't know what, if anything, was inside the barn, and he'd be dammed if he was going to let her be the canary in the coal mine, so to speak.

Quietly they moved ahead, and he peeked his head around the doorframe to see into the opening. He felt Naomi at his back, but he held her there as he scoped out the space.

"Jay?"

He let out a breath and straightened. "You want the good news or the bad news?"

He turned to look at her. She cocked her head and returned his gaze quizzically. "The good news," he continued, not waiting for her answer, "is that the space is mostly empty, no one is hiding in there."

"The bad news?"

He stepped back into the opening, allowing her to move forward as well. He watched her face as her eyes landed on the only thing in the barn to hold their attention and she sucked in a breath. Russ had texted her the particulars of Damian's rental car and a navy blue sedan with the same license plate sat parked in the middle of the packed, dirt floor.

For several seconds, she did nothing but stare at it, but then she started forward, dragging him along. When they got close, she let go of his hand and began circling the vehicle without touching anything. He did the same, and when they met up again at the back of the car he could tell from the look in her eye that like him, she'd found nothing suspicious.

"We need to open that," she said with a nod to the trunk. Then before he could react, she pulled her jacket sleeve down over her fingertips, stepped forward, and reached for the latch. She gave him one last glance over her shoulder, before popping the lock and lifting the lid. Taking a quick step back, she landed against his chest as they watched it open.

Revealing nothing.

They both let out a deep breath. Jay wrapped his arms around Naomi and they stood together, letting their heart rates slow.

After a beat, she spoke. "I need to let Russ and Brian know," she said pulling out her phone from the back pocket of her jeans. Over her shoulder, he watched her key in the note then hit send. She didn't bother sliding it back into her pocket, no doubt knowing one or the other would be texting back shortly. She turned in his arms and looked up. He could see the worry dancing in her eyes.

"We need to check the house," she said, her hands curling around his biceps.

"He could be out in the forest," Jay offered.

She gave him the ghost of a smile. "I wish, but I think we both know something has happened. He wouldn't have parked his own car here, which means someone did it for him."

"Should we call for back-up or something now?" he asked.

As if on cue, her phone vibrated in her hand, then vibrated a second time. "Russ is sending someone from the Atlanta office," she read out loud.

"And your brother? I assume the second message is from him?"

She nodded. "He wants me to wait for back-up. Or, I guess it's not really back-up is it?" she pondered absentmindedly, "That assumes we're the first line of defense, and I don't think we even qualify for that."

He dropped his arms and reached for her free hand again. He didn't like the defeated tone he heard in her voice. "Come on, let's go see what we can find at the house. It will take the team, or whoever is coming from Atlanta, a while to get here. We can be productive until then."

He pulled her with him as they stepped from the barn, and after a few yards, she was walking determinedly beside him.

"The back first," Naomi said, pointing to some barely discernible tracks he hadn't even noticed until she'd called his attention to them.

"Do you want to take pictures?" he asked.

She shook her head. "The grass will obscure the tread, it's not worth it, not right now anyway," she said as they continued. Now that she'd pointed them out, he could also see the small depressions in the damp earth, leading to—or perhaps away from—the house.

With his attention focused on the footprints, he was the first to see something that he wasn't too manly enough to admit caused his stomach to drop and the hairs on the back of his neck stand on end. He hauled Naomi to a stop, pulling her back to his side. "Look," he said, pointing to a spot about fifteen feet in front of them and about equidistant to the back porch, or what was left of the back porch.

She stilled beside him, then let go of his hand and slowly began to follow the trail he'd pointed out. The one that looked to end in some kind of confrontation if the trampled grass and weeds were anything to go by.

Even from where they stood, it was obvious more than one person had been in the area at the same time. Blades of grass were broken and trampled in a roughly circular pattern, as if a fight had taken place.

He watched Naomi kneel down and examine something. Not liking the look on her face, he approached and knelt beside her. Now the sinking in his stomach had turned into full blown rebellion.

"Maybe it's not his blood," Jay said, staring at the rust colored, damp smears along the blades of grass. "Maybe it's the other guy's."

Naomi said nothing just raised her head and scanned the area. He saw a flash of fear—not for herself, but for Damian—cross her features as her attention fixed on something. Dragging his eyes away from her, he followed her gaze and saw what had caused the reaction. Lying beside the cellar door lay a discarded and bloody two-by-four, one ripped from the porch railing an arm's reach away.

She rose and pulled out her phone, her hand shaking as she called Russ. "We need to check the cellar," she said, talking to both Russ and him. As she spoke, she pointed to the door that had yet another railing board shoved between the two handles, effectively locking it from outside.

Jay knew it wasn't a great idea, but he also knew that if Damian were down there, he'd need help, and they might not have time to wait for the Atlanta FBI to show up. Focusing his attention on the thought of helping Damian rather than his own unease, he nodded and approached the door. Not wanting to mess up any DNA or anything already on the wood—not even knowing if it was possible to leave DNA on such a porous surface—he eyed the two-by-four. Deciding not to second guess himself, he opted to simply kick the board out from the side rather than bend down and try to tug it out of place.

It moved an entire four inches with his first kick, but by the third, it went sailing a good five feet across the grass. He looked at the door, trying to keep his mind from imagining what might lie beyond, then looked to Naomi who stood just a few feet away.

"Ready?" he asked.

"We're going in," she said to Russ who was still on the line. Naomi slid her phone into her jacket pocket then she and Jay each reached for a handle. On a near silent count of three, they both pulled.

The two side-by-side doors flew open, and both Jay and Naomi jumped back in surprise. They stared at the dark, gaping hole, and when nothing came bounding out—no human or bullet—they looked at each other.

"Okay," Naomi drew out the word. "On to step two, checking it out. I'll go first."

"Not a chance," he said, stepping in front of her and pulling out his own phone. He found the flashlight function and flicked it on as he stepped down onto the second of seven stairs leading to the packed dirt floor of the house's old root cellar. Reaching behind him, but keeping an eye on the crumbling concrete steps, he felt Naomi's hand curl into his.

Together they made their way down and into a space filled with empty shelves. Ducking his head to avoid the low ceiling, he took a few steps in as he moved the light around. The shelving cast shadows across the room making it difficult to see the far reaches, but from where they stood, it looked mostly empty. Of course, he knew neither of them believed that no one would lock the door unless there was a reason.

He had a fleeting thought that maybe the blood did belong to someone other than Damian and that Damian had locked that person up in the cellar while he went for help. It was a nice thought, thinking of Damian safe somewhere, but that hope died when they heard a moan—and Jay remembered that Damian wouldn't have needed to lock anyone in a cellar, he had handcuffs.

"Back there," Naomi said pointing to a corner on the other end of the cellar. He gripped her hand and led her toward the noise, weaving in between the ancient wooden shelves that seemed to have been placed in the room with the maximum amount of inefficiency.

Suddenly, Naomi dropped his hand and whipped by him. A second later, she was on her knees beside Damian who lay prone on the floor, unmoving. The hairs on the back of Jay's neck were on full alert now, and the need to get out of the cellar nearly strangled him.

"We need to get out now," he said. "Can we carry him between the two of us?" he asked, kneeling on the other side of the agent. He didn't know the extent of damage Damian had sustained, but at least he could tell from Naomi's expression that the man was still alive.

"At the very least, he has a concussion," she said, holding up her hand for him to see. Her normally fair, soft skin was now bathed in blood, and for the first time in Jay's life, something other than the flu made him feel like he was going to throw up. Not even his first major league game had affected him like the sight of Naomi's blood-drenched hand.

"He's alive, though, and his pulse is pretty strong, too. I'm worried about any other injuries he might have. Hold on," she said, unceremoniously wiping her palm on her jeans then pulling her phone out of her pocket. They weren't that deep underground, and she had a signal. In fact, Russ had been on the line the entire time.

"Did you hear that?" she asked. Jay watched her as she listened. "How far out are they?" she paused again. "I see, well, I think it might be best to wait for the EMTs. Maybe we can—"

Her comment was cut off by the sound of the cellar doors slamming shut and the sickening grind of the board being slid under the handles again. Whatever minor light had seeped in through the shelving disappeared, and he and Naomi were cast into deep shadows from the glow of their phones.

He saw her swallow. "Okay, now we don't have a choice. I guess we'll be waiting for back up," she said, speaking into the phone but holding Jay's eyes.

On the floor, Damian moaned again, and his hand shot up to wrap around Jay's wrist. After telling Russ that Damian was waking, she dropped the phone back in her pocket and leaned over her friend.

"Damian," she said softly but with a firmness that reminded Jay of his mother. "Can you open your eyes?"

They both kept their eyes riveted on the agent's, and though they could see his eyes moving beneath his lids, they never opened.

"Damian, I know you can hear me," she said. He grunted in response. "You have a concussion. A severe one is my guess." She cast Jay a worried look. He reached across Damian and gave her shoulder a squeeze.

"I don't get concussions," Damian slurred, drawing their attention back to him.

"Um, you do now," she said, "Can you open your eyes?"

Damian took several breaths, then opened not his eyes but his mouth. "I've been shot at and nearly blown up so many times, you'd think I'd know if I had a concussion." All his words bled together rendering his insistence almost childlike. Or like that of a drunk.

"Well clearly at least one of those explosions blew your good sense away because you most definitely have a concussion," Naomi said with all the patience of a parent dealing with a five-year-old in the middle of a tantrum.

A line formed between Damian's eyes as his brows dipped, then slowly his eyes opened. For a beat, he stared straight ahead at the ceiling but then his gaze slid to Naomi.

"Naomi? What are you doing here?"

Once again, she glanced at him and Jay could read her uncertainty. Surely, it was a good thing he was awake and recognizing her, but the fact that he hadn't realized he'd already *been* talking to her was a bit of a concern.

"I finished the clinic and we thought we'd come looking for you," Jay answered. His years in sports had taught him that the best way to manage someone with a concussion was to keep things simple. "You had a little confrontation with someone. We don't know who, but we found you here in the cellar of the Robinsons' old farmhouse," he said. "Do you remember driving to the Robinsons'?"

Damian's eyes had slid from looking to his left at Naomi to his right, and Jay could see he was still trying to focus. "Jay?"

"Yeah, it's me. We've got help on the way."

"Do you remember driving here?" Naomi asked, stepping back into the conversation.

Damian tried to nod then winced and held very still before answering. "I do. I pulled around back and was walking toward the porch and someone came up behind me." He paused then managed a little shake of his head. "I let my guard down. It was so quiet when I got here, not a soul in sight, and I let my guard down."

"It doesn't matter. We're here now, and Russ has back-up on the way. We'll be out of here soon," Naomi said, brushing some of Damian's hair off his forehead. The touch was tender, but Jay also knew she was trying to examine a gash along his hairline.

"How soon?" Damian asked.

"Not more than another twenty minutes," she said. "Thirty at tops. He sent a team from the Atlanta field office, and though he could have had local EMTs here in much less time, he didn't want the EMTs arriving without armed and trained agents here first."

"Uh, Naomi…" Jay said.

"But we still have a signal down here, and Russ is still on the line, so all we have to do is make sure you don't drift off to sleep," she continued.

"Naomi," Jay said, a bit more insistently. Her gaze jerked up.

"I don't think we have twenty minutes. I don't even think we have ten."

CHAPTER TWENTY

JAY SNIFFED THE AIR, catching a stronger scent of what had teased his nostrils moments ago. Catching on, Naomi did the same, her eyes widening in horror as she, too, caught scent of gasoline fueled smoke.

"The door," she said. "I know it's blocked from the other side, but what about the hinges? Damian usually carries a utility knife; it should have a screwdriver on it."

"No time," Jay said, pushing himself back onto his feet. "And besides, don't you think that if we somehow manage to get the door open there's a good chance that whoever did this is still out there and then we'd be sitting ducks?"

Her face drained of any color it had left, but then she gathered herself up before his eyes and began scanning the area.

"I have a plan, you just work on getting Damian up," Jay said, moving toward the opposite corner.

"What kind of plan could you possibly have—" Naomi cut herself off when he shot her a look. Taking another deep breath, she placed her hands on Damian's shoulders in preparation for helping him rise. "Right, you have a plan and I shouldn't waste our time making you reiterate it to me."

"Especially not when the house is going to burn down around us," Damian said startling Naomi but making Jay laugh —it was one of those hysterical kinds of laughs, but it was a laugh nonetheless.

"Obviously he's better now," Jay said, feeling along the wall.

"Obviously he's better now," Damian repeated.

"Fine then, get up," he heard Naomi say, but he kept his attention on the wall in front of him as he stretched his mind back to a third grade field trip he'd taken to this very farm.

"I am up," Damian snapped. That surprised Jay, and he turned to see Damian still on the floor, his knees raised. It turned out that when someone had a concussion "up" became a subjective word.

"I'm going to tell Ian and Dave about this. About you letting your guard down and almost getting us killed," Naomi snapped at Damian. The words weren't those of comfort, but Jay knew what she was doing. Egging each other on was how the two seemed to communicate best.

"Who's Dave?" he called, as his fingers, caught on something.

"No one," they both answered. He smiled. He hadn't had a chance to ask Naomi about Dave Gregory the night he'd first heard the man's name. The moment he'd walked back into the guest house after visiting with his mom, Naomi had made it very clear that talking wasn't what she had planned for the night. And he had been more than happy to go along with her plan.

Finally, his finger found what he'd been searching for, and he pressed the hidden latch hard enough to cause an indent that would last some time. But none of that mattered when he heard the lock give. Relief flooded through him—he hadn't been sure his plan would work. It had been a long time since he'd been to the Robinson farm.

"Ready?" he asked turning around to see Damian on his knees and Naomi on her feet struggling to get him standing.

He took a step toward them and froze when heat shot down through the cracks in the floorboards above him and he heard the crash of something from inside the house.

"Shit," he said, bursting into action. Rushing to Damian's side, he pushed Naomi away, hefted Damian's arm over his shoulder, and lifted. Damian did his best to help, and though he could bear weight, he wasn't particularly stable.

"Go, Naomi," he said, motioning toward the spot he'd just left.

"Where, Jay? Where am I going?" she asked, looking at the solid wall before them.

Rather than explain, he half walked, half dragged Damian toward the secret door. When he was within reach, he kicked it open. Just as a beam collapsed into the cellar from the first floor of the house, blocking the door they had come in through.

"Go," he repeated.

"No, give me your phone and I'll light the way. You take Damian first and I'll stabilize him from behind."

Another crash sounded above them, and he was more than grateful that smoke tended to rise. It was getting thick in the cellar, but not nearly as deadly as it would have been had they been locked on the first floor.

Not wanting to argue, he handed her his phone and began guiding the agent down the eight steps to the floor of the tunnel. Naomi did her best to light the way, but the pitch of the stairs and the complete darkness in front of them cast unusual and deceiving shadows; shadows that slowed him down and made it so that he could only safely take one step down with both feet at a time before inching one foot forward to find the next.

Conscious that with every delay, the fire burned hotter against Naomi's back, he tried to balance speed with safety. Two steps from the bottom a loud explosion followed by a whoosh of hot air filled with sparks flew past them. He heard

Naomi let out a gasp, and at her strangled cry of pain, he took a misstep.

Landing with a foot precariously balanced on the edge between the second and bottom step, Jay struggled to stay upright as Damian's weight pitched him forward. Stumbling, he barely managed to get one foot out in front of him, preventing him from falling on his face as it found purchase on the solid floor. But momentum wasn't done with him yet, and he knew he was heading toward the wall.

Turning his body to protect Damian, he slammed into the brick wall, hitting it with his face and his shoulder in a bone crunching thud. Stumbling back, he righted himself, his cheek smarting from the contact and his shoulder aching.

"Oh my God, Jay, your shoulder. Let me take Damian, I'm stronger than you think," she said, trying to wedge her way under Damian's other arm.

"Don't, Naomi," he ordered. Thankfully, she froze. He took three deep breaths and mentally inventoried the potential damage to his left shoulder, his pitching shoulder. It ached and protested the treatment, but after rolling it back and forth a few times, he was confident there hadn't been any serious damage. Although at the moment, he was more worried about getting them out alive than his career.

"The passage is too narrow to make those kinds of adjustments," he said. "As it is, I will have to crab walk so we can stay single file," he explained, as he began to do just that. Turning with his back against one wall and facing the other, he then took a few steps sideways, all but dragging Damian. Even if Naomi had been able to carry Damian, she couldn't have done it from her position behind him, she would have needed the same leverage as he did, the ability to *pull* Damian forward rather than push him from behind.

"What is this?" she asked after they'd gone several more steps. The light in her hand bobbed as they walked but didn't waver from where he needed it to be as he led them down the narrow tunnel.

"This farm used to be part of the Underground Railroad," he said. "We came here for a field trip when I was in third grade, and Mrs. Robinson showed us the tunnel and told us the story."

"So, I'm guessing that while the person we're looking for has ties to the area, they obviously must not be as deep as yours if he, or she, didn't know about this."

"Maybe," Jay grunted as Damian, in an effort to help moved a foot right into Jay's path. "Hold up," he directed and immediately Naomi stopped. They'd traveled about forty feet from the house, and though they could still feel the heat and smell the smoke, they were no longer at risk of getting incinerated.

"Can you stand now, Damian?" Jay asked. If the man had had the presence of mind to try to take a step, the least he could do was try to coordinate those steps with Jay's own. Slowly, Damian straightened, and though he didn't remove his arm from around Jay's shoulder, he took more of his own weight until he was more or less standing on his own.

"Now," Jay started, "we're going to take small steps, one foot at a time to the side." The first few steps were awkward with Damian's lead foot smashing into the foot Jay used to anchor himself, but after a few tries, they managed to get into a rhythm.

"It's not well known that this house has this tunnel," Jay said as their progress picked up. "I knew about it because of the tour, but unless someone went to our school, I'm not sure many other people would know about it."

"I don't know," Naomi said. "It's a pretty cool thing to have a house that was part of something so historic. It seems like it would be something people talked about."

"Says the Yankee," Jay said.

"Meaning?" Naomi asked as he caught a glimmer of light ahead of them and felt a gentle presence of fresh, cool air.

"Meaning while many in the South recognize the importance, both from a historic and from a humane perspective, of the Underground Railroad, to some it's a reminder of the war of northern aggression. Having a house that's part of the Railroad, or coming from a family that supported it, wouldn't necessarily be something people would talk about." He paused and inhaled a lungful of clean air; the tunnel's exit wasn't far. "And not to mention that until fairly recently," he continued both talking and walking, "being a sympathizer, or kin to sympathizers could get a person killed."

"Nice," Naomi said, the sarcasm in her voice as heavy as the damp air around them.

"The good news is," he said as the walls around him changed from brick to rock, "that the people who built it built it to last, and built it to get people safely away from the house. Which, one hundred and fifty-some-odd-years-later, it's still doing. You ready to be out of here?" he asked, flashing a smile at her over his shoulder.

"You have no idea," she said. The tunnel led into a cave and from there, they'd emerge into the woods about hundred and fifty yards from the house. He couldn't remember if the cave had been natural and the original owners had built the tunnel to leverage the natural formation, or if they'd built the tunnel then created something that looked like it belonged there. Either way, he was just glad it was still doing the job it had been built for all those years ago.

After several more strides, the space widened enough for the three of them to walk side by side, and Naomi slipped next to Damian and draped his other arm around her shoulder. Jay shifted his gaze from the ground and glanced up. Damian was sweating with the effort to stay upright, his jaw locked and his eyes drilling into the ground as if willing his feet where to go next. But he was carrying more of his own weight now, even if his stability still wasn't one hundred percent there.

Peering around him, Jay caught Naomi's eye and, having also

seen the pain and intensity in Damian's expression, she nodded. By unspoken agreement, they paused and let some of the tension of the past fifteen minutes slip from their shoulders.

"How are you doing Damian?" Naomi asked softly.

"Like my head had a head-on with a semi, but other than that I'm peachy."

Naomi flicked Jay another glance. Over the next few days, the rest of his body would catch up with the hurt but right now, they both knew his head injury was the biggest concern.

"Well, let's see if those agents are here, I don't know about you, but I could really use a piece of Maisy's pie," Jay said. Of course they hadn't had a chance to pick one up yet, but Damian didn't need to know that.

"And a shot of whiskey, thank you very much," Naomi muttered making him smile.

"I knew you were my kind of woman from the minute you sat next to me that night at your cousin's pub," Jay said with a grin, part of which was due to the thought of sinking into a big hot bath as soon as they got home with nothing but her and a glass of whiskey.

"Seriously, guys. I could be dying over here, and you'd still be making googly eyes at each other," Damian groaned, his words a little less slurred than before.

"At least we haven't dropped you so we could celebrate surviving by making out," Naomi pointed out.

"Although that's not a bad idea," Jay interjected feinting a step away.

"I will kill you, Greene," Damian said, his arm flexing instinctively to keep him close. For a second, well, for more than a second, Jay felt just a bit bad about teasing the agent. To make up for it, he hitched Damian's arm a little higher across his shoulders and dipped down to get a better angle and support him.

"We're a little more than a hundred yards from where we

parked, but maybe it's worth just getting out of the forest and to the other side of the tree line so the agents from Atlanta can see us when they arrive," Jay suggested as they stepped out of the cave.

"I have to admit, I wouldn't mind..." Damian's voice trailed off and Jay, who'd been focused on watching where he set his feet, was pulled to a stop.

"There a probl..." his own voice failed as he looked up. He stared for a good long, tense moment before daring to speak. "Uh, Naomi? Any ideas?" he whispered.

Because he sure as shit didn't know what to do about the woman standing in front of them holding a gun.

CHAPTER TWENTY-ONE

NAOMI STARED at Agent Jacinda Brown standing before them. She knew beyond a doubt that it was Brown—she'd looked at enough pictures of the elegant, athletic agent to recognize her. But between the shadows of the woods, her black clothing, and the dark tone of her skin, it was hard to make out the woman's expression; and so what she couldn't immediately recognize was Agent Brown's intent.

Glancing back at Jay, Naomi wished she could ask his opinion, he was much better at reading people than she was, but that wasn't really an option at the moment. Her eyes then fell on Damian's shoulder holster. Taking a shot wouldn't be a problem, she had enough training to know that she'd hit her target if she fired. The problem was, there was no way she'd be able to draw Damian's weapon from its holster and take aim before Agent Brown got off her own shot.

If that was what she was planning.

Naomi's eyes rested again on the woman who stood watching them. Brown's weapon was drawn, but she didn't look particularly interested in using it. Naomi opened her mouth to say something, but then to her surprise, Agent Brown raised a finger to her lips, the universal sign to stay quiet.

Naomi, Damian, and Jay all froze. Agent Brown stood still and silent as well. And then she cocked her head, as if to hear something better. Following her lead, Naomi did the same, and to her dismay, she heard the sound of someone trying to move quietly through the woods.

Agent Brown didn't re-holster her weapon, but she did drop it, and Naomi heard Damian and Jay both let out a long breath. Keeping her eyes on Agent Brown, she waited for some idea, some sign, of what to do next.

She had not expected that that sign would, literally, be a sign, and it took her a few seconds to realize that Agent Brown was, in fact signing to her using a one-handed version of American Sign Language. Caught unaware, Naomi immediately fell behind in making the mental translation, but quickly signed back, asking her to slow down and repeat.

With a nod of acknowledgement, Agent Brown did just that. Naomi watched raptly, not wanting to miss a thing. It had been several years since she'd signed, and like any language, she felt a bit rusty. But the gist of what Agent Brown was saying was clear. She needed them to get back into the cave.

Silently, Naomi caught Damian and Jay's attention and gestured to the cave behind them with her head. They returned identical skeptical looks, but thankfully neither protested and, as quiet as two people managing a third with a concussion could, they back stepped into the shadows. Agent Brown gestured for them to stay put then took off up the hill behind them, her stride silent and sure.

"What the hell?" Damian whispered as she and Jay lowered him to the ground to lean against the cave wall. They were well out of sight now, and unless whoever was out there walked right up to the mouth of the cave, they wouldn't be seen.

"She used to work on Joe's old team," Naomi said. Surprise

flickered in Damian's eyes, but she didn't miss how the news seemed to ease some of his tension.

"Joe who?" Jay asked. "I thought you weren't sure whether to trust her or not. And why didn't I know you know ASL?"

"Joe is a friend of friend," Naomi said, keeping her voice pitched low. "He used to work counter intelligence in the FBI before retiring up to Windsor. That was one option we were considering when trying to figure Agent Brown out, she confirmed it just now. And as for ASL, I know five languages, not including the computer ones; Boston Brahmin, remember, and the education to go with it."

Jay looked momentarily confused by the reminder of her background but then he shook his head as if to clear it. "And you trust her?" he asked.

"Take it," Damian said, interjecting himself into the conversation, though how he knew she'd been eyeing his service weapon she hadn't a clue; his eyes had slid closed the second he'd sat and hadn't opened yet.

"I trust she's on our side," Naomi said, sliding the weapon from its holster under Damian's arm. "I don't know her enough to trust her with my secret cookie recipe, but I do trust she's not going to kill us."

She glanced up just in time to see Jay gaping at her. "Okay, that cookie thing was a joke. I don't have a secret cookie recipe. I just meant that I don't trust her like I trust Damian as an agent and a friend, but I do believe she's here to protect us, not harm us."

"You just disarmed an FBI agent and are holding his service weapon," Jay said, his voice oddly flat.

"He gave it to me and yes, before you ask, I am licensed, and I do know how to shoot."

"She's really good, too," Damian mumbled, his words starting to slur together again.

Jay's eyes searched her face, then he let out a little huff. "I'm not sure whether to be concerned that you think you need that or turned on, because, well, I'll admit that a few inappropriate policewoman fantasies are flashing through my mind right now."

"And yet again, I have to remind you two I'm still here. I may feel like I've died, or like my head exploded, but I assure you, I'm still breathing." As if to prove a point, Damian took a deep breath and let it out. "Then again, maybe I am dead. Maybe I am in hell. Maybe that's my punishment, to have to listen to all the lovey couples I know rhapsodize about each other."

"Don't be such a baby," Naomi said, bending down to brush his hair off his forehead and surreptitiously examine the gash there.

"I'm definitely still alive," Damian said, wincing away from her touch. "Not even hell would be as cruel as you."

Naomi rolled her eyes though Damian still had his lids closed. Rising from her position beside Damian, she stood next to Jay, both of them getting more worried by the minute about the agent's concussion. Surely, the Atlanta agents would be there soon? And then the EMTs could take care of him?

"How much longer do you think?" Jay asked, jamming his hands on his hips. He quickly lowered them, and though he did his best to disguise it, she didn't miss the grimace of pain that had flashed across his face.

"Not long," she said. "I don't know this area well enough, but I also wonder if the fire department might get here first; assuming someone sees the smoke and calls them. How's your shoulder?"

He rolled it back at her question. "It's fine," he said. "Someone probably will see the smoke, but I don't know how far away the nearest fire department is. Regardless, I'm pretty sure it will be a volunteer one so it might take a while to get the firefighters to the station before they can then get out here."

They both watched Damian for several more seconds but

then a rustling in the woods caught their attention. "I'm going out there," Naomi said as she began to move past Jay toward the mouth of the cave.

"Like hell," Jay said, wrapping an arm around her waist and holding her in place. Given his size and hers, she knew it didn't take much effort on his part, which, oddly enough, annoyed her more than his actual manhandling did.

Not backing down an inch, she met his stormy gaze. "I'm not going to go far, just to the opening of the cave. I don't know who is out there but if Agent Brown needs back up, someone has to do it."

"Then that someone should be me," Jay said, holding his hand out for the gun she gripped. She didn't doubt his sincerity or think he was being guided by anything other than fear for her, but even so, she didn't bother to hide the exasperation she felt.

"What kind of experience do you have with this type of gun?" She held it up for him to see.

He swallowed. "I've not shot with that specific kind, but I have shot a handgun before," he replied.

"In a shooting gallery?"

He nodded.

"But not in simulated combat?"

His brows dipped. "No, why would I shoot in simulated combat?"

"Because it's the only way to train for the real thing without actually engaging in the real thing," she replied.

"And you have?" She heard the skepticism in his voice but was pretty sure he wasn't doubting she'd done it, just questioning the reasoning behind it.

"Yes, many times. It's what you do when practically everyone in your family is in law enforcement."

"She's really good," Damian all but groaned, his voice rising from the floor surprising both of them.

"You're not helping," Jay shot back.

"Between the two of you, I'd put my money on her," Damian slurred, his eyes never opening though he did try to raise a hand and point in her general direction. "Probably been shooting since before she could walk."

Jay's eyes came back to hers. "Is that true?"

She wagged her head. "Well, not since before I could walk, but young enough that I don't ever remember *not* being able to shoot or handle guns."

"I'm not even sure what to say to that," he said, the honest confusion in his expression giving him an adorably perplexed look.

Taking pity, she smiled and went up on her tiptoes to give him a quick, and silent, kiss on his cheek—one that wouldn't annoy Damian—then moved out of his arms.

"You don't have to like it, but I am asking you to put aside your concerns for me—"

"Not possible," he said with a decisive shake of his head.

She exhaled. "Fair enough. Then I'm asking you to *manage* your concerns about me. I need to go out there for two reasons. The first is that Agent Brown may need back-up; I'm not going to go running around the woods, but I do want to be ready if she needs assistance. And the second reason is because she's also probably the only person standing between the three of us and whoever tried to set us on fire. I don't know about you, but I'd prefer for her to *stay* between us, and in order to do that she needs to stay alive."

She'd wasted a lot of time laying it all out for Jay, but she needed him to understand the logic of what she was doing, she needed him to understand that her decision wasn't based on a whim or any misguided belief that she could, or would want to be, their savior. No, she had no hero complex, she just wanted to make sure that someone else could stay alive long enough to play the hero.

She watched him struggle with the decision—she was going to go whether he approved or not, but he still had to decide whether to at least pretend to accept it or continue to fight it. Finally, he gave a sharp nod and then, as if he were afraid he might change his mind, he jerked his head toward the mouth of the cave.

"Go," he said. "Stay in sight if you can. I want to stand where I can see you, but I know I need to take care of him, too," he said with a nod in Damian's direction.

"I know you know this but please make sure he doesn't fall asleep," she said.

"Not shleeping," Damian mumbled.

"I got it," Jay said moving to crouch by Damian's side.

"Naomi?" She paused as she was almost out of his sight. "Please be careful," he said quietly.

There was a lot not said in those three words. Her gaze locked with his blue eyes, then she nodded in acknowledgement of it all. She longed to stay, to deny what was happening and just remain cozy in the cave and tucked in his arms. But she hadn't been raised that way nor was it part of her natural disposition. Shit needed to be taken care of, and she was the one to get it done.

Taking a deep breath, she thought of all her family members and all the different badges they wore, and then she stepped out into the woods.

CHAPTER TWENTY-TWO

SILENCE GREETED her exit from the cave, and she inched along, keeping the stone against her back until she came to a stop under the ledge of a boulder about twenty feet from where she'd started. The stillness of the woods seemed anticlimactic to the scene she'd just left, and she felt a moment's let down—*not* that she wanted to see any action, at least not the kind that would involve her using Damian's weapon.

Though tall enough for her to stand, she crouched under the ledge, leaning against the rough stone at her back. The gun she held rested heavy—and ready—in her hand. With the safety off, she could either just raise the muzzle or, if she needed to stand, she could bring it up with her body in one fluid motion.

What felt like several minutes, but was probably less than one, passed when it dawned on her that it was too quiet. A forest, even one as small as the one she was in, should have *some* noise. Which meant that something was scaring the animals either away or into stillness.

Craning her head, she strained to hear anything. Slowly, she recognized the crackling sound of the house still burning and the faint scent of smoke. Then, to her left, something flashed in the shadows. Focusing with her peripheral vision, she caught sight of movement not twenty yards away. She didn't have much to go on, but instinct told her it wasn't Agent Brown—the color of the clothing and the fleeting glimpse of the figure she'd seen—had been off.

She adjusted her grip on the gun; a heavier version than what she usually shot with, but still one that felt comfortable in her hands. Having no desire to call attention to herself and only wanting to be there if Agent Brown absolutely needed her, she remained still.

Suddenly the form stopped. An instant later, Naomi understood why. In the distance, the siren of a fire engine could be heard echoing into the woods.

"Don't move," Naomi heard Agent Brown say from somewhere to her right. Naomi froze and didn't dare turn even just her head.

The figure paused at Agent Brown's voice, then leapt into action, darting not down the hill or up it, as Naomi had expected, but almost directly toward her. As he came closer, she recognized the form before the face. Slightly overweight, but still fit, receding blond hair, and not more than five foot ten, Kevin Farlow headed straight for her.

With his attention split between his own feet and looking for Agent Brown, he didn't see her. Not at first anyway.

"Stop, FBI," Agent Brown called, much closer this time. Naomi fought the urge to turn and look for the woman.

"Kevin Farlow, you are under arrest for the murders of Carl Rogers, Kevin Beekman, and Michael 'Smitty' Smith," Agent Brown continued. Naomi still couldn't see her, but assumed the woman was somewhere where she could see Farlow.

Naomi watched Farlow slow his pace down as he scanned the area, presumably to look for either an escape route or, at the least, a place to hide. He seemed to make a decision and began to move down the hill rather than closer to her.

She let out a quiet breath, thankful that he hadn't spotted her, but just as she began to inhale, a small cascade of rocks came tumbling over the ledge, landing in her hair, and falling down her shoulders. The assault, as gentle as it was, startled her and her foot slid in the dirt as she ducked.

Between the sound of the tumbling rocks and, no doubt, her own muffled shuffle, Farlow's attention shot back in her direction. He slipped behind a tree, not quite big enough to cover his entire form, but big enough to protect his vitals, and peered around.

It took less than five seconds for his gaze to focus on her. He froze in surprise, and then she watched in horror as a smile spread across his lips and he raised his gun. From his position, she didn't think he'd seen her own weapon and in his mind, he was shooting at a sitting duck.

Only she wasn't a sitting duck. Without hesitation, she dove to the side as a shot rang out. Rock splintered above her, and she felt a few shards hit her face, but so focused was she on raising her own weapon that the sharp pain registered only nominally. In one smooth motion, she brought her gun into position and fired on Farlow at the spot that would cause him the most damage. Tucked back behind the tree that left one location to hit, his ass as it stuck out the other side.

She wasn't sure if she grazed him or he made a sharp move realizing just how exposed he was and that she was armed, but he leapt forward several inches. And to her great pleasure, he unintentionally stepped right into her line of fire.

She focused on his face and saw a dawning realization that she wasn't afraid of shooting back. She half expected him to leap back behind the tree but to her surprise, he hesitated only the briefest moment, before bringing his weapon back up and firing right at her.

Her own weapon went off as did another. She'd ducked her head to protect her eyes from any more rock splinters, but in the silence that followed, she raised it again.

About twenty feet in front of her, Kevin Farlow lay on the ground. Agent Brown hadn't bothered with a body shot and had gone straight for his head, half of which was now scattered across the forest floor.

"You okay, Agent Brown?" Naomi called, still not knowing exactly where the woman was.

"I thought I told you to get back into the cave," came the reply from above her.

"Naomi?" she heard Jay's frantic voice as she rose and slipped the safety of the gun back on.

"I'm here. And fine." She shook the rocks and dirt from her jacket. "You can come out now," she said to Jay as Agent Brown leapt down from the ledge landing as nimbly as a cat but startling Naomi.

"Anyone ever tell you not to startle someone with a gun?" Naomi muttered. Anything the agent might have said in return was lost when Jay strode out of the cave, eyed her from head to toe, then promptly closed the distance between them, sank his hands into her hair and kissed her.

Slowly he pulled away, but only far enough to look at her again. "Don't ever ask me to do that again," he said, his voice gravelly. She could still feel the tension in his body as his hands cradled her face. She nodded.

Behind her, Agent Brown cleared her throat. Jay speared Naomi with one more look then lowered his hands, reminding her that a big ass spark of flaming something had landed on her neck as they'd made their way out of the cellar and into the tunnel. She sucked in a sudden breath at the sharp pain Jay's touch had elicited.

"What the hell, you didn't get shot, did you?" Jay said, whipping back around and turning her away from him to examine the back of her body.

Naomi sighed. "No, a big ember landed on me when the roof collapsed as we were leaving through the tunnel. It's not serious, just a burn that hurts a bit." Or a burn that hurt like hell, but she wasn't about to say that. "By the way, Agent Brown, this is Jason Evans Greene. Jay, that's Agent Brown."

She managed to step out from Jay's examination of her neck and turned to see the agent eyeing them. The sounds of the fire trucks were getting louder, but it was hard to tell how close they were.

"Did you shoot the bad guy, Naomi?" Damian said, stumbling a bit as he emerged from the cave. "Agent Brown. I assume?"

"Agent Rodriguez," she returned with a nod. "And you must be Naomi DeMarco?"

Naomi nodded. Beside her, Jay had taken her free hand and didn't appear interested in letting it go. "Agent Brown shot him," Naomi said as a little shiver went through her at the memory of Kevin Farlow raising his weapon to fire on her.

"You missed?" Damian asked. She couldn't help it, the surprise in his voice made her laugh.

"I did," she said.

"You didn't," Agent Brown said. "Your first shot grazed him in the ass, which is a pretty good shot considering the angle you had. And your second shot got him in the leg, which would have been enough to bring him down if I hadn't also shot."

Naomi hadn't hesitated to fire the weapon and wouldn't have changed a thing, but still, she didn't feel the need to linger on the idea that she'd just shot a man, twice. Damian held out his hand, and she happily handed him his gun back.

"There are agents on their way from Atlanta, and he needs medical attention," Naomi said, jerking her head in Damian's direction. Saying that reminded her that her line with Russ was still open, or should be unless she'd accidentally shut it off somewhere along the way. Pulling her phone out of her pocket she glanced at the screen then lifted the device to her ear.

"I assume you got all that and know everyone is fine. With the exception of Kevin Farlow." She glanced over to the body as she spoke. All she could see from her position was the soles of his feet, his hands laying palm up beside him, and the slight paunch of his stomach.

"I thought I was done listening to firefights over telecommunications lines," Russ replied. She didn't know him well enough to tell if that was sarcasm or annoyance in his voice.

"The agents are ten minutes out," he added with a huff. It was definitely annoyance she heard.

"Agent Jacinda Brown is here too," she confirmed.

"Got it. You good now?" he asked.

She glanced around at the three of them. Jay looked more stressed than she'd ever seen him, Damian had dried blood caked along his forehead, and her body was starting to ache, and her burn was starting to throb.

"Yeah, we're good. I'll call you once we get Damian checked out," she said. Russ agreed, and she finally severed the connection between them.

"I think it might be best for you two to, well, not be here when everyone else arrives," Agent Brown said, her eyes darting between her and Jay. "We still want to keep this quiet, and well, I know you're not one to shy away from the press, but you need to rethink that strategy if just for today." Her suggestion bordered on being an order and she shot them both a flat, do-not-mess-with-me look. Naomi saw his jaw work, and his hand jerked in hers.

"I'm not hiding from the press because this is going to be uncomfortable," he said.

Agent Brown raised a hand in a conciliatory gesture. "That's not what I'm saying. I'm *asking* you to not be here when everyone else arrives. It will be distracting. Not to the FBI, but to the locals who are sure to show up. This is an FBI case and firmly within FBI jurisdiction, and no one has the right to interview you or take your statement but us. There's a side road that you can take out of here," she said pointing to a spot beyond the barn. "I'll stay here with Agent Rodriguez until the EMTs arrive and let you know what hospital they take him to. I also know where you're staying, and we can talk later."

Naomi could feel Jay wanting to protest. It did feel wrong to be leaving not only the scene of a crime, but also Damian.

"Go, you two," Damian said. "She's right. There is going to be enough talk about this that we don't need to add any fuel to the fire."

She felt Jay waver. "Come on," she said, tugging his hand. "They know what they're doing. Let's let them do their job. You will call me about the hospital?" Naomi gave Agent Brown a pointed look. The agent nodded.

"Jay?" she said, looking at him to make the final decision.

After a heartbeat, he gave a sharp nod and without a word, they began their quick descent from the woods to his truck. A few minutes later they were inside the cab of his truck and pulling out the side road, just as the fire trucks began to show up. Most of the house had already burned out, though, and they wouldn't have too much of a job ahead of them.

Jay had only let go of her hand long enough to be seated in his truck, and he held it firmly in his grasp now as he navigated the barely visible way back to the main road. With her free hand, she reached across and cranked up the heat in the cab. It wasn't particularly cold, but the post adrenaline shakes were starting.

Sensing Jay wasn't in a place to talk, they rode in silence. Rather than take Route 15 back to Highway 441, he chose the back roads, and twenty minutes later, much to Naomi's surprise, they were pulling into his mom's driveway from the opposite direction they usually came.

Naomi was beginning to get a little worried about Jay, who still hadn't spoken a word. She didn't think he was angry, not truly, but he was acting out of sorts.

"Jay," she said as soon as they'd parked. He'd pulled up closer to the guest house than to his mom's, and she could see the cozy little building peeking through the trees. "Are you okay?" she asked.

"Not really, no," he said as he climbed out of the cab. She made to follow and opened her door, but before she had her seatbelt off, he was there, helping her out. Keeping a firm grip on her hand, he tugged her toward the house. She had to admit, her heart tumbled a little more into something with this man when she realized that even with all the drama of the past hour, he hadn't forgotten to grab her computer bag.

He unlocked the door and pulled her in. Setting her computer bag down, he toed off his dirty boots and watched as she did the same, trying to hide the shakes that had taken over her body.

"Shower," he said, pulling her through the living room and the bedroom and into the attached bath. Flipping the water on to hot, he turned toward her. Pausing, he just looked, his eyes traveling up and down her body. And then he began to strip her.

She didn't need help undressing but she sensed he needed to do it, so she stood docilely as he gently removed her jacket, followed by her shirt and bra. He then moved to her jeans, tugging them down along with her panties and socks. By the time she was completely naked, the room was starting to fill with steam.

"Let me see it," he said.

She didn't have to ask what and, lifting her messy ponytail, she dutifully turned for him to see the burn on the back of her neck. His hands came up to her shoulders, but he didn't make any moves to touch or examine it. In truth, she didn't know how bad the burn was. It had hurt like hell when it had happened, and it was now throbbing like a mutant blob but in the heat of the moment, she'd all but forgotten about it.

"It's going to hurt like hell in the shower," he said reaching for a washcloth hanging on the rack. Wetting it in the sink, he gently laid the folded cloth across the injury. The cool of the terry cloth instantly relieved some of the pain, but she knew it would be short lived. "You should leave this on in the shower so the spray doesn't hit it directly," he said.

"So, I don't need a trip to the ER?" she asked.

His eyes darkened but he shook his head.

"I don't think so. We'll clean it up, put some antibiotic cream on it once it cools down a bit, and patch it up. Now into the shower, you're still shaking." He guided her into the walk-in shower, and holding the washcloth in place against her burn, she stepped under the hot spray.

"Are you joining me?" she asked, her eyes closed as the water washed over her head and down her body. In response, she felt his arms come around her from behind and his lips touch her bare shoulder. They stood like that for a long time, letting the water wash away more than the dirt and sweat and soot.

Eventually, Jay reached for the soap and they washed their bodies and hair, ridding it all of the smell of smoke. When they were done, they dried off, and by unspoken agreement, they both collapsed in bed. Naomi lay on her stomach in order to stay off her injured shoulder and Jay on his side, an arm draped over her lower back.

After a moment, he rose and found their phones. He placed them within reach on the bedside tables, climbed back into bed and pulled the covers over both of them. It was still early, the sun was still up, though starting to fade, but even so, exhaustion seemed to take them, and they drifted in and out of sleep as they stayed close to each other, waiting for the phone to ring with news of Damian.

"Who is Dave Gregory?" Jay asked, his pondering question quiet in the stillness of the room.

Naomi rolled to her side to better look at Jay. "You really want to know?" she replied, her lips involuntarily quirking at the memory.

Jay chuckled. "I thought I did, but now maybe I'm not so sure." He pulled one of her legs over his hip then ran his hand up her thigh until it rested again at her waist, his finger brushing the small of her back. "No, I do, tell me," he said.

"Just remember you asked," she said, tucking her hands under her pillow to raise her head a little.

When Jay nodded, she answered, "Dave was a Ranger with Damian and Ian. He's older than both of them, maybe by twelve or so years. He really took Ian under his wing, and Ian always says he wouldn't have lasted that first deployment without everything Dave had taught him."

"So, he feels pretty indebted to him, I get it," Jay said. "But what does that have to do with you?"

Naomi gave him a look that tried to convey that patience was a virtue. Jay just cocked an eyebrow and stared at her. "Fine," she said with a huff. "I'll get to the point. A couple of years ago, Dave and his team were caught in a bad situation. I mean a really bad situation," she paused, realizing what she was about to say. "This has to remain between the two of us," she said. "Some of what I'm going to say isn't really public knowledge, but some of it is also deeply personal to Dave and not really my story to tell, though I do have a part in it." She slipped a hand from under her pillow and laid it on his bicep. "Damian and I may laugh and tease about it now, but it's truly not a laughing matter, if you know what I mean?"

His blue eyes bored into hers, and he nodded. "After years of dealing with the press, I know how to keep a secret. I wouldn't have any friends otherwise."

Naomi considered this, then nodded as well. She supposed there had to be a lot of truth to that. The press was always after some sort of gossip about professional athletes, it made sense that in order to protect some of their own privacy, they'd learn to protect each other's—if they didn't, if they talked about the private lives of their teammates, she had no difficulty seeing that person finding themselves isolated and without friends.

"Okay, well, then," she continued. "He and his team were caught in a blockade situation. They'd gone into a small town to do nothing more than safety check for the Red Cross, who had plans to come in and do a health check the next day. Only it turned out that the town, unbeknownst to everyone, harbored an Al Qaeda leader. What started as a simple security check—as simple as they get—turned into a two day siege. Eventually, Dave and the team were assigned back-up, and between the teams assigned they were able to contain the situation, but not without a cost. Of the twelve people Dave took in that day, they lost four and Dave himself was shot, here," she said, sliding her hand from Jay's arm to touch a spot on Jay's lower back, right where the spine ended.

"He was medevac'd out to Germany and then back to the states. They weren't sure if he'd ever walk again, and between that and depression and PTSD, he was in a pretty bad spot."

"I can imagine," Jay murmured, stroking his hand up her spine.

"Ian had struggled a bit with some of that too," she said. "He was discharged after an IED nearly blew his leg off, and then he started experiencing PTSD symptoms when he came home to Windsor. With time, therapy, and a lot of support from my cousin, Vivi, his wife who he also met around the same time, he's doing really well. And then when Dave was injured and experiencing some of the same life changing things, Ian wanted to be able to help the man who'd helped him so much."

"Makes sense, I've been able to do the same with some of the coaches that worked with me when I was younger, those that invested and believed in me. It means a lot to be able to, well, not so much as repay them, but to do something for them that has an impact. I get that, but again, what does that have to do with you?" he repeated as he pulled her closer and dropped a kiss on her forehead.

"So impatient," she said, but snuggled closer and finished her story. "Well, Ian invited him up to stay with them in Windsor for a few weeks. They hadn't been sure he would walk, but with a lot of work and some luck, he'd managed to get back on his feet. But he was still wrapped in pretty deep depression and well, that's where I come in," she said, a slightly embarrassed grin made its way onto her face. She didn't regret what had happened between her and Dave, but she wasn't particularly comfortable talking to Jay about it.

"This is going to be a weird story, isn't it?" Jay said with a small shake of his head.

Naomi cleared her throat. "Not really. Just, well, the long and short of it is when they told him he likely wouldn't walk again, it wasn't just his legs that had been affected. It was, well— and this absolutely stays between us," she said with a pointed look to Jay who shot her a "yeah-I-get-it" look before she continued. "Well, they told him it would affect his sexual func-tion. So there he was, struggling to get back on his feet, literally, his entire world had changed, his career gone, some of his men gone, not to mention some of what he'd seen during the siege, and then, to top it all off, he thought he'd be facing a life with no sex. I don't think it was the end of the world for him, but I think it felt like the final 'fuck you' in a series of bad 'fuck-yous,' if you know what I mean."

Jay nodded.

"Anyway, where I come in is this. I didn't like how grumbly and pissy he was being toward Ian. You have to know that Vivi, though she's my cousin, is like a sister to me and so Ian, by extension, is like a brother. As far as I was concerned, Dave should have been grateful for everything Ian was trying to do to help him, and when he wasn't, well, I might have gone off on him a little bit."

"A little?"

"Okay, maybe a lot. I'll admit, it was not one of my better days, I mean, my god, he'd lost so much and had so many unknowns ahead of him, but I, well, I got a bee in my bonnet and picked a fight with him when Ian and Vivi were out of the house. Apparently, I pushed him far enough that eventually he shouted back at me about not ever being able to have sex again."

"I bet that was unexpected," Jay chuckled again, and she sensed he knew where this was going.

"It was and it shut me up for about twenty seconds. And then, of course I told him he was being ridiculous. He'd learned to walk again, he'd get his other functions back. He was still so mad—mad that I'd pushed him, and mad at what he'd admitted, and just generally mad at the situation. When I told him he was being ridiculous, I think I sent him over the edge."

"And let me guess, he dared you to prove him wrong?" Jay said, his chuckle turning into a soft laugh. She liked that he didn't seem to mind having this somewhat bizarre conversation.

"He did," she said.

"And I take it you did?"

She grimaced a little at talking about being with another man while she was lying in bed with Jay, but she nodded.

"Without going into details—"

"I thank you for that," Jay said.

"By the time we had our shouting match, his dysfunction was more in his head. It didn't take much to prove him wrong, but then once I had, well, he was grateful. Enthusiastically so. I stayed for another week and we parted friends. His outlook on life changed a lot that week."

"And Ian thinks the change was due to his friendship and help?"

Naomi lifted a shoulder. "He does. Not that he takes credit for Dave's complete shift in attitude. Having been through it, he knew that most of Dave's recovery would be, and was, driven by Dave's own work, but he felt really good about being able to provide the space and friendship to enable him to do that."

"And you don't want Ian to know that really it was just good old-fashioned nookie that helped Dave," Jay said with a laugh as he rolled onto his back.

Naomi rose and came up over him. "No one uses the word 'nookie' anymore, old man," she said dipping her lips down to his. "And for the record," she said, pulling back. "Dave's recovery had very little to do with the actual sex. I think it just reminded him that some of our worst enemies are inside our own heads, and if we can conquer those demons, well, we may not be able to conquer the world, but we can do a whole lot with our lives."

His chest rumbled under her and she traced the line of his cheek with her forefinger. Suddenly, the day caught up with her, and an intense wave of panic washed over her. She took several deep breaths, focusing on the feel of Jay's skin under her fingertips.

"I'm sorry you got pulled into this mess," she said, finally meeting his eyes.

He brushed her hair back from her face and tangled his fingers in it as his hand rested on her good shoulder. "I'd never seen a dead body before meeting you and now, in the space of less than a month, I've seen two—first Smitty and now Farlow. Having you in my life has definitely opened up a whole new world."

"I told you when we first met that I might not be worth your time," she said.

"You did, and I'll say now what I said then, you're a smart woman, one of the smartest I've ever met. Don't start being dumb now. It doesn't suit you."

She held his eyes then gave him a soft smile. "Good, I'm glad you think so because I think it's too late for you to change your mind. I don't think I'd let you."

He smiled back as he rolled her over, protecting her shoulder as he did. "Now how about a little nookie to help me get over the trauma of the day?"

CHAPTER TWENTY-THREE

NAOMI WAS GETTING NERVOUS. He could see it in her jerky movements and the way her head came up at every sound. Only three hours had passed since they'd returned home to the guest house, but Agent Brown still hadn't called about Damian.

"Why don't you call her?" he asked, knowing she could easily locate the agent's number if she didn't already have it. "And while we're speaking of being on the phone, have you called your brother?"

Brian had called twice while they were otherwise engaged. Knowing Brian was likely worried about his sister, Jay had felt a twinge of guilt letting the calls go unanswered, but his guilt wasn't enough to stop him—or Naomi—from taking and giving what they needed most from each other.

"I texted him on our way home, so he knows we're safe. I'll call him as soon as I know anything about Damian."

He handed her a glass of wine. "And Agent Brown?"

"She was *not* happy to find us there. I don't want to poke the bear," she said. "It's making me crazy, but I need to let her call when she can. But, if she doesn't call in the next few hours, I'm going to start calling all the hospitals to see if I can find him."

She took a sip of wine and gave him a look that dared him to challenge her. He was a smarter man than that, though and he was not about to question her loyalty to—and fear for— Damian.

Her phone pinged, and she glanced at the incoming call. "Russ," she said, picking it up.

Jay watched her take in whatever the analyst was saying to her; a minute or two passed as she listened, then she grabbed her computer and turned it on. After a dizzying flurry of her fingers flying across the keyboard, her screen came to life. He had no idea what she was clicking on, but she looked as though she could have found her way there blindfolded; and "there" turned out to be a series of images displayed on her screen.

Naomi, lost in her conversation, didn't seem to notice when someone knocked at his door. Assuming it was his mom, he made his way over and was surprised to find Brian standing on the other side.

The two men stared at each other, then Brian shot Jay a self-deprecating smile. "She's my sister. I had to come."

Jay opened the door wider and held out his hand. Brian shook it as he moved inside the guest house carrying a small duffle bag and a computer case.

Naomi looked up then did a double take. A small crease formed between her eyes, then with a little shake of her head as if to wake herself up, she motioned him over. "Russ thinks he may have a lead on the RV and is tracking a vehicle," she said.

Brian dropped all his things and came to his sister's side. Jay picked up the bags and placed the computer one beside Brian on his way to delivering the other one to the second bedroom of the guesthouse. When he returned, Naomi's phone was on speaker and the three of them were discussing where the RV might be headed next.

"They are clearly moving out of the area," Russ said.

"Well after what happened today, that's hardly a surprise,"

Brian said. Satellite imagery had been able to positively identify the RV that had been at the Robinsons', so they now knew exactly what to track.

"But where are they going? It looked like they were headed into Athens, but they've started to veer west," Russ said.

"Toward Atlanta," Naomi pointed out. "Where there are lots of highways."

Jay stood behind Naomi, his hand on her shoulder, watching three different images spread across her laptop screen.

"Any leads on who rented the planes that brought them to this area?" Brian asked to no one in particular. "If we know who was involved in that, maybe it will give us a lead as to where the RV might be headed."

"Where who's going?"

Brian, Naomi, and Jay all turned to see Damian stride into the room, Agent Brown behind him.

"He was making the hospital staff crazy and couldn't drive himself—didn't have a car anyway—so I just brought him back," Agent Brown explained as surprised silence greeted their entrance.

"Who's going where?" Damian repeated, joining the three in front of Naomi's laptop.

"The RV is on the move. I don't think I'll be able to reach Lucy, but I'm going to try," Brian said, pulling out his own laptop and setting it up next to Naomi's.

"Anything you can tell us that will help, Agent Brown?" Naomi asked as the woman joined them.

"Call me Jackie, and no not really. I was sent in to investigate because a similar incident to what happened in the DC office happened in the Miami office."

"How similar?" Russ's voice came through the phone still lying on the table.

"The same," Naomi interjected, obviously surprising Agent Brown. "It happened in New York and Chicago, too. But other than the initial disturbance, nothing more happened at any office."

Jay watched Brian and Naomi share a look, then suddenly her eyes widened, but it was Brian who spoke. "This happened about four months ago didn't it?" he asked.

"It did," Naomi confirmed and the two shared another look.

"Another person we know went missing around then," Naomi said. "He's prone to disappearing on his own, he once just up and went to Thailand for six months without telling anyone or bothering to keep in touch, and so we didn't think much of it."

"But no one's seen him since June," Brian picked up. "He didn't show up for a job he had scheduled and, well, we had it on our radar to look into, but we just hadn't gotten around to it," he said.

Naomi shook her head. "I discovered the Miami disturbance a few days ago, and I can't believe I didn't put two and two together."

"Russ, can you look into Jerome's movements? His full name is Jerome Whittaker. Our priority is Lucy, but if something happened to Jerome, we need to know that, too," Brian said.

"On it," Russ responded.

"And Russ, any luck in tracking my computer? Or Phone?" Damian added.

"Negative, boss," Russ answered. "I wiped both, remotely, so whoever has them won't get anything off of them, but I think they are lost to the gods by now."

Damian cast Jackie a long look. She sighed. "I'll have someone from the Atlanta office run one up to you. But it will be a couple of hours," she said stepping away and pulling out her phone.

"Want me to take over the traffic cams?" Brian asked, returning their attention to the task at hand.

Russ muttered a response Brian must have taken as "yes,"

because he keyed in several commands that Jay's eyes weren't fast enough to catch—which was saying a lot since he'd hit a homerun off a ninety-eight mile an hour fast ball not one week ago. Images similar to those on Naomi's screen popped up on Brian's computer.

"What happened to the satellite?" Jay asked, remembering that was how they'd gotten the information on the Robinson place earlier.

"It moved on," Naomi said. "We'll have another one come online in about..." she paused and looked at the time on her phone, "...in about fourteen minutes. But until then, we're doing it the old-fashioned way."

"Hacking into traffic cams?" he asked, not a little bit sarcastically. Naomi flashed him a smile but said nothing, and for a few moments, everyone just watched the screens.

"And now the RV appears to be turning south," Brian said. "Your images are useless, Nano," Brian said leaning over to his sister and tapping an outdated image, expanding it on contact. "That's from fifteen minutes ago. Why don't I track the images while Russ tracks Jerome and you can go back to digging into the plane rentals?"

"And what about monitoring Lucy's activity?" she asked, though she was already closing the images.

"I've got that, too," he said.

Naomi shot her brother a look, but his attention was back on his screen and so she turned back to her own, bringing up several files as she did.

"They appear to be headed toward Florida, could there be some tie to what happened in Miami? Maybe Miami is our ground zero?" Damian suggested.

"They've been headed in that direction for all of two minutes, I suggest we don't jump to conclusions," Naomi said.

"I also wouldn't dismiss how well they know this area," Jackie interjected. "Miami might be somewhere they are comfortable, if all this started there, but clearly they have ties here."

"Damian, I have an extra computer you can use," Naomi said. "It's in the bedroom. Can you go into the HR files and see if there is anyone linked to the Miami office who has ties to this area?"

"I'll get it," Jay said as Damian started toward the room. A minute later, he set the computer down in front of Damian who'd taken the third of four seats around the small breakfast table.

Naomi reached for the device, logged in, brought up a few documents and databases then slid it back over to Damian. "That's me logged into those systems so don't do anything dumb," she said.

Damian shot her a flat look, but otherwise said nothing, opting instead to focus on the information now at his fingertips.

"Any news from Lucy?" Damian asked. "And by the way, I filled Jackie in on everything we know on our way here."

Everyone flicked a glance in her direction, but no one said anything. Jay, deciding he wasn't going to keep up with all the information flying around the room and across the screens, headed into the kitchen to grab a beer. Thirty minutes later, he was reclined in a chair, his feet up on an ottoman, listening to a debate about whether to stop the RV or not. Jackie and Brian were arguing *for*, stating that a reason could be found to justify the stop. But Naomi and Damian were just as adamant that unless Lucy was in imminent danger, they needed to give the people in charge of the crime enough rope to hang themselves with. It didn't help that in that thirty minutes, the direction of the RV had changed another two times.

"I have a question," Jay said, interrupting Brian and Naomi. He wasn't sure if it was the fact that he'd spoken or the fact that they'd forgotten he was there and the surprise got to them, but all four people stopped talking instantly.

"Yes," Naomi said after a beat.

"Obviously someone familiar with this area is involved, they also probably know you're looking for them. And now the RV you *think* is holding Lucy is driving all over kingdom come and back—doesn't it seem like maybe they might be leading you on a wild goose chase? I don't know, if it were me orchestrating all this, and I will grant you that I'm not that devious—"

"I don't know, I saw that game in LA three years ago..." Jackie interrupted, making him smile. Okay, that pitch switch *had* been a little devious, but he'd been certain someone had been giving the batters a heads up on his incoming pitches and there had been only one way to find out. He and his catcher had been right, and as soon as they'd figured out how to thwart the other team, the Rebels had coasted to a clean victory.

"Be that as it may," Jay continued, raising his bottle in acknowledgement of the compliment from the agent. "If it were me, I would have sent the RV away to draw your attention and then tucked Lucy into some cozy—and I use that word loosely —place where I could keep an eye on her while you all are running around trying to find me. Either that or I'd leave the area altogether. Remember they do have access to planes." He took a sip of his drink as four sets of eyes stared at him.

Silence greeted his half-question, half-comment. Any doubt they might have had about the RV holding Lucy, at least at some point, had been dispelled by the vehicle being sent all over the state. But if whoever was organizing the escapade was now feeling the pressure to wrap it up, which he assumed they were, given what had happened to Kevin Farlow earlier that day, it seemed to him that they'd go into either lockdown mode or flee mode.

"Russ, where was the RV last seen before it left this area?" Naomi asked, breaking the silence.

"Actually, where was it from about noon onward today?" Brian added as some alert on his computer dinged. "That's about when Damian made his way out to the Robinson farm and probably the earliest they would have known their work wasn't going undetected," he said, his fingers flying over the keyboard. "Fuck," Brian suddenly muttered.

Jay's eyes fell to Naomi, who held up a hand, keeping everyone quiet while Brian furiously tapped the keys on his computer, his attention focused only on what was in front of him.

"Why didn't you say anything earlier?" Brian demanded suddenly, his eyes burning a hole into Jay.

"Brian," Naomi warned.

Jay blinked, but recognized the fear in Brian's accusatory gaze. "Would you tell me how to play baseball?" he asked. "No, you wouldn't, not really," he said, answering for Brian. "I didn't say anything earlier because this," he said continuing with a wave of his hand toward the table, "isn't anything I have any experience with and I'm well aware people's lives are at stake. For fuck's sake, I watched your sister, a woman I care a great deal about, get into a gun fight today. I have no interest in diverting your attention with my questions, and *that* is why I didn't say anything earlier."

With the memories of a few hours ago suddenly pressing in on him, he rose and walked to the kitchen. "I only said something now because it seemed like you guys were in a lull and it wouldn't be distracting. And now that we've cleared that up, if I'm not mistaken, something has happened with Lucy, hasn't it? Why don't you tell everyone so the people who can *do something* about it can help you?" He tossed his beer bottle in the recycle bin with a little more force than necessary.

Brian's eyes narrowed back at him, but Naomi put her hand on her brother's arm and spoke. "What has happened, Brian? What did Lucy say?"

Jay watched as the fire in Brian's eyes changed to something far bleaker, "It's not what she said," he said as he slid his computer over to Naomi. Jay watched as the expression on Naomi's face went from curious to thoughtful to horrified. In silence, she showed whatever was on the screen to the two FBI agents whose expressions went through the exact same series. Curious, Jay went to stand behind Naomi.

He had expected to see a line of code or something equally unintelligible to him as he knew that was how Lucy and Brian had been communicating up until that point. But instead of number, letters, or symbols, an image greeted him. At first glance, it looked to be just a field at dusk with a couple of cows grazing. Taken from maybe the second or third floor of a house, the angle was looking down and there wasn't much to see. He assumed it was her way of sending some sort of clue as to where she was, but that wouldn't explain the grim looks he'd seen. Nor why Brian currently had his head bowed, his hands buried in his hair, and was taking several intentionally deep breaths.

And so, he looked closer. And then closer still. And then to his horror, he soon saw what the others had more easily grasped.

In the reflection of the window through which the picture had been taken, he could see the image of a woman. Her dark hair pulled back, her eyes haunted, she stared at the window, making it appear she was looking right at them. And making it hard to miss the swollen, dark bruising that marred her left eye, or the gash across her right cheek, or the bloody and swollen lip.

He couldn't suppress the wave of nausea that washed over him—the sight was terrible, and he couldn't imagine the agony that gripped Brian. God knew if he had seen Naomi like that, it would have wrecked him. As if sensing his distress, Naomi's hand came up and entwined with his. Jay's eyes traveled to Brian, who now sat ramrod straight.

"We need to find where she is," he said.

"Let me send the picture to Russ," Damian said, reaching for

Brian's computer. It was a testament to Brian's distress that he didn't protest one single bit, not even a second glance.

"Maybe we can match the geography. We need comparison images and topography maps," Damian said.

As the other four jumped into action, Jay quickly slipped his phone from his pocket and snapped a picture of the image.

"Give me a minute, I might be able to help," he said quietly for Naomi's ears only. The pleading look she gave him made his stomach flip in ways it hadn't in years. He didn't want to promise anything, but he really wanted to be able to give her something.

"If there's anything," she said.

"If there's anything I can do, I'll do it," he said, dropping a kiss on her lips, then he slipped from the house, mostly unnoticed.

CHAPTER TWENTY-FOUR

NAOMI HEARD the door of the guest house open, and a soft gust of cool night air preceded its closing. Looking up, she saw Jay walking toward them carrying a piece of paper in his hands. Around her, Damian, Brian, and Jackie were all engaged in a variety of tasks in an attempt to locate where Lucy was being held.

They assumed it was close by, but nothing was guaranteed. There was something to be said about Jay's comment regarding the ease with which they could have left the area, and it was entirely possible that Lucy was now a couple hours' flight away. Russ was looking into air traffic, but it had been a surprisingly busy day at the number of regional and private airfields.

"Here," Jay said, laying a piece of paper down on the table. "It may not lead to anything, but I took that picture to my mom and we talked about where it might be. I know we don't have confirmation she's still in the area, but if she is, these are the farms we thought best fit the picture she sent."

Everyone else in the room turned to look at him. He shoved his hands into his back pockets and met their gaze. "Look, like I said, it may not help at all, but after what we just learned, I couldn't sit here and not do something. Those cattle in the picture?" he continued. "They're dairy cattle, and there are too many for them to be for private use only. There aren't that many farms around here that raise commercial dairy cattle. Most are beef," he said.

Again, a beat passed and then Brian all but lunged for the list. "There are four farms on this list," he said rattling off the addresses. By unspoken agreement, each person at the table took one.

"Do you or your mom have a favorite, one you'd look at first?" Brian asked.

"This one," Jay said, leaning over and pointing to an address. "The dairy farm belongs to the Wallaces, but the property that abuts it was sold about eight months ago, and though people have seen lights on and cars going in and out of the driveway, no one—well, no one that we know of—has met the new owners yet. And yes, I know it's possible that my mom doesn't know *everything* that happens in this county, but I wouldn't want to be the one to tell *her* that," he said with an affectionate smile.

"I'm on it," Naomi said turning her attention to her computer and bringing up mapping programs to see if the layout of the house and land could align with the image.

"I'll pull the satellite images," Russ said.

"I'm on the record of sale," Damian offered.

Five minutes later, Damian sat back abruptly in his chair.

"What?" everyone but Russ said.

"The house was bought by Lodestone Industries, which is, coincidentally, the parent company of Stonemark Industries, one of the companies that rented one of the planes used to get Lucy from Hawaii to Georgia."

"And do we know who is behind that company?" Jackie asked.

"Unfortunately, *that* is something I haven't been able to find yet," he responded.

"And it doesn't matter, not for what we need," Brian said, rising from his seat. "You," he said pointing to Jackie and Damian, "need to get a warrant to search that house. Given that we have proof that Lucy was taken, and that she's being held, and we have a connection between the house and the plane, it should be enough for a warrant," he finished.

Jackie and Damian shared a look Naomi recognized. The evidence wasn't as clear cut as Brian viewed it, and in order to meet the criteria a judge would require, the FBI would have to reveal more of the investigation—the internal investigation—than they might feel comfortable with. And Naomi doubted even Damian could make that call, in fact she was pretty sure that decision would rest solely with Agent Brown.

The woman held Damian's gaze for a long, tense moment then pursed her lips. "I know a judge in Atlanta that might be willing to hear us out."

"I'll fill out the paperwork," Damian said as he turned back to the computer.

"We can't wait that long," Brian said.

"We don't have a choice," Jackie snapped, picking up her phone. "Not if you want to keep working for any government agency, and not if you want to be able go after the people who are doing this once we save Lucy. Don't forget three people have died, Brian. Their families deserve justice, and if we don't do this right, we put that at risk."

"I can't sit here and wait for you two to drive to Atlanta."

"If you shut up and let me do my job, you won't have to." Jackie said and then, in a much different tone of voice, she turned to her phone. "Hey Willa, it's Jackie," and she proceeded to fill in who they assumed to be the judge. When she finished, she glanced at Damian, "We can have the paperwork to you in…"

Damian didn't even bother looking up. "Fifteen minutes," he answered.

Jackie repeated the timeline then after a few pleasantries, she ended the call. "I think we have a pretty good chance she'll grant it, but we still have to wait."

"But we don't have to wait here," Brian said. "We can get into position and be ready when she makes the call."

"Whoa, slow down there, Swifty," Jackie said rising from her seat. "You aren't going anywhere. You are not an agent, you're not even FBI. Rodriguez is out but we have a team of four from Atlanta still in the area. Unless we get information that there are more people involved than we currently think, I have who I need."

"I'm not out," Damian said. "And I agree, the six of us should be sufficient. Whoever is orchestrating this situation has kept the people involved to a minimum, and we've seen the same folks pop up in every scenario. Now they are down Kevin Farlow, the group will be even smaller. I suspect, other than Lucy, there won't be more than two, maybe three other people at the house."

"If they are at the house," Jackie said.

"They are," Brian said definitively, but Naomi knew he spoke only because he *needed* Lucy to be there, not because he had any proof—or not any more than what Jay had provided.

"You'd stop everything you're doing to go on what could be a wild goose chase?" Jackie challenged him. "If we're wrong, think of all the time you'd be wasting."

"I'll keep working on my end," Russ piped up from the phone that still lay on the table.

Brian looked at her. Naomi's heart stuttered. She didn't like the idea of sending her twin out to the property without her. She'd been without him earlier today, but that was only because he hadn't arrived yet. She had no illusions that had he been in

Georgia, he would never have let her and Jay go to the Robinson farm alone.

"I know the Wallaces," Jay said, placing a hand on her shoulder. "If I'm there, if Naomi and I are there, I'll be able to talk them into giving you permission to use their land to come in from the back of the neighboring house. If you don't cross the Wallace land, you'll have to come up the drive and I can tell you that on a still night like tonight, unless you park a mile away they will hear you."

Jackie didn't like that little nugget of truth Jay had dropped and her lips thinned. "And if we go in from the Wallace property?" she asked, the tone of her voice indicating she already knew she wouldn't like the answer.

"There's a small rise behind the Wallace house that lies between their place and the house where we think Lucy is that would block both light and sound. If you park on the Wallace property, you'll be about a quarter of a mile away, and even if someone in the house is watching, they'd never see or hear you." He pointed to the picture Lucy had sent, indicating the slight rise in land on the left side of the image. "Not to mention that the fields are dark, and if you skirt the edges where there is a line of trees and hedges, you should have pretty good cover most of the way." Again, he pointed to the image, tracing the line of hedges barely visible in the frame.

Naomi looked up at him, impressed with his use of the word "cover"—he almost sounded like one of them. He squeezed her shoulder.

"It's done," Damian said, breaking the tension in the room. "The paperwork is done," he clarified. "Who should I send it to that can take it to your judge?"

Jackie's eyes bounced between Brian and Naomi before she rattled off an email to Damian. "I'll call him and have him run it over to Willa, Judge Barkley's, house," she said.

Damian typed in the email, hit a couple more strokes, then

closed his computer down. "What are we waiting for?" he asked, coming to his feet.

Agent Brown glared at each of them, then acceptance seemed to finally settle in. "Fine," she said. "But you three," she pointed to Naomi, Brian, and Jay, "will stay on the Wallace property. And you," she said, pointing to Damian, "will be relegated to the perimeter. We don't know who or what's inside, and you've already had your head bashed in once today. As annoying as you all are, I don't want any of you getting hurt."

As she spoke, they all started to close computers and don jackets. "Your concern warms my heart," Damian said, shooting a grin to the room in general. Agent Brown glared at him, and he winked at her. "I know, the paperwork would be a bitch," he added with a grin.

"Not to mention it would ruin my chances of becoming Director if I broke two of the FBI's prized consultants." She nodded to Naomi and Brian.

They exited the guesthouse and made their way to the cars, Naomi, Brian, and Jay climbing into Jay's truck and Damian and Jackie into her government issued sedan. A few minutes later, they were caravanning down dark country roads in the direction of the Wallace property.

About ten minutes into the drive, Damian texted Naomi to let her know the agent in Atlanta was on his way to the judge's house and that they'd likely have to wait for an answer when they arrived. She relayed this information to Brian and Jay, and while Jay didn't seem to think much of anything about it, Brian's expression grew even grimmer. She desperately wanted to know what it was between him and Lucy, for it was obvious Lucy was much more than a colleague, but now was not the time or the place. His bleak look even assuaged the indignation that came with having been kept in the dark by her own twin.

"She'll be okay," she managed to say. She turned to face him, and his eyes flitted to hers but just as quickly darted back to the blackness outside his window. Jay reached over and took her hand. She opened her mouth to say something to her brother, but Jay gave a gentle squeeze, and she didn't need a billboard to know he was suggesting she leave it be, even if only for the time being.

Another ten minutes passed in a silence that would have been tenser had Jay not been there to absorb some of her own anxiety. Then suddenly they were turning onto a driveway, and within seconds, a small, gabled farmhouse came into view. Jay pulled his truck up in front of the front porch and Agent Brown came to a stop beside them. Naomi was barely out of the car when an elderly man opened the front door and stepped out.

"Mr. Wallace, it's Jason Greene, Margaret Greene's boy," he said loudly enough for the man standing in the doorway to hear. Naomi saw Mr. Wallace's head turn as he took in the two vehicles and five people who'd unexpectedly shown up at his front door.

"The baseball player?" Mr. Wallace said.

"Yes, sir," Jay answered.

"I took my grandson to watch you play when your college team came to Athens and played the Dawgs. You pitched a perfect game."

"I remember that game, sir. I was a little conflicted, I admit. I played my best, but I'm still a Dawg at heart," Jay said. Naomi could hear the smile in his voice when he spoke of the University of Georgia Bull Dogs—Georgia was nothing if not the Bull Dog Nation.

The man chuckled. "You done your mama proud, boy. She's a good woman, and I know you've been looking out for her. Why don't you and your friends come on in and tell me why you're here tonight."

"Thank you, sir. We'd be obliged." Jay led the group of five into the cozy farmhouse. Once inside, Mr. Wallace directed them into the living room to the right of the foyer where he offered them seats. Naomi, Jay, and Damian sat, but Brian and Jackie remained standing.

"Is Mrs. Wallace in tonight?" Jay asked. "My mama wanted me to thank her for the donation of the quilt to the church fundraiser."

Mr. Wallace shook his head. "She's gone to Augusta to visit her sister, but I'll let her know you said so. Can I get you any coffee or tea?" he offered.

Jay thanked him but declined. After a moment, Mr. Wallace sat down in a chair opposite the couch she and Jay had taken, and he studied them.

"Now, son, what can I do for you?" he asked. And at that, Jay told him everything—or nearly everything—they suspected about the house across the way.

When he was done, Mr. Wallace didn't express surprise or dismay, he simply let his wise eyes travel around the room before they landed on Agent Brown. "You have more people waiting?" he asked.

She nodded. "I do, sir. The search warrant just came through, but I didn't want the other agents to join us here until we had your permission," she said.

Mr. Wallace seemed to consider this, then abruptly, he gave a sharp nod. "Can't say as I'm surprised to hear something might be going on with that house—I've seen lights over there at odd times but never seen any actual people," he said. "You and your agents have permission to park here and cross my land."

Jackie barely got a "thank you" out before she had her phone in her hand and was calling her colleagues in to join them. A few minutes later two cars pulled in and three agents exited an SUV while a fourth agent climbed out of a sedan. Jackie jogged down the porch stairs to meet them, not wasting any time with introductions. Immediately, the five began pulling vests and other supplies from the back of the SUV. Leaving Naomi, Jay, and Brian standing on the porch with Mr.

Wallace, Damian trailed his colleagues at a much more measured pace.

Other than the warning Jackie issued to Damian to stay on the perimeter, the six agents kitted themselves out in silence. Naomi didn't need to see Damian's face to know what he thought about that order, but for his sake, she hoped he listened.

The yard was cast into darkness when Jackie closed the trunk and the interior lights of the car shut off. Naomi barely managed to make out the silhouettes of the agents as they gathered around in a circle, no doubt to make a plan of approach.

No one said a word as the shadows began to move away, but to Naomi's surprise, a form she recognized broke away and came toward them.

"Jay," Damian called as he came to a stop about forty feet from the porch. Jay shot her a look but then jogged down the stairs.

"You think Damian is telling him to sit on us while they're gone?" Brian asked from beside her.

"Undoubtedly," she responded as Jay leaned in to listen to whatever the agent was saying.

"He gonna be able to do that?" Mr. Wallace asked, startling Naomi who had more or less forgotten the older man had joined them on the porch.

"Probably not," Brian answered, his eyes still locked on the two men.

"I'd like to say yes, but if I'm being honest, I'd have to agree with my brother," Naomi chimed in.

Damian finished whatever he was saying and Jay nodded. Beside her, Mr. Wallace sighed. "Just be careful, an arm like his only comes along once in a lifetime. I figure allowing you guys on my property tonight is worth at least a couple of good seats to the next game the Rebs play against the Braves. I'd like my grandson to see him pitch in the big leagues at least once."

Naomi turned to look at the older man. He gave her a plaintive look then smiled. "Don't get me wrong, if something's going on in that house, I want it stopped, but if it happens to mean Jason Greene is indebted to me, even just a little bit, I'm not above taking a few tickets in thanks."

Naomi chuckled as Jay joined them. "I'm sure he'd be happy to oblige, wouldn't you, Jay?"

"What's that," he said, dropping an arm around her shoulder.

"Mr. Wallace and his grandson would like tickets right behind the dugout along the third base line next time you come to play down here," she said.

Jay blinked at the shift from government operation to baseball. Then he smiled. "Does he play?" Jay asked.

Mr. Wallace nodded. "He's good, too. Ranked fourth in the state in his age. He'll be at your clinic in a few days," he said.

"How would he feel about being a bat boy for a day?" Jay asked.

"I think I should invite you all in for a drink," Mr. Wallace said with a grin.

CHAPTER TWENTY-FIVE

Fifteen minutes later, Jay was standing by the fire, a tumbler of Jack Daniels in his hand discussing the Bulldogs baseball team with Mr. Wallace. Brian, having already knocked back his own drink, paced the room with the empty tumbler dangling between his fingers.

Perched on the edge of an upholstered chair herself, near enough to the fire to feel its warmth but not so close as to be drawn into Jay's conversation, she rolled her own glass between her hands. Having no stomach for the drink, she hadn't taken a single sip.

"I can't do it," Brian said suddenly. He drew to a stop and the look he gave her nearly broke her heart. She glanced back at Jay, who had stopped talking to their host, his eyes now on Brian. She knew that if the situation was different, and there was a chance Jay was in that house, and she was being asked to sit and wait, she wouldn't have been as accommodating as Brian.

"Did Damian tell you to sit on us?" he asked Jay.

Jay took a sip, finishing his drink, and nodded.

"I can't do it," Brian said. "I don't want to get in their way, but I can't just sit here and wait."

Jay looked at his empty tumbler then raised his gaze to Brian as he handed the empty glass to his host. "I know. And Damian knows, too," Jay said, surprising both her and Brian.

"What does that mean?" Brian asked, his body having gone still.

"It means," Jay said, moving away from the fireplace, "that he told me what Agent Brown told him to tell you, that you are to stay here. But what he also told me was that he knew neither of you would listen, and so he said to wait until you said something and then to let you know that there are night vision goggles and vests in the back of Jackie's car. He did ask that we travel unarmed, though."

"Not a problem," Brian said as she rose from her seat. "I didn't bring any weapons, and I know the one Naomi used today was Damian's, so I doubt she has any of hers either," he said, striding to the coat tree that held their coats.

"'Any' of hers?" Jay asked, gathering the glasses from the twins. Mr. Wallace stopped him from heading toward the kitchen and took the tumblers from his hand. "How many do you have?" he asked her as they donned their jackets.

Naomi mentally sifted her gun locker as she zipped her coat. "Four usable handguns and two antiques," she said.

Mr. Wallace let out a whistle. "A woman after my own heart."

Jay chuckled. "She's taken, and Mrs. Wallace might use one of hers on you if she heard you say that."

"I *am* a lucky man," Mr. Wallace said as he opened the front door. "You kids be careful," he added as the three filed out.

"Thank you for your hospitality, Mr. Wallace," Naomi said, the two men already heading down the steps.

He nodded. "You'll be careful?"

Naomi smiled. "Of course. Jay all but promised to pitch for your grandson. I don't intend for him to do anything that might risk that."

Mr. Wallace inclined his head. "It's not just his arm I'd worry about. I think if something happened to you it would throw his game off more than a little bit."

On impulse, Naomi leaned over and kissed the man's cheek. "Thank you, and I assure you, I don't intend to let anything happen to any of us."

Mr. Wallace smiled. "I think you might be just the one to see that's the case."

"Nano!" her brother called. She glanced over her shoulder to see the two men in vests. Brian holding an extra one for her as well as a pair of goggles.

"Because God knows it's not going to be either one of them," she said turning back to Mr. Wallace and shooting him an exasperated look.

"You'll let me know how it goes?"

She smiled again. "Promise. And thank you."

She didn't wait to hear his response as she bounded down the steps and joined Jay and Brian. She donned a vest but held the goggles Brian had handed her in her hand. Aside from being too bright near the house, she knew her eyes would adjust well enough to see once they moved into the darkness.

Following Jay to the edge of a field, the three climbed over a stile and began to make their way across the property while keeping to the shadows created by some sort of hedge-like bush.

Not surprisingly, Brian took the lead once on the path to the house where they believed Lucy was being held. Jay held the middle position, but only by virtue of his longer stride and Naomi, who held his hand in hers, followed half a step behind. Thinking she had been following pretty closely in both Brian and Jay's footsteps, the sudden catch of something on her toe caught Naomi by double surprise—surprise that something was in the path her two companions had just passed and surprise to see the ground rapidly approaching her face as she stumbled forward.

She heard her brother's exasperated call and from Jay a

much more concerned one, but none of it registered as she brought her other foot forward to steady herself and failed to find the ground beneath it. With her left foot swiftly disappearing into a hole of unknown depth and her right foot still hobbled from whatever she had tripped on, Naomi went down.

"Ummph." The sound expelled from her lungs. Thankfully, even in the surprise—and pain—she had the presence of mind to remain as quiet as possible.

"You okay?" Jay asked, at her side in an instant.

She stilled; her hands flat against the dew dampened grass, one leg stretched out behind her and the other buried in a hole up to about mid-calf. She took a few deep breaths as she catalogued her body. Her hands were fine, though they stung a bit from the sudden landing. The muscle in the inner thigh of her right leg felt strained but she thought she could probably walk it out. But it was her left foot, the one in the hole, that caused her some concern.

Turning to a seated position, she freed her right leg from where it had gotten caught on what appeared to be an old fence post.

"My left ankle," she said. Now that she was seated on the ground, the foot no longer held any weight and it dangled uselessly over the hole as her calf rested on the edge.

Jay studied her face then moved down to the ankle in question. Gently he lifted her leg and probed her injury. She sucked in a breath and stiffened at his touch.

"Scoot back," Jay said.

It took a second for her to understand what he'd said but then it sunk in and she did what he asked while he steadied her ankle. Once she moved enough, he set it softly on the ground.

"Is it swelling?" She could feel it pulsing and starting to generate its own heat, but she couldn't see it from her position.

"A little," Jay answered, his tone making it clear he knew that wasn't what she'd wanted to hear.

"Nano," Brian said, his voice conflicted.

"Go," she said. She didn't want him to go. They'd made a promise to stick together—the saying "safety in numbers" hadn't taken hold in the lexicon for nothing—but she knew she couldn't hold him back anyway. If Jay had been in that house, she would have felt the same.

"You'll stay with her?" Brian said turning to Jay.

Jay nodded. "When the initial pain wears off, I'll get her back to the house. I don't want to jog that ankle too much right now."

Brian glanced between the two of them, clearly conflicted, but after a beat, he gave a sharp nod and moved off toward the house leaving Jay and Naomi in moonlit darkness. Within seconds, the sound of his footsteps faded, and the crickets began their chirping to fill the silence.

"I don't think you're ready to make it back to the house yet, but I'm also not sure we want to just sit out here in the middle of the path," Jay said quietly. Still kneeling at her ankle, she could see the worry in his expression.

She didn't think they were in any danger, not this far from the house, but like Jay, she didn't like feeling so exposed. "Any suggestions?"

Jay glanced around then his attention landed somewhere behind her. "You're not very squeamish are you?" he asked.

She shook her head. "I loathe snakes that swim—it's an abomination against nature—but other than that, not really, no," she said.

"Good," he said rising and walking behind her. She craned her neck to see what he was doing, and though she couldn't see much from the angle she had, she heard him rustling in the brush. A few moments later, he returned to her side.

"Think you can scoot backwards about six feet?" he asked. "I can steady your ankle," he added.

She nodded. "To where, though?"

"This hedge is a wild grapevine. I just cleared a little gap in the bush that we can tuck ourselves into. We had one beside our house growing up, and my sister and I used to build forts in it all the time, they provide a surprisingly good hiding place."

Well, at least now she knew what kind of plant made the hedge, she thought as she glanced over her shoulder at the dark hole Jay had created. Without another word, she braced her hands and more or less crab walked back into the gap with Jay steadying her injured leg the entire way.

"I know I said I wasn't really squeamish, but how many venomous spiders do you have around here? I'm asking for purely practical reasons, of course. It wouldn't be good if one of us got bit."

Jay chuckled but didn't answer as he tucked her farther into the opening. Once she was settled, he took his own seat under the leaves, placing himself between her and the pathway.

For a long while, they heard nothing but crickets and the occasional night bird calling in the night. Sitting in the shadowed hiding place, it felt like eons had passed since Brian had left, though Naomi knew it had only been a few minutes. She'd been counting the seconds—the interminable seconds.

"Why can't we hear anything?" she asked, more of a whine than an actual question.

"The only thing we'd be able to hear from here is a gunshot, so I think it's probably a good thing it's quiet."

"Please don't be so practical, it makes me feel irrational, and I'm not normally an irrational person."

Again, Jay chuckled, but this time he wrapped an arm around her shoulder and pulled her against him. "You're worried about your brother and Damian and Lucy, too. There is nothing irrational about that." He dropped a kiss on the top of her head.

A few more minutes of quiet passed when Naomi couldn't take it anymore. "Can you take a pair of the night vision goggles and go to the top of that hill and see if you can see anything?"

she asked, gesturing to the hill that rose beside them. They'd been in the shadows of the hedge on the edge of the field as they'd walked the path, but now she saw the more exposed hill opposite the field as having a different advantage.

"Naomi," Jay said. Just her name.

"I know," she replied. "I know we need to stick together but it's only forty feet or so. And it's my brother…" She was not above playing the sympathy card.

"That was low," Jay said even as he moved away.

"When used judiciously, emotional pleas are very effective. What if your sister was in there?" she said, driving the nail in a little farther.

Jay lowered a single brow as if to say "really", then grunted as he maneuvered out of the hiding place he'd created. "Stay here," he commanded.

Naomi opened her mouth to point out that she wasn't likely to go anywhere then promptly shut it deciding a little graciousness wouldn't hurt. "Please be careful and of course, I won't move an inch." He rose to his feet as she spoke, the night vision goggles in his left hand. He shot her a look as if he wasn't quite sure whether to believe her or not, but after a beat, he moved away and into the shadows.

She watched his form make its way up the gentle hill, more just a soft rise than an actual hill, but she hoped it would give him vantage enough to see the house. Even with the night vision goggles, Jay wouldn't be able to see much more than indistinguishable people, but at least he'd be able to tell if they were moving or not. Reason told her that without having heard gunshots it was unlikely anyone was seriously injured, but she was also painfully aware of the thousands of other ways her brother or Damian or Lucy could get hurt that didn't involve a gun.

With his back pressed against a tree, all Naomi could see of Jay was an occasional glimpse of various parts of his silhouette

—a shoulder here, a knee there—as he shifted in the cool night air. But then suddenly, she saw nothing. Her heart leapt into her throat as she realized he must have straightened and stilled, and she knew the only reason for that would be if he'd seen something.

In an instant, she became aware of two things. The first was that she was very much alone, and though she was strong, she recognized her own vulnerability. The second was that she never should have asked Jay to leave, not because she didn't want to be alone, but because she'd *sent him* out alone. He was exposed, more so than she, and had no training for this kind of thing. Not that she had a ton either, but she did know a thing or two about covert activities.

Her heart raced as she very quietly brought her own night vision goggles up and trained them on Jay. He stood still as a sentry, watching something. She hesitated, then, as quietly as she could, she shifted on the ground and followed Jay's line of sight.

She let out a long slow breath when she recognized Brian headed back their way. The relief she anticipated at seeing her brother didn't come though when she realized he wasn't alone, he was half carrying, half guiding a stumbling, limping Lucy James. Naomi's heart caught in her throat as she watched Brian slowly guide Lucy along the dark path. Lucy's head hung forward and moved like a rag doll's with each jostling step, the arm that Brian wasn't holding around his shoulder swung loosely at her side, and with nearly every step, her toes dragged then she lurched forward. She looked drunk—beyond drunk, really—but Naomi more than suspected that she'd been drugged instead.

The couple made slow progress, and they were about ten feet away when Naomi shifted so as to better alert them to her presence. If she could get their attention, maybe Brian could tuck Lucy safely in with her amongst the wild grapevines and then return unimpeded to the Wallace farm for help. But no sooner had she opened her mouth to whisper to Brian than a shot rang out, rupturing the quiet of the night.

On instinct, Naomi ducked deeper into the grapevines but sought Jay out with her eyes even as she moved. She scanned the trees and her stomach flipped when she didn't immediately find him. But as she willed herself to calm, she caught a glimpse of his shoulders. Relief like she'd never felt before washed through her as she realized he'd moved to the relative safety of the other side of the tree. No doubt, growing up hunting as a kid had helped him discern where the shot had come from, and he'd put the tree between himself and the shooter. It wasn't ideal, she'd have preferred there to be something more substantial like a boulder, or better yet, no shooter at all, but as it was, Jay was doing his best to take care of himself.

Swinging her eyes to where she'd last seen Brian and Lucy, the relief she'd felt quickly evaporated. Brian and Lucy both lay on the ground, Lucy flat on her stomach and Brian covering her the best he could with his own body. She scanned the scene, and though she could see her brother making small movements, as if he were checking Lucy for injuries, she couldn't tell if either of them had been hit.

She cursed the fact that she didn't have any weapons on her —she wasn't a huge fan of carrying a concealed weapon, but she should have known better than to not carry one on a night like this. As it was, Brian, Lucy, Jay, and she were now sitting ducks —no one was armed, and no one had any way to defend themselves. The one saving grace was that the sound of the shot would no doubt bring the agents back their way. She just hoped they weren't too late.

Taking a gamble that she wouldn't make too much noise, she rolled to her stomach and inched her way farther out of the opening of the grapevines to see if she could get a glimpse of the shooter. Scanning the area, she saw nothing to give his—or her

—position away; either they were out of sight, or had taken cover themselves.

Creeping forward another few feet, she caught a glimpse of movement off to her right, about midway up the hill and less than a hundred feet from where Jay stood. Frantically, her mind raced to think of what she could do to distract whoever it was because not only were they close to Jay—too close for her comfort—they also had an excellent vantage point to take another shot at Brian and Lucy.

She watched the figure emerge from the shadow of a tree and saw that it was a man. She admitted to herself that she had expected to see the second man who had traveled with Kevin Farlow—the one she'd yet to identify—and was surprised to see someone else. She didn't have a clear view of his features, but his build was markedly different, and there was no doubt the man who had caught sight of her brother was someone she hadn't yet encountered in their investigation.

With no thought other than to draw attention away from Brian and Lucy, she kicked out with her good leg, connected with what felt like a fairly sizable stone, and sent it careening from the hedge. The rustle and disturbance did exactly what she'd hoped, and the man dissolved back into the shadow. She didn't kid herself into thinking she'd done more than buy them a little time, but sometimes that was all it took. Her tactic had even caused the animals of the dark to still, and the night had fallen deafeningly silent.

As she watched the tree that concealed the shooter, she counted her breaths, willing them to remain steady. She counted to fifteen then to twenty. The man was patient, she had to give him that. But he couldn't be too patient; they all knew the shot he'd fired earlier would bring the other agents. And so he had two options, he could simply flee, or he could stay and try to finish the job he'd obviously set out to do and risk getting caught, or even killed.

Since she hadn't seen him leave the slim protection of the tree he'd moved behind, she had a sinking feeling he'd chosen option number two.

Which also meant he saw himself as a man with nothing left to lose—the worst kind of opponent.

Twenty-two breaths in, she saw him move. This time, she knew if she tried the same stunt, he wouldn't fall for it again. Her heart pounded as she watched him sight his weapon, he wore no night vision goggles so only had the dim light of the moon to guide him, but still, he raised his gun with a level of confidence that sent shivers down her spine. But brushing off the eeriness of their opponent, and desperate to do something to protect her brother, Naomi moved to stand up.

And three things happened at once.

The hedges around where she sat shook with her movements. The sound of something ricocheting off a tree up the hill echoed around her. And the report of a gunshot filled the air.

CHAPTER TWENTY-SIX

NAOMI DIDN'T DUCK BACK into her hideout this time. This time, she pulled herself to her knees and crawled to her brother. Dimly, she was aware of the sounds of people yelling, beams of light bouncing off of trees, and the silence that had previously filled the area evaporating into something more familiar. But her focus remained on her brother.

"Brian!" she called, frantic with worry. "Brian!" she called again as she reached him. "Are you all right? Are you hit? Is Lucy hit?" she battered him with questions.

"I'm fine, I'm..." his voice trailed off as he rose from his position atop Lucy and began to search her for wounds as she lay still beneath his touch.

"Naomi," Jay said, his voice startling her by its nearness. She looked up to find him beside her. Jay was here, Brian was sitting up, and no one was getting shot at anymore. She blinked at Jay then launched herself into his arms, well, as best she could with her injured ankle.

"It's okay, everything is going to be fine," he said, though he held her tight.

She jerked back and examined him.

"I'm fine," he said.

She ran her hands over his waist and torso then up over his shoulders. "You're fine? You're really fine? I'm so sorry I sent you up there..." she managed to say the words before Jay silenced her by pressing his lips to hers. It wasn't a passionate kiss, it was barely a kiss at all, it was just a contact, a contact between two people who needed to feel something familiar and good.

"I'm fine," Jay said on an exhale when he drew his lips from hers. "You're fine and so is your brother."

"But what about Lucy?" she asked, then she turned back to her brother. "What about Lucy, Brian? Is she okay?"

She took in the sight before her as she waited for her brother to answer. Brian knelt on the ground beside Lucy holding one of her hands, gently he brushed a lock of her long black hair from her pale face—her pale, battered face.

"Brian?" Naomi asked, suddenly afraid to hear his response.

Brian took a long breath that all but shuddered out of him. "She's going to be okay, I think. She wasn't shot, and I think most of her physical wounds are superficial, but I'm pretty sure they drugged her. I don't know with what, but as soon as we get her to a hospital we'll know more."

"Which is going to be within the next five minutes," Damian said, joining the four of them. Naomi looked up, and though the look on Damian's face held concern, she could tell the night had ended far better than he had anticipated.

"Good," was all Brian had to say, never once taking his attention from the woman on the ground before him.

"Damian?" Naomi said, asking without asking.

"I'll tell you more later, but now you can thank Jay for causing the distraction we needed to get to you all in time."

"It was Naomi's idea," Jay said.

"What was my idea?" she asked, completely confused as to

how she could have given Jay any ideas given they were forty feet away from each other.

"I saw you make that first distraction, I saw you kick the rock out from beneath the hedge. It made whoever that was,' he said with a jerk of his head toward the tree where the gunman had hidden, "pause and take stock. When I saw him step out again, I knew that even if you did the same thing it probably wouldn't have the same effect, so I picked up a good sized rock and winged it in his direction."

"You hit him?" Naomi asked, still struggling to unwind the events of the past few minutes.

Jay shook his head. "Although that would have been awesomely cliché for a pitcher like me, no I didn't hit him. I didn't even aim for him. Instead, I picked a larger, unmoving target, the live oak tree about ten yards behind him and to his right. I figured such a loud sound coming from the opposite direction would confuse him. The first sound, the one you made, might have been confused as an animal, but the sound of a rock hitting a tree most definitely wouldn't be."

"And the shot?" she asked.

"Mine," Agent Brown said, joining their five-some and gesturing as she spoke. Naomi turned to see three FBI EMTs approaching them. "I don't know who he is yet, but we'll find out." She stepped back as the two women and one man knelt and began taking Lucy's vitals.

Jay stood and brought Naomi up with him, swinging him into her arms. She wasn't heavy, but carrying someone was never as graceful as the books or movies made it out to be and so she wiggled to be let down.

"We need another stretcher," Jay said. One of the EMTs glanced at him and Naomi saw his eyes widen, probably in recognition. To his credit, he said nothing other than to order additional assistance even as his attention returned to Lucy.

"Don't even say it," Jay said as she opened her mouth to insist she could walk. Which was stupid because really, she couldn't. But unlike Lucy, Naomi was stable and hadn't been beaten or kidnapped or drugged or anything like that—relatively speaking she was in great shape.

Instead of arguing or conceding, she turned her attention to her brother. He stood still and strong, watching every move the EMTs made; watched as they monitored Lucy's vitals, watched as they ran their hands over her scalp looking for injuries, watched as they began hooking up an IV and drawing blood.

Finally, they loaded Lucy onto the backboard, which was far easier to maneuver than a stretcher, and Naomi watched them walk away—her brother walking alongside with his fingers wrapped around Lucy's unresponsive hand. As they made their way back toward the Wallace farm, she spied the second group of EMTs coming for her.

"Don't you dare give them a hard time, Naomi," Jay said, still holding her. Tightly.

"I wouldn't dream of doing such a thing. They are just doing their job after all." That last comment drew his attention—which had previously been focused on the coming aid—to her. One eyebrow winged up.

"I wouldn't," she insisted.

A hint of a smile teased at his lips. "Right," he said.

In the end, she didn't give anyone a hard time figuring that the sooner she answered every question—those posed by the EMTs as well as the FBI who seemed to have taken up permanent residence in the small room in the ER the hospital had assigned to her—the sooner she'd be out, and she and Jay could return to the quiet solitude of the guesthouse.

Especially now that she knew Lucy would be okay.

Brian's assessment had been accurate, her physical wounds were painful but superficial, and the drug they'd given her, some bizarre mix of sedative and Rohypnol usually seen in eastern China, was working its way out of her system. A full recovery was expected, although Naomi wasn't as optimistic as the twenty-something ER doctor that the "full recovery" would be as speedy as he anticipated. No one, not even the indomitable Lucy James, could walk away from a violent kidnapping without some lingering effects.

But still, she knew that whatever Lucy would go through in the coming weeks, months, or even years, she wouldn't be alone. She'd known it even before Jay had wheeled her to the door of Lucy's room and they'd caught the tail end of a private conversation between the two.

"This doesn't change things," Lucy had said.

"Like hell it doesn't," Brian had responded, the harshness of the words softened by the tenderness in his voice.

"Brian," Lucy said. She'd spoken on a long exhale, and Naomi hadn't been sure if that was because she had been exasperated or still exhausted from the drugs.

"Lucy," her brother had said. "I love you and you love me. We've each known our own feelings for a while, now we know each other's. That changes things."

"I don't," Lucy mumbled.

"Love me?" Brian countered "Try again, Luce."

For a moment, Lucy had said nothing, and then she'd let out a long breath. "You know this isn't over," she said instead of answering.

Brian sighed. "Yeah, I know it's not over. But we'll tackle that when you're ready."

"We can't do it alone. We'll need help," she said, her words starting to slur.

"And we'll have it," Brian said. "You know Naomi's in, and now we have Agent Brown and Damian, too."

"Will it be enough?" she asked.

"Will you just focus on healing?" Brian countered.

But no answer had come, Lucy had fallen back asleep. Naomi had watched, not feeling one ounce of remorse for playing the voyeur on her brother, as he took Lucy's hand in his and raised it to his lips. When he'd lain his head down on the side of Lucy's bed, Naomi had silently signaled Jay that it was time for them to leave. She hadn't a clue what her brother and Lucy had been alluding to, but she knew they'd figure it out together.

She'd call her brother later, they had a lot to talk about, and there were still so many unanswered questions, but for now, he needed this time with Lucy just as she needed time with Jay.

When the doors to the hospital swished open, and Jay wheeled her outside, she inhaled deeply, the fall air filling her lungs. Closing her eyes, she savored the sting of the cool air against her cheeks and the sounds of the bustling hospital behind her.

"You okay?" Jay asked.

She opened her eyes and looked up at him as he leaned over her. She smiled.

"I'm fine, but please, can you take me home?"

EPILOGUE

Naomi stood to the side of the room, her arms crossed as she leaned against the wall watching Jay. Out of sight from most of the others who occupied the space, she smiled just watching him. Manny sat to his right and then flanking the two seasoned Rebels were Aaron Huffman and Matt Ridder, two of the team's rookies. Light flashed as cameras went off, a couple of champagne bottles, a birthday cake, and a row of microphones lined the table in front of the four players. Three of their coaches and the owner stood behind.

Winning a second pennant in a row called for such a celebration.

Not to mention it was Aaron's twenty-third birthday. The baby of the team, the others loved to tease him. Hence the "It's a boy" baby cake.

Seeing Jay laughing with his teammates, completely at ease made her reflect on everything that had happened in the last year...

Following Lucy's rescue, she, Brian and Lucy had spearheaded a covert task force to identify and stop the people behind the entire operation—an operation that had far more

343

nefarious—and horrifying—goals than she'd ever imagined. The work had been arduous and dangerous and more than one secret had been revealed, including a few from her own brother. But in the end, Naomi hadn't much cared about his secrets. She'd almost lost her brother twice before they were finally able to stop the operation that would have left hundreds dead. That tended to put things in perspective.

Just less than three months after Smitty had been shot, they'd brought everything to closure—closure that included being able to tell the families of the victims just what had happened to their loved ones. The knowledge would never bring those they'd lost back, but at least Carl's and Smitty's families knew what heroes they'd been.

But that hadn't been the only thing that had happened in the last year.

One of the reporters at the press conference said something that made those on the dais laugh, drawing her attention back to the present. "So, what now?" one of the reporters shouted out. "You going for a third pennant next year?"

The four players looked at each other, each laughing and shaking their heads. "Man, what kind of question is that?" Manny shot back. "No team would be a team if they didn't enter the season thinking this would be the one they'd take the pennant. Of course the Rebels will be going for a third," he answered.

Naomi smiled at his wording—even in the heat of the moment, Manny had carefully worded his response.

"The Rebels may be going for their third, but I'll be cheering them on from the third-base line," Jay cut in. He smiled at his teammates. They'd been told ahead of time what Jay would announce during this press conference. Manny had known for a while, but Aaron and Matt had learned less than thirty minutes before stepping in front of the press. To give credit where credit was due, both of the young players wore an appropriate expression of sorrow at losing their teammate and pleasure for what he had planned next.

At Jay's comment, the room erupted. Reporters shouted questions, each drowning the next out. Flashes went off like strobes. Jay glanced her way and grinned. Never one to shy away from attention, he was going to enjoy his last night in the limelight.

They'd talked about this endlessly, this decision. But in the end, Naomi had done nothing but make clear that whatever decision he made, she'd support. And she had to trust that the decision he'd landed on was the one he felt good about standing behind.

Jay raised his hands to quiet the crowds and eventually they fell silent. Finally, he pointed to someone she couldn't see. "Amber, go ahead," he said.

"Are you telling us you're retiring, Jason?" the reporter asked.

Jay took a moment to answer, no doubt building the suspense. If he'd glanced her way, she would have rolled her eyes at him and pulled a face. As it was, all she could do was shake her head and smile to herself.

Finally, he nodded. "I am. I spoke to management a few weeks ago and we've come to an agreement. I'm going to spend the last few years of my contract working with the young pitchers in the Rebels' farm teams. The team took a chance on me a little over ten years ago, just like they took a chance on Aaron and Matt," he said, gesturing to his teammates who were nodding. "It's one of the practices I admire most about management and the ownership," he said gesturing to the men behind them. "They know the importance of investing in young talent, and their investment is why we're here today. I'm looking forward to being a part of that and mentoring and working with the young pitchers in the line-up."

"But why now?" one of the reporters shouted out.

Jay grinned. "Well, um, that's kind of an interesting question. So, my wife and I are expecting twins in about four and a half months, and my mother-in-law promises they will keep us well occupied. And since my wife, her daughter, is a twin, I tend to believe her. So that's 'why now.' I have other obligations I want to focus on in my life now."

Deafening silence filled the room at that pronouncement. Since their wedding nearly eight months ago, they'd managed to keep it quiet; only the people who'd attended the ceremony and a few select others knew. Knowing they couldn't keep it from the press forever, Jay had picked this time to drop the bomb. He knew the gossip rags wouldn't be at the press conference so they wouldn't get the scoop and drag it out. And he believed that by announcing it to the sports reporters, they'd take the scoop and run with it, but not in the way the entertainment reporters would. And judging by the sound of the silence, Jay hadn't been wrong in his tactic.

"You're married?" a reporter finally managed to ask. "When did that happen?"

Jay glanced her way and she smiled at him as one, or maybe both of the twins kicked and her hand came to rest on her belly.

"I was married last February. It was a small ceremony in the town her father's family is from in Italy. Just family and a few close friends," he said. Beside him, Manny, who'd been one of the guests with Liz and their children, couldn't wipe the smile from his face.

"February," one of the reporters repeated.

Jay nodded.

"We haven't seen her at any games though," another reporter said. Naomi almost laughed at the whine she heard in his voice.

Jay smiled his charming smile. "She's been to most home games. She works, has a life of her own, and comes when she can. When she does, she tends to come with her family, especially her twin brother, and they like to sit in the bleachers like they did as kids." He added that last part sounding a bit confused. It was a little bone of contention between the two. He didn't understand why she didn't want to sit closer or, better yet, in the family box. But growing up, she and Brian had spent many a game with their dad in the bleachers. They liked it in the bleachers with the smell of hotdogs and beer in the air and feel of popcorn crunching under their feet.

"But wait, February?" yet another reporter piped up. "Late February? Is that why you were a few days late for spring training?" he demanded.

Jay wasn't one to blush, but he did duck his head a bit and rub the back of his neck with his hand before he raised his eyes. "Uh, yeah," he said, a sheepish grin stealing over his expression. "We were on our honeymoon and kind of lost track of time."

That elicited a laugh from the crowd and with that, it seemed the topic had run its course and they were back to asking about stats and plays and what the players were thinking at every given moment of the seven games it took to win this pennant. Again, Jay stole a glance at her, silently pointing out how right he'd been to announce their marriage tonight, when it would be so overshadowed by the team's second World Series Win.

She sketched a mock curtsy, conceding his win then straightened and placed her hand on her stomach. It was almost as if the twins knew it was a big night for their father and they were having a little celebration of their own.

Twenty minutes later, the press conference ended and the players, the managers, and the owner filed off stage. Jay, being the last, stopped in front of her.

Wrapping his arms around her, all of "her" being a bit bigger than most women only four and a half months pregnant thanks to the twins and the real estate they were creating in her body.

"Nice job," she said, slipping her own arms around his neck. He leaned down to kiss her.

"I told you—"

"Yes, I know you told me tonight would be a good night to let the information slip, and yes, you were right," she said with a laugh, her lips still brushing his as she spoke.

"Say that again," he said, pressing his lips more firmly against her.

She smiled. "You were right," she dutifully repeated.

He grinned and suddenly dropped to his knees. "You hear that girls," he said to her stomach. "Your mom says I'm right." She ran her hand through his hair as he spoke. He kissed her stomach then looked up.

"I'll not begrudge you your victory tonight but just know that once they are released into this world, you may never be right again," she said with a smile.

He grinned back. "Or if I am I'll learn to keep my own counsel?"

Naomi laughed as he rose. "Perhaps," she said, wrapping her arms around his neck again. "Have I congratulated you again on your win?" she said pulling him down into a kiss.

"Yes, but I feel obliged to point out two things," he said.

"Oh yeah? What's that?" she said.

"First," he said kissing her again. "It wasn't me who won, it was a team effort."

"Of course," she said. "And second?"

"Second, you can congratulate me as often as you like," he said, sinking into a real kiss.

"I'm happy to do that," she said pulling away as the twins kicked between them. "But why don't you take me home and we can take it up from there."

"Best thing I've heard all day," he said backing her away from the press room and toward the exit.

"You mean other than that last strike call that finished that last game," she teased. "You know, the one that let you know you won game seven." She smiled up at him.

"Nope," he said, dropping another kiss on her lips. "Like I said, hearing you say, 'take me home' is the best thing I've heard all day."

THE END

Did you enjoy Naomi's and Jay's story?
Leave your review here!
Care to find out what happens next in Windsor?
Read on to find out in the first chapters of the second Windsor book
Into The Dawn

INTO THE DAWN

Stunned. Brian DeMarco doesn't know what to think when he's recalled home from a top secret government project—he only knows that it can't be good. What awaits him is something beyond his wildest nightmares. The woman he loves has been kidnapped, two friends have been killed, and there's a traitor in the FBI willing to sell secrets that will kill thousands.

Compelled. Lucy James knows exactly why she's been kidnapped; just as she knows that Brian is the only one she can trust to find her. Their personal history is murky at best, but there's no one who understands more what's at stake than her one time lover. He won't give up or back down—of that she has no doubt—but the price of reaching out to him might be more than she's ever been prepared to give.

Driven. Together, Lucy and Brian race to stop an attack that will kill countless Americans and scar the nation. They think they're ready. They think they've covered their bases. But nothing can prepare them for the final message the killer intends to deliver.

PART I

CHAPTER ONE

THE SUN WAS COMING UP, and as it did, Lucy shut down the computer her captors had provided. It was top of the line and completely out of place in the grungy, aging room in the back of the RV where they kept her.

It had been three days since she'd started to do as they'd asked and began hacking into the FBI systems that would ultimately lead them to information hidden deep in Smitty's network. Whoever these people were, they didn't speak enough for her to have any idea what their plan *was* for the information. But the fact that they even knew it existed told her this was something bigger than just a hack job. And there was no way she was going to let them anywhere near it.

She was fighting back—they just didn't know it.

She'd started her campaign to protect the information by convincing them she needed time if they wanted her to get into the system undetected. That they believed her spoke to their ignorance about who she was and her skills. But their ignorance was her bliss...it meant that so long as she kept to some schedule and showed some progress, she could more or less do whatever else she needed to do.

Like contact Brian.

Each night that she'd accessed Smitty's files, she'd left a few special character strings embedded in the code that she hoped Brian would find. It wasn't a foolproof plan, but he had systems set up to monitor the network and a penchant for leaving an "I was here" mark in the systems that he worked in—something only she and his sister, Naomi, knew about. The characters she'd left mimicked his style, and she hoped that he'd see the rogue lines of code soon and look into just how something that was his signature had made its way into the system when he hadn't put it there.

Hopefully.

Staring at the soothingly smooth black of the screen, Lucy linked her hands overhead and stretched her back. Her captors had more or less let her be since she'd acquiesced to their demands, and they'd even tolerated her habit of working through the night and sleeping during the day. She *was* a night owl by nature, but she'd taken it to the extremes, mostly to make it more uncomfortable for the people who guarded her. And more than once, she'd smiled as one snorted and jerked awake in the chair they had planted outside her open door.

Calling to the current guard, a man named Farlow and the only one whose name she knew, Lucy let him know she was coming out to use the restroom. He grunted in response then rose and stepped back when she appeared in the doorway. His pig-like eyes trailed over her body and lingered on the bruise on her cheek. A sick smile teased the corners of his mouth. She wondered if he got off on causing people pain, in general, or if it was just hurting women that did it for him.

In response to his perusal, she glared at him and was gratified when he shifted uncomfortably and took a step back. Her bright gray eyes often disconcerted people, and she wasn't afraid to take advantage of that.

Without a word, she slipped by him and stepped into the

bathroom, closing the door behind her. A few minutes later, she was back out and climbing into the ratty bed they'd assigned her in the same room where she worked. With minimal showers and only three changes of clothes, the room was starting to smell. But at least it wasn't summer. At least the cooler fall temperatures kept her room from turning too rank. Thank god for the small things, she told herself with a wry bent to the sound of her voice in her own head.

Turning away from the door, she did what she usually did before falling asleep. She thought of Brian.

She thought of his smile and the way he and his twin sister constantly teased each other. She thought about how there was always a little thrill that went through her body whenever she learned they'd be working together. She thought about the one other time he'd stepped into the fray and rescued her. And last, before she drifted off, she thought about that night two years ago; that one night when he'd offered her everything and she'd taken it.

Then run the next day.

CHAPTER TWO

BRIAN DEMARCO LEANED back in his chair and tossed a peanut up in the air. The thought that it was a choking hazard flitted through his mind as its trajectory turned back toward him. But then he caught it between his teeth, and he smiled as he chewed.

"You're going to choke," Allen Digby said.

The aging vinyl of Brian's chair creaked as he leaned forward. Barely visible over the top of a behemoth monitor, Allen sat about ten feet away.

"You're never going to crack it," Brian said.

A middle finger appeared over the monitor making him laugh. He, Allen, and four more of the world's top white-hat hackers were currently sequestered in the northern reaches of Newfoundland conducting secret tests on the technology infrastructures of just about every alphabet agency in the United States. It was a once-a-year gig organized by the National Security Agency, and this year he'd drawn the short straw, leaving his sister, Naomi, home to manage their business.

"I'm close," Allen said.

"Sure you are," Brian said. Allen was good, one of the best, but his specialty was how to move around once *inside* a system.

Brian specialized in detecting and preventing *access* to the systems, and he was confident that the program he'd put in place to protect access to a certain unremarkable server housed in a nameless location within the Pentagon could only successfully be hacked by one other person. Well, maybe two.

To be fair, it was possible that Allen might be able to get through—given enough time just about anything could be hacked. But "time" wasn't something hackers often had and actually, Brian's own system had already detected Allen's presence forty-two minutes ago. He'd kept silent though, partly because he wanted to see if Allen *could* break through, but mostly because he was waiting until Allen got *really* close and then Brian would shut him down just to piss him off. He had to entertain himself somehow up in the wilds of Newfoundland.

"DeMarco!" a voice barked through the intercom. Brian jerked back in his chair and Allen's head popped into view. His colleague raised an eyebrow in question, but Brian shook his head and shrugged in response. He had no idea why General Jakes was calling for him; the man tended to interact with Brian and the other hackers as little as possible.

"You have a phone call," Jakes followed up. "In my office, now!"

"He has an office?" Allen asked as Brian stood.

"Fuck if I know. I thought he just sat alone and played a one-man game of Battleship all day."

Allen snickered.

"Now, DeMarco. And I heard that," the intercom bellowed.

Allen's snicker turned into a laugh, and Brian grinned. Jakes might be an asshole but he had no authority over the project so Brian wasn't worried.

After a quick survey of the options, Brian headed for the one door that he hadn't ever been through. The room he and the other hackers worked in was about fifty feet by fifty feet with white walls and a white ceiling. It had three doors—one led to a bathroom and another to their sleeping quarters, but the third— located next to the one-way mirror—had never been opened.

As he approached, General Jakes flung it open. The solid metal slab flew at Brian, and he drew up short so as not to catch an edge in the face.

"It's nice to see you too, General." Brian grinned at the dour-faced man. Perhaps in his late fifties, General Jakes was not a man to whom time had been kind; wisps of hair were brushed over a sun-spotted head, the bags under his eyes sagged, and his mouth was improbably tiny. Although, oddly, the few strands of hair he had were still a rich, dark color.

"General Marsh is holding the line for you," Jakes said.

Brian's stomach plummeted and any frivolity he'd felt vanished. Getting a call from General Marsh—one of the three people who *had* authority over the project—was akin to that two-in-the-morning call. There was no reason other than a bad reason for her to need to speak to him.

He stepped around Jakes and hurried through another open door and into what he assumed to be Jakes's office. Seeing a phone lying on the desk, he snatched it up before Jakes even entered the room.

"General Marsh?" Brian asked, feeling his heart rate kick up. If something had happened to his family...

"Naomi called me moments ago," she said without preamble. "You need to come home. A helicopter is on its way already, and a plane will meet you in St. John."

"Is everything..." He couldn't even get the rest of that sentence out. If Naomi had been well enough to call the General, then at least she was okay. But the rest of his family was huge and every single one of those mother-fuckers meant the world to him.

"Everyone is fine," General Marsh said. "Or at least she didn't indicate otherwise. She simply said she needed you home. She's never asked anything of me before, and when she assured me it was necessary I agreed to pull you from the project. The helicopter will be landing in twenty minutes. Be ready," she added.

The fear that had gripped him and squeezed his chest since Jakes had first told him Marsh was on the line eased. But just a little bit. Even if everyone in his family was fine, it would take a lot for Naomi to ask to have him pulled from the project. In fact, short of a massive security breach that threatened national security, he couldn't think of a reason why she'd go to such an extreme. And if that had been the situation, Brian wouldn't be the only one being pulled out of Newfoundland.

"I'll be ready," he said, hanging up before Marsh responded.

A grim feeling settled over his shoulders as he made his way back through the main room and toward his private quarters. He hadn't a clue what his sister was into, but he couldn't get back to Boston fast enough to find out.

* * *

*T*hree hours later, Brian rode the elevator directly to the fourth floor of the building he owned with Naomi on Boston's Beacon Street. Naomi's apartment occupied the fourth and fifth floors, his the two floors below, and below that was a public office area and then a garden level apartment they let their employees use when needed.

The door slid open, and he stepped onto the thick carpet of her foyer. Within seconds, Naomi appeared from her bedroom, wearing a robe and exclaiming his name. Things couldn't be so bad if she were in a robe, right?

She hugged him then pulled him into her office. Caught in the whirlwind of her energy, he followed along until she pulled him to a stop in the middle of the room. Unbidden, his gaze traveled to the far wall.

Unlike him, Naomi preferred big open spaces, and she'd turned almost the entire front of this floor into one big work area. Her desk sat behind them, but the wall that now drew his attention—a wall about thirty feet long and fifteen feet high—was lined with floor-to-ceiling computer screens.

His attention jumped from one to the other as he took in the images projecting back at him; some were static but others contained scrolling code.

"Naomi?" he asked, studying what she clearly wanted him to.

"Just look," she said.

Incongruously she also called out "Jay?" but he ignored that and focused his attention on two of the static screens as they contained a few highlighted lines of code. He frowned, that looked like his signature…but it couldn't be.

"Naomi?" a voice came from the door.

Startled by the fact that his sister hadn't been alone, Brian jerked his attention to her then to the man who was walking into the room. Naomi smiled and held out a hand. He took it in his as he came within reach.

"Brian I want you to meet Jay. Jay this is my brother, Brian," she said.

Brian drew back as he recognized him. Then his eyes went from the man to his smiling sister then back again. "Jay?" His brow raised.

"Jay Evans," he said, holding out his free hand. With a slight hesitation, Brian took the offered hand.

"It's nice to meet you. Jay."

"I need to go get dressed. I'll be right back," Naomi said, as she released Jay's hand and bustled out of the room.

The two men stared awkwardly at each other.

"She's glad you're back," Jay said, with a nod toward the bedroom.

Brian's brow went up. "Been seeing my sister long, *Jay*?"

Jay cleared his throat. "We met at your cousin's pub while I was watching game seven of the American League championships."

At that, a smile tugged at Brian's lips, the first since he'd received the call from General Marsh. "She has no idea who you are, does she?"

Jay tried to hide his grimace as he shook his head. "She thinks I'm just a businessman who's been negotiating a deal with his team over the past week."

Brian snorted then turned his attention back to the screen. "I'm gonna get so much mileage out of this," he muttered.

Before Jay could say anything more, a loud, strangled curse came from Naomi. Brian glanced at Jay, then both men strode toward her room. Naomi emerged into the foyer dressed in yoga pants and sweater. She paused to pull on a slipper and started hopping around as she tugged at it.

"Problem, Nano?" Brian asked using his nickname for her.

Jay walked over and grabbed her outstretched arm to steady her. She flashed him a grateful smile then turned and made a face at Brian.

"Tonight is that charity event for the children's hospital that I promised Mom I'd go to. I'd completely forgot," she said.

Brian laughed, he couldn't help it. Their mother was always dragging them to one society event or another. They usually tried to tag team them and this particular event had been a trade-off—he'd go to Newfoundland for the hacker project and she'd go to the gala. Despite his lack of enthusiasm about the government contract, he still believed he'd gotten the better end of the deal.

"I swear to god, Brian, I will call Mom and tell her you're home if you don't shut up," she said, now standing with two feet firmly planted on the ground.

"You wouldn't," he said.

Naomi shot him a sickly smile. "I understand Millie Rossiter will be there. Her divorce was final last month."

Brian wasn't too proud to admit that a little sweat might have broken out on his brow at Naomi's words. "I'm going to…

go, to, uh, get back to things." He pointed to the monitors before he turned his back on the couple.

He was aware of a muted conversation going on between the two, but his attention focused on the images before him—Naomi would tell him what had raised such an alarm that she'd called him home, but while she finished talking to Jay, he tried to puzzle it out himself.

Two of the monitors were clearly scanning traffic into and out of certain FBI servers—he recognized the numeric names of both pieces of hardware. But the still images…those were out of context and harder to identify. Something beeped and one of the scrolling screens froze in place, but he hadn't a clue what had triggered the sound.

Hearing a rustle behind him, he turned to find Naomi leaning over one of her keyboards, Jay nowhere in sight. Her gaze went to the now-frozen screen and two lines formed between her brows in an expression that was all too familiar.

"Naomi—"

"There," she said, cutting him off and pointing to the screen. "Third line, eight characters in."

He walked closer to the image and followed her direction. Not believing what he was seeing, he re-read the line of code. Shocked, he stumbled back then studied all the screen shots she had displayed, again. Sure enough, he saw the pattern now.

"Naomi." His voice sounded distant even to himself. "You are the only person who knows my signature and the pattern behind it. How is it getting into the code flowing into and out of the FBI servers? I'm here, you're here, and neither of us did that," he said, pointing the code that had rightfully triggered his sister's concern.

Naomi said nothing and he turned to find her contemplating the wall of images. But he didn't think it was the code that she focused on.

"Naomi?"

She stared at him, saying nothing.

"What the hell is going on?" he asked.

Her gaze flitted to the screen then back again. "There's one more person who knows you well enough to know your signature and your pattern, and it appears she's trying to hack her way into the FBI."

At Naomi's words, his brain froze, just like the monitor she now studied had done moments ago.

"It's not possible. She wouldn't do anything like this," he said, waving to the wall behind him. Because there *was* one other person who knew him that well; he'd never shared his signature with her or the pattern behind it, but with her, he wouldn't have had to.

Sympathy flashed crossed her face. "I think it is possible, and that's the problem, Brian. I agree she wouldn't be doing something like this on her own, but Lucy James is missing. No one's seen her for weeks, and not only that, but Carl Rogers is dead and—" Naomi's voice broke, but she cleared her throat and continued. "So is Smitty."

CHAPTER THREE

BRIAN STARED AT HIS SISTER, who was blinking furiously, trying not to let her tears fall. Feeling a bit helpless and way out of the loop, he walked to the corner of the room and sank into one of the two upholstered chairs. Part of the deal of the Newfoundland project had been complete isolation; it had never seemed like such a big thing to give up before. But now...now that the hollow shock of loss—and fear—echoed through his body, he made a promise to himself to never be out of reach from his sister again.

Or Lucy.

Naomi pressed her palms to her eyes, wiping them dry, then joined him.

"Tell me," he managed to say. He could barely breathe at the thought of Lucy in the hands of killers. He would not contemplate a world where she was not in it.

"Naomi?" he demanded, when she didn't immediately answer.

Thankfully, she cleared her throat and began talking. "A little less than two weeks ago, I got home from DC to find a letter from Smitty asking me to meet him at The Swan," she said, referring to their cousin Kate's pub in Salem, just north of Boston. "I showed up and he wasn't there."

"That's when you met Jay?"

She nodded but didn't raise her eyes. "We were leaving the bar when I noticed what I thought could be Smitty's car. It was and he was inside." A hand came up as she wiped a tear. "He, uh, he'd been shot several hours before I even arrived."

"Jesus, Naomi, do they know why?"

She bobbed her head. "I'm not sure *they* do," she said, referring to the authorities. "But I think I do. He left me a USB drive that he'd stuck under the bar top much earlier in the day. It contained two security scans of his systems."

"What does this have to do with Lucy?" Brian asked, interrupting. He should let Naomi tell him the entire story in her way but as the reality of Smitty being murdered sank in, his anxiety ratcheted up.

Naomi's eyes searched his but then she nodded. "The files Smitty left me led me to a man named Corbin Beekman, an IT guy for the FBI. His group manages the day-to-day operations of Smitty's department. Only by the time I tracked him down, Beekman hadn't been at work for a while. Damian and I were already in DC," she said, referring to their mutual friend who was an FBI agent. "So we went to find him. He's dead," she said flatly. "We thought he might be when we realized no one had heard from him since the day he ran a scan on Smitty's systems. I wish he weren't, but I think he had something to do with Smitty's death so my sympathy for him is a bit short."

"Lucy," Brian said. "I need to know about Lucy." Heat crept up his neck as adrenaline began to course through his body.

"When they pulled Beekman's body from the reservoir they also found Carl Rogers's body. *That* was a shock." She paused and he was just about to prompt her again when she spoke. "As to Lucy and what made me call you home, well, it wasn't until earlier today that I think I finally understood the scope of what we're up against."

"The down and dirty, Naomi. I know Smitty and Carl's deaths are important and a great loss and I'm not minimizing that, *but what is going on?*"

She pursed her lips at him but then rose, walked to her desk, and hit a few buttons on her computer. Instantly, the images of all the code disappeared and in their place was a single image of a network infrastructure. He recognized it as the FBI infrastructure —the entire infrastructure—with four nodules lit up.

"That's what's going on, Brian. I believe that several weeks ago, someone coerced Carl Rogers to test the security of the FBI offices in Miami, New York, and Chicago before trying DC." She pointed to each node as she spoke. "We were called in to help in DC, remember that?"

He hadn't known about the other three offices, but he did remember the quick patch job they'd done in DC at the request of the field office there before he'd left for Newfoundland. Both he and Naomi thought the FBI should have funded a more thorough investigation, but they'd been overruled.

He nodded in response to her question, and she continued. "In addition to the security changes we made to the division in general, I added a few extra things to Smitty's system, because, well, you know," she said with a small shrug. And he did. In addition to all the expected case files Smitty had, he was also the keeper of certain government secrets—secrets that gave the government leverage outside of legal channels when needed.

Naomi cleared her throat. "And I think when I did that, I put a big neon sign up telling whoever is behind this, that Smitty's system had information worth extra protection. And so it was only then that they went after Smitty."

"And they killed Carl once they had a name? Once they knew it was Smitty that they needed to target?"

Naomi nodded then she approached the screen with the highlighted code.

"And now, now I think they have Lucy, Brian," she said quietly. "You and I both know the kind of information Smitty has—had—access to and they'd need someone like Lucy—or you or me—to get it. But Lucy would be the best option." Naomi was right about that. Like Allen, whom he'd left behind in Newfoundland, Lucy's specialty was moving around within stored data; Brian couldn't think of a single person in their world who wouldn't consider her the best of the best. That would have put a big target on her back for a project like the one Naomi was describing.

"And so you think they've taken Lucy and those lines of codes she's dropping are what? Hints? Clues?"

Naomi nodded. "I think she's warning us. I think she's trying to talk to you." Naomi hesitated, then her gaze met his. "And I think she's stalling. And I'm worried that if we don't find her fast, she won't be able to stall any longer."

"And once they have what they want, they'll kill her," Brian said, forcing the words from his mouth.

"Three people are already dead, Brian. We need to find her, and you're the best person to do it."

* * *

Three hours later and two floors down from his sister's, Brian sat in his own office staring at a bank of monitors. Unlike Naomi, he tended to prefer more traditional stylings, and his office, with its rich oak book shelves, coffered ceiling, and Aubusson carpet, reflected that. Of course, the aesthetic, though soothing for him, was somewhat marred by the six computer screens mounted at different depths on the wall across from his large mahogany desk.

Culling through the files Naomi had shared with him, it was

crystal clear now why she'd called him back. Losing Smitty was one thing if it had just been him, his death would likely have been written off as a casualty of the ongoing information wars —an extreme casualty, true, but nothing to suggest what Naomi, and now he, thought was going on.

No one, not even the most desperate man or woman, would kill three people and kidnap another for just the information most people thought resided in Smitty's network. No, whoever was behind all this definitely knew there was more to Smitty than meets the eye. The problem was, how much did they know? He and Naomi had buried certain files in Smitty's network—information that could easily be sold to the highest bidder for a pretty penny. But there was another layer of information not even Naomi knew about. Lucy did though. Because she'd helped him bury it.

His chest tightened at the thought of her, but he forced his attention back to the monitors. Lucy was definitely trying to tell him something, now he just had to figure out how to tell her he was listening. It sounded easier said than done, but leaving a message inside a system as closely monitored as the one Lucy was in would be tricky. Not to mention, he had no idea how sophisticated the people who had Lucy were. Given that they'd resorted to kidnapping her for her talents, obviously they weren't as smart as she. But still, he didn't want to do anything that might make them suspicious—anything that might put her at risk.

God knew she'd had enough of that in her life already. He'd rather die than be the one who caused her more pain.

Shoving away from his chair, he rose and stalked to the window. Opening the blinds, he stared out, watching the light rain gather on the window and the drops collect and fall, leaving streaks of water down the pane.

He wasn't a violent man by nature, but he couldn't deny the burning urge coursing through him to hit something, to destroy something, to rage and howl. At his side, he clenched his hand into a fist, his short nails digging into his palm.

The pain and the anger were nothing but scapegoats for his own helplessness. And the best way to combat these feelings was to focus on the problem at hand and figure out a way to contact Lucy, figure out a way to tell the woman he loved, had loved for years, that he was listening. But even knowing all this, he'd never found it so hard to sit down in front of his computer.

CHAPTER FOUR

Having been summoned for a final check-in, Brian waited in the foyer of Naomi's apartment debating whether to encourage her to give their parents an excuse and duck out of the night's event. He needed more time to catch up on everything he'd learned, but even so, he knew she was struggling with leaving him on his own tonight.

A wave of guilt washed over him as he waited. Smitty's death had shocked him, as had everything Naomi had told him, and he wished he'd been here with her from the start. She'd had Damian and Jay, of course. But she hadn't had him, her own brother.

She did now, though. And so did Lucy. So while Naomi spent the evening dancing and making nice, he had every intention of finding Lucy and getting to the bottom of whatever the hell was going on.

At the thought of Lucy, the now familiar pitch in his stomach kicked in again. He didn't doubt her ability to take care of herself, but she'd experienced enough in her life that she didn't need whatever shit was happening to her now. True to

Lucy form, she was fighting back, sending him messages and clues, but the fact that she had to fight at all, infuriated him.

And terrified him. In his mind, he'd always had the time to convince her to give him a shot. He's always had the time to let her come to the same conclusion he'd come to years ago about them being better together than apart. But the last few hours had been a sucker punch to the gut—a stark reminder that they all lived on borrowed time and that he and Lucy might never have their chance.

The elevator door slid open, pulling him from his thoughts. Jay stepped into the foyer just as Naomi walked out of her bedroom wearing a dress the same color as their eyes. Jay's attention darted to him then traveled like a pilgrim to Naomi. The man's gaze drank in Naomi's appearance, her beauty to be sure, but a little something relaxed in Brian's chest when Jay only really smiled when his gaze met Naomi's and she smiled back.

"My shoes!" she said suddenly, then spun and turned back toward her room.

Jay cast him an amused smile—only Naomi could forget her shoes—but Brian fell serious.

"She needs to know who you are. Before you walk into the event tonight," he said.

Jay's smile faltered. "I know."

"I don't think you do," Brian countered. "We are part of a prominent family but the work we do is private," he said. "It's vital that we keep a low profile. We *can't* have people digging into our lives any more than what we give them in the public without jeopardizing the work we do. We don't *need* to work, but we are good at it and what we do is important. She needs to know who you are in order to protect who she is." He held Jay's gaze and the corners of the man's mouth tightened and his jaw clenched. Brian's speech had probably irritated him, but if his sister was truly interested in the man standing before him, which she appeared to be, then Jay wasn't a thoughtless man.

After a moment, Jay gave a curt nod just as Naomi returned to join them. "Ready?" she said, pulling a black wrap around her shoulders.

Jay held out his hand and his sister slipped hers into it as if they'd been doing this for years. Neither of the two people in front of him seemed to notice the easy familiarity. On one hand, he was glad of it—Naomi had had a number of relationships throughout the years but none appeared as *easy* as this one. On the other hand, who Jay was and what he did would throw a wrench in the game—not an insurmountable wrench, but a wrench nonetheless.

Brian stepped forward and kissed his sister on the cheek, surprising her into a smile.

"Have fun, kids," he said.

She rolled her eyes at him as Jay called the elevator. "It's your turn next year. And I'm only going for a few hours to make Mom happy. When I get back, we'll need to figure out what to do about..." She was still gesturing toward her office when Jay ushered her into the elevator.

"I'll be here," he said as the elevator doors closed behind the couple.

He wasn't about to call a justice of the peace, but, for the first time in his life, he contemplated the fact that it wouldn't always be just the two of them.

* * *

*L*ucy James snuck a glance over her shoulder at the man seated in the hallway outside her door. He was one of the men who'd originally kidnapped her, but he was also the one whose patterns she hadn't figured out yet. They all had them, though—the shift that came with the sigh, the glance at the time then the check of their gun. For all except her current guard, Lucy could even predict when they'd call for backup so they could have a bathroom break.

Pushing aside the questions of her current guard, she let her gaze skate around the room. She'd been able to suppress it so far, but she had a thing about small spaces. Having been packed in a shipping container with sixty other undocumented immigrants making their way from China to the United States when she was four would do that to a person. She didn't know how many people had died on that trip but the stench of human sweat and suffering (and excrement) was not one she'd ever forget.

She closed her eyes and took a deep breath through her mouth, counting to three on the exhale and remembering the day they'd finally arrived in Los Angeles. When the doors had been thrown open and waves of the fresh night air flowed in, a joy so intense had washed over her, as though anything was possible now that she could see the sky again.

Slamming the mental door on those long dormant memories, Lucy turned her attention back to the computer screen in front of her. She couldn't put her captors off much longer. Being one of the best white hat hackers out there sucked sometimes. They may not know the extent of her talents, but her reputation had definitely preceded her. It was something she was usually proud of, but since that was also what had landed her here in the first place, she was rethinking Brian's more under-the-radar approach.

Brian.

With another quick glance over her shoulder, Lucy found the man staring at the wall opposite from where he sat. She'd have to take a chance that he either couldn't see what she was doing or, if he could, he wouldn't understand it.

With a couple of quick keystrokes, she pulled open a file from the database she was in and scanned the contents. Her captors had told her to pull a file just to be sure she could do it without raising any alarms. She didn't intend to countermand that order; she just wanted to find the right file—one that if Brian noticed, would give him some clue as to where she was.

He hadn't responded to any of her prior tries though, and so, in truth, she had no idea if he was even aware that she'd been kidnapped. But she had to put her faith in something. And experience had taught her that he had always been there for her, even when she hadn't wanted him to be.

"Farlow," the man at the door said. Lucy let out a small sigh of relief. Farlow was more brawn than brain, and she'd much rather have him standing over her shoulder than any of the others.

The RV rocked as Farlow made his way from the front to the back of the vehicle. Her previous guard, a man who reminded her a little of Rod Serling from the Twilight Zone, rose from his seat and stepped into the room. Quickly, she closed the file—it was perfect for what she needed, but she wanted to delay officially pulling it from the system to give Brian more time to find her. Ideally, she'd wait until she had his attention. Although if he didn't reach out to her in the next day or two, that might not be an option.

The man took another step closer to her and Lucy tensed as she felt his focus on her monitor. To distract him, she typed a line of code and in response, the screen flashed and brought up a new file. If he had any idea what she was doing, he would have seen that she'd just made one more step toward the database they'd directed her to access. Not a big step, no she'd orchestrated just small, convoluted steps, but a step nonetheless.

A little bit of tension left her shoulders when he moved away. The chair in the hallway creaked as Farlow took a seat. She didn't turn around but kept her eyes focused on the screen. Although her mind once again drifted to Brian.

It had been a week since she'd dropped her first clue to him.

She hadn't expected him to come charging in the door the next day, but she had hoped she'd at least hear from him, that she'd at least have some indication that he'd noticed her presence in the system. And *that* was the disconcerting thought—if Brian hadn't even noticed she was trying to talk to him, she'd have to start all over with someone else, probably his sister, Naomi. And while she trusted Naomi, only Brian knew what was truly at stake.

She was scrolling down her screen, trying to appear busy and mulling over whether or not to cover her bases and figure out how to reach out to Naomi when suddenly a single symbol showed up in a line of code.

Lucy wasn't one for weeping, but tears pricked her eyes and damn if she didn't sniffle a little bit.

She didn't know what had taken him so long, but Brian had her back now.

* * *

A short-lived thrill pierced Brian when a single letter response popped up in a string of code, before it disappeared just as quickly. He was probably imagining things but it was as if he could feel Lucy's relief in just that one little letter.

Jesus he wanted to find her. And hold her. And keep her with him. She didn't know it yet, but once he found her—and he would find her—his days of waiting patiently for her to work through her shit and realize everything they could be together were over. Granted, she had a lot a shit to work through, he'd give her that. But she was a smart woman, and he intended to make the work worth her while.

His mind drifted to the many ways he would make it worth her while, but his screen filled with new code and drew his attention back to the task at hand. Now that he had a trail to follow, every bit of electronic data he captured would help him find her. But even then, he wasn't putting all his eggs in that basket.

Grabbing his phone, he dialed a familiar number.

"Brian," Damian Rodriguez answered after the first ring.

"You and my sister had quite a little adventure while I was gone," Brian commented.

"Much as I wish it weren't so," Damian acknowledged.

Brian hesitated.

"You need my help," Damian said, anticipating what Brian had been about to say.

A flash of guilt lanced through Brian. Damian was both a friend and an FBI agent, and though he never hesitated to travel the thin line that separated the two, Brian hated to put him in that position. But he didn't hate it enough to not ask, not when Lucy's safety was at risk.

"I do. We do," he said. "Because of the way the attacks were orchestrated, we think someone on the inside is involved, someone who knows people like Smitty exist, and well..."

"I'm your go-to guy," Damian finished.

"You're one of the few we know we can trust," Brian clarified. It was a little bit of ego stroking, but both men knew the statement was one hundred percent true. Damian had proven himself to the tight-knit DeMarco clan on more than one occasion.

"What do you need?" Damian asked, getting to the heart of the matter.

"I need to focus on communicating with Lucy so that we can find her. I need someone to track Lucy's movements before she disappeared. I also need someone to dig into the FBI and watch our backs."

Damian chuckled. "Thought that might turn out to be the case. I just landed in Boston. It's a good thing I have so many vacation days stored up."

Brian's lips quirked into a smile but before he could even offer his thanks, Damian ended the call.

He started to type a note to his sister letting her know about Damian's involvement but paused when his computer chirped. He looked at the code streaming on one of his screens and the thrill of the hunt coursed through him. Lucy had just pulled a file from Smitty's database. It was possible she had pulled it at the specific direction of the people holding her, but when she followed up with another single letter embedded in the code that scrolled on his screen, he knew she'd pulled it for him—to give him a clue.

Again, his heart stuttered. She'd been trying to contact him for at least seven days. Of all the people she could have reached out to, she'd put her faith in him—and continued to keep it there even when she'd had no idea if he'd ever respond.

Not wanting her to ever feel abandoned by him, to feel like she might have misplaced her faith, he quickly typed in a similar response to let her know he'd received the message. Then switching to another computer, he carefully extracted the same file, covering his tracks so that no one would notice what he'd done.

Just over twenty minutes later, he thought he understood what Lucy was telling him but he really wanted a second, and maybe even third, set of eyes on the information.

Picking up his phone, he texted Naomi. "I have a lead. I know you can't rush out, but as soon as you can, do. I've called in reinforcements."

"What reinforcements?" she typed back fifteen minutes later, just as Damian buzzed to be let in.

"Can't text, working on something, just come when you can," he wrote.

An hour and a half later, Brian was at his desk, triangulating some data, when Naomi and Jay walked into his apartment.

Damian opened the guest room door and greeted the couple in the foyer.

"Nano!" he exclaimed with over the top enthusiasm.

"Ugh, no one calls me that but Brian," she responded. Brian glanced up as she strode into his office, Damian and Jay traveling in her wake.

"I know, that's why I did it of course. Are you going to introduce me?" Damian asked. Not surprising, her attention had immediately gone to the myriad screens Brian had up and running. Having monitors placed at different heights and depths helped him track information better, but it always disorientated Naomi a bit at first.

"Jay, this is Damian, Damian, Jay," she said waving a hand between the two men as her eyes scanned a screen.

"Jay?" Damian repeated. "You've got to be fucking kidding me, Naomi."

That got her attention. She straightened and looked at the agent. "What?"

"You're dating Jason Greene, and you didn't bother to tell me?"

Brian almost laughed at the expression on her face; she was clearly confused as to why Damian was taking issue. Although he was happy that Jay had taken his advice and told her who he was.

"Oh, wait, don't even tell me," Damian continued as he turned to Jay. "She didn't even know who you were when you met, did she?"

Jay glanced at Naomi then shook his head. She flashed Jay an apologetic smile but still appeared unclear what the issue was. Damian pulled out his phone, tapped in a few keys and brought up a picture.

"Who is this, Naomi?" he asked, holding the phone out for her to see. She frowned at him but then looked at the picture on the device.

"That's Grace Hopper," she said then turned back to the data she'd been studying. Damian showed Jay the picture. Jay shook his head, obviously not recognizing the woman.

"She recognizes someone who's been dead for more than twenty-five years and a computer scientist at that, but not one of the greatest pitchers of modern times." Damian shook his head in dismay. "That's one hell of a Series you and Rebs just won," Damian said, referring to the shut-out Series win the New England Rebels had just cinched the day before.

"Thanks, team effort," Jay said. His words were humble, but pride gleamed in his eye. Brian couldn't blame the man—from what little he'd gleaned in his few hours home, it had been a hell of a Series, in no small part thanks to some epic pitching on Jay's behalf.

"Are you sure you want to date her?" Damian said, casting Jay a dubious look. "There's something not quite right with both of them." He waved between Brian and Naomi. Brian considered objecting, but then Naomi took a step closer to one of the screens and his attention went back to her.

"Then again," Damian continued. "Between your athletic prowess and Naomi's super genius, if you guys ever have kids they'll probably turn out to be some sort of mutant super hero species."

"Is there a reason you're here, Damian?" Naomi interjected, flicking a glance at Damian.

"I called him," Brian said. "We need someone on the inside and, well, he's our go-to guy."

Damian gave Naomi and Jay a toothy smile. "Lucky me."

Naomi considered Damian, then she turned back to the monitors. "Talk to me," she said to Brian as she gestured for Jay to have a seat in one of the upholstered chairs scattered around the room.

"What do you think of that?" Brian asked, pointing to several highlighted characters.

Naomi leaned closer. "She's already extracted a file," she said, zeroing in on one of his screens.

"She has," Brian said, sending the information from the file in question up onto another screen. Naomi approached the new image. Her eyes scanned the snippets he'd isolated, then she moved to the screen beside it. "Although it's one from the department, not one of Smitty's special ones," he added.

"Uh, Brian, we have a civilian in here," Damian reminded them all.

Brian looked at Naomi then to Jay, who was lounging in a chair, an ankle resting on his knee.

"I can leave," Jay offered.

"Or you can understand that if a word of this gets out we can make your bank accounts disappear," Brian countered.

"Brian!" Naomi admonished.

"Fair enough," Jay said. Brian eyed the man then switched his attention to Damian, who wasn't *quite* scowling. He also didn't appear surprised, and after a beat just lifted his eyes and shook his head.

"So the file?" Naomi said.

"Low level embezzler. Embezzled a couple of million from a small insurance company in the aftermath of Katrina," Brian said.

"Was he caught?"

Brian nodded. "He's serving eight years in prison."

"That's an odd file to pull given what else she should be able to access," she said.

"Why's that?" Jay asked.

"The file she copied sits with files of people who have embezzled tens and even hundreds of millions of dollars, most of which are ongoing investigations," Naomi said then pursed her lips. "Why go for such a small, closed case?"

"My guess is that whoever has Lucy told her to pull a test file to see if she could do it without raising any alarms." Brian said.

"And I think she pulled this specific file for *that* reason," he said, pointing to a screen on the opposite side of the room.

"Madison, Athens, Union Point, and Stephens," Naomi said, reading off the information.

"Those are all towns in Georgia. If you were to draw lines between them they form a sort of square," Jay said, drawing the shape in the air with his finger.

"That's right, you're from Georgia, aren't you?" Damian asked.

Jay nodded. "Born and raised not far from that area."

"How did you get from here to here?" Naomi asked Brian, pointing first to the file then to the list of locations.

"Anton Petrov, the man who owned the business that was embezzled from, has a home base in Athens, Greece. The man who embezzled from him is named Harold Madison. The woman who ran the operations was named Natalie Stephens, and check out the name of the company."

"Union Insurance," Naomi read it off. "If this is a clue as to where Lucy is being kept, how in the hell did she find a single file with enough coincidences to give us a general location?"

Brian grinned. "I'm not sure she did. I pulled up the backup file from three weeks ago and at that time, the woman running it was named Natalia Stepov. The other three are still accurate."

"Okay, so do we assume she's in that area? And if so, how do we find her?" Damian asked.

"And I hate to interrupt, but are you sure she was even taken?" Jay piped in.

Brian let out a long exhale. "She's definitely been taken, but sorting out how and by whom is one of the reasons I called Damian in. I need to focus on the computer stuff. She's talking to me, and I need to figure out how to keep listening without raising any flags. Damian has started tracking everything else, like her last known movements, her credit cards, phone usage, those sorts of the things," he said.

"All we know right now is that she returned from her walkabout in New Zealand, flew through Honolulu, and then disappeared," Damian said, sharing with Naomi and Jay what little he'd already tracked down.

"Her mother said she received a call from her saying she'd decided to hike some of the Appalachian Trail," Naomi said.

"There's been no activity on her phone since she landed in Hawaii, but I'll run a backward trace on her mom's phone and see if we can find anything there," Damian said.

Silence reigned for a long moment then Naomi spoke. "So what now?"

Damian eyed the twins then slowly grinned. "Now we go to Georgia to find Lucy," he said.

"What? That's a needle in a haystack!" Naomi said.

"No," Brian said. Naomi started to flash Damian a smug look, but he cut her off with his next words.

"Naomi goes to Georgia to find Lucy," he said. "Everyone else stays here."

CHAPTER FIVE

"No!" both Damian and Jay spoke at the same time. Brian had expected the protest but the strength of it seemed to startle Naomi.

Her eyes narrowed on them. "And just why shouldn't I go to Georgia?"

"Because it's dangerous. Jesus, they've already killed three people, Naomi," Jay said, straightening in his chair.

"That and I'm the only actual field agent here," Damian said.

"But I need you to be running the investigation into Lucy's disappearance and *I* need to stay focused on this," Brian said, waving toward his computers. "Which just leaves Naomi."

"Or any other agent I bring in," Damian snapped back.

"With someone on the inside do you really think that's a good idea, Damian?" Brian said. "Even if you do, I don't. Given the way they tested the Miami, New York, and Chicago office before hitting gold with the DC office, the way they involved Corbin Beekman, and the speed with which they picked up Lucy, you *know* it's someone higher up on the food chain.

"The FBI is officially investigating the deaths of Smitty, Carl Rogers, and Beekman," he continued. "And it's probably best to let whoever is behind this think that that investigation is the extent of what is going on. If you bring in someone else to help us, there's a high probability that the insider will know there's a second investigation going on. With three people already dead, I don't want to corner the bear and risk Lucy. I know none of you do either," he added, fixing his attention on Damian, challenging the agent to contradict him.

Damian jammed his hands on his hips and glared at the floor. Naomi stood unmoving in the middle of the room, though she did risk a glance at Jay, who was glowering at the room in general. The tension crept up as the seconds ticked by, finally Jay spoke.

"If you're going, I'm going."

Naomi's head drew back. "You can't just take off," she said. "You just won the World Series. You have press conferences and a parade or something, don't you?"

He smiled. "I do have a parade. It's tomorrow by the way."

She gave him a rueful smile then mumbled something about watching it on TV, but he cut her off. "Press conferences are all morning, the parade starts at two. It will be over by three-thirty and then there is a reception. We can be out of here by six. I'll charter a flight so we don't have to fly separately in order to not be seen together," he said, impressing Brian with his quick resolution.

"I have a cousin who can fly us down," Naomi said. "I'm not concerned about getting down to Georgia, but how would we move around without calling too much attention to ourselves?" Naomi asked.

"We'll hide in plain sight," Jay said "A couple of high schools in the area have reached out to me a few times asking if I would come down and give some clinics to their young players. I've never had the time before, but now is as good as any. Damian can travel with us. If needed, we'll tell everyone you two are my support staff, and no one will bat an eye. That is, of course, if you can run the investigation stuff Brian needs you to handle from the road?" Jay said, turning to Damian. The three of them remained silent, waiting for the agent to reply.

Damian seemed to be pondering the idea, but even if he hadn't taken the time, Brian knew he was on board—he'd be able to continue focusing on his piece of the investigation but still be in Georgia if needed.

After a few moments, Damian met everyone's eyes, one by one. Then he nodded.

"We'll leave tomorrow," he said.

* * *

*B*rian embraced his frustration. It was either that or give into the fear that threatened to claw its way out of his chest and consume him. Lucy James was an enigma in his life. Over the years they'd known each other, they seemed to go from warily circling each other, to being able to finish each other's sentences, to being as close as two people could be, and then back again.

He couldn't explain what it was between them—wasn't sure he needed to. But there was no hiding from the fact that her kidnapping had ripped a hole in his heart.

Rubbing his chest, he let his eyes drift to the screens in his office. He'd seen nothing from her since that last little acknowledgement letting him know she recognized that he'd seen the file she'd pulled. By nature Lucy was more nocturnal than most; he hoped her silence simply meant she went offline in the mornings. Maybe she was sleeping.

The intercom system between his and Naomi's office chimed, and Naomi's voice came through. "Have you been able to reach her yet?"

He appreciated his sister's vigilance and concern, but what he appreciated even more was her forbearance. From the pitch of her voice, he could tell that she knew Lucy was more to him than just a colleague. She was worried about him, but she hadn't opened that door yet, and for that, he was grateful.

He took a measured breath then answered. "You asked an hour ago, Nano. I've left a few more signs she'll recognize, but I haven't heard anything. I don't know if that's because she's not in the system right now or because she's not seeing them or because she's seeing them but can't respond," he replied.

She sighed, then cut the intercom off. His attention traveled back to the screens. Some were static images, others showed lines of code streaming by documenting the activity of certain databases.

There was nothing.

But there was something else he could do. He let his gaze drift to the paper file on his left, a file he'd ignored so far despite having asked Damian for it. It tugged on him with a dark thread.

Inside were the details of Carl Rogers's and Corbin Beekman's deaths. Corbin Beekman had been the IT specialist at the FBI that Damian and Naomi had found murdered. They suspected he was involved somehow with the people who had killed Smitty and kidnapped Lucy. But given Beekman's background, they now also suspected he might have been tricked into doing what he'd done. Regardless of why he had done what he'd done, he'd ended up dead. Shot in the head and his body dumped in a reservoir in Virginia.

Carl Rogers. Now that was one that caused hitch in his heart. He hadn't known Beekman, but Rogers had been a friend.

Telling himself he owed it to Carl, Brian reached for the file and opened it. Filled only with photos and the initial police report—including the autopsy information—the file lacked many details. But what was there was just the torture he needed.

Picturing Lucy rolled up in a blanket, tossed in the water, with a bullet hole in her head wasn't hard when the image of

Carl Rogers stared up at him. Carl's hair had been thinning and wispy strands were plastered to his forehead, covering the bullet hole. Lucy's hair was long and thick, and she usually wore it pulled up into a ponytail. She did have bangs though and, like Carl's hair, those strands of hair fell limp against her skin when wet. He knew this because they'd been caught out in the rain a time or two together.

Drawing his finger over the picture of Carl, as if he could swipe the hair to the side, Brian thought of the last time he'd seen Lucy. They'd been on a job together in New Orleans, and on their way back to their hotel rooms, the elevator had stopped midway, trapping them inside. She had an aversion to small spaces, and he'd had just enough wine with dinner to give him the courage to kiss her. He'd meant it as a distraction, but he'd also kissed her because he'd wanted to—had for years. And she had kissed him back; long and deep, with her back pressed up against the cool wall of the elevator. Sitting in his office, he could all but feel her fingers sliding through his hair, her lips on his.

He *had* distracted her, but not nearly enough. When the elevator finally started moving again, Lucy had been pale and shaky. And so instead of letting her go to her room alone, he'd pulled her into his and led her through a pair of French doors where they'd stepped out onto a terrace and under the wide night sky.

It had been raining that night and they'd stood for fifteen minutes in the cool night air, feeling the water pouring over their skin, absorbing the openness around them. And then he'd done something he'd never done before—he'd slipped inside, turned on some music, kicked off his soaking shoes, and returned to Lucy. Wrapping his arms around her, they'd danced. More of a gentle sway than a true dance, but they'd moved together slowly in the rain, just the two of them, his body offering her warmth and safety under the night sky.

Lost in the memories of that night, he started when the intercom chimed. "Brian?" Naomi's voice came through.

"Still no word," he said, his voice sharp at the sudden intrusion.

"Does Lucy have any ties to Georgia?" Naomi asked, ignoring his tone.

"No, not that I know of," he said. "Why?" He set Carl's file down and straightened in his seat. Clearly, his sister was onto something.

"I'm just thinking about how she came to *identify* those four towns," Naomi said. "Athens is a pretty big town and Madison is historic, so sort of well-known in the area, but the other two are really small towns. Even if she knew she'd landed in Athens, there's no way she'd know about the other three towns unless she saw them. And I think she did, but not on a map," Naomi said, answering her own question.

"You think they're moving her from place to place," Brian said, excitement stirring in his veins. Sometimes it was harder to track a moving target, but just as often it was easier. With more data points, they could run things like predictive programs that might be able to help them determine where she might be *next*. Or, with each new piece of data, they might be able to compile a better picture of who had taken Lucy and through identifying her captors, find her.

"Or she's mobile in general, like an RV or mobile tech van," Naomi said. "If they are moving her, it would help explain the sporadic timing of her incursions into the system and maybe why she hasn't responded to you yet."

"What are you thinking?" he asked.

"I'm thinking that if they are moving her from location to location then we might be able to run searches to look for common property owners in each town," she said "Or, alternatively online rental sites in the area. I don't want to discount the possibility of an RV or something like that though, too," she added.

"Why didn't I think of that?" Brian grumbled as he started typing. He wanted to focus on communicating with Lucy, but since she didn't appear to be online, this would give him something to fill the dangerous empty time.

"What are you taking?" Naomi asked.

"I'll take the common property owners. You search the online rental sites and RV rentals."

"Will do."

"You're the best," Brian said, already working this new line of investigation.

"Brian?" Naomi's voice startled him, reminding him their connection was still open.

"Yeah," he said, distracted by his new task.

"We'll find her," she said, her voice quiet but certain. "You know we will."

He paused his typing and let his sister's certainty wash over him. "I know and I have to believe we'll find her in time. But even so, while I wouldn't wish what's happening on anyone, I hate even more that it's happening to her." It was as close as he'd come to admitting anything more than friendship with Lucy to his sister. Naomi seemed to sense the fragility of these new revelations, and without another word, she muted the connection and they both went back to work.

* * *

$\mathscr{L}$ucy kept her breathing even and her back to the door as she curled up under the blankets and feigned sleep. Attuned to each footfall, she knew the one woman amongst her kidnappers now stood at the doorway. It was a pitiful show; if Lucy had wanted to get away she could have done so many times already. But it served her purpose to let them think she was afraid, to let them think they had her cowed.

Truth be told, when it had taken Brian so long to respond, she *had* worried. But now that he was listening, and that meant Naomi was too and maybe even a few more of the DeMarco clan, nothing was going to stop her from stopping these people. Oh, she acted the part of the victim, crying crocodile tears and cowering when they came near, but inside, rage was boiling. If they thought she was going to lie down and let her friends' killers get away with it, they'd kidnapped the wrong woman.

Not to mention the fact that she'd die before she let anyone near the data she suspected they were truly after. In the grand scheme of things, she was but one person. If the people behind her kidnapping were after what she thought they might ultimately be, the lives of many more would be at stake.

But in the hours she stayed huddled on her bed, feigning sleep so as to reduce the time she had to be online at night, she acknowledged that even though there were several good reasons for fighting back, there was just one that was woven into her soul.

Brian.

If she didn't manage this situation in the right way, they'd likely go after Brian next; he was the one other person, other than two people at the FBI, who knew the true type of data Smitty had access to. She didn't want to think about how her kidnappers had known to target her—she'd leave that for another day—but if they knew about her, they probably knew about Brian too.

The world was a better place with him in it, and she intended to do everything possible to make sure he remained. Besides, dying didn't really scare her—she wasn't looking forward to it, but she didn't fear it. Unlike the idea of someone going after Brian, which caused her heart to hitch more than just a little bit.

The RV creaked, and the woman moved away. Rolling onto her back, Lucy strained to hear any conversation that the four might be having. Not surprisingly, she heard nothing. Of the four, only two seemed to get along and even that was a stretch. They didn't argue; they just didn't talk. Which was a complete pain in the ass since it meant she had to guess and glean what was going on rather than have any real idea.

Letting her eyes drift to the ceiling above her, she started to make her plan for the coming night. After she'd successfully pulled the Union Insurance file the night before, they'd directed her to pull the file of an investigation of a business-man out of Miami. She didn't know anything about the case, but she had to drag her feet on it. It wasn't that she couldn't do it or really even cared if they had the information, but once she was successful at that, they'd eventually move onto asking her for what they really wanted.

Her chest squeezed as she thought about the information buried deep in Smitty's system. As she stared at the faded and warped ceiling above her, she contemplated whether or not she could move the files altogether. She could, of course she could, but it would take time, something she suspected she might be running out of.

She sighed and rolled onto her side again. It was nearing four in the afternoon. She had a few hours left to figure out just what she needed to tell Brian tonight and how to do it in such a way to best protect him.

* * *

*B*rian rubbed his eyes then reached for his now cold coffee. The late morning light filtered through the two windows of his office and he considered whether or not he should grab a few hours of sleep. The building was eerily quiet with Naomi having left the night before.

He'd stayed up through the night monitoring various systems for signs of Lucy. At three in the morning, he'd finally made contact. Sort of. She hadn't been able to tell him much other than what he already feared—that whoever was behind all this was going for the information he and Lucy had buried deep in the network.

But then, for the next few hours, her actions seemed to contradict what she'd told him and she'd ended up pulling the file of another embezzler from Smitty's system. He didn't much care about the content of the file—in the grand scheme of things, the guy was a minor player—but the fact that she'd pulled it was, well, not really in opposition to what she'd told him, but definitely not in furtherance of it. True, the file was buried deeper than the Union Insurance file, but it wouldn't get her—or the people holding her—closer to that last layer of information.

Because in truth, they weren't really layers at all. They weren't stacked on top of each other, with someone needing to get through one in order to get to the next. No, they were more like nodes or nodules buried deeper and deeper in the system; each self-contained, but successively harder to access.

She'd gone offline shortly after extracting the file, and he'd spent the dawn hours culling through online rental sites in the Athens area as he pondered Lucy's actions. He could write off her pulling the Union Insurance file as a test, but the file last night? It didn't make much sense if what they were really after was that deepest layer.

That realization gave him pause, and his fingers stilled over his keyboard as his mind turned an idea over. Was it possible there were different factions of *people* involved, each wanting access to the different kinds of data?

The idea had merit, and he was turning it over in his mind when his email beeped with an incoming message and video file from Naomi.

"I found how they got Lucy from Honolulu to Athens—multiple planes over two days, all rented by different companies. Damian is on it."

He opened the video file to see Lucy being led by three people through the door of a private airport and onto a waiting plane. He recognized Kevin Farlow, a man Naomi had identified as being one of the two she'd seen at their cousin's pub the night Smitty had been killed. The other man from that night was also in the video, he had an iron grip on Lucy's elbow, and if Brian wasn't mistaken, a weapon pointed at her side.

He brought up an IM window. "Who's the guy?" he typed, knowing Naomi would know which of the three he was referring to.

"Hell if I know," she typed back. "I've run him through every system and I still don't have an ID. I'm starting to take this as a personal challenge."

"Every system?" he asked, instantly regretting the question. Of course she meant *every system*, not every system but a few.

Thankfully, she seemed to forgive his slip and simply typed back, "Yes."

"John Taylor's record was breached early this morning," he typed, giving her the name of the file Lucy had pulled.

His IM remained quiet, then Naomi responded. "Shit, she's in the system, isn't she?" Taylor had stolen about three million dollars from a prominent real estate developer in Miami.

"Yes, she is."

"Where is Taylor now?" she asked.

"Living the life on Curacao."

"Any reason his file was targeted?" He could sense her confusion too. Of all the records on Smitty's computer, Taylor's didn't register as a particularly important one. He was part of Smitty's special files—the ones Naomi knew about—but he was also just a guy who embezzled some money from another rich, but ethically challenged, guy and now lived the Life of Riley on a

Caribbean island. Okay, he was a little more than that, but not much.

"Working on that," Brian wrote.

"She knows you're there, though, right?"

"Yes."

He could feel her restraint and appreciated that she didn't ask about what he and Lucy had communicated about. He didn't have many secrets from Naomi—aside from being his twin, she was also his best friend—but the one he shared with Lucy was one of them.

"Let me know if you need me to do anything more, anything different," she wrote. Then she followed the message up with another letting him know she, Damian, and Jay were out visiting all the local campgrounds where an RV could be parked.

A wave of fatigue washed over him and he recognized that the long hours might be getting the better of him. "Thanks," he typed. "I know you're working on figuring out who that guy is, I think he could be the key."

"I'll call you tonight unless we find anything game changing."

"I'll keep you posted if I hear anything from her that I can pass on."

A beat passed and then another IM popped up. "Love you. And get some sleep if you can," she said before closing the IM window.

He smiled. Lucy seemed to be working at night; maybe Naomi's advice had some merit.

* * *

*B*rian woke early in the evening to a few messages on his voicemail. He'd managed to get a few hours of sleep thanks to some good information Damian had passed on just before lunch. They now felt fairly certain that Lucy was being kept in an RV and they believed they'd found a campground where it might have been parked. It wasn't a sure thing, but the tire tracks were recent enough that Damian had brought in an analyst—a newbie to the FBI, but a recruit from a SEAL Ops Support team—to look for satellite images of the vehicle that had been parked there. It was hands down, the most solid lead they had in terms of physically finding Lucy, or so he hoped.

Damian had also asked him to give some thought as to who in the FBI would work with consultants like Carl and Lucy and also suggested that he reach out to a few other hackers in their circle to check if anyone had been approached to do the kind of work Lucy had been kidnapped to do. He didn't think the effort would yield anything, but he'd put out a few feelers. And in the time he'd slept, three of them had returned his calls.

He rolled out of bed and padded into the kitchen as he listened to the first message. Helen Fodor said she hadn't been approached, but had heard about Carl and Smitty and if he needed her for anything to give her a call. As he made a pot of coffee, he listened to the next two messages which were variations of the same theme. He liked to think they were being sincere in their offers to help, but he wasn't about to trust any of them enough to bring them in.

After filling a large mug, he made his way to his office, reading a series of text messages from Naomi. Most of which did little more than inform him of their progress throughout the day, although the most interesting of the lot was a message letting him know that John Taylor, the embezzler from the file Lucy had pulled, had been found murdered in Curacao.

A fleeting moment of guilt pricked his conscience as he booted up his computer, but that sentiment was quickly replaced with curiosity—how had they gotten to Taylor so fast? And *who* had gotten to him? His mind touched again on the theory he'd just started to formulate when Naomi had sent him the video of Lucy's abduction.

The information contained in what he always referred to as Smitty's second layer, was information the US government used as bargaining chips. At its heart, the information was nothing but currency—the government maintained files on US citizens that they couldn't prosecute for one reason or another, and they traded that with businesses and individuals for information that was more useful to them.

The only person Brian could imagine finding the information on John Taylor useful was the man he'd embezzled from in the first place. A man who would likely pay to know where Taylor had holed up after absconding with his money.

He dashed off a quick text to Naomi, but not surprisingly, she'd come to the same conclusion earlier in the day and was already digging into the owner of Coastal Development, the company from which the man had been embezzled. She also let him know that Russ, Damian's analyst, had found a few satellite images of the RV they thought might be holding Lucy—he hadn't been able to get a license plate yet, but he was working on it.

With everything under control on the data and information front, he did what he did best; he hunkered down and waited to hear from Lucy.

ALSO BY TAMSEN SCHULTZ

2) Six

3) Devil

4) Nora

The mystery lake Series

1) Defenseless

2) Exposed

3) Relentless

4) Shattered

5) Hidden

6) Broken

7) Burned

8) Tangled

9) Vindctive

10) Forbidden (coming August 7, 2024)

www.ingramcontent.com/pod-product-compliance
Lightning Source LLC
Chambersburg PA
CBHW021126260626
47169CB00005B/1470